This Changes Everything

This Changes Everything

A Novel

Danielle McKechnie

HARPER PERENNIAL

NEW YORK • LONDON • TORONTO • SYDNEY • NEW DELHI • AUCKLAND

HARPER PERENNIAL

hc.com

First published in Canada in 2026 by HarperCollins Publishers Ltd.

FIRST US EDITION

Library of Congress Cataloging-in-Publication Data has been applied for.

ISBN 978-0-06-351939-8 (pbk.)

Printed in the United States of America

26 27 28 29 30 LBC 5 4 3 2 1

To Mike

And Elijah Wood
Because if not now, when?

Prologue

VANCOUVER

20 years old

"ELLIE, WHAT DID WE DO?" RORY'S HEAD WAS ON MY SHOULDER. His face was buried in my collarbone. His loose dark curls plastered against my cheek, clinging to my skin in the same mindless, desperate hold that my limbs were clinging to him.

I stopped breathing, and my eyes flew open. I must have misheard him.

Rory's hot breath steamed my neck. We were in the passenger seat of his musty, old black Jeep Cherokee, and it dawned on me that all my parents needed to do was look out my sister's second-story bay window to find me and Rory Campbell, tangled up and naked, perfectly lit under the streetlight that loomed at the end of our driveway. The passenger seat was reclined all the way down, and I didn't know how he wasn't suffocating as he pushed his face even further into my neck. Our thrashing heartbeats bashed against each other in unison.

"What did you say?" I asked. He didn't answer, so I repeated myself. "Rory, what did you say?" He didn't move, but I felt his lips tremble against my skin, and I had to actively stop myself from filling his Jeep with vomit. Why wasn't he talking to me?

"What's going on?" Tears started materializing in my eyes. "Look at me," I pleaded. I could hear my voice getting weaker the longer he hid his face.

When Rory eventually lifted his head, his pained expression burned through me. My eyes trailed over the faint freckles across the bridge of his nose and the tops of his cheeks. I called it his Summer Skin and had obsessed over his soft, subtle freckles, which multiplied under the summer sun, since we were twelve. In eight years, I could count on one hand how many times Rory Campbell and I had purposefully touched each other, and touching him so intimately now, with what we had just done, combined with *that* look on his face, felt like both a dream and a nightmare. He kept his eyes closed and lightly touched his nose to mine.

"Look at me. Please," I begged.

He opened his sad, coffee-brown eyes, which I had memorized long ago, and then quickly squeezed them shut again as tears rolled down his cheeks. He kissed me softly. I assumed the kiss was to stop his bottom lip from quivering, but it didn't work. When I heard him inhale a choppy breath, I asked more urgently, "What's wrong?"

"This was a mistake." He dropped his head as if he had lost all the muscles in his neck.

"What?" I blinked. There was no way he could possibly have said—

"This was a mistake," he said again.

"What do you mean?" My heartbeat filled my head, clouding my hearing with its heavy thumping.

"We shouldn't have done that . . ."

"You're still inside me, Rory." I swallowed, entirely unable to comprehend what was happening.

With a sudden surge of energy, Rory tore himself off me and quickly shuffled over to the driver's seat. He leaned down and pulled on his underwear, then his pants, then his black T-shirt over his head. I tried to do the same, but my fingers stopped working, my hands, my legs, my brain, everything.

Rory wiped his tears with the back of his hand and looked out the window, facing away from me. He looked down the dark street I grew up on.

"What did I do?" I asked, staring blankly at my sleepy house.

"Nothing. You did nothing. That was . . ." He ran both hands through his floppy hair. "You did nothing."

"What's happening right now?"

"Please. Ellie." He sucked in a shallow gasp. "Stop."

"Rory, what did I do? What is going on right now?" I must have asked one too many times, because he then slammed his hands into the steering wheel.

"You're leaving!" Rory practically shouted at me, rocking me back in my seat with his unexpected burst of fury, lighting a fire under my ass to get my clothes on. "Tomorrow. You're moving away tomorrow, and I feel like I'm dying!"

"It's only two years." I fumbled with my shirt. I couldn't look at him.

"It's not. You've wanted to leave for as long as I've known you. I knew it would happen, it's finally happening, and you're not coming back."

"I'm coming back," I insisted.

"No, you're not!" Rory yelled. He closed his eyes, trying to control himself.

"It's just school. This is my home. I *will* come back."

"We both know that's not true. I *know* you, Ellie. You're leaving, and I'm going to be left with nothing."

I could feel my body recoil even though I didn't move a muscle.

"I . . . I can't do this," he finished.

"But we've already done it . . ." My eyes were stinging. I swallowed the last of the air inside the Jeep, and my stomach fell to my feet. I could still feel him inside me. I could still feel his mouth, and tongue, and breath, and teeth all over me. I could still feel him digging into my skin and hair.

"So, what, then?" I choked. "Did you come here to finally fuck me, then send me on my way?"

"I can't believe you just said that," he answered quietly, sounding sickened, unable to meet my eyes. "Is that what you think?"

"How can I not?" I was in disbelief.

"I came tonight to say goodbye . . ."

A lost memory of Rory when we were fourteen surged through me. I had walked through the front door of the busy juniors' lounge at Juniper Golf Club. He was sitting with his hands clamped behind his head, and he was leaning back comfortably. He had flipped his black hat backward, and his eyes widened, then darted away from mine the moment they connected. I watched his chest lift, and his breathing pick up. An empty seat sat next to him with his rain jacket hanging over the back, and I didn't have to ask to know he was holding it for me. It was always for me.

The Jeep Cherokee was steaming up, so Rory turned on the engine and rolled down his window.

"I haven't been able to think since you told me about New York. Whatever you and I have ever been, that's when it all ended. It's over, and it didn't even start." Rory could barely get the words out as he white-knuckled the steering wheel.

I stopped recognizing my own reality. I looked carefully at my house. Had my sister's bedroom light been on this whole time?

"This is it, Rory. It's us. We're choosing each other. I choose you, and you choose me."

"I can't do this . . . I won't. I'm not choosing this. I'm not choosing you." He started hyperventilating, burying his face in his hands. "I can't spend the rest of my life—" He inhaled sharply, having lost his words. "None of this is real, Ellie. You. Me. Us. None of it. We've never been anything real." Rory heaved, and his voice sounded like it came straight out of his gut.

"Rory . . ."

"I can't love you, Ellie! I'm not doing it!"

I sat back in my seat. Finally, totally, and entirely composed. I grabbed my shoes and opened the door. With my hands full, I stepped outside the Jeep. I looked up at my sister's window, overlooking the driveway, and saw her blinds move.

"What was I thinking?" Rory said quietly to himself as I slammed the door.

I sobbed with my sister throughout the entire night. I finally stopped the next morning when the plane took off, the wheels were up, and I got the fuck out of Vancouver.

Part 1

Everything Before

Chapter 1

NEW YORK
20 years old

I EMERGED FROM THE SUBWAY AT 72ND STREET BETWEEN BROADWAY and Amsterdam. My dad stopped me at the top of the stairs before we were snuffed out by historic buildings and blinding lights. The smell of garbage, sewer, perfume, body odor, and street food was already wafting around me and sinking into my pores. The violent rumble of trains beneath the staircase reverberated through my feet, and the constant hum of traffic and people was a symphony that landed squarely in my chest.

"Ellie, there's before this moment, and everything after. For the rest of your life, you're living in the after."

I wasn't going to tell my dad that he was wrong, and that specific, monumental moment that divided my life in two happened the night before, on the ripped fabric in the passenger side of a hand-me-down classic black Jeep Cherokee with Rory Campbell.

"I got it from here, Dad. I love you, but no one can see me with you. I won't be Ellie McCain. I'll be the pathetic little girl from Canada who needed her dad to bring her to orientation." I tried to push my dad back down the stairs to the train platform, but he bested me with a bear hug. His salt-and-pepper hair pressed into my face as he breathed in his little-girl-no-more one last time.

My dad and I stood at the same height. It was jarring how much we looked like one another now that I had grown into an adult-ish kind of person. We both had blue eyes that random people would comment on. I had wavy dark-blond hair that reached down my back and teetered on the verge of a color often referred to as "mousy." We both had smiles that pulled creases into our cheeks. But my biggest inherited trait from my father was my occasionally damaging, often delusional, blinding ambition. We were both determined to rip our roots from the ground and fly into the unknown, come hell or high water. My dad had moved out of Canmore, Alberta, to study medicine in Toronto and become a doctor. And I was going to move out of Vancouver, British Columbia, and become a goddamn movie star!

The moment I knew that I was on my way out of Canada is as clear to me as if it happened yesterday. I was fourteen. We were driving down Sepulveda Boulevard in LA on a family holiday and cruised through the Airport Tunnel. I could feel the yellow lights inside the tunnel burn into my soul as I watched them blur around our car. My dad was driving, my mom sat in the passenger seat, and my older sister, Hannah, was beside me. I closed my eyes in the sudden darkness and rolled down my window to let the warm air push into my face and rip through my hair. I said aloud, "This is it. It's LA. I'm going to live here one day. I'm going to *be* somebody." I didn't have to open my eyes. I could feel my parents smiling to themselves from the front seat, as if they were patting my head condescendingly and saying, "That's nice, dear." My sister snorted out her annoyance. But I meant it, and that indescribable pull of "this is it" tugged on me and had me chasing dragons ever since, as my parents liked to say.

Yes, I was aware that New York wasn't Los Angeles, but I had made it to the States. I was one step closer. I was on my way to orientation at Bronwyn School for the Arts. "Good luck pouring coffee for the rest of your life," my uncle told me when I got accepted into the theater program at the prestigious conservatory. "How does it feel going into something when you already know you'll never make your money back?" a friend asked at my going-away party. "It's so funny how some people think they're special," my cousin quipped passive-aggressively. "My friends complain about having to drive over the bridge to North Vancouver to see their kids, and you want to go to *New York*?" my mom cried after I went to the audition.

Two years, I told them.

It's only two years, I told Rory.

I had been in New York for a total of three hours, and I already felt like a different version of myself. I wasn't sure how much of that had to do with my traumatizing night before, but I was different nonetheless. I didn't know who this new person was yet, but I was free, scared, and excited. I also pretended I wasn't instantaneously homesick and so overwhelmingly heartbroken that I could hardly catch my breath.

A wave of heat hurtled toward me and my dad on the staircase like we had been blasted inside a wind tunnel. Another train had come into the station below. The warmth washed over me and propelled me into a memory of Rory and me standing at my door, sixteen years old and flushed with nerves, excitement, awe, and fear. His brother, Cameron, and my best friend, Kara, were waiting for him in the driveway, ready to go.

"I don't know what to do right now." Rory carefully moved his forehead to mine. His sweet, shallow breath seeped into my bones.

"Rory, let's go!" Cameron called out the Jeep's window and honked.

I wanted so badly to lean in, skim my nose along his, part my lips, and see what would happen. I wanted so badly to move my hands into his dark-brown, loose curls, but I didn't. I closed my eyes instead and felt his warm breath steadily coat my skin.

"Rory, they can see us." I kept my voice small and quiet, and my words only for him.

"I don't think I care . . ."

Cameron honked louder and longer this time. I could hear Rory's lips pull into a smile, and we both started laughing.

"On your left!" A stranger bumped my shoulder, rushing down the stairs to catch the next train, slapping me back to reality.

"Oh, sorry," I said instinctively, even though she was the one who hit me. I watched her work blazer flap in the wind as she clutched onto the railing with one hand, barreling down the stairs. Her other hand popped above her head, and her middle finger raised high and proud. I pulled my face back, surprised that someone had just randomly told me to "fuck off" minutes after getting off the train.

My dad and I had taken the E train from our hotel, which sat near the Empire State Building, before I moved into a converted hotel-turned-apartment building called Grayrock on the Upper West Side. It was one of the very few buildings in the affluent neighborhood that had yet to be bought by a developer and renovated. Two beds sat in the middle of the tiny studio apartment, divided by a small nightstand. The walls were made of concrete, so that no one could hear my screams. There was a small fridge, an electric grill, and an oven at the foot of the beds that was considered unsafe for use but too big to move. The kitchen sink was also the bathroom sink. Oh, and there were most definitely what one would assume to be murder stains all over the gray carpet.

After I found the apartment on my own, my overprotective parents were on high alert and weren't about to let me vet a roommate on my own. I had to agree to let them come with me to New York to help me settle in. It was the only way they would support my taking on this irresponsible (in their opinion), yet inevitable (in my opinion) adventure. I needed a roommate and a job, but because I was Canadian and only had a student visa, I promised my parents that I would find a roommate and take on internships to build real-world connections and work on a backup plan should I never catch that pesky little dragon. My parents and my sister were the realists. I was the asshole.

My dad cupped the back of my neck to pull me in and kiss the top of my head. "Okay. I'll go. But before I go back down there"—my dad nodded down the stairs into the busy subway station—"and you're off in the wind up there . . ." We both looked up at the enormous buildings blocking the late-summer, early-evening sky. "I love you." I saw my dad shift his weight and prepare to tell me his next sentence. "Your mom's flying back tonight."

"What?" I almost fell over from whiplash. "We just got here! We *literally* just got here."

"Your grandma had a fall—"

"What?!" My eyes twitched.

"She's okay, take it down three notches. Your mom got a voicemail when we were on the plane, and we didn't say anything until now because we didn't want to interfere with your big night. But she's not going to be there when you get back tonight, so that's why I'm telling you."

"She didn't say goodbye." I searched my brain for exactly what transpired when we left my mom in Bryant Park. Well . . . Now that I thought about it, she did seem to cry an unusual amount over her lukewarm afternoon coffee. She wished me good luck, and she squeezed my face between her palms with an intense look in her eyes that I had shrugged off as "Mom is nuts." Come to think of it, she did scream "I love you, Ellie-Bee" so loud that everyone in the park stopped what they were doing to slowly look at the overly emotional crazy lady sobbing into her pain au chocolat.

"Your mom knew if she said a proper goodbye, she wouldn't be able to leave, but all is good. I'm staying until we find your roommate, so it's fine. It's all fine." My dad was trying to sound like he had things under control. He didn't.

"You don't know how to do that," I declared accusingly. "You don't know how to be a person like that."

"What's that supposed to mean?" my dad asked defensively.

"Life stuff is Mom. You're here for the fun."

"It's okay, I have a plan. You find a roommate. I'll humanize you by showing them you have a family, so they'll think twice before killing you." My dad grinned mischievously.

"This is just . . . a lot of information." I blinked heavily. There was too much swirling around my mind.

Mom. New York. Orientation. Rory. No friends. Grandma. Roommate. Rory.

I looked down, feeling the weight of everything at my feet. Nope. Never mind. It was a rat. There was a rat on my shoe.

"Ahhhhhhh!" I screamed then booted the rat against the stairwell's wall. As it scurried away back down the stairs, I looked at my dad with my eyes wide open, and he doubled over with laughter.

"Okay, honey." My dad kept chuckling. "I can't wait to hear about how it all goes tonight. Also, your mom wanted you to have this. Please, I'm begging you, read it when I'm gone. You'll see what I'm talking about."

My dad handed me a letter and gave me a quick kiss on the cheek before turning back to catch the next train.

I may have failed at concealing my cry as I choked out "Dad?"

He turned back around from the bottom of the stairs to see me silhouetted by the scary super-city filled with bad people behind me. I fiddled nervously with my delicate rose gold bracelet. I didn't have words, but it didn't matter. My dad nodded, holding in his tears, and gave his fist a pump.

"Give 'em hell, Ellie."

I watched my dad disappear beneath the city, then read my mom's letter.

My Ellie-Bee,

I am so, so, so proud of you. Remember these four rules:

1. Zip up your purse.
2. Have big feelings. Make big choices.
3. Stop what you're doing and recognize what you're doing.
4. No licky-dicky.

Vancouver will always be home, but it's not your life. Live your life and don't look back. I love you.

Mama

"No licky-dicky?" My snort turned into a full-blown, tears-spilling-down-my-face laugh. I sucked in a shaky inhale and pocketed the letter.

No licky-dicky. Christ . . .

I shook my head with another chuckle. It took five seconds for my smile to fade. To my parents, New York was Gotham City. To me, it was something hugely different. I knew when I turned around and walked onto the streets, toward those suffocating skyscrapers and blinding lights, I was letting go of my "everything before" and heading directly into my "everything after."

I closed my eyes and dragged in a slow, shuddering breath.

Don't think about him. Don't think about him . . . Don't look back.

I looked up one last time, and before I stepped into the unknown, I quietly said, "Goodbye, me. I'll miss you."

Chapter 2

VANCOUVER
12 years old

THE FIRST TIME I SAW RORY CAMPBELL, I HAD WHAT MANY PEOple horrifyingly refer to as "buds"—rubbery, disc-shaped nipples that popped out of my twelve-year-old chest like a dropped soda can that failed to explode on impact. What was supposed to be my second day wearing a training bra became the chilly November day I spent walking around Juniper Golf Club having forgotten my jacket and holding my youth-size golf bag over my front to save the embarrassment of my sudden nips poking out like two mismatched pushpins.

My dad took me to Juniper's two-storied, covered driving range for the first time, and it was so much fancier than all the other ranges my sister and I had been going to since I was six. A range picker plowed through an enormous field littered with white, yellow, and the occasional orange balls. The first level had about twenty or so stalls with wooden dividers separating each person, and the entire range was enclosed by mile-high Douglas firs and Japanese maples lining hidden fences and nets.

It started to rain. I breathed in deeply and could feel my body cleanse. I tucked away the scent of sap mixed with damp grass into my memory bank. In the not-too-distant background, there was a churning rumble of balls from the ball dispenser and a popping sound as balls dropped from the machine into the bucket. This was followed by the click-clacking of golf spikes making their way down the path toward the range.

My dad was in the stall behind me, hitting balls while simultaneously chirping away about my foot placement, my grip, my distribution of weight, you name it. Every now and then, I would swing and really smack the ball a good distance, but my aim was always horrendous. I wasn't consistent in the slightest, but when magic struck, I could really hit the crap out of a golf ball. I was competitive and determined, and that determination rocketed through most aspects of my life, including my swing.

THWACK!

"That's it, Ellie! What are you hitting?" my dad asked.

The sound of spikes on the cement softened as footsteps grew closer. Clearly, the golfers closing in didn't want to distract us.

"Is that a six iron?" my dad prodded.

I picked up the club, flipped it around to have another look, though I already knew the answer. "Nine iron," I said casually, feigning modesty.

My dad's eyes brightened. He nodded. That was all he was going to give, but it was enough for me to puff out my braless chest.

"Not bad, right, boys?" My dad turned to the golfers who were slowly walking toward us.

"Not bad." A boy's voice cracked from behind me.

Three teenage boys had golf bags slung over their shoulders, their clubs cracking together as they walked. The spikes at the bottom of their shoes clattered like a chorus over the rain. Not many people wore spikes at the club, as they were becoming outdated and even banned on some courses, but these guys still did. The two oldest boys confidently strode up to my dad and me, while the youngest trailed behind.

"Hi, Dr. McCain." The oldest boy's wobbly voice broke through his wide smile.

The youngest looked directly at me, and I had to look away, as if

I had caught myself accidentally staring at an eclipse. He had coffee-colored eyes and unruly brown hair with streaks of auburn hidden beneath his wild, wet curls. His nose and cheeks were delicately freckled, as if they had been painted on by hand. When I gathered the courage to look at him again, it felt like I knew him. It was like he had already been in my life, circling the outside, knocking on my door as steadfast as my heartbeat, and when we actually *looked* at each other for the very first time, the quiet knocking stopped.

I felt so deeply exposed in my white Costco polo.

White shirt, no jacket, forgotten training bra, Dad, cute boy, buds. For the love of God, someone kill me.

Hopefully the boys couldn't hear me curse my boobs and my lack of foresight to cover them the hell up.

"You boys playing in the rain today?" My dad pulled out his enormous driver in its protective sleeve. I was incredibly thrilled when he didn't forget to grab my dinky three wood, hidden beneath a stuffed orange tiger sleeve. "Try this one now, Ellie-Bee," my dad insisted, handing me my club and throwing the tiger over the top of my bag.

Nooooooo! Not the tiger stuffy!

The oldest boy flicked his eyes over to me briefly before answering my dad. "We're just out to hit some balls."

After hitting a shot straight down the center of the range, my dad decided it was time to introduce us. "Ellie, these are the Campbell boys. Blair, Cameron, and Rory."

I looked over, and all three boys stood wearing rain jackets and khakis, looking back at me as if I were an alien.

Blair, the oldest at fifteen, had chestnut-brown hair that swooped and brown eyes with long lashes. He had noodle-like arms and legs, and you could tell in an instant that he was the flirt, with a smile that overtook his entire face. Cameron, the middle brother at thirteen, was lanky, like Blair, and had short, blondish-brown hair and gray-blue eyes. He was looking at me like he wasn't sure about me, with a slightly confused frown. Rory, the youngest, was twelve like me, and pretending not to look at me at all through his curly tresses.

"Wanna go again, Ellie? Show 'em the goods?" my dad asked, breaking my hypnosis and absolutely demolishing my vibe. I couldn't bear the idea of my father saying "Show 'em the goods," and yet here we were.

"Nope. Not at all." I shook my head like it was on a swivel and then bent down to put a ball on the rubber tee.

"Alright, well. Let us know if you need any tips on your swing, Dr. McCain," Blair teased.

My dad chuckled, flicking the driver in his wrists. "Didn't you need to borrow one of my balls the last time you played because of all the ones you lost over the summer? Oh, and speaking of balls, have yours dropped yet?" My dad's grin lit him up like a firecracker.

Blair and Cameron doubled over with laughter, while Rory blushed. His lips twitched at the edges, and a hidden dimple appeared. I can only imagine what my face looked like when my dad dropped the testicle bomb. I diverted Rory's quick glance like I was under attack on the battlefield.

"Make sure you don't accidentally hit your old-man danglers instead of the ball, Dr. McCain," Cameron shot back like a devil.

"Cameron Campbell!" My dad let out a belly laugh that rumbled through the tall evergreens. "Them's fightin' words." It was clear my dad already loved these boys, whom I had never met before, and the feeling was mutual. He turned to me. "Stay away from these boys, Ellie, or you'll be forever branded a traitor in our family. Got it?"

I looked over at Rory once more, and his dimple deepened. Everything inside me dropped to the pit of my stomach at the sight of his shy, downturned smile. My heart thunked. Just . . . *thunk*.

"Got it," I said quietly. I brought my attention back to my mat as the boys finally made their way past us. I kept my head down but slowly raised my eyes.

Blair had ducked into an opening three stalls away, Cameron was beside him, and Rory placed his bag on the stand directly in front of mine in the next stall. He was left-handed. I was right-handed. He was facing me, and I was facing him, while we were about to hit balls in total and complete silence with nothing but a waist-high green wooden divider between us.

Settle down, Ellie. Just breathe. Hit the ball. He'll sneak a peek, and there's nothing you can do about it, so calm down and swing. Calm down and swing. Calm down, Ellie. CALM DOWN!

I took a deep breath, swung my three wood back, and—

SMACK!

I shanked it. I shanked it so badly that the ball didn't fly out into the grass, it flew ninety degrees from where it was supposed to and directly in front of me, hitting the wooden divider that separated me from Rory.

Oh. My. God.

A woman at the end of the line cried out when the smack heard round the world rattled the tree line. I knew I was fire engine red, but when my dad chimed in with "You gotta hit the ball *that way,* honey," and pointed out toward the range with his club, I thought I would combust.

I looked up to see Rory, looking down, holding back a smile as he dumped his bucket of balls into the tray in front of him. Blair and Cameron were both right-handed, so I could only see the backs of them, but their shoulders were shaking while they tried to suppress their laughter.

I placed another ball on the tee.

Back on the horse. It's out of my system. Trade the bad for the good. Calm down. Calm down, Ellie. Calm down and swing. Calm down and—

SMACK!

Well, I did it again. The lady yelped a little louder. My eyes shot up to Rory, who had just hit a ball and had squared his body to the range. His eyes were wide. He pretended not to have seen or heard what happened. His club was over his shoulders . . . which were . . . shaking. Rory held back a smile so tight that it looked like he might strain something.

Awesome. Super awesome.

"Ellie, be careful," my dad said in a not-so-whispery whisper. "Rory's right in front of you. Six inches higher and you've killed the kid."

I could hear Cameron start to wheeze. I looked all the way over to Blair, and he was the only one looking back at me, shaking his head with a playful smirk.

Here we go again. I placed another ball onto the tee. *I have to hit at least one solid, mind-blowing shot, or I, 100 percent, will die. Let's do this. No more messing around. Here we go.*

WHIFF!

Not only did I miss the ball entirely, but my club slipped out of my hand, and I accidentally threw it into the rain. My whole body spun wildly with my momentum, and the wind delicately knocked the ball off the tee.

"That's one," my dad joked as if those two inches were my intended shot.

"Isn't the ball supposed to go farther than the club?" an elderly man grumbled with a condescending chuckle as he walked past us, his empty bucket in hand.

I could hear the boys laughing now. I looked up. Blair and Cameron had fully spun around to enjoy the show. Rory was standing, holding his club in front of him and leaning it against his shoulder. He was looking directly at me with a tight-lipped smile, staring straight into my soul. His dark-brown eyes sparkled as brightly as a Christmas tree.

My insides shriveled as I stepped out into the grass to retrieve my club. The rain was dumping on me, and everyone at the range had to stop what they were doing so as not to hit me with their flying balls.

So this is how I die. This will be on the news, no doubt. "Ellie McCain, twelve, died in the rain on the fourth of November from embarrassment at Juniper Golf Club."

I couldn't lift my head or connect with the ten or so sets of eyeballs that lit me on fire as I made my way back to my stall. I set my jaw, picked up my whiffed ball, and popped it back onto the tee. I was stubborn and furious and swung for dear life.

SMACK!

This time, I shanked it so hard that the ball left a dent in the barrier between me and Rory.

"Ellie!" My dad couldn't control his shout. The woman screamed. Blair threw his body forward in hysterics, clutching his belly. Cameron cackled, "Oh my god! It's like a magic trick!" And Rory tossed his head backward from laughing so hard. He threw his free hand over his eyes, which were squeezed shut.

I stopped and held my club to my chest with crossed arms. I waited for the laughter to subside. Rory pulled at his sleeve and wiped away his tears, his smile taking over his entire face, building up his cheeks, and pouring out of his eyes.

Once he, Cameron, and Blair finally settled, Rory and I locked eyes.

"You done?" I attempted to conceal my mortification.

"I don't know. *Are you?*" Rory quipped back. We held each other's stare for a moment longer than I was prepared for, and my heart rate quickened.

"How about this," my dad interrupted. "How about once you boys are all finished up here, you come and have some hot dogs with Ellie and me in the clubhouse? Her sister, Hannah, will be up there, too. It'll be fun!"

Blair responded with an enthusiastic "That would be great! Thank you, Dr. McCain!"

Rory looked down. He bit his bottom lip to stop himself from breaking into another full-blown, face-morphing smile, but it wasn't working. Once everyone resumed positions, I heard Rory whisper, "You're funny." He pulled a ball out with the head of his iron, then took a smooth swing, cracking the ball perfectly down the middle. "Anyway, we saw that other shot when you didn't know we were watching." His eyes flicked up to meet mine, which dropped like boulders.

I looked down at my last ball, took a deep breath, squared my body, and swung.

THWACK!

My attention darted to Rory. He was watching my ball arc through the air. Once my ball hit the ground, he glanced back over at me and smiled. Impressing Rory somehow suddenly meant so much more than impressing anyone else ever. I would never be the same. He quickly looked over the barrier between us at my empty bucket.

"You're already finished?" Rory asked quietly.

I nodded, taking longer than necessary to put my club back in my bag. "You gonna come up and have a hot dog with us later?" I asked nonchalantly, simulating confidence.

"Yeah." He dug into his tray for another ball. "You gonna come back tomorrow?" He avoided eye contact.

I looked back at my dad, who had grown increasingly quiet. The swell of his smile was unmistakable—he was eavesdropping as he packed up.

I turned back to Rory. "Yeah, I think so."

Rory took a deep breath, as if he had been holding it. He kept his eyes down and nodded. "Good, you need the practice." He smacked another perfect shot. I saw Blair and Cameron sneak glances at each other, also eavesdropping. Once Blair saw me notice him, he tucked his head back down and took another swing.

Chapter 3

NEW YORK
20 years old

WE SAT IN A CIRCLE OF CHAIRS, IN A SMALL ROOM, WITH FLOOR-to-ceiling windows that beautifully showcased the prewar building next door. The walls in the classroom were white, the floors were painted black, the ceilings were high, and I was out of my element. It had seemed so ridiculous that I was accepted into Bronwyn School for the Arts that I'd continued to say "We'll see" with a shoulder shrug and a head shake whenever someone in Vancouver asked if I was really moving to New York.

Rory had driven me to Seattle for the audition seven months earlier. I cried the whole drive home, believing I'd absolutely tanked my comedic monologue that I had decided to write myself. I was Humpty Dumpty trying to coax all the King's men into touching me inappropriately while putting me back together again. It was a big swing for a prestigious school.

"What was I thinking?" I scream-cried the whole way home, while Rory suppressed his smile. I could see his face contort, choking down his laughter as I explained how I accidentally made eye contact with the school's director and flirted with him in character, calling him a "dirty little pervert."

"What was I thinking?" was also the last thing Rory said to me before I left. I gripped my chest, trying to protect my heart, which I could physically feel breaking every time I thought about him.

I looked around the room of student actors as we all introduced ourselves, sharing our names, ages, hometowns, and one fun fact. There were about twenty of us in our group.

"Hi, I'm Zoë Reyes. Twenty-one. I'm from Connecticut and I hate cheese." Zoë had emerald eyes and long, dark-brown hair pulled back into a clip. She was gorgeous, with thick curtain bangs and a tight green V-neck shirt that showed her curves with precision. Her voice was raspy. We made eye contact, and she pulled a small, uncertain face, then chuckled at her silent admission of nervousness. Somehow, she oozed sex appeal, and all she had said was "I hate cheese." I liked Zoë instantly. She was cool, but the likelihood of her connecting with a Canadian who wore a Bionator and headgear until she was ten felt improbable.

"I'm Lucas Martin. Twenty-four. I'm from Paris. I can get anyone underage into a bar, guaranteed." Lucas's quick but playful tone, combined with his rolls-off-the-tongue Parisian accent, brought everyone to attention. He wore a soft-blue long-sleeved shirt rolled up, showcasing his strong, tattooed forearms. His dark-brown, almost black hair was styled with a side part but also pushed casually behind his ears. He was leaning forward, arms pressed into his thighs, and his eyes penetrated every person in the circle. He was clean-cut, but you could tell he had to shave every morning and maybe every night to stay that way. I could have sworn I heard Zoë from across the circle exhale a noise through her nose when his stare connected with hers. She then shifted, uncrossing and then recrossing her legs, and I wondered if she had just accidentally come in her seat.

I pulled a face while looking at Zoë, silently communicating, *You good, girl?*

A surprised expression spread across her face, and she slowly shook her head. *Nope.*

I snorted, then my eyes shifted to the person sitting next to Zoë. He was looking at me, not Zoë or Lucas, and his eyebrows popped upward when we made eye contact.

Shake it off, Ellie. You're up.

"Good to know, Lucas, because the drinking age in Vancouver is nineteen, but here, sadly, I'm only twenty. Also, I'm Ellie. McCain. If you see a cougar, it's probably been stalking you for forty-five minutes . . . I think. So, yup. That's the thing I've chosen to say." I looked over the room and could see everyone barely listening as they prepared their own answers. All but three: Zoë, Lucas, and . . .

"I'm Ben Winters." Ben's voice was deep, but soft. He sounded like he knew what it was like to camp under a tarp. He kept his forest-green eyes on mine. "I'm twenty-three. From Seattle. Think of it as a better Vancouver."

My face snapped into a frown. The. Gall. Ben held my gaze, refusing to turn away as the next person stepped up to the plate. They could have been speaking another language. I genuinely have no clue who they were or what they said. I was so immediately in my own head. I scrunched my nose and squinted suspiciously at Ben. I popped two fingers toward my eyes, then pointed them at whoever was talking, encouraging Ben to pay attention to *that person*. Whoever they were.

Beneath his crossed arms, Ben's chest lifted with a silent chuckle. My eyes shifted back to Zoë, sitting beside him. She was mirroring the exact contorted expression that I had given her when she unintentionally groaned for Lucas. *Girl. You good?*

I tried to keep my focus on the class but found myself studying Ben from across the circle instead. He had dark-blond, thick, slightly wavy hair. I suspected that it took him forever to perfect his "casual, just-out-of-bed" strategically messy coif. He looked more formal than anyone else in the group, wearing a crisp white button-down shirt that had a couple of buttons open at the top, revealing a hint of his muscular chest. I would have put a thousand dollars down that this Seattleite grew up playing hockey or football—one of the cool kids.

He caught me looking at him, and his lips twitched.

Crap! I wasn't ogling. I really wasn't, and he probably thought I was.

He lifted his fingers to meet his eyes and threw them out at the teacher, this time telling *me* to pay attention. My face burned, but his silent laugh kept me grounded.

At the end of the orientation, our Acting Technique teacher, Jess Munch, a sixty-year-old silver-haired goddess, encouraged us to memorize the face of each person in our group. She said we would be together day and night, leaning on each other, sharing our darkest secrets, trusting each other, using each other, and needing each other for the next two years. She said we'd become more than simply the best of friends. We'd love each other and be bound by this moment because this was the moment we found out who we were.

I didn't know how to feel. In theory, that all sounded great—if it had been with the people I grew up with, like Kara and Jacob Griffin, or my sister, Hannah . . .

Don't think about the Campbells, Ellie.

I looked around the room at all the students gathering, talking, and laughing with each other. It felt like such a performance. Everyone was already performing whatever version of themselves they'd decided to be at Bronwyn but hadn't yet become, including me.

I caught Zoë's eye from the drinks table. She waved at me, then mouthed, *What are we doing?*

I mouthed back, *I have no fucking idea.* My face twisted the second I said it.

What the hell was that? Why did I swear? Is that a thing I do? My first sentence to her, and I swear?

It was just another performance, but I had no idea the part I was playing. I was starting to sweat from so much trying. I guess Jess Munch was right: I was already finding out who I really was, and apparently, I was a moron.

The evening was over, and Ben finally made his way to me. Instead of officially introducing himself, he simply said, "You hungry?"

Ben and I walked into the brightly lit pizza place across the street from the school. The display case featured enormous, tourist-size slices covering all the basics from cheese to pepperoni to meat lover's and Hawaiian. There were a couple of specialty slices ranging from shrimp and lobster to turkey, stuffing, and cranberry.

Ben leaned over the counter but kept his body open to me so I could view the display case. He pointed at the "Thanksgiving Special" and grimaced. "That can't be good, right?"

"Who knows, but do we try it now or wait for Thanksgiving?" I said, then ordered a spicy Hawaiian with a drizzle of hot honey and chili oil.

"You just told me everything I need to know about you with that order," Ben said without looking at me. "Can I get the one with mushroom ragù sauce?" he asked the guy behind the counter.

"Seriously? Blech." I gave the hardest stink face imaginable, and the worker threw up his middle finger at me, causing Ben to chuckle.

My jaw dropped. *Seriously?!* The worker turned his back to me, and I leaned in to Ben. "That guy just fingered me."

Ben's laugh blasted throughout the small space. "What? Jesus. Don't say that again."

"What?" I could feel my own laugh bubbling from within as I pulled out my card to pay for my slice. Ben swatted my hand away and handed his card to the teller, steamrolling me.

Ben turned back to me. "You said that guy *fingered* you."

I pointed at the server, disgruntled. "He did! Did you not see that?"

"Is that a Canadian thing?"

"Is it an American thing to just finger people?!" I spat out defensively.

"Oh my god, Ellie." Ben laughed again, covering his face this time.

"Girl. Stop saying that," a stranger behind us in line said with a giggle.

"What's going on? *He's* the asshole here!" My face tightened with confusion.

Ben looked me straight in the eyes. "He *gave you* the finger. Gave. You. Or he flipped you the bird. It's not 'He fingered me.' How do you not know that?"

"I'm not saying anything wrong. What I'm saying is normal." I started to blush, but I carried on, deciding to be stubborn. The guy handed us our greasy pizza on paper plates, and I said it once more for good measure, with my hardest stare. "You fingered me, and I didn't like it!"

Ben and the stranger in line both laughed. I smacked Ben's shoulder with a smile but refused to give an inch, like the McCain I was raised to be.

"Come on. I asked Lucas if he wanted to meet us here in a bit, too." Ben tilted his head to the side so I would follow him to a seat along the window bar.

"How'd you feel about tonight?" I asked as we took our seats.

"I don't know. I kinda can't believe I'm here," he answered honestly, folding his pizza in half. "I helped Lucas move a couch through the East Village the other night, and it felt like I was in a movie."

"Oh, do you know him from before?" I took a bite of my pizza.

"We did the summer program together and were invited to join full-time. So, yeah." Ben took off his jacket and draped it over another barstool. "I thought I was going back to Seattle to my girlfriend and our dog, because I moved here for six weeks on a whim, but then I had two weeks to decide if I was going to throw my old life away and start again. It wouldn't be the first time, so I went for it."

"Wait! Let me guess!" I said excitedly. "You were an athlete who got injured and became an actor."

Ben stared me down, bothered. "Well, that was disturbing. Am I a cliché?"

"Football or hockey?"

"I don't like this," he paused, then narrowed his eyes at me. "D-1 baseball. Pitcher. Torn labrum."

I nodded, somewhat proud of myself, taking a sip of water and watching Lucas and Zoë scurry across the street, heading toward the pizza place to join us.

"Anyway, yeah. Take a guess as to whether or not my girlfriend and I decided to stay together and do long distance," he said sarcastically, with his mouth full of food. With his low register, it sounded a lot like garbled gibberish.

I snorted out some water from my nose and grabbed a napkin, muttering, "Jesus Christ."

Ben smirked at my reaction. He shook his head again as he dipped his pizza in some ranch dressing. "What's his name?"

"Rory," I grumbled. "You?"

"Sasha," he groaned.

"Is that the girl or the dog?" I asked, and he laughed. Ben lifted his slice of pizza in my direction for a cheers, and I reciprocated by tapping it with my own.

"Where are you living?"

"In a studio on the Upper West Side. Looking for a roommate, so if you know anyone . . ."

"Yeah." Ben laughed again, with his mouth full of ranch dressing this time. "Me. I'm staying on a family friend's couch in Dobbs Ferry until I get my shit together."

I scoffed. "Okay, Stranger Danger, you can't live with me." My mouth was jam-packed with pineapple.

"Why not?"

"Because you heard the worst version of what I said earlier instead of assuming the best. You *saw* that guy finger me!" Ben choked on his pizza. "You went negative. Now I can only assume that there's a ten percent chance that you might murder me. My parents would be so annoying if I picked a murderer to live with. They think I'm going to, and I can't prove them right. I just can't. I'm too stubborn. If you don't kill me, that would."

Ben turned to me, analyzing me. "Fair enough."

Two minutes later, Lucas and Zoë pulled up a seat next to us. My dad joined us an hour later. And Ben was my roommate by the end of the week.

Chapter 4

VANCOUVER
14 years old

IT WAS OFFICIALLY THE LAST DAY OF SUMMER, AND RORY AND I had been spending almost every day together. It would have been unusual if a day had gone by at Juniper and the regular junior golfers weren't all there. When it was sunny, we were golfing. When it was raining, we were in the clubhouse eating, playing games, or watching movies in the small games room. Rory and I would fight over which movie to watch, and our squabbles had become so common that we were often overruled.

Whenever Rory looked at me and asked, "Do you wanna watch a movie?" I would look back at him and scowl, knowing he would never agree to my movie choice no matter what I suggested. Those spirited debates lit me on fire.

I was looking in the woods for my lost ball, which happened to be the very last ball in my bag. There was a coyote den between the sixteenth and seventeenth holes, so Rory left his ball, perfectly placed in the center of the sixteenth fairway, and came to help me look for mine. His brother Blair and the club's newest junior, Jacob Griffin, were already ahead of us, making their way to their own balls. Everyone was smack dab in the center of the fairway, and I was hacking at the brush, sidestepping tree roots, and making shrill *ca-caw* sounds to ward off hungry wild animals looking for a feast. Rory chuckled when my last *ca-caw* caught in my throat and turned into a cough.

Rory never made me feel bad for hitting a terrible shot. It was probably because it happened so frequently in front of him. Aside from the driving range debacle two years earlier, I'd had one other horrifying display of terrible golf that I was certain would be etched into my tombstone.

I had signed up for the Women's Long Drive competition at the beginning of the summer after my dad and Rory spent two weeks convincing me that I would place. I had no hope in the junior category when people like Rory, his brother Blair, and another junior named Caleb Davis, the rich kid, were competing. But when it came to the ladies, I was okay. I constantly had older men at the driving range commenting to my dad (never to me) about how impressive my swing was.

I had five chances. I just had to hit it far and within bounds. Rory volunteered to be the person who'd stake where my ball landed. About a hundred people showed up to watch the competition, including my mom. My sister and my best friend, Kara, Jacob's sister, were sitting on top of golf carts with some other juniors, lining the rough. Competitors gathered around the first tee.

I had auditioned for a bunch of commercials, was a body double for a lead in a made-for-TV movie, and had been the lead in two school plays, but the Long Drive competition felt like I was in a pressure cooker. I had the nervous poops for thirty minutes before they called my name.

"Let's go, Cainey!" Cameron Campbell shouted as he climbed onto the hood of Kara's golf cart. The Campbell brothers had started calling me Cainey, sometimes Cains, two years earlier, after I trounced them in a hot-dog-eating contest. Only my sister knew how violently ill I was after that exhibition of competitive assholery.

"Come on, Hollywood!" Orson Whitlock, another junior, the same age as me, called out—yet another nickname he started after learning that I liked to act. I turned around to smile at Orson. He was standing behind me with Blair, Jacob, and Caleb. They were ready to compete.

Rory jogged up to me at the tee box, his brownish curly hair swooped along the sides of his black Titleist hat, which he had flipped backward. His dark-brown eyes sparkled with excitement, and his dimple dipped into his cheek. He handed me five balls.

"You got this, Ellie." Rory said my name. He never said my real name. My throat closed. He tossed me a wink and ran down the fairway to capture my drives.

Rory Campbell called me Ellie. Rory Campbell only calls me Cainey. Why was Rory Campbell calling me Ellie, and why did he wink? A wink? He really did wink, right? Did I imagine that?

DUFF. DUFF. DUFF. DUFF. And DUFF.

I didn't hit any of my balls. I hit the ground behind them, taking chunks out of the grass every time. All five balls rolled into the hedge at the front of the first tee box. Rory didn't see a single shot and only knew my turn was over once another player was called. I came in last place—thirty-fifth, to be exact. I went and picked up one of my five duffed balls and put it in my pocket to bring it home with me. I wouldn't be able to tape it to a diary, but I was certainly going to keep it, to remind myself that I was a piece of shit.

"The plan is the theater program at UCLA. I'm gonna get a yellow Jeep. I'll wear a bright-blue Dodgers hat, like, every day." I swung my club in the tall grass next to the sand trap, looking for my lost ball. "I'll marry a celebrity, and every time I come back, I'll have to get my dad to remind me what your name is because I won't be able to keep all the normies straight. You'll understand," I teased.

"Oh, will I?" Rory took his trusty black hat off to readjust. The sporadic sunlight caught in his auburn streaks, making him look like the quintessential teenage heartthrob.

"That's the plan."

"Which celebrity are you marrying?" Rory played along with my game and trudged farther into the weeds to look for my ball.

"Elijah Wood," I answered with absolute certainty.

"Is that the hobbit?" Rory smirked.

"Yes. And?" I popped my foot out and leaned on my club.

Watching Rory laugh always sent a shock wave through my system. I could see his dimple form, his eyes blaze. He would run his fingers through his curly hair or adjust his hat mid-laugh, and I would think, "That was because of me."

The sky rumbled overhead.

"Alright, three questions each. Go." I checked behind a random tree along the rough.

"Hmm . . ." Rory swung his club through the thick grass, smacking a log. "What's your favorite movie? And what's your favorite song?"

"*Scream*, and . . ." I had to think carefully about what to say for the song. Something older, and mature, maybe? Something unexpected and maybe even a little abstract or unpopular. The perfect answer would make me sound like I was cool, unique, and an interesting conversationalist with lots of provocative and sexy thoughts. "Maybe . . . anything by . . . I don't know, the Beatles?"

"The Beatles? You hang out with your friends listening to the Beatles? I think you've been spending a little bit too much time with your dad. I don't know your grandparents, but I'm guessing them, too." His smile twitched, teasing me.

Goddamn it.

Instead of embarrassing me further, he dropped his gaze and then dropped a grenade. "I have some music that reminds me of you, you know."

"You do?!" I said, louder than I meant to, scaring away a flock of birds. "What music?" I heard my voice go up an octave and told myself to chill out.

He shook his head and doubled back, checking to see if my ball was nestled by a rake in the sand trap. "Nope. I still have one more question."

"What is it?"

Rory kept his back to me as he asked, "Do you have a boyfriend?"

My heart pounded through the top of my head. There may have been ringing in my ears. I may have been levitating. "Um." I choked over my spit, then cleared my throat. So far, I was nailing this. "No. No boyfriend."

Rory turned back to me, unfazed and unbothered. "Alright, your turn."

I took a deep breath. "Um, okay . . . What's your favorite movie? Do you have a girlfriend? And what song makes you think of me?" I think I died.

I could see Rory holding back his smile as he pressed his lips together. "Favorite movie will always be *Terminator 2*. No, I don't have a girlfriend." He flicked his eyes up to me very briefly and then flipped his hat around. "And the song 'November Rain.' You know it?"

"No." But you better believe I was going to listen to that song on repeat every day for the rest of my life. Rory's eyes hooked on to mine, and we both released small, shy smiles.

"Hurry up, ya freakin' turtles!" Jacob bellowed from a hundred yards ahead of us, jolting us back to Earth. I looked up to the dark clouds that had seemingly come out of nowhere.

"It's going to rain. It's super warm, too. I bet there's a storm." Things were looking ominous. "Do I just forget the ball and walk?" I looked at Rory and knew he could see humiliation dripping from me. I slammed my club into the inside of my foot, mortified.

"No, don't be stupid. I'll give you a ball."

"This is so embarrassing." I threw my face into my hands and sighed. "Why do I keep embarrassing myself in front of you?"

"Why would that matter?"

"What do you mean?" I straightened. My organs all contracted at the exact same time.

"Embarrassing yourself in front of me. Why would that matter?"

"I don't know." I diverted my attention back to the forest. "Just does, I guess."

"But you're so good at it." Rory's smile tightened.

"Whatever." I kept my eyes locked on the deep, deep woods and frowned. "Jacob's wrong. I'm not a turtle."

"I know you're not," Rory declared as he dug into his pocket to give me his spare ball. "You're a bird." He tossed it on the ground, flipped his hat around again so it was forward-facing, then nodded toward the ball that lay neatly in the grass. "Hit the ball," he insisted.

"I'm a bird?" I asked, and he nodded. "What kind of bird do you think I am?"

I took a reluctant swing, and in the exact moment I connected with the ball, he said, "Maybe an ostrich?"

SHANK!

The ball flew ninety degrees in front of me, and right in Rory's direction. Rory screamed as he dropped to the ground, ducking out of the way. The ball rocketed into the forest.

"Shut it, children! We're on a golf course!" It was Blair shouting this time.

"You almost hit me!" Rory's eyes were wild. I threw my club into my bag with an embarrassed giggle. "How are you so good, but also so bad?" His smile had taken over his entire face as he grabbed his bag.

"You. That's how, you dummy. You make me nervous, and you give me the frickin' yips!" I realized my confession and carefully lifted my eyes to meet his.

"Why do I make you nervous?" His gently sloped, closed-mouth smile had him glowing from the inside out.

"You just do, Rory." I shook my head dismissively while pulling the backpack-style straps of my bag over my shoulders, then yanking my ponytail free. "We should go. I'm not hitting another ball. I've accepted my fate." We slowly walked toward his ball in the middle of the fairway in silence before I finally said, "I can't believe you said I'm an ostrich."

"What?" Rory couldn't help but laugh. "Is that bad?"

"Yes. That's bad. Have you ever *seen* an ostrich?"

"They're cool!" Rory defended. "Okay, fine. California condor, seeing as that's where you'll live one day. Is that better?"

My face scrunched. "I don't like the idea of being a bird. They're either all neck or no neck, you know?"

"What do you think I am?" Rory gripped the straps of his bag, his knuckles tensing. All I could hear was the sound of our clubs clanking into each other as we walked.

"Oh man." I exhaled. I wanted to get this right. I scanned my brain, trying to think of an animal that could somehow secretly convey to Rory exactly who he was and that he was perfect, but without appearing obvious or pathetic. "Maybe a sheep?"

"A sheep?!" he bellowed.

Oh, fuck. I blew it.

"Like, I just follow the crowd?"

"No! Not at all. I didn't even think about that." I started to sweat. "You're calm, and cool, and nothing ever bothers you. And there's all this stuff under your layers that you hide away."

Stop talking, Ellie.

"Everyone loves you and your brothers, so you've got your herd. And you're warm and fuzzy and . . . good."

Stop. Talking.

Rory kept his eyes on his feet as we walked. "So, you think I have no bite?"

"SO, YOU THINK I'M AN OSTRICH?!"

Rory laughed again, tipping his head back and pinching his nose between his fingers. "No. I take it back, okay? California condor."

"Why are you so sure I'm a bird?" I twisted my waist and bumped his bag with my own from behind our backs.

"Because eventually you're gonna fly away."

"Damn right. Right down south to Los Angeles. The die has been cast." I smiled. "I can't help that she calls to me."

"Los Angeles is a girl?"

"She is now." I giggled.

"Did I tell you that I saw you in the background of a Colgate commercial the other day?" Rory looked down at his feet and kicked a chunk of loose grass.

"You did?"

"Yeah. You looked . . ." He trailed off, stopping himself from saying anything he shouldn't be saying. "It was cool." After about a minute of walking in silence, Rory asked, "Are you excited for tomorrow?"

"For school? No."

For school? Never. No one at Juniper knew about my alter ego, where I was an obnoxious theater kid, and such a bloody try-hard that even the teachers rolled their eyes at me. Rory and I didn't go to the same school. And even though I was an awkward, boy-crazy little turd, and had a different crush every other week, absolutely everyone in my class knew about Rory.

"Are *you* excited for tomorrow?"

"No," Rory answered.

My throat went dry as I thought about how my time with Rory was going to change drastically as of the next day. We'd see each other on weekends, but school friends and other sports would slowly start to get in the way. Eventually, Rory and I wouldn't have an easy banter because we wouldn't be part of each other's everyday lives. I'd get a random crush on some boy, but would still end each day thinking, "But he's not Rory." The winter would be a dead zone, and then, hopefully, when spring bloomed, we would bloom again.

"Are you gonna miss . . . summer?" He pressed his lips together. Each step we took along the fairway closed our distance until our arms were brushing against each other.

"Yeah." I felt a drop on my nose. And then another. And another. "Are you gonna miss . . . summer?"

Rory stopped walking, then locked his big brown eyes on mine. I could see honey around his pupils. The light rain made his Summer Skin freckles look like they were moving.

"I'm gonna miss it a lot." He narrowed his eyes at me playfully. "Summer."

Our smiles faded, and we held our stare. It was the longest I had ever looked at anyone outside of a family member. A crack of lightning and a quick boom of thunder startled us into the present.

"Oh no!" My panic sprang up without warning, and I told myself it had nothing to do with Rory. "There's lightning! We're in these massive trees, we've got metal clubs, and we're the only dummies left at the club with metal spikes on our shoes! Doesn't lightning come from the ground?" I shrieked.

Rory grinned, amused by my mayhem. He kept his eyes on mine, then bent down and took off his shoes.

"What are you doing?!" I squealed. His socks were instantly soaked as he tossed his bag and shoes to the side.

"If one of us is going to be a lightning rod, Cains, it's not gonna be me." He shot off like a bullet, sprinting down the golf course.

"Rory!" I dropped my bag on the ground and ripped my shoes from my feet, throwing them violently at my bag.

"Blair!" Rory shouted at his brother. "No one will care if you die. Get our stuff!"

"What are you two doing, you assholes?!" Blair called back.

We sprinted past Blair and Jacob, with our socks sloshing through puddles, and ran the final three holes together, laughing in the rain.

Chapter 5

NEW YORK
20 years old

BEING BEN'S ROOMMATE WAS STRANGE. I HAD NEVER LIVED WITH anyone other than my family, and the only man I'd lived with was my dad.

Not only was our space small, but it was entirely shared. We had no room for ourselves except for on the toilet or in the shower, and even then, it was hampered because we didn't have a kitchen sink. Within the first month, I was sitting on the ledge of the bathtub shaving my legs, while Ben was doing the dishes right next to me. The number of times that my stomach cramped in the night from holding in gas had become obscene.

Our comfort level was tested the first time I got sick. I turned on the sink and the shower to drown out the noises, but Ben knocked on the door, and instead of offering his support, he quietly said, "Don't think I don't know what's going on in there."

Ben would wake up early to make breakfast, and I would get ready in the bathroom first. We liked to walk down Broadway to school, always stopping for coffee. In those walks, we told each other everything, then would pick the conversation back up on our walks home.

I got a job as an unpaid intern at a film production company that was run by a young, up-and-coming actor named Justin Bordin, who was only a couple of years older than I was. Other than panicking over stocking the kitchen with kombucha and the exact right energy drinks, my job was to answer the phones and make sure the printer always had paper. The goal was to eventually get miraculously discovered, but I quickly learned that Justin didn't give two craps about the nobodies in his office when he fired his assistant mid mood swing because he "didn't like her haircut."

At night, Ben and I would run lines. We would often meet for dinner on the days that I had shifts at my internship, at either the diner across the street or the Indian restaurant attached to our building. We had a system in place, and it worked. On nights when he didn't come home, I assumed he was staying over at a friend's place or a girl's place. On nights when I didn't come home, he assumed I was dead, because I always came home.

It had only been a month, but there was an ease to our instant friendship. Ben and I drifted toward each other like two magnets snapping into position. At school, we were scene partners and were always standing or sitting next to each other.

Most classes were held in small, old-fashioned, original rooms spread across four floors of the historic Upper West Side building. The ground floor was Bronwyn's newly renovated six-hundred-seat theater, and because there was a show in the middle of a run on our theater's main stage, we rarely, if ever, had access to that theater. We practiced Alexander Technique, Speech and Dialect, Classical Text, Mask, Dance, everything, in those small rooms. The exceptions were Movement for Actors and Stage Combat, which always ran early in the morning and onstage to save our bodies from being run ragged against the lead-painted floors. So we were all taken aback when our Combat teacher, Don Gomez, sent us upstairs and into one of the old rooms, where he would be teaching us how to roll safely.

Ben and I coupled up. The yellow chairs that usually lined the walls for Scene Study were stacked and pushed into the corner, and individual mats were placed in front of us. Ben was wearing shorts and a white tank top, while I was in black leggings and a black top, with my hair tied into a ponytail. Ben tugged at my ponytail, and I hip-checked him as Don made his way around the room, weaving in and out of the pairs.

"Tuck your head inside your shoulder, then hit the ground, or you'll break your wrists. Easy." Don demonstrated by rolling against the hard ground like a teenager.

Ben extended his hand for me to go first. "You heard the man. Easy."

"That's all we get? Just tuck my head? I'm going to land on my ear." I watched everyone around us start throwing themselves to the ground. It was moments like this when I often thought about what Kara was doing back home in her Introduction to Environmental Science class. Or what Hannah was doing in her Cognitive Neuroscience class. I wondered what my parents would think if they knew this was what their child was getting up to on her big New York adventure. The week before, I'd had to actively prevent a premature quarter-life crisis. As I lay on the ground next to Ben and all my new friends while we birthed our inner clowns, I found myself thinking, "What am I doing with my life?"

"Don't land on your face or your wrists, and you'll be fine. Like this." Ben flipped himself over and landed back on his feet like he was a gymnast.

"It's hilarious that you think I can do that," I said, straight-faced.

"Turn your body on the way down, Ellie." Don stopped at Ben and me. "Start on your knees and let your shoulder lead the way."

I dropped down on one knee and placed my hands on the mat in front of me. Don put his hand on the top of my head, tucked my chin into my chest, then playfully kicked me in the ass to roll me over. Don had become one of my favorite teachers at Bronwyn. He was the only teacher who appeared to realize that we were all spending two years of our lives delaying reality and just wanted us to have some fun. I got back up, and Ben threw himself over again, accidentally knocking into Lucas, who had coupled up with Zoë.

"You alright there, Lucas?" Don asked.

Lucas tossed a thumbs-up and then put his hands back on Zoë to help her.

"I see what you're doing, Zoë," I snarked.

"What?" Zoë cooed.

Lucas's black hair fell into his face as he bent her over. They weren't fooling anyone as they enjoyed their sneaky little public groping session.

"Alright, go for it, babe." Don clapped my back.

Once Don moved on to another pair, I turned to Ben, who had his hands on his hips, waiting impatiently for me. "Don Gomez just called me babe."

Ben shrugged. "Come on. Let's go. You being a chicken-shit here isn't cute."

"Fine." I turned my palms inward, so they faced my body, hoping that would stop me from landing on my hands. The last thing I wanted was to snap my wrist in my first month in New York. I leaned forward, shoulder first, and I missed the mat and inadvertently slid hard against the floor. Somehow, as fate would have it, an old chunk of the chipped lead paint that coated the floors jammed under the first layer of skin beneath my index finger. It was like bamboo had been rammed beneath my fingernail, only it wasn't bamboo, it was hardened, poisonous paint.

"AHHHHHHH! FUUCKKK!" I screamed.

"What?! What happened?!" Ben dropped to the ground and grabbed my shoulder.

"Hoooooooooly shiiiiit," I said, losing clarity in my speech. I was drowsy and nauseated. It was as if I were drunk. The class stopped, and I lifted my trembling hand to show Don and Ben my finger.

"What is that?" Don asked.

"It's paint. It's chipped paint. Under my nail."

"Oh. Okay. We've got to get that out." Don lifted me to my feet, and Ben put his arm around my waist to steady me. "Everyone, keep going." Don pretended he wasn't in a full-blown panic.

Ben held on to me, and Don took us down in the elevator to the director of the theater department's office, where he sat me in a chair. It was there that they decided the best course of action was for Don to try to take the chipped paint out from beneath my fingernail . . . with a needle.

"A needle?!" Ben's face turned white. "What are you gonna do?"

Don pulled out a needle from a sewing kit inside one of the office closets, where random twenty-year-old wardrobe items from plays of Bronwyn's past were left to decompose. The director of the theater department, Jeffrey Rander, stood behind his office desk, bent over, watching the entire ordeal unfold with a pained expression on his face, his hands on his knees.

"We're just going to press the tip of the needle against the chip underneath your nail. Then the chip will slide out as we pull," Don said.

"But I don't have long nails!" I replied incredulously, tears squirting from my eyes.

Ben's face went from white to green. "This is literal torture. You can't do this."

"The cut has already happened, so we're just going to go a little bit under the cut with the needle." Don swallowed. His eyes widened as the words came out of his mouth and he saw my look of pure terror. He gulped, then forced me to bear witness to the world's fakest smile. I guffawed as aggressively as I could.

"I thought you were a teacher at an acting school!" I pointed at Don's smile. "What the hell is that shit?"

"Um, uh . . ." Don was startled by my instant snap of personality.

"Do better!" I demanded, and Don tried his hardest to soften his smile, offering me comfort. "That's worse, Don! Boo!" I cried.

Ben patted my leg. "She's not herself right now."

Don realigned in his seat, tightening his muscles as he settled his body closer to mine. He fastened our legs together like we were a zipper and carefully took my injured hand in his. He raised the needle.

"Hey, hey, hey!" Ben sat next to me. "I don't like this."

"Ellie, dear . . . It's Ellie, right? Do you want something to bite on?" Jeffrey Rander, whom we mostly saw when shit hit the fan, made the very considerate and lovely suggestion without looking at me.

"Jesus Christ. What is this, a war movie?" Ben asked disbelievingly. "Want some cotton in your ears to drown out her screaming, too, *Jeff*?" Ben hissed, unaware of how angry he sounded.

Don disinfected the needle, and Ben's face looked stricken. "I can't watch, Ellie."

"Don't leave, Ben!" I turned to him, panicked. "Please don't leave."

"I'm not leaving." He grabbed my good hand and squeezed. "I'm just not watching." Ben closed his eyes as Don moved the needle to my fingernail.

"You ready, babe?" Don asked.

"Stop calling me babe, you monster," I cried, causing Ben to chuckle, with his eyes still closed. I hung my head and then nodded.

Don buried the needle beneath my nail. I didn't writhe in pain, but my whole body swayed like I was on a pendulum. I tipped my head back, and my eyes rolled to the back of my head as I groaned in agony. "Fuuuck . . ." I whispered, having promptly lost all the wind in my lungs. "I can't do this . . ."

"Don't pass out, Ellie. Do not pass out." Ben still wasn't watching. He was clutching me with both of his hands now.

After about a minute of Don digging for treasure like he was Blackbeard searching for gold, I had to end it. "You gotta stop . . . Don. Stop," I hissed breathlessly.

Tears spilled from my eyes. Don's face contorted into a thousand wrinkles. Eventually, he put the needle down on Jeffrey's desk. I slumped over, and my head dropped between my legs.

"It'll just come out on its own eventually. I think. I'm guessing. I'm certain." Don turned to Jeffrey, who was nodding. A tense smile was plastered across his face, but he looked like a standing corpse.

"But it's lead paint. Shouldn't it, you know, *not* be in my body?" I mumbled. I had lost all strength from the torture I had just endured.

"It'll probably just come out on its own," Jeffrey said through gritted teeth. "Excuse me." He smiled, then left. To vomit, I assumed.

I finished my classes, suffering in pain like a goddamn champion, and when Ben and I got back to our Grayrock apartment, he sat on my bed with me, waiting to see what my next move would be. Anything touching my finger was still excruciating, so I left my hand out on the bedside table while hiding the rest of my body beneath the hideous fish-in-a-martini-glass bedsheet that I got for 80 percent off at Macy's.

"Maybe we could try . . . the needle thing again? Or is it hospital time? I genuinely don't know what to do right now, buddy. Do you have insurance? Do we just assume it'll come out? It'll come out, right?" Ben shook his head, perplexed. "Here, let me make you dinner. That's something I can do." Ben stood and opened our small, empty fridge. "We have no food! What's wrong with us?"

I sprung up. I went into the bathroom and pulled out my makeup kit, then fished around with my good hand until I found my metal nail file.

"Ellie, what are you doing?" Ben gasped, wide-eyed. He zeroed in on my nail file.

By this point, I was a machine. "I'm getting it out." There was zero lightness to my voice. I started filing my nail the usual way, screamed bloody murder, and realized I was just pushing the chip in farther and sculpting it beneath my first layer of skin.

I looked at the file, then my nail again. Removing my entire nail was the only way to get the lead paint out. So I started filing my nail from the top down. Once again, my body began swaying with torment, and my eyes rolled to the back of my head. Ben was watching me, stunned, as if he were living inside a horror movie.

"I'm gonna faint." Ben looked dead behind the eyes.

"Don't. Don't do it. If you faint, I'll decapitate you in your sleep with my nail file."

Ben couldn't hold my hands because they were busy, but he sat on his bed, across from me, and held on to the outside of my thighs. "W-what am I supposed to do?"

"I don't know. Just be with me," I whispered with my eyes closed. I pressed down on my wound harder, sawing my nail off, needing it all to just be over with. Fire shot up my arm with every stroke of the nail file. The nerves in my neck pinched, twisting my body uncontrollably.

Ben brought his hands from my legs to the sides of my head, and he held me in place. He pressed his forehead to mine and swayed with me. I kept my eyes closed as he slowed his breath down.

"Deep breaths, buddy." He took a long, deep inhale and started counting, forcing me to slow down with him until we were breathing together. He held my head against his and moved with me until I'd filed off my entire nail.

Both of our eyes were on my finger, and he quietly said, "Holy shit," as I peeled back my first layer of skin. Ben brought his lips to my forehead and kept them there while still holding my head. He counted again with his mouth against my skin, trying to keep me calm as I pulled out the piece of chipped lead paint.

"I did it." I finally let out a breathless laugh. Ben's forehead fell into my lap. I instinctively threaded the fingers on my good hand through his hair. I closed my eyes and tilted my head back, trying to catch my breath. Ben eventually looked up at me and shook his head. His mouth was open. He was struggling to find the words he wanted to say.

"You're a maniac." He smiled, then moved away from me. "Let me get you a Band-Aid. And a bucket of disinfectant."

"Okay . . ." I climbed beneath my sheet once again and looked over at the discarded paint chip. I couldn't control my feeble laughter. "Ben?"

"Yeah?" he said, coming out of the bathroom with a Band-Aid.

"I filed off my nail."

Ben matched my laughter as he tended to my finger. "Damn right you did. You're Ellie Fucking McCain. Remind me never to underestimate you." Ben gave my hand a quick kiss and surprised me when he didn't let go.

"Thank you for being there with me today. And for just now, too."

Ben opened his mouth, but whatever he was about to say, he decided against it. He snapped his mouth shut again and let out a quick recovery breath before asking, "Want me to run downstairs and grab us some dinner?"

"Yes, please." I nodded, then leaned back against my headboard. Other than a clown, I had never birthed anything before, but the feeling of expelling that paint chip from my body was euphoric and otherworldly. I had two choices. I could tape the paint chip into my diary, or I could keep it on the bedside table, next to my lucky golf ball.

Chapter 6

VANCOUVER
15 years old

HANNAH, KARA, AND I WALKED INTO JUNIPER'S BALLROOM, AND it was buzzing with boys. It was our first time attending Junior Night, which was a ruse pulled off by management at the start of the season to have the juniors run around the course after hours and fill in all the divots, holes, and damaged grass. Afterward, a buffet was set out for a juniors-only dinner and movie night.

It was the first time I had ever walked into Juniper wearing jeans and a regular shirt. I had decided to wear a black tank top with a boat neck that sat just below my collarbone. It was the absolute most amount of skin I had ever shown to the golf club boys, and I was both terrified and titillated knowing that they might look at me just a little bit differently than they usually did. Hannah even put makeup on me and told me to wear my wavy hair down.

"He's going to like it. He's only ever seen you in a ponytail," she insisted.

"Who's he?" I said, and Hannah rolled her eyes at me.

I had barely seen Rory since the previous summer. Once the weather turned, our weekends at the course were off. Our timing was never right, and then life got in the way. I was nervous. I was more than nervous. I had to take a deep breath, feeling warmth rise to my cheeks as we stepped into the massive room with cherry wood floors, a cathedral ceiling, and twinkly white lights strung around the windows. "Scar Tissue" by the Red Hot Chili Peppers was playing through the speakers embedded in the walls.

A slideshow was playing on a projector, showing photos taken last summer. Jacob and Blair with their arms over each other's shoulders in a huddle, sticking their tongues out for the camera. Cameron putting on the twelfth green, with Hannah holding the flag in the background. Caleb on the practice green, with a group of boys clustered behind him. My breath hitched when I saw a photo of Rory pop up. He was sitting with his arms behind his head in the games room of the clubhouse, tilted back. His black golf hat was flipped backward, and his eyes were shut as he laughed. He was sitting beside Orson, who had doubled over, busting a gut. The picture faded into one of Kara and Hannah smiling inside a golf cart.

"Oh no. It's me. Look at that zit." Kara's head snapped back, causing her shiny brown bob to shimmy over her shoulders. Their picture shifted into a solo shot of me from behind. I was silhouetted and leaning against the bag stand by the driveway, where I would wait for my mom to pick me up, looking down the road with my ponytail flying in the wind.

I puffed out my cheeks and tightened my lips, traumatized.

"Oh wow. I love that photo of you, Ellie!" Hannah knocked me with her hip. Hannah was seventeen, and as the firstborn, it was evident she had stolen all the good traits from my parents, leaving me the leftovers. She was the "put together" sister. I was always "the mess."

Once I was sure the picture was off the screen, I slowly raised my eyes back up to the group of juniors. Not so hidden inside the sea of boys, I found Rory standing with Orson and Cameron. He was wearing a moss-green T-shirt and dark-brown corduroy pants. I had never seen him in anything other than khakis and a polo. His smile was downturned, and he was staring at me. His curls flipped over his ears.

He looked taller, too. He seemed calm and confident as he lifted his left hand from his pocket, keeping his wrist against his hip, and flicked me a small, almost invisible wave. I smiled and lifted my hand, giving him a tiny two-finger salute. His soft smile widened, and the moment his dimple revealed itself, he looked away.

I needed to calm down.

The music cut off, and a speaker shrilled sadistically with feedback. "Alright, everyone," a high voice screeched throughout the ballroom.

I stepped onto my tiptoes to look over the crowd and see the club's event manager holding the mic. She told us we would be broken into groups of five and given three holes to clean up, with six teams in total. The oldest junior on each team would drive the pickup truck. That statement led to a few rowdy whistles in the crowd, which had Hannah, Kara, and me giggling. The event manager paused, clearly already annoyed by the room full of teenagers. She then told us that the driver was solely responsible should anyone from their team experience an untimely death. This brought on another laugh. I looked over at Rory, standing with Cameron and Orson, and he was looking at me again. The moment our eyes met, he quickly snapped his head back to the event manager, and I watched his lips press firmly into each other, stopping himself from smiling. The event manager then pulled out a folded piece of paper and started listing off the groups. I held my breath. Team after team was called as I waited for my name.

Then it happened.

"Jacob, you'll be driving. Your team is Orson, Blair, Rory, and Cainey."

My sister, who was still standing on the other side of me, covertly grabbed my thigh and gave me a little squeeze. I couldn't prepare myself for the squeak that popped out of my mouth.

"Cainey? Why did she call me Cainey? I write my name on all the sign-ups as Ellie." I dropped my head into my neck, confused. "That's weird, right?"

I turned back to Rory. He was standing off to the side, leaning against the back wall, and his eyes were on me again. He shifted his weight, but didn't look away this time. It was the first time I ever had true, honest-to-God heart palpitations where it felt like a legitimate medical condition.

"Dammit. We're not together," Kara exclaimed, pulling my attention away from Rory.

"You're with Cameron, though. That'll be fun." Hannah grabbed a pop can from the drinks table.

"He grabbed my boob the last time I saw him," Kara said sulkily.

"What?" Hannah laughed.

"Not on purpose. He was reaching for the score sheet. I dropped it just as he went to grab it. I, like, bent into him. My entire boob went into his hand." Kara grabbed my hand to demonstrate.

"You've acted this out for me three times already. Why are we doing this again?" I scowled.

"It doesn't surprise me that you guys are starting to get all touchy. You're fifteen." Hannah smirked at Kara and me as if she knew she was about to blow our minds. "You know, I was fifteen when Blair kissed me."

She was right. Mind blown.

"What?!" I shrieked. More than a few people looked over at us, including Blair. Hannah smacked me, with a laugh, but I was . . . *not* laughing. "Are you joking right now?"

I was . . . I was . . . I was . . . *jealous.*

She shook her head and sipped her drink casually like a goddamn villain. "No, I'm not joking, and I didn't tell you because it's not a story. It happened once in the parking lot, no tongue, so random." She laughed again, and my jaw dropped.

"Ooooo." Kara's almond-shaped brown eyes were rapidly darting between us. "Are you mad? Are you jealous?" Kara appeared thrilled at the thought. "What are you right now? You're definitely something." She turned to Hannah. "You know Ellie has a *massive* crush on Rory, right?" Kara blurted out, not at all concerned with the boys that surrounded us, and I wanted to murder her.

"Kara!" I covered my face with my hands, mortified.

"Yes, obviously, I'm aware," Hannah answered in a hushed tone, trying to temper her laughter.

"Can we stop now, please?!" I begged.

"Alright, everyone." The event manager raised her hands to try to calm the growing restlessness of the crowd. "It's still light enough for us to do this, but that sun is on its way out, so no one on the course after dark, and be back here by seven for dinner."

"Have fun." Hannah grabbed my hand and looked over my shoulder with a smile. "Bye, Rory." Her eyes flipped back to me, and she gave my hand one quick squeeze.

I turned around to see Rory standing so close that I could have sworn I heard him thinking. He took a deep breath. I noticed that, for the first time, he was taller than me.

Before I could say anything, Blair flung his arms around us both and slammed all three of our heads together.

"Hey, Rore, what are the chances that we would get our little Cainey all to ourselves tonight? How did we get so lucky? It's almost like someone rigged the teams." Blair gave Rory a shake, with his arm wrapped around his neck. Rory's cheeks flushed. Blair turned his face toward mine, closer than ever.

Wrong brother. WRONG BROTHER!

"Are you wearing makeup?" Blair's face scrunched.

"Um, yup." I breathed, intensely aware of the ketchup chips I'd eaten earlier.

Blair let Rory and me go. "Nice. You look pretty." He gently brushed my hair over my shoulder, and that right there was the most intimate touch I had ever experienced from the opposite sex. "Let's do this." Blair winked and then walked away, leaving me stunned in his wake.

My eyes lifted to meet Rory's. His smile was gone. His body had tensed. He nodded without looking at me, then turned around and walked out of the ballroom.

Our team had holes ten, eleven, and twelve. Rory and I hadn't spoken during the entire cleanup portion of the night. He kept his distance as he dropped sand from his plastic bucket, staying on the other side of the fairway the entire time. I had seen him and Blair talking, walking together in the distance. Rory's shoulders were down, and his chest looked sunken. Blair had put his arm around his brother at one point during the conversation, half wrestling, half hugging. It was the only time I saw Rory smile.

I climbed into the truck's open box bed and tossed my bucket half-heartedly onto the mound of sand. We had all been sitting in the back of the truck whenever we needed to move longish distances. I would take that time to close my eyes, listen to whatever song Jacob had been blasting through his open windows, and feel the wind dance in my hair. There was one time I opened my eyes, hair whipping around my face, and found Rory watching me.

I leaned my legs over the back of the bed, sitting squarely on the dirt, and waited for everyone to come back. The night was done. I was done.

"What do you want to listen to, Ellie-Bee?" Jacob called from the driver's seat. He was eighteen, like Blair, and had always felt like a brother to me. Jacob had spent his entire life taking care of me, Kara, and Hannah. We fought like brother and sisters as well, but it was the kind of familial love that moved mountains.

"I don't know. Something cool." I pulled on my toes, stretching my sore feet.

"Well, you and I have two very different ideas of what's cool." Jacob shuffled through the truck's ancient CD collection.

"Okay, then *your* cool. It's probably the real one anyway."

Blair saddled up next to Jacob in the passenger seat and quickly grabbed the CD organizer from his hands. "Wait! I saw something before. I know which one." Blair flipped through the pages until he found exactly what he was looking for. He started playing Guns N' Roses' iconic power ballad "November Rain." He looked out devilishly at his younger brother, who was still working along the edge of the twelfth green. Rory lifted his head and closed his eyes when he heard the song choice. He collected himself before directing a death glare at Blair.

It was the song that Rory had said reminded him of me. My whole body hollowed out. I burned bright red. It was a song I had now listened to about a hundred thousand times. I had dissected the lyrics over and over, trying to figure out what it was about *this* song that made him think of me.

Orson jumped into the back of the truck and leaned against the cabin's frame. After three more minutes of Rory wasting everyone's time, Jacob shouted, "Time to go, Rore! Let's move it!"

Rory stalled for one last minute, just looking at his feet. I wondered what he was doing. What was he thinking? I couldn't take my eyes off him, especially after he stopped moving altogether and looked out at the sky, which was transforming into a lavender hue.

"Rory." Blair's calm voice pulled Rory from his trance. Rory's eyes finally lifted to mine. Between our eyes connecting and the music—not to be dramatic or anything—it's possible my spirit lifted from my body in that moment. I may have blacked out.

Rory slowly made his way from the green to the back of the truck. He tossed his bucket in the sand. I noticed that beneath his T-shirt, his arms were freckled and slightly flexed as he pulled himself into the truck. I was surprised when he sat next to me. Still, he said nothing. I could feel my pulse in my neck and wondered if he could see it nervously thumping away. Rory and I looked out at the multicolored sky revealed against the tall Douglas firs. Some stars had burned through the sunset. I should say something. Anything.

Say literally anything, Ellie.

Neither of us spoke. Blair did instead. He leaned out the truck's passenger window. "You kids ready?"

"Ready," Rory answered.

"Cool." Blair nodded. "Now, Rory, when are you going to tell Cainey you missed her?"

My heart thumped into my stomach. My throat went dry. I slowly turned my head to Rory, speechless. Blair ducked back into the truck, and Orson turned his head, looking away from us with a taut smile. Rory closed his eyes and sighed. He tilted his head back with an embarrassed laugh. After a couple of seconds of both of us just sitting there in silence, he leaned in to me ever so slightly.

"So . . ." It was the first thing he'd said to me all night. It was the first thing he'd said to me in weeks. Hell, in months! Rory's leg was stiff beside mine. He pressed his hands into his thighs and wiped. We were uncomfortably close, and it felt like we were supposed to be touching, but instead we were charging each other with energy.

"So . . ." I answered.

"I missed you." He whispered it quietly so no one else could hear. "Your turn," he prodded, not letting anyone in on our private confessions. I was barely breathing as we shared a smile. It was soft. It was small. And it was only for each other.

"I missed you, too."

He shuffled his body and inched closer to me until his leg was lightly pressing against mine. Neither of us moved. It felt like I had been electrocuted, and the press of his knee was the only thing I could feel or focus on. The rest of my body had numbed.

It was this small moment that changed my life. It was right then that I gave it all away. Wind in my hair, "November Rain" blasting, legs touching and knocking into each other, clutching onto the back of the pickup truck as it sped across Juniper's rolling hills . . . That was when my heart no longer belonged to me. It belonged to Rory Campbell.

Chapter 7

NEW YORK
20 years old

"HE'S TAKING A BATH." I WAS PACING BETWEEN BEN'S AND MY twin beds and holding my phone hard against my ear. I could tell from his huffing through the phone that Ben was dodging piles of garbage as he walked home from his shift at Lifers Bar & Grill.

"A bath?! What happened to drinks?"

Ben and I had been living together for three months. We had already fallen into a comfortable routine of texting, weekend date days, pushing our beds together to watch TV, and then separating them again for sleep.

"We did that already!" My whisper was harsh. I looked at the bathroom door. My date, Ethan, was still in there. It was my first date since I'd moved to New York. No, that's wrong. Technically, it was my first date in *years*. I had met Ethan at my internship and thought he was cute, witty, and charming. We had a fun back-and-forth.

"Ethan said it had been years since he took a bath and that his apartment only had a shower. I offered it up as a joke." I raked my hand through my hair and gave it a frustrated pull.

"Ellie, he didn't hear it as a joke. He heard it as an invitation, you absolute dumbass," Ben hissed through the phone.

"I realize that now! But it's been sixteen minutes. I can hear his ass squeaking against the fiberglass." I grabbed my lucky golf ball that

I'd held on to since the Women's Long Drive and rubbed it across my strained forehead.

"If you want to get in there, then get in there!" Ben barked.

"It's too late! I haven't slept with a thousand men. My number is two. TWO! I don't know what I'm doing!"

"Does he know you live with a guy? Bold of him to take a bath in *my* tub."

"I think so. I don't know. He's nice. He's from Nebraska. He's twenty-five. He was a magician in college—"

"Ellie, no!" I could hear Ben stifle his laughter through the phone and traded the golf ball for a glass of wine.

"He told me he has a washer and dryer inside his apartment, and I can't stop thinking about it. I can't let that go! What am I supposed to do, go back to the laundromat? Fuck that, Ben. Fuck. That." I shivered, thinking about our four-block trek to the laundromat every two weeks. Ben and I would sit in horribly mismatched clothing and inside-out underwear for hours, claiming our machines like hungry vultures and watching them spin hypnotically. The laundromat felt like a literal death spiral where we were both the predators and the prey.

"What's that noise in the background? Are you watching TV?"

My eyes widened, and I threw my face into my wine. "He said he's a history buff," I muttered. "I thought I'd put on a documentary for after he got out of the bath, as a special surprise and to make him think I'm smart, too."

"What did you put on?"

"Um . . ." My eyes darted toward the television. "*Fahrenheit 9/11.*" I waited ten seconds before breaking the silence. "Ben?"

"This is dire, buddy." Ben snorted. I just knew he was clutching his stomach. I could practically see his delight shine through my phone.

"I told you, I don't know what I'm doing! I didn't even realize how much of a date this was until *after* he got in the bath. I. Am. Bad. At. This!" I whispered aggressively.

"No. Shit."

"You can't come home," I begged.

"I can see Grayrock. I'm looking at our Christmas lights right now. I've had a long shift and I'm tired, so I am, one hundred percent, coming home to see this shitshow. You either get in there and take a bath with your magician—"

"Ben!" I couldn't help but laugh.

"Or it's gonna be so awkward when he comes out all wet and you're sitting there watching *Fahrenheit 9/11* with your full-grown-man roommate." Ben was howling now. "Holy shit. I'm so excited!" His laugh was infectious.

"I can hear how naked he is." My eyes fell to the closed bathroom door, knowing Ethan was behind it. For a moment, I put myself in Ethan's shoes. He was probably sitting uncomfortably in the tiny tub, cold water barely covering his body, his dick and balls floating to the surface of the filmy water, and wondering what I was doing. I had to cover my mouth to keep from spitting out my wine with laughter.

"I mean it, I'm coming! And I'm really close!" I could hear Ben's breath quicken.

"Stop running!"

Ben was laughing again, and I hung up as angrily as I could with an iPhone. I chugged my full glass of wine and, like a clumsy child, took off my clothes. I stood in front of the closed bathroom door and drew in a strained breath as I reached for the door handle.

"I'm going in. This is what people do. I'm cool. I'm casual. This isn't weird." I realized I was talking out loud. "Shut up, you idiot, you're talking to yourself!" Code Red. I was losing it.

From behind the bathroom door, I could hear a muffled "What?"

"What?!" I shouted back in a blind panic.

The front door swung open. The surprising movement caused me to jump. My instinct was to swing the bathroom door open and hide inside, concealing my nude body from Ben as he stormed through the front door. I slammed the bathroom door shut just as I heard Ben sing out, "Honey, I'm home!"

I faced the inside of the bathroom door, feeling relieved that Ben hadn't discovered me standing in the middle of the apartment naked and talking to myself. Then I heard Ethan's small voice behind me. "Ellie?"

Aghhh! I forgot about Ethan!

I spun around slowly with a fake smile plastered across my face. "Hey, Ethan. What's up, bud?"

He looked me over and stammered, "What are you doing?"

"Just hanging out." I leaned awkwardly against the door.

"Was that another guy I heard?" Ethan sat up in the bath, and I could see everything beneath the water's surface.

"My roommate. He's super cool, though, you know, with this whole thing." My strangled laugh sounded like a dying whale.

An agonizingly long moment passed before another word was spoken. "It's just, I've been in here for a while, and after the first five minutes, I didn't think you were coming in. Then I didn't know how to leave."

"Oh, totally. Totally, totally. Totally." I nodded like a bobblehead.

"I'm just surprised. Your nipples . . . This is all surprising at this point. Have you had kids?"

"THERE'S NOTHING WRONG WITH MY NIPPLES, YA FUCKIN' MAGICIAN!" I screamed. I looked at Ethan, naked, and he looked back at me, naked.

KNOCK. KNOCK. KNOCK.

"How's everything going in there?" Ben asked through the bathroom door. I could hear him swallowing his laughter as I burned brighter than the sun.

Later that night, Ben, Lucas, Zoë, and I were in line to get into Key One Lounge, a live blues bar on Bleecker that Lucas swore by. He promised he would get me in, but I had my doubts. We were twenty people deep in the line, but it was still moving.

"When did he leave?" Zoë asked before blowing warm air into her gloves.

Zoë had quickly become one of my all-time favorite people. She was the type of girl who always went for what she wanted. I envied her gumption. If she wanted to see someone naked, she would have no problem.

Zoë was invited to everything, but she didn't always go. Being social fed her and fulfilled her, like every other extrovert, but she had dueling personalities that I found fascinating. She was soft and hard, sugar and salt, bold and terrified. Her traits constantly battled each other. I couldn't wait to introduce Zoë to Hannah and Kara, and I worried about how quickly Jacob would take off his clothes if I ever introduced the two of them.

"Oh, Ethan took off right away. It was horrifying." I opened my jacket and fixed my boobs in my bra. I saw Lucas's eyes slip down to my chest, and I glared back. "See anything you like there, pal?"

Lucas shrugged. "They're fine, I guess."

Ben tossed his head back with a chuckle.

Zoë smacked Lucas in his puffy jacket's shoulder, then asked, "Did Ben see you naked?"

"No naked Ellie for me. Though, trust me, I'm trying." Ben smiled teasingly.

"It's not an easy feat. Just ask everyone from my high school. That was always a fun joke. I mean, it took years for Rory to see me naked." I shook my head, laughing at myself to cover the embarrassment.

"You're not in high school anymore, and I'm not Rory."

"You're also not my boyfriend," I bit back smugly.

"Neither was he." Ben leveled his eyes at me.

Zoë wrapped her arms around my waist. "Don't be a dick, Benjamin." She squeezed me. "Besides, it doesn't matter how long it took for your childhood sweetheart to see you naked. It took Ethan one bath, which is quite the exceptional magic trick, if you ask me."

"It wasn't Ethan. It was the alcohol." I mined my purse and started applying lipstick. My hands cramped in the cold. "And I took off my clothes with Rory long before we actually got naked together. My mom was there. It was a thing," I mumbled, hoping no one was listening. They were. All faces were showing repulsion, but no one asked questions.

"Are you going to keep seeing Ethan at your internship?" Ben swiftly moved the topic away from Rory.

"Yup. Definitely. Big lesson for your girl. Do not date your coworkers. It will never happen again." The idea of seeing Ethan and picturing his floating dick and balls while he walked past my desk made me ill.

"I don't want to love this, but I do." Zoë giggled.

"He's Justin's producing partner's assistant. I can't get away from him. We have a good banter at the office, too. I don't know what happened," I shuddered, then grabbed a water bottle from my bag and took a sip.

"You didn't realize you were on a date. I'm fairly sure *that's* what happened," Ben quipped.

"Story of my life," I sighed.

"Happens to the best of us." Lucas jumped up and down to warm himself up. "I once tried to have a rebound after Louise and I broke up, but she accidentally turned into my girlfriend because I stayed too long and ended up watching TV on her couch. Then she invited me to a rugby game that afternoon, and I thought, 'Why not?' Her parents were in the box, and somehow, four months later, we were on the phone, and I was sitting on the toilet, just needing to shit, but having to hold it in because she was crying."

Ben, Zoë, and I laughed at Lucas's poker-faced delivery.

"Oh no." I giggled, then handed Zoë my water. "How did you break up?"

"Also on the phone. I was at a crêperie and had to keep pausing the breakup to make sure they got my order right."

"Jesus, Lucas. Remind me never to sleep with you," Zoë said, sneering. She took a sip from my water bottle, and Lucas stilled. He looked at Zoë pointedly, and she choked on her water. Her cough attack came in hard. It almost sounded like she was gagging. She pointed to her throat and rasped, "Sorry, choking."

Lucas grinned, then opened his hands to his crotch and said, "How's that possible? My dick's down here."

I scream-laughed, and Zoë had instant tears as her coughing transitioned to laughter. Ben bent at the waist and had to hold his chest from laughing so hard. Lucas's filthy comeback was so lightning fast that no one saw it coming.

"You're the worst." Zoë leveled her eyes at Lucas, then turned back to me. "Is your boss letting you take some time off so you can go home for the break?" Zoë handed me back my water.

"Yeah, I'm going back for eight days. Christmas Eve to New Year's." I stepped backward to Ben's body for warmth, and he wrapped his arms around me. I was nervous to go back to Vancouver, but other than my family and the Griffins, I hadn't told anyone I was coming home. No one needed to know. Kara, Jacob, and Hannah were sworn to secrecy.

"Oh, Ellie! I forgot to tell you!" Ben squeezed me from behind. "I saw your lottery commercial on the TV in the back of a cab."

"You did?" I beamed.

"If Anne Hathaway had lighter hair, alien-size eyes, too many teeth, and no distinctive personality, I would definitely think you sort of reminded me of Anne Hathaway," Ben teased. I smacked his thighs with my fist.

"So, what's the plan here? How am I getting into this bar?" I asked Lucas. We were getting closer to the front of the line, and I needed to prepare.

"I'm going to teach you five French phrases. When the bouncer asks for your ID, look at me like you're confused. I'll 'translate,' then you act like you forgot your wallet and repeat the phrases over and over like you have a fever." Lucas pulled his beanie down to cover his ears.

We got to the front of the line and kicked it into high gear. "My girlfriend forgot her passport at the hotel. I'm sorry. Hold on." Lucas turned to me and spoke in a flurry of French. When our back-and-forth turned heated, loud, and utterly incomprehensible, the bouncer waved me through, unwilling to put up with us any longer.

"I can't believe that worked. Kara would die!" I exclaimed as I looped my arm through Lucas's. We made our way to the bar for our first round of drinks. Key One Lounge was loud and overcrowded. My body squished as I leaned against the bar. Ben once again stood behind me. He placed both arms protectively around me as he held on to the railing, trapping me.

"Two whiskey sours," Ben said to the bartender, already knowing my order, while Zoë looked over the cocktail menu.

Lucas turned to me as I stood half hidden inside Ben's arms. "When do we meet this little Canadian best friend of yours?"

"My twenty-first birthday is in March. My sister and Kara are both coming out for it."

"I can't wait!" Zoë said giddily.

"What are they like?" Lucas asked.

"Hannah is studying psychology and is the beacon of light and hope for our family." Hannah and I were close, closer than we had been as kids, and I knew now, as an adult, how lucky I was to have a sister like her. We couldn't have been more different, and yet somehow, we had only grown closer the farther away I moved. "And Kara can be unpredictable. She's not sure what she wants to do or who she wants to be yet, so she tries everything. She can pick up any sport within a day, and she doesn't back down from a fight."

"Sounds like my kind of girl." Zoë nodded approvingly.

"Are they single?" Lucas asked curiously.

"Hannah is single. Kara is taken," I answered cautiously.

Ben popped his chin down onto my shoulder. "My birthday is in March, too. Do you want to do a joint thing?"

"For sure." I grabbed my drink and spun around to face everyone as Ben stepped back.

"Okay, good. I'm glad. Now I can start to forgive you." He reached over me to grab his drink.

"Forgive me? For what?" My eyes narrowed.

"You brought another guy into *my* bathtub, McCain." His dark, woodsy green eyes pierced mine.

"I told you about his washer and dryer. I'm simply doing the best I can to save us from another laundry day. It's all for you, Ben." I smiled playfully and poked his stomach.

"She makes good points," Ben said to Lucas.

Zoë stepped forward to take my hand and smiled smugly. "What else is yours in that apartment, Benjamin?" She arched her eyebrows beneath her thick curtain bangs like a tricky little pixie and led us toward a table next to the band.

Chapter 8

VANCOUVER

15 years old

RORY AND I WERE WAITING AT THE CURB FOR MY MOM TO PICK ME up. There was a black bear on the course that had somehow traversed bodies of water, highways, and suburbs to get to Juniper. Even though my sister, Blair, and Orson decided to keep playing, once the conservation officers showed up with rifles, I power-walked off the course and called my mom to pick me up. Luckily, the timing worked out. I needed to duck out after the fifth hole to get to an audition for a jeans commercial.

"Are you going home?" I asked Rory, turning my attention to the road, looking for my mom's SUV to pull into the long driveway.

"Nah, I have to wait for Blair to drive me." Rory bent down to sit on the curb below me and stretched out his legs. He leaned back on his hands. It was a relaxed position I couldn't pull off without looking like a gangly skeleton.

"Did you know he got Hannah cupcake-shaped earmuffs last Christmas?" I tapped my shoe on Rory's hand.

"Who? Blair?!" Rory barked. He cranked his neck to look up at me, and his mouth opened with a gasp.

"Yeah." I laughed. "They showed up at our door, out of nowhere, with a card."

"Blair bought Hannah a Christmas present?!" Rory blinked about five times, baffled.

"No, Rory. Blair bought Hannah . . . Cupcake. Shaped. Earmuffs." I stressed each word, trying not to laugh.

"What was he thinking?" Rory fell back onto the cement.

"We have no idea," I said as deadpan as possible, which made Rory laugh.

It had been months since Junior Night, since Rory told me he'd missed me, but since then, we had resumed our friendship as it had always been. There was no more leg pressing. There were no more declarations of anything. I tried to convince myself that it was better this way, us just being friends, even though "us just being friends" still strangely felt like we belonged to one another.

"You think he likes her?"

"Yes! Of course! You know he kissed her, right?"

Rory sat upright like he was a marionette doll and someone had just yanked on his string. "That's a joke, right?"

I sat down next to him on the curb and picked up a twig. "That is not a joke," I said, smiling at Rory's reaction.

"Are you kidding me?" Rory stared at me, shocked.

"Why does it matter?" I asked, testing him and wanting to see what I could pull out of him. I wondered if Rory didn't like the idea of Hannah and Blair for the same reasons that I didn't like the idea of Hannah and Blair. That was supposed to be us kissing, and they bloody well beat us to it. Our siblings weren't allowed to touch each other. They weren't meant to belong together. That was our thing!

"You know why it matters," he answered quickly, not running away from me in the slightest.

"No, I don't." I started directing a stream of ants toward a small mound of dirt next to the curb.

"Yes, you do, Cainey," he stated definitively.

Rory and I locked on to each other. His dark-brown eyes roamed my face, then landed on my mouth, just as Caleb Davis, the rich kid who lived on the periphery of everyone's friendship, drove past us in a cart with his dad on their way to the practice putting green.

"They shot the bear!" Caleb called out as they crossed the driveway. Mr. Davis stopped the cart so his son could talk to us.

"They did?!" Rory and I shouted back in unison from the curb.

"Is it dead?" Rory asked.

"No. Got it with some sort of tranquilizer dart, and it was right in front of Orson!"

"Poor bear!" I exclaimed. "Hannah's probably freaking out."

Rory leaned in to me. "Don't worry. Blair can comfort her with his earmuffs."

I playfully poked Rory's shoulder with my twig, and Mr. Davis smiled at me. "You look lovely today, Ellie." I felt a rush of discomfort as his eyes crawled over my body. Mr. Davis took off his hat to adjust his curly dark-brown hair, which had a spattering of gray at his temples. He kept smiling his creepy smile, and all I could see were his skinny, overcrowded bottom teeth.

"Oh, thanks." My voice was polite but clipped. Rory went rigid beside me.

"I was behind you at the driving range yesterday. I love watching you swing." Mr. Davis nodded as if we were having a two-sided, incredibly engaging conversation. We weren't.

"Oh, yeah. Thanks." My eyes flicked to Rory. I could see him looking uncomfortable and slightly surprised. His arms wrapped over his knees, and he was staring Mr. Davis down from the curb. I was uncomfortable, but not at all surprised. It wasn't the first time Mr. Davis had said he liked to watch me.

"Well, have a nice day. I'll see you later, Ellie. Bye, Rory." Mr. Davis nodded.

I continued to play with my stick while Rory watched them drive away to the putting green. In the distance, Caleb got out of the cart to putt. Mr. Davis's attention continued to jump between me and his son.

"That was weird, right?" Rory quietly asked.

"I don't know. I guess." Honestly, I didn't know how to answer that question. Of course it was weird that Albert Davis, Caleb's fifty-year-old dad, would tell me that he liked to watch me and then proceed to watch me from afar, literally, but in a way that I knew he was watching, and he knew I knew he was watching. It was also weird how Mr. Davis would run to catch up with me while I was walking toward the lounge. He would open the door, then stand in the way so I had to bend under his arm. It was weird that he would constantly find reasons to touch my arm or press his hand into my lower back. But it wasn't something I knew how to talk about, or even fully understood. "I've had worse, I guess."

"What does that mean?" Rory adjusted his hat, trying to tuck his curly, sweaty hair behind his ears.

"Like, I went to an audition the other day—it's where I'm heading now. I have a callback. Anyway, the casting director threw a pen on the ground and told me to turn around and pick it up. And that was the entire audition. I said my name, and he stared at my ass. After that, I was like, 'Buh-bye, everyone, have a great day!' " I said sarcastically.

"Are you serious?" Rory's face looked both upset and confused. I could see him nervously running his hands over his knees. "What did your parents say about it?"

"I can't tell them that. What are they going to do? And besides, every other person in there auditioning has to do the same thing. If I'm the one complaining, I'm the one not getting the job. I once had to pretend to . . . enjoy myself, if you know what I mean, while a director burped behind a camera. It was for an independent film, and the whole thing was awful. It was just the two of us in this small room, and he was burping, and I had to pretend to like it. You know, *like* it." I lowered my voice, starting to feel ashamed. But it was an audition. "It's just an audition" was what I told myself constantly. I only knew what an orgasm sounded like from TV and movies, so I was certain I looked like a fool and sounded like a walrus. Knowing that audition tape forevermore lived out there somewhere haunted my fifteen-year-old nightmares. "Anyway, the auditioning process isn't the best. It can be uncomfortable. It would be nice to have backup with me sometimes. But it's okay. It's fine," I said, trying to sound as casual as possible.

Rory's jaw flexed. I looked up, and Albert Davis was still watching me from his golf cart. I could feel myself shrink.

"Why do you do it if it makes you uncomfortable?" Rory's eyes remained on the ground.

"Why do I act? Because I love it?" I rolled my eyes. Even I knew how ridiculous I sounded, but if I had booked the job, I would have been on set for a month, surrounded by passionate, like-minded people, getting paid to play pretend, feeling alive because I was a part of something bigger than myself. I placed my hand down on the curb and gripped the edge.

"Doesn't sound like you love it," Rory said softly before carefully placing his index finger on top of mine. He gently brushed my skin, sending a fire drill throughout my entire nervous system.

"Well, I don't love auditioning, but I don't know . . ." I had no idea how I was talking. I don't even think I could hear my words come out of my mouth. Rory moved his finger to circle the delicate rose gold and amethyst ring I was wearing on my middle finger. I didn't dare move as I stuttered through my next thought. "I . . . I like getting lost inside my head sometimes. It's why I like writing in my diaries, too. I can go back in time or imagine different . . ." He placed two more fingers down on top of my hand and started slowly sliding them in the spaces between my fingers. I was short-circuiting. I looked up, and Rory's eyes were focused on our hands. "I just . . . I like . . . I like . . . Um, I like . . ."

Rory smiled softly, likely recognizing that my brain was falling apart from his touch, and my mom's SUV finally appeared. I stiffened, and Rory dragged his hand away from mine. We both stood.

"So, you're going back to that jeans audition now?" Rory asked as my mom pulled up. "Will you have to pick up another pen?"

"Maybe," I said, while clenching and flexing my now permanently branded hand.

"Well, do you want . . ." Rory laughed quietly. "I don't know, a friend there? Or, like, I don't know . . ." He scrunched his face and pinched the bridge of his nose. "I can be your backup if you want? I don't even know what I'm trying to say." He laughed a little louder as my mom parked in front of us. "Do you want me to come with you, and then we can hang out after or something?" He strung his sentence together as quickly as possible, and before I could wrap my mind around what was happening, my mom rolled down the window.

"Hey, Rory," she said brightly.

"Hi, Mrs. McCain," he said. His face slowly reddened.

"Um . . ." I looked back at Rory and swallowed. "That would be nice, but you don't have to. I'll be okay." I tossed my golf bag into the trunk and opened the front passenger door. "Um . . ." I was about to say something else, but had no idea what.

"Sorry, Ellie-Bee. I've got a ton of stuff up front. Get in the back." My mom shuffled paperwork around on the front seat, but without making space for me.

I opened the door to the back seat, and as I got in the car, Rory's hand landed on my back, pushing me farther in. He jumped in behind me, then closed the door behind him. I whipped my head around, surprised by his hijacking.

"Whatcha doing, hon?" my mom asked with a smile.

"Rory?" I asked, trying to control my smile.

"You said it would be nice." Rory clicked in his seat belt, and his eyebrows flew up his forehead nervously, looking at my mom. "Is it okay if I come, Mrs. McCain?"

"That's on Ellie," my mom answered, turning back around to face the front. She watched us through the rearview mirror. I snapped my lips together quickly. Rory and I had never hung out beyond Juniper before. He was taking us out into the real world. My heart heaved into my throat.

"Yeah, of course," I mumbled, trying not to explode. Rory glanced over at me briefly as he slouched in his seat. "You're crazy," I breathed, and he laughed softly through his nose, squeezing his eyes shut. Another blush crept up his neck.

"Is this weird?" he asked, then flicked his attention to my mom, who was avoiding eye contact through the rearview mirror.

"Yes." I laughed.

Rory covered his face with his hands and silently chuckled to himself.

My mom grabbed my backpack from the floor of the front seat and tossed it at my feet. "We'll be there in twenty minutes. I have your clothes to change into once you get there."

My chest emptied, and my stomach churned. "It's a one-room studio, Mom, and we wait outside to get called in. It's not like a normal audition space. There are no bathrooms." My body went stiff. Rory was silent beside me.

Oh god . . . Oh god, oh god, oh god.

I was going to have to change in the car. I knew it. My mom knew it. Rory knew it.

I very slowly turned my head to Rory, and he kept his eyes forward. "I won't look, I promise," he whispered, trying to keep our conversation private. My eyes went back to my mom in the rearview mirror, and her face twisted with concern.

"There are some beach towels in a bag in the trunk. You can reach them, Rory. Lift a towel between you two so Ellie can have some privacy," my mom instructed.

Rory and I looked at each other with our eyes deadened as he sluggishly swiveled in his seat and reached into the trunk to grab an extra-large pin-striped towel. He bunched it on his lap as I dug into my backpack, grabbing my clothes. My breathing became heavy, and my mom turned up the music to create an extra barrier between her and us.

"I'll just do it quickly at a red light."

After a couple of minutes, we crept up to our first red light.

Rory took a deep breath. "Cainey?" His voice trailed off. He refused to look in my direction.

"Rory, look at me," I whispered. His brown eyes found mine, his face softened, and we both started laughing. I wanted to say more, but didn't know what to say. We stopped at the light, and Rory dropped his head, closed his eyes, and lifted the towel. He held it over the middle seat, separating us, and I quickly unbuckled and ripped my polo shirt off, then yanked on my T-shirt as fast as I could. The light turned green, and my mom hit the gas, but Rory kept the towel between us until I gently touched his hand. He brought the towel down and looked at me.

"Is this second base? Did we beat Hannah and Blair?" I joked, and Rory's eyes widened. A stunned smile crept across his face, and his eyes darted to my mom in the rearview mirror to see if she was listening.

We approached the next red light, and he raised the towel again. I unbuckled, lifted my ass, and shimmied out of my khakis with a grunt. I reached for my jeans, and the light turned green. "Oh shit," I muttered, and could hear Rory laughing quietly from the other side of the towel. I pulled on my pants but struggled momentarily as my mom started driving again. "Ah! Crap!" I panicked, and Rory laughed a little bit louder. I buttoned up and buckled in, and my body sank into my seat with relief. "I'm done."

Rory crumpled the towel into his lap, taking a deep breath.

When we stepped out of the car at the studio and mixed into a sea of beautiful teenage girls, I realized that Rory experienced life on the outside every day. He didn't exist solely at the golf club, and probably had girlfriends, kissed girls, looked at girls, and dated girls. He wasn't mine, like I wasn't his. My face must have shown the distress of my inner monologue, because Rory gently poked my side.

"Nervous?"

"No." I felt rejected before I'd even stepped into the audition room. "You can't come in with me when they call my name."

"Why not?" His face fell. "Can't I watch?"

Looking at Rory as he leaned against the brick building, lit up by the sun and removed from how I knew him, turned him into another version of himself, leaving me feeling lightheaded. I scanned the group of girls and noticed at least half of them were looking at him, too.

"It doesn't work like that."

"What are you going to do in there?" he asked curiously.

"I don't know. They're probably going to make me dance. I can't tell you how many auditions I've been to where I'm dancing in front of people judging me. They want to look at my body to make sure it looks the way they want on camera. Commercial auditions are weird like that. It's filling a quota. It's not actually about me." I told Rory the spiel I often told myself.

I don't know what came over me. I brushed my knuckle against the back of his hand. He reacted by taking his index finger and hooking it around mine. I looked down at our hands, and everything inside me seized.

I was called into the studio, and they asked me to do the same as always. I danced and they watched. But this time it was different. This time, I had backup.

Chapter 9

NEW YORK
20 years old

BEN AND I STOPPED AT TRADER JOE'S ON OUR WAY HOME FROM school, and he grabbed the ingredients to make a creamy Tuscan chicken dinner from our electric skillet, which sat near the end of our beds. I was to make the salad.

In just five months, Ben had become my closest friend. He and I had already exchanged a lifetime of words. I don't know if it was our intimate classes together as scene partners, sharing our darkest moments and most vulnerable sides, or if it was our middle-of-the-night, pitch-black laughing fits from our separate beds. Still, somehow along the way, Ben had come to know me better than anyone. He knew me better than my sister, better than Kara, better than Zoë, better than . . . well, a lot of people. He caught my faraway stare when I was thinking about Rory on countless occasions and would take his dirty socks off and shove them in my face unexpectedly to snap me out of it. We would take each other to Central Park when we were having bad days. If it rained, we would pack snacks and sit under the Glen Span Arch at 102nd Street. He would memorize lines or study, and I often found myself writing short stories in one of my school notebooks, inspired by the spooky stone arch trapped in the woods.

Ben knew who I was and who I wanted to be. He knew what made me happy. He knew when I was sad before I did. He knew what made me tick, because it made him tick, too. Our friendship came as naturally and as comfortably as the rising sun.

I came out of the hot shower and pulled on my striped pajama bottoms and an old swim club tank top. Ben was standing over our skillet in a thin gray T-shirt that draped over his muscular build, and his pajama pants hung. His dark-blond hair had grown out a bit and waved into a mess.

"It smells so good!" I breathed in deeply.

"Can you pull out the table?"

I giggled as I took off the lamp that sat on our nightstand. I cleared our schoolbooks, plays, and notes, my lucky golf ball, my jewelry, and his phone. I then dragged the nightstand toward the foot of our beds and pulled out a tealight from the drawer. I lit the candle and put it in the center of the tiny, square, makeshift table.

"Oh shit. We're cute." Ben looked at my setup while plating the chicken.

I knelt on the floor as Ben placed our dinner down on the table, then sat cross-legged across from me. My first bite almost knocked me over. It was creamy and shockingly delicious, considering it was made in our non-kitchen and cooked in an electric skillet.

"Ben," I said with my mouth full, looking him dead in the eyes. "Yum."

He chuckled softly and took a bite for himself. "Have you decided if you're going to ask Justin to meet his agent, or, like . . . give them your résumé or something?" Ben picked our conversation right back up from earlier in the day, after I told him my boss's LA agents were coming into town to discuss a strategy to get Justin's production company more press and better scripts.

"I'm worried it would look bad. I'm just an intern."

"What's the worst that could happen, he says no?"

"I'm pretty sure the worst that could happen is looking like an asshole," I retorted. But I considered Ben's argument. Justin was a dick, but we were close in age, and he knew I was trying to be an actor, too. I didn't feel like an actor in Vancouver, to the point where I had become embarrassed to admit that's what I wanted for my life. There were no real, meaningful credits to my name, and I constantly felt like an imposter when I told people that's what I was, because I wasn't. I was a student. I was a fraud. In Vancouver, I wasn't real. In New York, I was.

"Stop worrying what people think about you," Ben said with his mouth full. "You're not asking for a part or anything. You're asking for an introduction to his agent, and for him to see you as something other than an intern. Stop being so Canadian and be bold."

"Oh, I'm Ben. I walk into a room like an American. I'm beautiful and take up space. Make way, world!" I pitched my voice up and rolled my eyes to the ceiling. Ben dropped his fork and leveled his glare at me.

"I walk in the room like an American? What does that mean?" His look was a mix of amusement and annoyance.

"Like you know you belong there." I lifted my finger and booped him on the nose. I surged to my feet, pressed my hands into my pajama bottoms, straightening them, then charged out the front door, leaving Ben on the floor at our tiny table.

Coming back into the room, I flung the front door open with so much bravado that it slammed into the wall, knocking down our framed *Fight Club* movie poster.

"Oh no." I broke character and lifted my hands to my mouth.

"Great demonstration. A-plus," Ben said sarcastically while popping another forkful into his mouth.

"Sorry," I said, picking up the fallen frame and leaning it against the wall.

"Still so Canadian." He wagged his fork, making fun of my instant apology. "Are you *sorry*?" he mocked.

"Fine, I'm not." I decided with a confident nod, then dug back into my salad.

"You know, this whole apartment looks like you. Do you think I want twinkly lights over my bed? You sleep with a comforter that has a goldfish swimming inside a martini glass. And I can't escape that shit because we live in the world's smallest studio that *you* found. That frame cost me eighty bucks. It's an original, studio-printed poster, and it was the only thing I put up on the wall that was mine." Ben looked up at me again and pressed his lips together. "Don't you think you should be sorry?"

". . . No?" My voice wavered, and my face twisted with discomfort.

"That sucks, Ellie." Ben held firm, and I could swear I saw his heart break.

This is a test. He's testing me, right?

Ben pushed his plate away and stood. "I'm not that hungry anymore. Just go ahead and finish without me." He walked over to his poster to hang it back on the wall.

He was torturing me. This was one of the seven layers of hell, where I'd meet my maker and they'd say, "But you didn't say you were sorry." I'd spend an eternity living in shame and guilt as I watched that poster drop on an everlasting loop. Each crack in the glass would crack my soul, and I'd forever relive that time I saw the light leave Ben's eyes and I did nothing to revive him.

"Ben . . ." I began, but Ben cut me off as he spun back around to face me.

"Pussy." Ben's grin stretched across his face.

I deadened my expression. "Really? *Pussy*? Is that necessary?"

Ben walked out of the apartment, then swung the door open again just as vigorously as I had, crashing the poster to the ground once more, with a bounce to his step.

I shook my head and returned to my food. "You're a doofus."

"A *doofus*?" Ben laughed.

"Yes, a doofus. Deal with it."

Ben chuckled as he sat back down. "So, I've been thinking about Los Angeles."

Welcome to the club, buddy.

"What are your thoughts about making our way out there once we're done with school? I know we're establishing our network here, but then there's more opportunity there. We'd have to start all over if we left. I don't know."

I felt my heart jump up into my throat, then shoved it back down with another forkful of food. Moving to Los Angeles had been my goal since I was fourteen. Did Ben really want to go with me one day?

"First off, we're only in our first year. We've got loads of time." I tried to temper my expectations. "Secondly, what's with all this 'we' business?"

Ben smacked my fork with his. "Have you thought about it? Because I'm not going if you don't. I'm not taking a chance with another roommate. You're locked in, kid."

"You're asking me if I've thought about moving to LA? Hmm, yes. Every day of my life since I was in utero, and I have the diaries to prove it," I said, nodding at a box under my bed between chews of food and gulps of wine.

"OoooOOOoo! You have *diaries*?! Here?! What's in your diaries?" Ben asked enthusiastically.

"There is *a lot* of Rory. Like, it's disturbing." I had scanned my diaries in the weeks leading up to my move, and Rory Campbell had managed to work his way into almost every entry since I was twelve, like a goddamn psychopath.

Ben snorted. "Do you still diary?"

"Yes, I still diary." I smiled, looking down at my food.

"Have I made an appearance in said diary?" Ben's smile was wicked as he scraped up sauce with his fork.

"Here and there." I smirked.

"Here and there and everywhere?"

"Alright, that's enough of that."

"I wanna read!" Ben whined and dropped his fork with a clang.

"*You want to read my diaries?*" I cackled. "You're an idiot. Yeah, okay. Sure there, bud. Let's go read my diaries," I said mockingly.

"Oh, come on. How bad can it be?" He poured himself another glass of wine.

"Oh, it can be pretty bad, Ben." I held out my glass for a top-up as well.

"I'm reading them," he teased as he filled my glass, his eyes dancing all over mine.

"No, you're not." I accepted his staring contest and dug in deep, furrowing my brow.

"Yes, I am." He imitated my faux-serious expression.

"No. You're not."

"Yes. I am." He was so confident it killed me.

"No, Ben. You're not."

An hour later, Ben was five diaries deep. He sat on the edge of his bed and was howling, clutching his chest every other page. A surprising shock wave of thrill shot up my spine every time he looked at me, appalled, bewildered, or in awe at the ridiculousness laid bare in my diaries.

After reading one entry, Ben looked over at the bottom of my bed, where all our bedside table items had been discarded. "Interesting . . ." I could tell he was slightly alarmed but still eager for more.

"What?" I threw my head back onto my martini fish pillow.

Ben stretched over my bed to pick up my lucky golf ball. "Is this the ball you swiped from the Long Drive competition?"

"I don't want to say yes, but yes?" I pinched my face together and closed my eyes.

"Hmm," he hummed curiously and continued reading. I fiddled with my rose gold bracelet nervously. After a few minutes of chuckling through his nose, he eventually tossed his head back with tightly shut eyes and started snorting, attempting to prevent himself from letting out a bigger laugh.

I had to ask. "What now?"

"You're so mad at your sister because she got a Christmas present from Blair, and you got nothing from Rory. You eviscerate her."

"She didn't even like Blair! It still makes me mad." I pretended to be angry.

"You wrote a poem about cupcake earmuffs. You said it was an *affront*, then called her a *cunt*."

"I *DID*?!" I roared, then pulled my pillow out from under my head and threw it over my face.

"I like reading your stuff, Ellie. You're good at this. Your short stories are good, too. Why didn't you go for Bronwyn's writing program?"

"Well, loads of reasons," I scoffed. "First, I'm an actor. But also, the writing program is four years."

Ben nodded absent-mindedly, his eyes still on the page. "You're a writer, too, you know. Maybe we could write together sometime. Like, a play or something." Ben put the diary down. "Didn't you write one of your monologues for your audition? I don't think anyone else did that."

"Who knows," I sighed. "But yeah, I was a horny Humpty Dumpty. It was dumb."

Ben's smile was wide. "Must not have been *that* dumb. It got you here."

"I've never let anyone read my stuff before, not on purpose. Hannah and Kara have snooped once or twice, but I don't share this side of myself with people," I admitted.

Our eyes connected, and after a beat, he picked the diary back up. "Thank you for trusting me."

"There's a whole world inside my head that now only you know."

Ben's eyes flicked back up to mine from over the diary, and he let out a long, measured exhale. "I wish I knew you when you were a kid." He tapped the diary's cover with his finger. "I wish I knew you like this."

"Yeah, but you know me like *this*." I smiled softly.

"You're right. This Ellie is a little nutbar. My Ellie is better."

"Your Ellie has leveled the fuck out." I took a sip of my wine.

"Tell that to the magician in my bathtub," Ben quipped, and I spat out my wine into my glass. "Do you want to go golfing together sometime soon?" Ben asked, surprising me.

"Oh man." Another sigh escaped me. "I don't know."

"Why? I'm pretty good, and I want to see you play. I want to know how you're going to hit the ball in front of me. Rory made you nervous.

Do I?" Ben asked, and my stomach turned over. "The way you talk about him in here . . . It's pretty wild. It all feels really *real,* and you were just a kid."

"I have big feelings," I admitted.

"No kidding," Ben said quietly. "Do you still love him?" He brought his eyes back to my diary.

My heart fell through my chest. I could answer that question with anyone and everyone, but I didn't know how I felt about Ben being the one to ask it.

"Never mind. Don't answer that." Ben swallowed, clearly reading my mind. "Anyway, I want to go golfing with you. We can trade off. I can teach you how to hit a baseball. Or we should go to a game."

Ben moved our nightstand back between the heads of our two beds, placed the lamp in the center, and turned it on. He then climbed into his bed and leaned against the headboard, cracking open the next diary in my collection.

"I've been to a baseball game before."

"Yeah, but you've never been with me." Ben looked down at my diary, and his eyes went wide. He closed them again, tipped his head back, and tightened his mouth, and his shoulders shook.

"Do I even want to know?" My voice dropped.

He turned the open diary around to show me what he was looking at. It was an enlarged photo taped to the back of a page, taking up the entire space.

"Elijah Wood *as* Frodo?" Ben wheezed, and tears sprang from his eyes.

"I AM NOT ASHAMED OF THIS!"

Ben shook his head and looked back down at the diary, flipping to another page. "I love this so much." He let out a massive happy sigh before asking, "So, why did you stop playing golf?" His question was seemingly innocuous.

"I'm sure you'll get to that part. Give yourself a couple more diaries." I exhaled, unsure if I wanted to get into it. "How did it feel when you stopped playing baseball?"

Ben had told me about the shoulder injury that sent him into early retirement on our way to Connecticut when Zoë's family opened their house up to us for Thanksgiving.

"It felt like I didn't know who I was anymore, and I didn't know if I liked myself without it. What did I have to offer without baseball, you know? I wished for things to be different for so long even though I knew I could never get it back. I still wished."

"I'm a dreamer, too. I wish for the impossible all the time."

Ben leaned his head against his bed's headboard. "I lost a lot of myself, but then I found acting. Then I found Bronwyn . . . And then I found you." Ben held my eyes with his own, and my heart thunked. Just . . . *thunk*.

I let out a heavy exhale before saying, "I didn't stop playing golf. I went to the driving range all the time, just a public one. But I stopped going to Juniper when I was sixteen."

Chapter 10

VANCOUVER

16 years old

I LOOKED OVER AT THE OTHER END OF THE COUCH AND HOPED to hell that Rory didn't notice every time I caught myself staring at him sitting there, watching a movie, leaning against the sofa's arm. It was rare for us to be alone together.

Over the past year, Rory and I had spent a lot of time together, but we weren't actually a couple, and I often wondered if we would ever become one. We went to Juniper almost every weekend, even during fall and winter. I was convinced that the only reason we endured the rain and snow was to find an excuse to spend time together. We hardly played golf in the cold; instead, we played cards in the games room and argued over which movies to watch. Eventually, we would leave the club and grab lunch or hang out at each other's house. But since we always met up first at the golf club, I worried that Juniper was what kept us connected. Without it, what would we be?

There were only a few times when we saw each other away from Juniper. Kara and I went to watch Rory play basketball at his school, and it didn't surprise either of us when he moved around the court as comfortably as he did on the golf course. My dad had always said that Rory was the most gifted junior at the club, and it was as plain as day that he was better than most of the adult members, too, but his natural athleticism carried over into other sports as well. It also didn't surprise us when we weren't the only girls in the gym with our eyes on him. Rory had only grown increasingly gorgeous. The subtle auburn streaks glistened through his sweaty, unruly curly hair. He stood out from the rest of his team. He was the only one who looked like he belonged in a magazine. I assumed that other girls had to be the reason why we weren't holding hands, kissing, boyfriend and girlfriend, the works. He was at another school and had a whole life that had nothing to do with me. It killed me, but if having Rory at all meant having him as a "golf club friend," it was worth it.

Rory and Cameron had come to a handful of my swim meets and sat with my sister and sometimes Kara. Rory would wear his black Titleist hat, and I could hear him whistle as they called me to the starting blocks. He only ever saw me win. I hated to lose, and there was no chance in hell I was losing in front of Rory. If I was being forced to wear a swim cap in front of him, you bet your ass I was at least going to win.

Since I was impressing Rory in the pool, and my yips on the golf course had finally settled, there was no way I would allow any of the Campbells to see me in my school plays. I couldn't have Rory discovering how desperately uncool I really was. My tricking him into thinking otherwise was working. It would be certain death.

After an afternoon at the range, we went back to my house and were watching *The Wedding Singer* while Kara and Cameron played pool in our games room. Rory cleared his throat and stretched his body, tipping his head against the back of the couch. I stood to get myself some water from the adjoining kitchen. Rory's eyes shifted from the TV to me, but his body didn't move. I had to walk up three steps, so we were separated by a white wooden railing that divided the kitchen from the living room.

"Where's Hannah?" Rory asked.

"She's out with some guy she met at UBC," I called out from the kitchen. My sister was eighteen now and officially flawless.

"She like him?"

"I don't think so, but who knows. Hannah keeps it pretty close to the vest."

"Whatever. I hate that guy." Rory looked back at the TV with a cheeky grin. "Did *he* get her earmuffs?" I could hear him chortle from the couch. "What's the best present you ever got from someone you liked?"

"Oh man. I don't know. Someone from school once brought me chicken noodle soup when I was sick." I leaned my elbows on the railing. My arms stuck to the wood with nervous sweat.

"That's nice." His eyes remained glued to Drew Barrymore.

"What about you?"

"I've gone on some dates, but I haven't had a girlfriend yet, so . . . can't really answer that." He shrugged. He had gone on some dates . . . It was official. And I was officially going to be sick. I had gone on some dates, too, but Rory didn't need to know that.

"I haven't had a boyfriend yet," I responded, wanting to defend myself. Rory leaned even farther into the couch and kicked his feet onto the coffee table, still not looking at me.

"Chicken noodle soup," he quipped back.

"Yeah, but that's . . . That was just a nice thing for someone to do." I needed to retreat. I put my empty glass into the kitchen sink, then opened the fridge, looking for absolutely nothing. I felt a rush of cold air over my body. I'm going to assume that was what came over me when I asked, "Have you ever been in love?" I kept myself hidden in the fridge, waiting for Rory's answer from the living room.

After an uncomfortably prolonged silence, he said, "Yeah. Once, I think."

I closed the fridge and flicked my eyes over the railing to Rory, only to discover that he was looking back at me from the couch. His eyes flew to the TV as soon as mine made contact.

He adjusted his position. "Have you?"

I took a deep breath and could hear my heartbeat thump like a drum rattling my brain. "Yeah. Once, I think." I repeated his words.

Rory didn't look at me. He just tightened his mouth and nodded.

Kara's voice rang down the hallway. "Ellie, how do we play music throughout the house?"

"There's a stereo that's hooked up to the speakers in—" I started shouting back, but Beyoncé cut me off.

"Never mind! Got it!" Kara screamed back.

The music had overtaken the TV's speakers, and Rory looked at me, surprised. The song flipped to Nirvana. After the first verse, it shifted to Gwen Stefani. Rory and I laughed. Kara cried out, "Stop it!" to Cameron. The music changed to Coldplay, then went back to Nirvana's "Smells Like Teen Spirit." I started shimmying my body and dancing in the kitchen. Rory, with a smile plastered across his face, started bobbing his head and subtly bounced his chest up and down, with his eyes closed dramatically. We sang the song playfully to each other. The music turned off again, and both Rory's and my eyes flew open, landing on each other, anticipating what would happen next.

"Cameron!" Kara screamed from the other room, and Rory and I busted out laughing.

"She's gonna kill him. I don't think I can do it. I don't think I can hide a body." I moved back to the living room and sat down beside Rory, landing a little closer to him this time around.

Rory grabbed my arm and squeezed my bicep without realizing he had accidentally squeezed my heart as well. "You're right. You don't have the muscles."

Guns N' Roses' "November Rain" turned on, and Rory tensed beside me.

"This one's for you, Rore!" I heard Cameron bellow from the other room.

Rory's face was beet red. He dropped my arm, and it felt like the whole thing fell off my body.

"So . . . I need to ask." I gathered every ounce of courage I had bottled up inside my body since birth. "Why does this song remind you of me? I've tried to figure it out, and I can't."

Rory pinched his lips and looked down. "Okay." He lifted his coffee-colored eyes carefully, but didn't land them fully on mine. He wiped his palms on his pants. "Do you remember the first time we met? We were at the driving range, and you almost killed me because you kept hitting the divider?"

"Please don't remind me."

"Well." Rory smiled and raised his eyes a little more. He was almost there. We were almost connected. He shifted his body to face mine. "It was November, and it was raining, and I just . . ." He struggled to continue, and his eyes focused elsewhere. "Pretty much every Guns N' Roses song makes me think about you now, which I know is weird, but my brothers know this, and they bug me about it." Rory shifted his hand so it was closer to mine on the couch. I could feel the energy charging between us.

"Why do your brothers bug you about it?" I was going to barf.

"Come on, Cainey." He exhaled a small laugh.

"It's just . . . Rory." I laughed and rubbed my palm over my eye. "Do you like me?" I blurted. "Because sometimes I think I know, but most of the time I don't think I know anything about anything."

"Cains." I could hear the smile in Rory's voice, but I couldn't look.

"I genuinely have no idea. Like what's . . . Like . . . What . . . Like. What?" I was flustered and forgot my purpose in life.

"Ellie." Rory said my real name this time. "Look at me."

I lifted my eyes. Rory's smile sloped down, and his dimple deepened. His eyes pulled across my face until they landed on my mouth. Then, to both of our surprise, the music changed again. It flipped over to Radiohead, taking us out of the moment. Our eyes locked.

"Are you kidding me?" I was unable to hide my disappointment. "You're finally—"

I couldn't finish my thought because Rory's lips crashed into mine. His kiss was firm, exquisite, and desperate. My mind went blank, and the only thing I could hear was my heartbeat pounding through my eardrums. Rory was kissing me. Rory was kissing me. Oh my god.

Rory was kissing me. Everything inside me stopped, stunned, paralyzed, all of it, and all I could do was feel.

Rory parted my mouth with his tongue and rolled it into mine. We both lifted to our knees on the couch, and our bodies pressed into each other as if we had done exactly this in another life. I couldn't control a small whimper slipping from the back of my throat. I had never made a sound like that before in my life, and he instinctively brought both hands to my cheeks as if he were trying to capture it and take it from me.

His hands shifted to the back of my head, his fingers digging into my hair and securing me in place. I moved my hands up his back and trailed them over his shoulder blades until they found their way to the back of his neck. I brushed my thumbs against his jaw, feeling his movements, memorizing his touch and face with my eyes closed. Rory pulled back to take a breath, and we both smiled.

"Oh my god, Rory," I whispered.

He softly shushed me, peacefully and happily. His mouth reached for mine once more.

"Oh my god, it's happening again," I muttered, having entirely lost my mind.

Rory gently laughed, then murmured against my lips, "Kiss me, Ellie."

Rory saying my real name did something to me that I couldn't explain. It changed my brain chemistry. I pushed my hands into his curly hair, and our bodies shifted, fastening to each other. I kissed him slowly, deeply. I kissed him in a way I had never kissed anyone before. We took our time tasting each other. It was as if we were discovering who we really were for the very first time. His arms wrapped around my waist, pushing my shirt aside so his skin could feel mine. He enveloped me as if I were breakable yet he wanted to crush me.

The moment we parted, Rory dropped his forehead onto my shoulder. He collapsed into our embrace, and my face pressed into his hair. He smelled like shampoo and freshly cut grass.

"I have wanted to do that for so long," I whispered. I didn't know my insides could smile, but they were.

Rory turned his head into me. Our hug tightened. He lightly kissed my neck, then skimmed his lips along my skin to beneath my jaw and my cheek. He looked at me, searching my eyes and finding my heart. "Ellie . . . This is . . ." He shook his head, unable to process what was happening.

"I know."

We both silently laughed as our lips found each other again.

"Do you have anything to eat, Cains?" Cameron's voice appeared before his body as he walked down the hallway toward the living room. Rory and I threw ourselves off each other and ended up at either end of the couch. Rory grabbed a decorative pillow and slammed it down over his lap.

"Umm, yup. Pizza in the fridge." My voice was hurried. Rory slapped his hand over his mouth and snorted, trying to stop himself from laughing.

"Anything to drink?" Cameron asked as he turned the corner.

"Just look, dummy." Kara followed closely behind Cameron. They both pillaged the fridge. "You guys want anything to eat?"

"Sure," Rory answered. He stood, fiddled with his pants to collect himself, then took a deep breath and opened his hand for me to stand with him.

We looked at each other for just one more minute. Just two more minutes. Kara leaned back from the fridge to see what was taking us so long just as we dropped our hands and stare, then joined Kara and Cameron in the kitchen.

I couldn't have gotten to Juniper more quickly the next morning. It was 9 a.m., and I was on the practice putting green when Jacob and Orson joined me for a putting competition. Another couple of juniors joined us as well, "the randos," as Hannah called them. Caleb joined, and his dad, Albert Davis, decided to sit in his golf cart and watch us. Well, watch me. I was still waiting for the Campbells to show up when Mr. Davis called me over.

I didn't want to go over to him, but I did it anyway. After all, he was Caleb's dad, and he was a member of Juniper, where my parents trusted that I was safe. I had to go, right?

"Hi, Mr. Davis. What's up?" I turned my head back to my friends and could see Orson looking over at us.

"I went to Portland last weekend and found something that made me think of you." My stomach rolled as he spoke, his smile revealing his bottom row of crooked teeth.

"What?" I said, surprised. Why would he think of me? I literally never thought about this man, ever.

Mr. Davis reached into the back of his golf cart and pulled out a white bag. He opened it and pulled out a small jewelry box with a delicate green horse painted on top.

"What is this?"

"A jewelry box. Elegant. Effortless. Beautiful. Just like you. You're growing up into a beautiful young woman, Ellie, and I wanted you to know that I've noticed. I want you to have this."

What? Why would Caleb's dad want to give me a gift? I barely spoke to this man. Yes, he watched me. Yes, he made me uncomfortable. Yes, he would say things that I found confusing and had found reasons to touch me for over a year now. But . . . he thought I was . . . *elegant*? What did that mean? I tried to think about all the compliments my dad had given me over the years. This didn't feel anything like that. I needed Mr. Davis to know that I was not elegant, that I was not anything, but I didn't know how to say that with his narrowed eyes roaming all over me, burning through me.

I could feel my heart hammering at the base of my throat, growing and choking me with every beat, suffocating me. I lifted my head and looked at Orson, who was still clocking our interaction. He whispered to Jacob, who now had his brotherly attention on me as well. Why was everyone looking at me?

"I . . . I can't accept this, Mr. Davis. But that's nice of you." I didn't know what else to say. Was I supposed to thank him?

"That's okay. I understand. You'll have it one day."

What did *that* mean?

I started feeling chilled, and tiny black pinpricks came into view. My insides got hazy, like I could feel myself somehow start to blur. It wasn't my vision. It was me.

"Take this for now." Mr. Davis pulled off his wristband, grabbed my arm, and pushed the wristband over my hand and up my forearm. He didn't let go. His sweat wrapped around me, sunk into me, and everything got darker as his grip tightened around my wrist. It felt like I was doing something wrong, but I couldn't figure out what, and why did it feel like *everyone* was looking at me?

Suddenly, Rory, his black hat turned backward, was walking toward the putting green with Blair, but it was Jacob and Orson who walked toward me.

"You good, Hollywood?" Orson asked.

"Ummm . . . I . . ." I looked down at Mr. Davis's wristband wrapped around my arm and his hand wrapped around my wrist. I felt every particle, every square inch of his skin fusing into mine. I felt his sweat from the wristband, and every word I've ever known emptied out of my mind. I didn't just lose my voice; I lost the ability to think.

"We're just having a quick chat," Mr. Davis answered on my behalf, then slipped back into our one-sided conversation. "I saw your mom. I can't believe I didn't realize that my company does your family's taxes. Small world, isn't it? She mentioned that she and your dad were going to Palm Springs in a couple of weeks. That'll be fun. You can have the house to yourself. Do whatever you want." He smiled at me again.

I genuinely could not comprehend what was happening. It felt like everything inside me was being compressed, as if I were physically shrinking. I was so deeply confused, and I still couldn't speak. Why wasn't I talking?

Mr. Davis's eyes dropped, and right in front of Orson and Jacob, he brought his hand up to the sweatband he'd put on me. His finger hooked underneath and lightly swept my skin. "I'll hold on to the jewelry box for when you're ready." When he finally let go of my arm, the tips of his fingers trailed down my side to lightly graze my hip and leg. Was it an accident? Was I standing too close?

Jacob stepped into my personal space. "Let's go, Ellie-Bee." Jacob's voice was low.

Mr. Davis didn't drive away. He stayed in his golf cart and watched me standing awkwardly on the putting green, shrinking, and shrinking, and shrinking, until I felt like I had disappeared entirely.

Jacob brought me back to the juniors and stood me next to Rory. I think. I wasn't entirely sure, as everything looked blacked out around the sides, like I was in a dark tunnel, and I could only see the putting green at my feet.

"Hey. Do you want to do something with me tonight? Just us? Like . . . a date?" Rory asked. I think it was Rory's voice, at least. Whoever it was sounded nervous, but I couldn't be sure.

I shook my head, barely, more to try to shake off this feeling than to say no to whoever was speaking. My body still wasn't working. My mind felt as if it had shut off. And I walked away from whoever was talking to me, to try to collect myself, and I didn't turn back.

Rory didn't know why I walked away from him without a word. He didn't know why I went to find my dad and sister in tears. He didn't know that my dad spoke to the club's board of directors, and the only question they asked him was "But what did Albert Davis actually *do* that was harmful?"

Rory didn't know about the countless people who said that if I felt so uncomfortable, it was up to me to do something about it. It was up to me to choose not to see Mr. Davis again. "Just don't go back to the golf club," they said. "What's the big deal?" they asked.

Rory didn't know that I tried to go back but started having panic attacks, or that I constantly questioned myself. I started to believe I had blown it all out of proportion. I must have misunderstood his intentions. Maybe it *wasn't* a "big deal" that a middle-aged man I barely knew had been confusingly, uncomfortably observing me since I was fifteen. Maybe it wasn't a "big deal" that he wanted to buy me presents and have me wear articles of his clothing. I told myself that everyone was probably right; maybe I *was* just a dramatic, ridiculous, stupid, silly little girl. Echoing through my imagination, every single junior was saying the exact same thing: "Did you hear what Ellie said about Caleb's dad? Who does she think she is? She's not that special."

I was paralyzed at the thought of the people at Juniper talking about it, about me, people I had grown up with making fun of me, judging me like everyone else, like every audition I'd ever gone to.

Juniper was my childhood. It was the safest place in the world. And then it wasn't. It was my happy place. And then it wasn't. It was at Juniper where, for the very first time, I felt like I belonged. It was at Juniper where I fell in love before I knew what love was. And it was there, on the putting green, where I grew up.

My life at Juniper was everything to me, and then everything was gone.

Chapter 11

NEW YORK

20 years old

BRONWYN SCHOOL FOR THE ARTS WAS CLOSED DUE TO FLOODING. We were expected to be out for a week, and I was deeply unsettled when Ben told me he was going to Boston for his birthday to catch some basketball with Lucas and some other guys from school. I wondered if the thought of him leaving made me uncomfortable because it meant I would be living and sleeping alone, or if it was because it was *him* leaving.

I finished my Thursday evening shift at the production company. Ben and I were to meet at the diner across the street from Grayrock, and I waited for him in the vinyl booth, slumped in my seat, eyes on the sticky table. I didn't notice he'd entered the diner until he had already sat down across from me.

"What are we having?" Ben shook his arms out of his jacket and grabbed the menu.

"Um, I don't know, I haven't looked yet." I didn't look up, lost in my own moment. "When's Boston again?"

"Leaving the day after tomorrow. But I'll be back when Hannah and Kara get here for our birthday thing." He eyed me over the menu. "What's up? Everything okay?"

"Yeah," I said quietly. "I don't want to talk about it."

Ben put the menu down and sat back in his seat. "What happened?"

"Nothing." A tear slipped down my cheek, and I quickly pushed it away with the bottom of my palm, then ran my fingers through my hair. I picked up the menu, playing the part of "normal."

"You're crying." Ben grabbed the menu from my hands and put it behind his back so I couldn't reach it.

"I just had a bad day, okay? Justin's an asshole."

"Ellie. Stop it. What happened?"

I took a shaky inhale, another tear slipped, and Ben lifted from his seat and squeezed himself next to me. He pulled me in to his side.

I groaned. "I asked if he could introduce me to his agent. I gave him my two-year-old headshot and embarrassing résumé that only has, like, four commercials and body-double, stand-in shit on it. I felt like an idiot the entire time, but I did it."

"Okay . . . ?" Ben waited for me to finish.

"He brought me into his office, closed the door, and told me to do push-ups."

Ben's head snapped back. "What?"

I took in a wobbly breath. "He said he didn't believe that I wanted it enough. Then he laughed and said, 'Push-ups should do the trick.' So I did push-ups inside his tiny fucking office as he leaned against his desk and counted loudly so everyone at the company could hear what I was doing. I was just . . . on the ground, looking at his fucking feet." An uncontrollable sob escaped me. "I can't believe I did it. I hate him. I fucking hate him." Another sob fell out. "Fuck," I said, gasping for air and wiping my face with my hands. Saying it out loud made everything a bit more real, and I felt sick not just at what happened, but at admitting to myself and someone else what happened. I don't know what made me feel worse, holding it in or letting it out.

"Ellie, I don't know what to say." Ben held on to my shoulder as if I might float away. After a long moment, he stood up, taking me with him. He reached over the table and grabbed his coat. "Come on, let's go home."

He held my hand as we walked across the street. The red *R* in the Grayrock sign was blinking.

"Do you want to watch TV tonight and just eat chips?" he asked as we pushed our way through the revolving doors.

We moved the nightstand and pushed our beds together. We lay under the covers and watched absolutely nothing that mattered. I barely paid attention to the TV's blue humming light. Ben put his arm around me, and I cuddled into his chest.

"You tired?" We had devoured a family-size bag of chips, Diet Cokes, and leftover Chinese food, and watched a couple of hours of television. We had already changed into our pajamas and brushed our teeth. It was past midnight.

"Yeah. Tired." I pushed my head to the side so I was resting in the crook of his armpit.

"Do you want me to move the beds back?" Ben asked quietly. He had never asked that before. He always just did it, assuming our usual solo sleeping positions.

"Can we just stay like this tonight?" I answered.

"Of course." He flicked the TV off and shuffled down his headboard to his pillow. I moved with him seamlessly and pressed my face into his body, breathing into his rib cage.

"You have to go back tomorrow," he murmured softly. It was the first time either of us had mentioned the incident with Justin since the diner.

"I can't." I shifted my position, internally uncomfortable, and flipped over on my side. He moved with me. It was as if we knew the same dance and he wasn't going to let me dance alone. He draped his arm over me and pulled my back into his chest and stomach. His breathing was labored at first, but then we settled into each other and began breathing together.

"You didn't do anything wrong . . ."

"I do everything wrong," I replied, accidentally saying my thoughts aloud.

"Don't say that. I promise you, that's not true. He may be a man-child, and only like two years older than you, but he's in a position of power. He's your boss. He's a fucking movie star, Ellie."

"He wishes." I choked.

"I can't believe he bullied you like that. You're an unpaid intern. I want to kill him." Ben's hold on me was tightening unintentionally.

"Please don't kill him. I'll get deported." I sighed, and Ben laughed softly into my hair.

"You think I'm gonna let you get deported? I'll marry you before that happens." Ben tucked his face into my neck and then murmured, "I can go with you tomorrow, if you want. You can show him that he didn't rattle you, and you're not someone to fuck with."

"But he did rattle me, and apparently I am someone to fuck with." My chest started to fill with heaviness. I didn't want to cry again.

"No, you're not. You're Ellie Fucking McCain. I watched you saw off your finger, and you took seventy-seventh place in the Women's Long Drive when you were fourteen, goddamn it," he said into the back of my head.

I let out a small laugh that sounded more like a wheeze. "Thirty-fifth place, you dick."

Ben pulled me in harder, squeezed me tighter. I could feel his quiet smile form through his breath, warming my neck. "I can come with you if you want. I can be there for you," he whispered. "Plus, I'm like . . . seven inches taller than that little fuck. He'll hate me. It'll be great."

I didn't answer Ben. Instead, I closed my eyes and eventually we both drifted off to sleep.

In the morning, Ben was still holding me. I felt his body stiffen when he woke. After a moment, he slowly and gently moved closer to me from behind. I shifted with him, revealing myself to be awake and very aware of our bodies pressing into each other. An electric current rippled across the small spaces between us, invisible to the eye.

Ben's breath was hot and shooting down my spine. I could hear his lips part as they brushed against the fine hairs on the back of my neck. He moved his fingers lightly down my arm until they reached my hand. We still hadn't said a word, and yet we carefully intertwined our fingers.

I held my breath and adjusted my hips, pushing them back against Ben's hardened body. We were silently testing each other, challenging each other on how far we would go. He brought his hand around to my front, where he gently slipped it beneath the hem of my shirt so his fingers could find my skin. I inhaled at his light touch, hollowing out my stomach. I was so instantly wide awake with his touch that I was practically buzzing. Our movements were tentative but deliberate. He spread his fingers across my stomach and pressed into me, guiding my body, and I rolled my hips into him. He felt so good against me, it felt like I was melting into him.

Holy shit. What am I doing? Does he want this? He does, right? I can feel how much he wants this. Do I want this? Yes, I definitely want this.

I wondered if I should turn and face Ben. If I did, I knew it would be a clear signal and an invitation for more. Ben was my friend and my roommate. But what would *more* mean?

I second-guessed myself and stopped slowly writhing my body against him, with him, together. Everything together. He stopped milliseconds after me, and I felt him tense. I pushed myself away, giving us several inches of space, then turned to face him. He kept his hand on me, letting it drag across my stomach to my hip as I turned. His green eyes were focused, and I could see hesitation behind his concerned brow.

"Good morning," I mumbled.

"Morning." His smile was crestfallen.

"Um . . ." I let a small, nervous laugh slip through my nose. Ben watched me closely, waiting for my next move. "I'm . . . going back to the internship after school," I decided to say.

"Yeah?" Ben rested his head up into his hand, leaning into his elbow.

Okay, we're going to ignore the fact that we were rubbing up against each other just now. Cool. I can do that.

"Yeah. And I don't need you to come with me."

"I know you don't, but can I anyway?" He moved his hand from my side and lightly brushed his finger against my arm hair.

"Ben . . ." I dropped my head to my arm, and Ben started playing with my hair, which was draped over the pillow.

"It's you and me, Ellie." Ben leaned down and lightly kissed my bare shoulder, surprising me. He was still testing me.

I lifted my head from my shoulder and found his face inches from mine. The last person I was an "us" with was Rory. Actually, no. I guess we were never an us. Not really. As Ben liked to remind me, Rory was never my boyfriend. Was Ben?

The lines between Ben and me were blurring, and I was sure we had already crossed a few of them. He kept his eyes on me as he kissed my shoulder again. With his lips still pressed against my skin, he said, "Okay, I won't come and be your bodyguard, but can I at least pick you up after work? Maybe we can go for a walk? Maybe talk?"

Our eyes locked. My heart was in my throat.

Don't kiss me, Ben. Don't kiss me. But also, please, dear god, kiss me.

I nodded cautiously and whispered, "Okay."

He kissed my shoulder for a third time, simultaneously warming me from the inside and confusing the shit out of me, then slipped out of bed to make us coffee.

Ben arrived to pick me up at my internship at 7 p.m. I had been through a gauntlet of horrors. Justin had explained that he was going to fire anyone who pissed him off that day, based on the three-strike rule. His assistant was out the door by 5 p.m. He then called me into his office, saying I was going to be the one to take over the assistant's desk because he liked the way I took initiative and color-coded the kombucha in the fridge.

The top of Justin's desk was already stacked with the CVs of people next in line to replace me should I screw up. He tasked me with getting him tickets to a Vegas fight that hadn't yet been announced and didn't yet "technically" exist to the outside world. He said if I figured out a way to get the tickets, then I could come back tomorrow. Needless to say, after crying in the bathroom for thirty minutes, I got scrappy. I got a hold of the third assistant to the CEO of the biggest talent agency in Los Angeles by lying my ass off, and once I connected with her executive assistant, I told them whom I worked for and my predicament.

Luckily, Justin's reputation extended across the country, and the executive assistant gave me the contact information for the assistant of the agent who represented one of the fighters. It went on from there, and in about an hour I received an email from the agent himself, guaranteeing Justin the tickets. Justin thanked me by squirting me with his water bottle and not firing me.

It made me forget about the push-ups from the day before entirely, and I felt like I had pulled a rabbit out of my ass. I may have accidentally given myself my very first ulcer, but I did it. I pulled it off, and I wondered for the first time if maybe there was something other than acting, other than writing, that I might actually be good at. Yes, Justin was a movie star, but in the moment, I didn't feel like an intern; I felt like his producer.

Ben gently tapped on my computer, surprising me with his arrival.

"You moved desks?"

My attention had been buried deep inside my phone, answering Justin's texts even though he was in the office next door. Another intern named Chase, my desk-mate before today's trial by fire, dropped off a stack of movie scripts that Justin had been offered. Chase gave Ben the ol' up-and-down.

"Security?" Chase laughed.

"Kinda." I returned the laugh half-heartedly. I looked toward Justin's open office door, then whispered, "I can't go until he goes."

"Okay. I can wait. But was today better, or do I lose my shit?" Ben asked, mirroring my hushed tone.

I smiled and felt myself fully inhale for the first time in hours.

Before I could answer Ben, Chase jumped in. "You Ellie's boyfriend?"

Ben held out his hand and shook Chase's. "What's up? I'm Ben," he said, not entirely answering the question.

"Oh, Ben! I'm Chase. Ellie talks about you all the time." Chase leaned against my new desk, oblivious to how he had just called me out.

Ben's eyebrows flew up his forehead, conveying his delight to be receiving this news. "Does she?"

"Settle down," I cautioned Ben with an eye roll.

Just then, Justin stalked out of his office. He once again shot me with a squirt from his water bottle, then barreled toward the exit door like a hurricane of pomp and ego. "Nighty-night, intern."

Thankfully, my computer was spared. I looked up at Ben, whose entire face had transformed.

"Ben. Don't," I warned, sensing he was about to blow. Ben carefully closed my laptop, then pulled on my hand, lifting me from my seat. He gently pushed back my damp hair and thumbed some water away from my face.

"Ellie." His voice trembled with an anger that I knew he was attempting to harness. "He just squirted you in the face with water like you're a cat he's trying to train."

"Please. It's fine. I'm fine." I clutched Ben's hand. He kept his intensifying gaze on mine. His mouth tightened into a firm line. "Let's go home," I implored, and Ben eventually nodded, reluctantly following my lead.

We walked up Central Park West. Ben hadn't let go of my hand.

"What happened today?" he said through gritted teeth. I could tell it was difficult for him to speak.

"Ben. Stop." I pulled on his hand, forcing him to stand with me on the street. He forced his eyes down to mine. I gently pushed the back of my hands into his rigid jaw. He closed his eyes and brought me into him, wrapping his arms around my neck.

"I'm okay. Today was really hard. Like, *really* hard. But I got through it. I did it." I turned my head to the side, resting it on his collarbone.

"I know you did. You're Ellie Fucking McCain." He repeated his words from the night before. I hummed softly and found myself quietly breathing him in. After a long moment of just holding each other, he cleared his throat and let out a long, slow breath. "What are we doing? Are we friends? Are we more? What's going on?"

My throat went dry. "Of all my friends, I like you the most."

"Is this how you are with all your friends?" Ben placed his chin on the top of my head. Cars whizzed past us, horns were blaring, but we stood on the sidewalk as still as the trees in Central Park.

Did he mean, do I secretly fall in love with my friends and suffer through intense feelings twisting me in knots, torturing me until the end of time? Then do I eventually mess everything up by holding on to something that wasn't real? Or maybe it was real, and I was too terrified to do anything about it because of how real it really was? I mean . . . Maybe? I feared that I was running directly toward a record-breaking two for two here.

"Somehow, in six months, you've become the most important person in my life. If we got together and it got bad, I'd lose you. And I can't lose you, Ben. I don't want you to wake up one day and . . . not choose me . . ." My voice wavered. Everything felt a little too familiar.

"I've already chosen you, Ellie. It's already happened. Now you have to choose me." Ben tipped his head down and brushed his lips against my temple. "Which is what I thought was happening this morning before you freaked out."

I pulled myself away from Ben's embrace but left my hands on his chest. "I did not freak out."

"You freaked the fuck out." He couldn't help but laugh.

"I don't want a day to come when you're not in my life anymore."

"I'm not Rory, Ellie." He said it. He went there. And by the crack in his voice, I would swear he sounded jealous. He took a deep breath. "I'm always going to be your friend."

Ben left for Boston the next day. I looked over at his empty bed, then out to the busy streets of New York. It was the first time I had ever been entirely and completely alone.

Chapter 12

VANCOUVER
18 years old

ONCE I STOPPED GOING TO JUNIPER, I STOPPED SEEING RORY. IT was exactly as I feared. The club was the thread that held us together. I had a difficult time thinking about what everyone thought of me at the golf club after it all went up in flames. The idea of the people I loved laughing at me absolutely terrified me, and facing the shame that I had placed on myself felt insurmountable. I was scared to call Rory, and eventually, too much time had passed. It didn't matter anyway; it's not like he called me.

Hannah stopped going to the club, too, and with me and Hannah not there, Kara was out. Any conversation involving Rory or Juniper had become off-limits. I declared that shoving my head in the sand was my only line of defense and my only chance at self-preservation.

I grew up a lot in two years. I even had a boyfriend named Matt. He was nice and sweet, and my parents liked him. It was with Matt that I lost my virginity, in my twin-size bed during one of my sister's house parties.

I was forced to choose between swimming and acting, and I decided to dedicate myself to the latter. Without hours at Juniper distracting me, I was reconnecting with that little girl who believed in big dreams and had made up her mind about herself a long time ago. My only problem was that no one else believed in my dreams, and it had started to feel like I couldn't get an audition if my life depended on it.

I would spend hours staring at the course descriptions for UCLA and daydreaming about what it would be like to sit in a lecture hall for Introduction to Musical Literacy for Singing Actors. I wrote three different personal essays to apply to the school, but leaving the shadow of Vancouver's mountains wasn't something my friends were doing. So I kept my dreams close and told myself, "Maybe not today, but one day."

Matt and I were very different. He wanted a beautiful, uncomplicated life. He wanted to go to school, get a job, get married, have kids, get a cabin, retire early, have grandkids, and . . . I guess die? The life Matt wanted sounded ideal, and I wished I wanted it, too. I just wasn't built that way. My parents worried I would spend my life chasing dragons. I guess I had always hoped that I would find someone who, instead of telling me that the dragon was a fairy tale, or asking me to slow down, or change directions, or stop altogether, would throw me a sword and fight by my side.

Matt was watching TV in the living room with a bowl of popcorn in his lap and my mom sitting next to him when the phone call came through the house's landline. No one called the landline except my dad, and even then, the ring startled us all.

"Hello?" I answered.

"Hi. Is Ellie there?" Rory's voice rocked through me, knocking me on my ass. It was deeper, but I knew it was him. I quickly walked into my dad's office, sat in his swivel chair, and turned my back on Matt and my mom.

"This is Ellie," I said, my eyes wide. I focused on a framed photo of me, Hannah, and my dad at Juniper from when I was twelve. My sister had a hole in one that day, and we celebrated with hamburgers and milkshakes.

Rory waited an agonizing few seconds before speaking again. "Hey, it's Rory."

"Hey." I pitched my voice up, trying to sound casual.

"Hi," he said again. I kept my mouth shut, so he continued. "How are you?"

"Ummm . . ."

After two years? How do I answer this?

"Good. How are you?"

"Good." He laughed nervously. I released an ocean's worth of tension with my exhale, joining him in the awkwardness.

"Hi, Cainey!" I heard Blair call from the background and started to tear up. He was twenty-one now. So much time had passed. I wasn't going to be able to get through this call. I heard Rory shut the door to whatever room he was in.

"Sorry," he said. "Umm . . . so, I know this is unexpected, and it's been a long time. But ummm . . . Okay, here we go." Rory struggled to find the words, and then finally, they all strung together. "My prom is coming up, and there has never been anyone in my life who's meant as much to me as you, so I was wondering if you'd go with me?"

I was speechless. My mouth dropped so far open that my jaw may as well have fallen off its hinges. Two years had come and gone. Two. Years. I hadn't known my heart had been sitting dormant, waiting for him to wake me up again, but here we were. I was awake.

"I heard you have a boyfriend, so just friends and all that, but what do you think?" Rory pressed on through my silence. I could hear his voice waver through his nerves.

I spun around in my chair slowly, like I was moving in molasses, and looked over my shoulder to see Matt zoned out on the TV. My eyes plummeted to the ground. All my blood rushed to my head. "Of course," I whispered with my eyes closed. "Yes, I'll go with you."

"Okay." I could hear the relief in his voice. "Great. We'll just stay in touch to figure it all out. But yeah. Thank you."

"You're welcome? Thank you?"

Ellie, don't you dare start crying.

"Alright, I'll talk to you later, Cainey," Rory said quietly.

I hung up the phone, and I saw stars.

"Who was that?" Matt called out, and I fell into a black hole.

Rory pulled into my parents' driveway to pick me up in his new-to-him, old-to-everyone-else Jeep Cherokee. Hannah, my mom, and I were hiding beneath my sister's bedroom bay window, secretly watching Rory step out of his Jeep. When he got out of the truck in his fitted black suit, crisp white shirt, thin dark-gray wool tie, and Ray-Ban sunglasses, I almost threw up. He pushed his hand into his loose curls, which were styled and off his forehead.

"Oh . . . Yikes. Has he always been that pretty?" Hannah asked.

"Yup." I gulped.

Utter delight penetrated Hannah's stare as she grinned at me like a lunatic. "This isn't good." She giggled like a goddamn monster.

"It's going to be fine. Don't scare your sister." My mom rubbed the back of my cream-colored, lacy, but structured dress, which I was starting to worry looked a lot like a wedding dress.

"I wonder what Blair looks like these days," Hannah mused, just as Rory looked up to the window we were peeking out from. The three of us dropped to the floor with a thud.

"Oh, Jesus. Did he see us?!" my mom said in a harsh whisper.

"I don't know. I have to crawl now. This is a nightmare." I slumped. "I think I'm gonna be sick."

"Don't barf. Get it together." Hannah crawled toward me and kissed me on the head. "Have fun." Her devilishness was disturbing. "We're going to be right here waiting for you when you get back, and you better remember every last detail. It's Rory, Ellie! *Rory! This is huge!*"

"Stop it!" I hissed. "I have a boyfriend."

"I know, you stupid idiot." My sister shook her head at me.

"No licky-dicky." My mom smiled, looking exactly like my sister.

I contorted my face. "I. Have. A. Boyfriend!" I growled, refusing to admit that I was reminding myself of that fact just as much as I was reminding my sister and mom.

"IT'S. RORY!" my sister exclaimed through gritted teeth.

What is wrong with these people?!

I awkwardly crawled out of the bedroom in my fancy dress on my hands and knees so Rory wouldn't know we had all been spying on him.

I opened the door to Rory, and the air was sucked out of my lungs. He looked at me standing in the doorway and appeared stunned for a moment, frozen in place. I must have looked different to him. I didn't have my hair in a ponytail. It was in loose waves down my back. It was also longer and darker than he was used to, making my blue eyes stand out a little more. I wasn't wearing a polo or the khaki pants that he had seen me in for all those years, and he had never seen me dressed up before. Not really. My lips were red, and my closed-mouth smile was instant. Rory pushed his sunglasses back into his hair like a headband. He looked like he couldn't form thoughts, so I formed mine instead.

"I made you a boutonniere." I reached over to the side table by the front door and pulled out a little box. I lifted out the boutonniere that I had made the day before. It was small, natural, and green. It had two sprigs of eucalyptus, a pop of baby's breath, and was wrapped in twine. He still hadn't said anything when I pulled it out of the box and got the pin. "Oh, I'm sorry. I'm just assuming. Do you even want this?"

"Yes," he said quietly.

Hearing his deep, grounded voice, even though it was still barely a whisper, made my hands tremble. I pinned the boutonniere to his lapel and pressed it down afterward. My eyes flicked up to his.

"You made this for me?" he asked, not looking away from me.

I nodded. "Yeah, it just . . . I wanted, umm . . . They just reminded me of you, or of . . . you know, what I used to know and all that," I breathed.

That was weird. I shouldn't have done that.

He cleared his throat and gave himself a couple of seconds before saying, "I didn't get you a corsage, but I did get you this." He pulled out a delicate rose gold bracelet. "Can I?" he asked. I had to center myself before holding out my hand to him. He barely touched me as he clasped the bracelet together. "I hope this isn't weird."

A smile spread across my face. "It's not weird. I was worried the boutonniere was weird."

He relaxed. "It's not weird."

He carefully watched me wrap my hand around my bracelet, fiddling nervously. "Come on, Cainey. Let's go." He tilted his head, calling me away from the front door, then thrust his hands deep into his pockets. He spun around toward the Jeep.

Just as I went to close the front door, my sister screamed from upstairs, "BYE, RORY!"

Without turning around, he tossed his head back and laughed.

"Wow. I'm sorry." I was burning bright red.

"You should have heard my brothers." He opened the car door for me.

As I climbed in, I looked up at my sister's bedroom window, and my mom and sister threw themselves back onto the ground.

The ballroom was stunning. Twinkly lights were scattered across the ceiling, illuminating the entire space. Massive flower centerpieces overflowed every round table, dangling over the edges.

Rory held his arm out for me as we entered the room, and I was surprised to feel his bicep beneath his suit. Rory was still lean, towering over me now, and his fitted suit hid nothing. He was beautiful.

When he was introducing me to people, he would say, "This is Ellie. We grew up together." It was true. It was also the same thing I had said to Matt to ensure he was okay with me being another guy's prom date. There were about three or four people who recognized my name, saying, "Oh, Ellie! Wait, do you mean Cainey?" Or "So *this* is Ellie!" They held their opinions to themselves in those moments of recognition, so I never knew if I had made a good impression through Rory's stories or a bad one.

Keane's "Somewhere Only We Know" started playing, and one guy came up to us at our table and said, "I heard this is Juniper-Ellie. I can't believe I'm meeting you."

I noticed Rory shift his body uncomfortably.

"Hey, Alex, you know what, don't sit. We were about to dance." Rory grabbed my hand, which felt like it was on fire.

But Alex continued, "Man, the things Rory used to say about you . . ."

I saw Rory's back stiffen, and he pulled me onto the dance floor.

Rory whipped me around, and our bodies collided. He held my right hand to his chest and wrapped his other arm around my waist. He was holding on to me tightly, as if I had only ever belonged to him. I did the same, and he dropped his forehead onto my shoulder. I was transported in time and sent back two years. Suddenly, we were on my couch, and I could feel us kissing all over again. It was as if we hadn't moved from the last time we held each other in this exact way, with his forehead on my shoulder.

Eventually, I asked, "What did you used to say about me?"

Rory let out a deep exhale. His breath coated my collarbone, wrapping me in warmth. He lifted his head and smiled. Our faces were so close. They had only been this close one other time.

He ignored my question and asked one in return. "Why'd you have to look so pretty?"

"I'm sorry." I scrunched my nose. "Do you want me to go . . . fuck up my face?"

Rory laughed through his nose, and his dimple finally made an appearance. He tilted his forehead down to place it on mine, closed his eyes, and sighed just as the song changed to "Drop It Like It's Hot" by Snoop Dogg. I snorted, unable to hold back my amusement at the ill-timed song.

"Brutal . . ." Rory chuckled. "We're pretty good at having terrible timing."

I tipped my head back, pulled out my dance face, and started popping my neck and shoulders to the beat of the song. Rory mirrored my expression and bobbed his head. He subtly bounced his body, and I let out a loud laugh. We slowed our silliness after only a few seconds, until we were swaying once more.

"Come on." Rory pulled on my hand to take me away from the ballroom. We went up to the hotel's roof, where there were already about thirty people from the prom hanging out. He gave me his jacket, and we lay out on the prickly roof. We looked up at the sky, and he finally asked about Matt.

"So, how long have you been with your boyfriend?" Rory stretched his arm back and bent his elbow, creating a pillow for himself.

"Almost a year," I answered carefully.

"Oh, wow . . . Is he going to LA with you?"

"Ha!" My laugh slipped out involuntarily. Rory turned his head to see what was so funny. "Sorry. That was a strange reaction. I'm going to UBC. I'll figure it out from there."

Rory turned his head back toward the sky, his mouth downturned. He nodded slightly. "Have you applied for any schools down there? UCLA? Or have you auditioned for anything?"

"No," I sighed.

"Not yet."

I smiled, keeping my eyes locked on a cloud that was shape-shifting overhead. I had been working as a host at a restaurant, and I was getting ready to attend the University of British Columbia, because that's where my sister had gone. My last audition was five months ago. Whenever someone asked about my acting, I tried to swallow my feelings of ridiculousness wrapped in a healthy dose of anxiety.

After a moment of silence, Rory said, "You're a bird, Cains. You'll fly away eventually."

"You know ostriches don't fly, right?" I turned my head toward Rory, recalling the accidental insult he'd thrown at me a long time ago.

Rory's laugh was so loud that his body twisted. He propped himself up on his elbows, and his eyes ignited. "You know you called me a sheep, right?" He smiled.

I pressed my hand over my eyes, horrified.

"That haunts me." Rory laughed again. "I can't even tell you how many people I've asked if they thought I was a sheep."

"Oh my god." I laughed. "Okay, yeah. Fine. That's worse." I crossed my arms, closing myself off, and took a deep breath. *Here we go.* "Rory, I owe you an apology. I feel like I've been careless with you over the years . . . I didn't know what to do with all the feelings I had. And I had a lot of feelings." My laugh was heavy and weighed down with guilt. "They were big. I was messy, and I'm sorry."

Rory's smile slipped into sadness. "Where did you go?" His dark-brown eyes knocked me out.

"What do you mean?" My heart sank, and my throat closed.

"You left, and you never came back."

"You never called, Rory. It wasn't just me," I said defensively.

"I know." Rory nodded and looked out at Vancouver's skyline. We were surrounded by glass buildings and the dim lights that penetrated their windows. "I freaked out when you walked away from me the day after we kissed. I asked you out, and you couldn't even look at me. I don't know what happened, but you didn't want to talk to me or be around me. You just left."

I took a deep breath. And then another.

Four. Three. Two . . .

"Something happened with Caleb Davis's dad that day that I didn't really understand. I still don't think I understand it," I admitted. The sky pushed down on me. "But after that, I didn't know how to *be* there." I let out a sharp, unexpected gasp. I hadn't thought about Albert Davis in over a year. Why was I gasping? "I tried to go back, but I didn't know how, you know?"

"I don't know. I don't know what you're trying to say. What happened with Caleb's dad?" Rory's face twisted with concern.

Four. Three. Two . . .

"I don't even know how to say it without feeling . . . ridiculous. But before that day, I was walking around Juniper with rose-colored glasses on, thinking everything was one way. When the glasses came off, I found out I had been walking around looking like an idiot the whole time. And everyone knew but me."

"Ellie, what happened?" Rory asked again, nervously.

Three. Two. One . . .

"He just . . . He . . ." Our eyes connected. "He liked me, Rory . . . And he tried to give me presents. He had this sweatband that he . . . tried to make me wear? He watched me, and he said things to me, and . . . He *liked* me, and he wanted me to know it."

Rory looked away from me, and distress clouded his face. He ran his fingers through his hair, and his eyes searched for the nonexistent horizon. "I wish I'd known that."

"I was . . ." I was currently blacking out, that's what I was doing. "I was embarrassed, and then I felt a lot of shame." I shook my head and bit the inside of my cheek. "Besides, you wouldn't have done anything. Nobody did. There was nothing to do. Nobody cared." It was hard for me to admit, but it was also the truth. I blinked back tears. "I thought I was special, which is stupid because I ended up being just like every other random junior that shows up there for a stint and then disappears. I was a blip. I was just another girl at the golf club, and then I wasn't, you know?"

Rory closed his eyes and released a wobbly breath. "You weren't a blip."

"I think a lot about where I would be if that all didn't happen. Would I still be at Juniper every weekend, waiting to see your Jeep pull up the driveway? I think I probably would be. When I really think about it, I wasn't up there golfing. That's not what I was doing. I was just up there . . . waiting for you."

His face pinched with sadness and then transformed with realization. "So that's why you all stopping going?"

I didn't answer. I didn't have to.

"I thought you changed your mind about me. Or you were bored with me. I thought you didn't like me."

I went numb.

"I loved you, Rory." My words fell out of my mouth, natural and necessary.

"Please don't say that." He kept his eyes closed, avoiding me.

"I'm sorry . . ."

What are you doing, Ellie? Stop it. He doesn't want to hear it, and you shouldn't be saying it. Calm down, Ellie. He doesn't want you. He doesn't love you. You have a boyfriend. What the fuck are you doing? Don't love him anymore, Ellie. Just stop. Stop.

After a hard swallow and a throat clear, I sat up. Rory opened his eyes to see what I was doing. I held out my hand, and he braced himself for a moment before taking it. I pulled him up so we were sitting face-to-face.

"Before anything else, we were friends. I miss you."

He didn't say anything. He just looked at me. I could have sworn his eyes looked a little glassy, a little watery.

"Your turn," I whispered.

His breath caught in his throat. "I miss you, too."

I pulled out my phone from my small purse and pressed one earbud into his ear, then one into mine. I flipped through some tracks, landed on Guns N' Roses' "November Rain," pressed play, then turned to him. "Want to start over?"

His eyebrows crinkled, as if he were in pain, and he pressed his lips together tightly. His dimple dug deep into his cheek. When he opened his eyes again, it felt like a shooting star had exploded overhead and pierced every inch of me.

"Let's start over," he answered, capturing my heart once more.

Chapter 13

NEW YORK

20 years old

IT WAS THE DAY BEFORE MY TWENTY-FIRST BIRTHDAY. HANNAH and Kara had arrived the night before. I was thrilled to show off New York to them, and everything that came along with my new life, especially Zoë, Lucas, and Ben.

It was March, yet we were visiting classic tourist destinations while battling a freak snowstorm. We trudged through ankle-deep, mucky, dirty sidewalk snow, bundled up so only our eyes were exposed.

Ben and Lucas had been in Boston for five days to catch two Celtics games and were caught in the storm overnight.

BEN: Train comes into Penn Station @ 7:30, so maybe I can meet you all once you're already out?

ELLIE: Let's go to Lifers and keep it local. Plus, you can hook us up with freebies. I have a feeling tomorrow will get expensive.

BEN: Sounds good. I'm looking forward to meeting them!

ELLIE: Okay, calm down over there.

BEN: I'm calm. You calm down.

ELLIE: I'm calm. YOU CALM DOWN!

BEN: I'M CALM! YOU CALM DOWN!!!!!!!!!!!!!!!!

"So, what exactly is going on between you and Ben?"

Hannah's quiet voice next to my ear startled me. My head snapped up to see both Hannah and Kara hunched over my shoulder, reading my text messages. We were at Battery Park, and not one of us was admiring the glory of the Statue of Liberty.

"What do you mean?"

Hannah snatched my phone from my death grip and pulled it up to her face. She read, "I'm so calm I've reached a new state of existence. I can't see any material things anymore, I'm so calm." Hannah flicked her eyes up to me.

"Yeah . . ." My face flushed. "He's a silly goose."

"You like him. I knew it." Kara's smirk was cracking, exposing her teeth. "You like your hot roommate. That is so sexy. Also, Cameron called it."

"Wait, what? What do you mean?" My head almost twisted off my neck as I spun to Kara, mouth gaping. I refused to admit how envious I was of Kara's closeness with the Campbell family since she and Cameron had started dating.

"I told Cameron that Ben was your roommate, and showed him that picture of you guys in the subway. The first thing he said was 'Well, if she wasn't gone before, she's gone now,' and that Rory blew it."

"Whatever." I shook my head, trying to steady my voice. "I can't listen to this. I haven't talked to Rory in . . ." I did the mental math. "Six months? And you're right, Kara. I do like Ben," I continued. "But he's just my friend, and I know we've all heard *that* before, but it's true." I rolled my eyes. "I was always one foot out in Vancouver, looking for something else, and I found it. I'm happy here. I'm actually happy."

"The fact that you *like* Ben after all these years of Rory is such a big deal, Ellie." Hannah pressed her finger into my puffy jacket. "You need to go for it."

"We're just friends," I muttered, shuffling my feet.

"No!" Kara's face morphed with frustration. She pushed me in the chest harder than either of us expected.

"Ow! You got my boob!"

"No, Ellie!" Kara waved me off. "Cameron's going to kill me for saying this, but I don't care! I'M IN NEW YORK, BABY!" Kara screamed out into the cold. Hannah and I both chuckled at her lunacy. "Before you left Vancouver, Rory broke your heart. Whatever's ticking inside your chest right now is new, and it's growing. And if whatever's in there belongs to Ben, then give him the whole thing. Don't give him bits and parts. You didn't tell Rory how you felt until it was too late. Don't make the same mistake with Ben."

Hannah and Kara had witnessed every step of my life. They watched me struggle to become a real person in Vancouver. They watched my childhood crumble the moment I stopped going to Juniper. They watched me become a new version of myself out of that heartbreak. They watched me fall in love, and never judged me for my inability to let that love go. They watched me decide to run away, and they didn't stop me when they knew I wouldn't look back. I couldn't. Not anymore. Hannah's and Kara's love for me, and my love for them, was unconditional, and if anyone could slap me in the face with reality, it was them.

My phone dinged.

I reached into my pocket, pulled out my phone, and opened the message.

"What does it say?" Hannah asked.

"He . . ." I tried to conceal my smile. "He photoshopped his face onto a picture of the Dalai Lama. And said, 'You calm down.'"

We got to Lifers, and I kept checking to see who was walking through the door every time it opened. When Ben finally pushed his way in, with Lucas following closely behind, the tension in my body released. Some of the last words he'd said to me before leaving for Boston hit me like a ton of bricks.

Now you have to choose me.

It always struck me like a thunderclap how beautiful Ben was. He wasn't a star yet, but everyone could read the tea leaves. He was wearing slacks, a cream shirt, and a gray peacoat that he took off as he walked toward us. The scruff on his face was thicker than usual, chiseling two long lines that creased his cheeks when he smiled. He pushed his hand through his hair, shaking away the snow.

"Oh, wow. Jesus Christ," Kara muttered while looking at him.

"You made it!" I threw my arms around Ben and hugged him tight.

"I made it." He took a minute to drag his eyes down my face, landing them on my mouth, before he turned to Hannah and Kara. They were already exchanging private looks with each other.

"Hi. I'm Ben."

"Yes, we know." Hannah smiled. "I'm Hannah."

"Kara." Kara took a sip of her gin and tonic and winked.

I narrowed my eyes and cocked my head at her.

"Okay, well. I'm happy to meet you. Gimme a second." Ben combed his hair with his fingers again, resetting it, then jumped over the bar.

"He works here." I justified his comfort level.

"Apparently." Hannah grabbed my waist and squeezed approvingly.

"I'm getting us some drinks. Go grab a seat," Ben called out as he grabbed a tray. I saw him pull out a bottle of champagne and then duck beneath the bar to pour everyone sneaky shots.

Lucas's lean body towered over the rest of us. He took off his black jacket to reveal his tattoos. "I'm Lucas. Lucas Martin." He smiled directly at Hannah, and I could see my sister's knees go weak when she heard his French accent.

"Well, shit." Kara looked Lucas up and down. "What do they put in the water here, Lucas Martin?"

By the time 2 a.m. rolled around, the five of us had finished two bottles of champagne, a bunch of cocktails, and two shots each. I was feeling loose from the alcohol. My jaw hurt from smiling, and my stomach was tender from laughing. Once Ben and I had a moment alone together, I turned to him. "I hope you're okay with them staying with us."

"Of course. We can push the beds together, and the three of you can take it. I'll go on the floor." Ben took a sip of his beer. "Or I can stay with Lucas, if you want?"

"No." I jumped over his question. "I want you there."

Ben's lips tugged at the edges, then he nodded toward Kara and Hannah, who were tearing up the makeshift dance floor. "I like them."

"They like you. Everybody likes you, Ben."

His smile grew. "You're drunk."

"I'm tipsy." I felt a sudden urge to be honest. "You look good tonight. Your face is pretty."

"*My* face is pretty?" Ben smirked.

"Yeah. I thought about your face a lot when you were gone." I placed my hand on his chest, and he covered it with his. I took a deep breath, then flexed my hand, opening my fingers. Without letting a second pass, he laced his fingers through mine, tying us together, and lightly stroked my thumb.

Ben softly exhaled. "I thought about *your* face a lot."

Now you have to choose me.

The choice was easy, and I didn't even realize it had already been made. I didn't want Ben to have bits and parts of me. And I didn't want bits and parts of him.

Ben's gaze dropped to my mouth. He very slowly moved his head toward mine. Instead of meeting him in the middle, I stood. He stilled, surprised by my sudden movement. All the blood rushed to my head, and the shots took over my better judgment. Ben's eyes followed me as I made my way to the DJ in the corner of the bar.

I turned back to see him mouth, *What are you doing?*

The music shut off, and more than a few boos could be heard throughout the crowd, who assumed a mistake had been made. The song "Dreams" by the Cranberries started playing through the speakers. I pulled a microphone up to my lips, and Ben's mouth dropped open. I began singing, and the soulful love song reverberated throughout the entire bar. Once I had people whistling and whooping, I slowly walked toward Ben, who was sitting in shock at the table. I flipped a chair around and planted myself in front of him, with the back of the chair between my legs. Ben covered his eyes with his hands and laughed.

"Can someone get this girl a glass of water?" Ben shouted out to no one, with the biggest smile I had ever seen.

I heard Lucas whistle at me from the bar. On the dance floor, Hannah's hands were covering her mouth, and Kara's eyes were bulging out of her head. I threw my hand into the air and shifted my body upward until I was standing on the chair, letting it all out.

Ben pulled his hand over his beautiful face and dragged down his mouth. He looked around the crowd to see people filming, people cheering for us, and almost everyone singing along. The entire bar was alive.

"I'm going to kiss you, Ellie!" Ben yelled over the music.

I laughed and shook my head *no*, still singing.

"It's happening."

I shook my head again. *No.*

He nodded. *Yes.*

I shook.

He nodded. His beautiful smile dipped at the edges, lighting up the entire room.

Oh fuck. I love him.

I hadn't even finished singing when Ben stood, never taking his eyes off me. Once he was on his feet, I stepped off the chair. He slipped one hand around the back of my neck and the other around my waist. I dropped the mic onto the table, and when he brought his face toward mine, the entire bar erupted. He paused for a moment to look into my eyes. I gently brushed my nose against his. And when he finally pressed his lips onto mine, we were both smiling.

We had pushed the beds together in our tiny studio apartment. Hannah, Kara, and I were cuddled up, while Ben lay below our feet on a twin-size, wobbly, overinflated air mattress. At 3 a.m., my sister and Kara were breathing deeply, and I heard Ben shuffle about with our spare comforter.

"Are you asleep?" I whispered.

"Yes," he whispered back. "Come down here."

"What?"

"Get your ass down here, Ellie."

My heart rose to my throat as I inched out of the bed. I crawled over to Ben, and he grabbed me around the waist and pulled my body toward him. My back pressed against his chest. A soft glow from the Grayrock sign shone through the curtains.

"I can't believe you sang to me."

"I know." I giggled. The air mattress swayed, but I relaxed into him as I settled between his arms.

"You sounded like a broken dishwasher."

I laughed loudly, and he shushed me with a light smack. The unsteadiness of the air mattress caused it to slip on the floor, pushing it forward and knocking Ben off with a thud. We looked up at Hannah and Kara, who were both drooling in their sleep.

"Whoops." Ben put the mattress back, then slipped into the small space next to the foot of the bed, holding me in front of him.

"You deserved that. I sounded amazing. It's all those drills in voice class."

"Ha! Caaaaaa, caaaaaaa." He quietly replicated one of the many vocal warm-ups we were forced to do every morning—to loosen our jaws, maybe? I think? I needed to pay more attention in voice class.

"Caaaaaaa, caaaaaaa!" I matched his energy and then some.

"Shhhhh! For Christ's sake, too loud!" He shook with laughter, jostling me around in his arms. His solid body flexed and tensed. My stomach hurt from holding back. After we calmed again, he pressed his face into my hair and breathed in deeply. "You smell like alcohol." His hot breath made it feel like he had kissed me softly behind my ear, but I couldn't be sure.

"Right back at you, buddy." My heart tripped. Ben squeezed me a little tighter, then brushed my hair away from his face. He pressed his lips into the back of my neck. There was no mistaking it this time. He kissed me. Every organ inside my body fluttered. "You never told me about Boston. How was it?"

"It was okay." His fingers slowly grazed my arm. He was connecting my freckles. After a long moment of silence, he said, "You're doing it this time."

"Doing what?" I turned my body to face Ben, pressing my hips and stomach into his.

"Kissing me."

"I am?" I smiled.

He nodded. "I know you pretty well, you know. I know when you're scared, because I am, too. I know when you're excited, because I am, too. And I know when you want something, because I want it, too."

I gently pulled Ben toward me, and our lips came together like a river to the ocean. From my prickling skin to the firmness of our kiss to every time he opened my mouth with his own, I was disappearing into him. We were disappearing into each other. I felt him everywhere. His teeth trailed against my bottom lip, and I twisted onto my back, letting his body take over mine.

He lifted my hands overhead, giving himself full access to my body. He slipped his free hand under my shirt, lifting it. He trailed his mouth across my rib cage, up to the bottom of my breast. His mouth wandered my body as I arched alongside him. It was as if we were moving in slow motion. He released my hands, and I moved them to the front of his pajama bottoms. My thumbs dipped below the elastic band, and I pulled his hips against mine. We started slowly grinding against each other, moving in tandem, and I felt like I was going to combust.

"Ben . . ." I breathed. "You're barely touching me, and I'm already close."

Ben lifted his head, his eyes glinting. He was clearly surprised by my admission. "Seriously?" He laughed softly. "We just started."

"I'm telling you right now, there's nothing I can do about this," I panted, and he laughed a little louder. "And yes, I'm aware that we're fully clothed, but . . . Jesus Christ, Ben." I was only half embarrassed. Ben's mouth roamed my neck, and I could feel him smiling.

"Don't you dare come," Ben whispered against my skin. "Not yet. I want to *live* in this moment." He pulled the drawstring of my pajamas and pushed his hands past my hips. A moan slipped out of me as he dug his fingers into my skin and dragged them roughly over me.

"Fuck, Ellie . . . You can't make that noise, or I'll lose it, too." When his hands discovered that I wasn't wearing any underwear, he pressed his fingers deep inside me, unable to stop himself.

"Oh god." My body started to tense. Every part of me was folding and throbbing.

"Keep your shit together, McCain." We both laughed into each other's mouths.

As Ben and I kissed, I felt like I was floating away from the person I was and into the body of someone entirely new. We both took off our shirts and started taking off our pajama pants. Unfortunately, we did so with a little too much enthusiasm, and the air mattress shifted beneath us. We toppled onto the floor with a thunderous crash. We had landed, fully exposed, with our pajamas trapped below our knees, and I somehow rolled on top of him.

Hannah and Kara both stirred.

"Oh shit!" I smacked my hand over Ben's mouth and, through the power of expression, told him to kindly shut the hell up. "How is it possible that I forgot they were here?" I whispered after they settled.

"We're in a dangerous position right now, Ellie." Ben's eyes softened with his smile. He leaned forward, kissing my collarbone, and carefully pulled my pajama pants all the way off. He then grabbed my leg to help me straddle him properly.

"Should we . . . go somewhere?" I asked deliriously.

He brought his mouth to my chest, exploring my body. I dropped my hands into his hair, holding him against my breasts, and he gripped my hips to help me drag myself against him. Ben was right; we were in a *very* dangerous position. Everything was warm, and hard, and wet, and we were close to giving ourselves over entirely. I dipped down and grunted softly into his ear as our movements quickened, heightened. I wanted more. I needed more. "Let's go somewhere."

"Fuck, yes," Ben groaned, far too loudly.

"Ellie?" My sister's groggy voice cut through the room.

Ben and I froze, and our eyes went wide.

"Yes?" I answered stiffly.

Ben's cheeks puffed out, restraining his laughter.

"Where are you?"

"I . . . I fell out of bed."

Ben and I looked at each other, and I shrugged, unsure how to handle things from here on out.

"Oh, okay." I could hear my sister turn over and settle herself back to sleep.

Is she going to ask if I'm okay? I mouthed to Ben, pulling a face.

Priorities, he mouthed back, then pointed to our naked bodies.

I quickly put my shirt back on, then leaned over to grab my pajama pants from the floor, but he ripped them from my hands and defiantly threw them across the room.

You idiot! I mouthed, suppressing my laugh.

Are you trying to kill me? he mouthed back. He popped his hips up in a playful fit of faux anger. I lifted myself off his body, and his eyes narrowed as I pulled up his pajama pants. I then stretched to grab my own.

Are we at least gonna talk about this? he mouthed as I put the pants on. I shook my head.

"Ellie McCain, do not freak out on me again," he whispered as he grabbed my hips and placed me back on his lap.

"I'm not freaking out. I'm trying not to come, you moron," I whispered harshly, through a strangled laugh. Ben hung his head, silently laughing with me. "Now, stop stalling, and move your extremely hard, distractingly big dick away from me unless you want *this* to be my first orgasm with you."

"Well, *my* first orgasm with *you* happened in the shower months ago, just thinking about you. Little did I know, at that same time, you were eating Brie and Triscuits in your bed like a goddamn Neanderthal. So this is a step up, Ellie! At least I'm here!"

We were both shaking from trying to rein in our laughter. We looked at each other for one more sloppy minute before Ben lifted me off him and tore himself away with a growl. "I can't wait to read about this in your diary."

"Good night, Ben." I crawled along the floor to my side of the bed, but was stopped by his hand gripping my ankle. I slid along the ground with his tug, as if I were on rollers, and collided with his body. We both sat up, and his eyes were sparkling. He traced my mouth with his thumb.

"Whatever this is, Ellie, whatever's happening between us, I want it." Ben kissed me one last time. "Happy birthday." He finally backed away from me, put his hands to his head, and mimed that his head had exploded.

"Good night." I laughed, then pulled myself back into bed. I most definitely did not sleep.

Chapter 14

VANCOUVER
20 years old

RORY AND I WERE ON THE SEAWALL AND MAKING OUR WAY UNDER the Lions Gate Bridge, walking past the massive greenish-blue anchorage near the tip of Stanley Park. We had done that a lot since rekindling our friendship after prom. For two years, we had been meeting up once or twice a month. We'd go for a walk or a hike, or we'd hit some balls at a public driving range. We always did something outside, letting the world come between us.

Kara and Cameron started joining us once Cameron finally came to his senses and asked her out. Hannah and Orson made appearances, too, and when Jacob came, he always brought a different girl. Usually, it was just me and Rory. My boyfriend, Matt, went to the driving range with us once. That was a goddamn nightmare. Rory never brought anyone else, though Kara told me there had been a couple of girls since prom.

Our conversation was surface-level, which was unusual for us. Even as kids, Rory and I had figured out a way to talk to each other without fear of being misunderstood, except, of course, when it came to our feelings. Then we said nothing.

I stared off into the ocean, unfocused, and Rory didn't say anything about it until we reached Third Beach.

"What's going on? I don't think you've formed a sentence in the last ten minutes." He looked out at the thirteen gigantic freighters in the water.

"I don't know." I sighed.

"Liar." He flicked his eyes over to me but kept his distance.

I was studying psychology at university, but only because it was what my sister was studying. I had stopped swimming competitively after high school. My auditions were few and far between, and they never progressed beyond one line or a dance. I had been studying with an acting coach since graduating high school, working on monologues I had written myself, but I feared no one would ever see them performed. I was also taking singing lessons, and my acting coach encouraged me to participate in community theater in and around Vancouver, which I kept secret from everyone. After my coach found out I was writing my own material, she started taking me seriously and began pushing different theater programs at me. I had finally applied to UCLA and was rejected. I could feel everything I believed myself to be slowly disassembling.

But I couldn't let it go. I wasn't finished, but without the dream of UCLA, I didn't know how to fill the phantom emptiness and unraveling inside me. I had felt this way for a long time and hadn't talked to anyone about it.

"I don't know, Rory . . . I think I'm . . ." I deflated. "I don't know." I moved over to one of the empty logs on the beach and sat. I didn't tell Rory about UCLA. I couldn't stomach him knowing I'd failed at the one thing I'd told everyone I would do.

"Is it school-related?" Rory sat next to me, and even though he was six inches away, I could feel all our years of distance keeping us as far apart as possible. He dipped the toes of his shoes into the sand, and let a long stretch of silence pass before saying, "You've got to work with me here, Cains." He tipped his body back. "Is it Matt?"

"No," I answered quickly, not wanting to go there.

"Well, then, what's going on? I can tell you're off."

I zeroed in on some grayish-white sand fleas near Rory's feet. "I just feel unsettled." I took a deep breath. "Things aren't what I thought they'd be, you know?"

Rory nodded, not looking at me, already understanding my train of thought. "You're not doing what you want to do," he stated definitively.

"I don't know what I want to do." I turned my head, not wanting him to see that I was on the edge of tears.

"Yeah, you do."

"It's like I have this ache inside me that won't go away. I thought it meant something to be so certain of who I was when I was young, but I'm not an actor. I say I am, but what have I done? It's like calling yourself a golfer when all you do is go to the driving range."

Rory put his hands down on the log, listening to me. I instinctively did the same, mirroring him, keeping our hands close but not touching.

I took a deep breath. "I thought I was this person, and I'm not. I'm a fraud. I know it, and everyone else is gonna figure it out eventually." Rory shifted his fingers on the log to gently cover mine, comforting me. "I'm not happy."

"You're only twenty," he said quietly. "And you are the farthest thing from a fraud."

He was going to figure it out eventually. I needed to change the subject, but he changed it for me. "Are you happy with Matt?" I could feel the blood drain from my body. Everything inside me went dry and calcified. The subtle, subconscious shake of my head was barely perceptible. "Are you gonna leave him?" We kept our fingers connected. He held his mouth in a tight line, not revealing a thing.

"I don't know," I breathed inaudibly, though I absolutely did know. I just didn't know when. "Are you gonna transfer?"

After graduating from high school, Rory decided to take golf seriously. Very seriously. He moved beyond Juniper, winning championships and awards all over the country and in the States. The University of British Columbia, Florida State, the University of Southern California, and the University of Texas all took notice.

"I don't know. I've got some time. So do you, you know."

"There's a program I've been looking at. They're holding auditions next week in Seattle. I was thinking about going and not telling anyone." I shook my head. "It would just be another thing to be embarrassed about if I put myself out there and got rejected by another school."

"Another school? What schools have you been rejected by?"

"N-no. Just . . . You know." I bit my lip. "Anyway, the audition is for a two-year intensive theater program at Bronwyn School for the Arts. It's in New York."

"New York?" Rory was holding his breath. "That's new . . . different," he muttered.

"It's ludicrous to think that I might get in. It's this prestigious performing arts school. It would never happen. But I don't know. I have this feeling in the pit of my stomach, just eating at me . . . I don't belong here. And maybe there's something else for me out there. Something more." I hung my head. "I'm mortified even to say that out loud, but I'm never going to be happy if I don't . . . if I don't . . ."

Try.

I looked back at Rory, and he was already looking at me. "Would you go to Seattle with me for the audition? For backup?" I asked meekly.

Rory let out a jagged breath. "Yeah, Cains. I'll go." He pulled his hand away from mine and stood to finish our walk.

Five months later, I was accepted into Bronwyn School for the Arts. I couldn't believe it. Nobody could, except for Rory.

"Are you breaking up with Matt? Or are you thinking about doing long distance with him?" Blair asked while slurping his spicy miso ramen.

"Oh man," I sighed.

Hannah, Kara, Cameron, Blair, Jacob, Orson, Rory, and I were grabbing a late-night snack at a hole-in-the-wall after-hours ramen spot just off Granville Street in downtown Vancouver. We'd gone to a concert at the Commodore Ballroom as part of my going-away festivities because I was leaving in a week. Rory and I had intentionally spent the entire night with someone standing between us, acting as a buffer. At least, that's what I was doing. I wasn't sure what he was doing because he looked so goddamn good with his hair all sweaty and his T-shirt clinging to him that I could barely look in his direction.

We crammed around the restaurant's small table. Blair was letting Hannah share his broth. Orson was still waiting for his meal because they had put the wrong order in and had to remake it. Jacob was inhaling his food. Kara's head was hanging low. She was drunk, and Cameron was preoccupied with taking care of her. Rory and I sat across from each other.

"Matt is on Salt Spring Island right now, but he's back tomorrow. I'll figure it out." I stuffed noodles into my mouth.

Jacob groaned. "Why don't you just pick up the phone and break up with him?"

I scoffed. "Nice. Classy, Jacob."

"Do you even love him?" Jacob asked with his mouth full.

"No. Ellie loves Rory," Kara announced.

Every muscle in my body contracted. My heart sank to the bottom of my stomach. She'd said it. She'd actually said it. Kara was known to let things slip out from time to time, but this was unfamiliar territory. Kara had said the thing that no one ever said.

Orson stiffened. Jacob's face warped into an "uh-oh" expression. Hannah's cheeks popped out like she was a blowfish. Cameron's eyes bugged out of his head as he wrapped his arm around Kara. Rory was the only one who didn't flinch. With a clenched jaw, he kept his eyes on the ground.

"Don't listen to her. She doesn't know what she's saying," Cameron said, trying to cover for Kara.

The silence that took over the table had a high-pitched ring attached to it.

"Ummm, so . . ." I laughed nervously. "So *this* is how I die." I nodded, still softly chuckling. "Okay, cool. I just need to— I'm gonna go outside and get some air. Get a cab and all that. I'll see you later." My voice was trembling.

I got up from my chair. Blair, now twenty-three, shot up like a rocket to stand with me.

"Cainey, don't be dumb," Blair implored. Blair and Jacob had moved into a downtown apartment, and the plan had been for us all to crash at their place. That clearly was no longer happening.

"It's okay," I said. Hannah grabbed my hand to steady me, and I pushed her away. "No, Hannah. Honestly, it's fine. We all know she's right." I shrugged and gestured flippantly toward Rory. His dark-brown eyes were now burning a hole into me. All my fucks officially went out the window. My vision went blurry. "Not like it's ever mattered, but there you have it."

"Not like it's ever mattered?" Rory repeated. "Is that a joke? You think that wouldn't matter to me? Ellie, you've had a boyfriend this whole time!" Rory stood.

"Why do you think that is, Rory? What the hell was I supposed to do?! Not live my life?" I couldn't stop myself from shouting. "You've never said that you actually like me. We've danced around it, but you've never said it. Never. Not once."

"Are you kidding me right now?" Rory looked stunned.

"You haven't."

"Neither have you!" he roared.

I scoffed. "I told you I loved you at prom, and you told me to stop talking."

The shocked silence from everyone around the table after I dropped the love bomb was almost laughable.

"*Loved*, Ellie! You said *loved*! Past-fucking-tense! Did you mean *love*?" Rory's voice boomed. His eyes went wide, and he threw his hands into his hair.

"Oh my god," Hannah whispered. Everyone, including drunk, sloppy, foot-in-her-mouth Kara, was watching us like we were in a tennis match.

"Two years have gone by since prom, and you said *loved*, but you meant *love*?! *Loved* or *love*?!"

"Please stop saying that. It's semantics. It doesn't matter."

"IT FUCKING MATTERS!" Rory shouted louder than I'd ever heard before.

"I'm not doing this. We're making a huge scene, and this needs to stop. Sorry, everyone." I twisted my body around to face the people inside the restaurant. We even had rubberneckers in the street looking at us through the windows.

"You love me?" Rory looked like he was going to faint.

"I'm a bad person. I'm . . . I'm a bad person." I nodded uncontrollably.

"ELLIE, DO YOU LOVE ME?!" Rory screamed.

"I have a boyfriend, Rory! I can't fucking say it!" Tears sprang from my eyes, and I lost focus.

"Well, *I* can't fucking say it!" Rory's eyes were wild.

I was pretty sure I was dead. I must have fallen on the dance floor and hit my head against the bar and died, because there was no way this long-awaited conversation was actually happening in front of my sister, his brothers, our friends, and a bunch of drunk strangers on Granville Street.

"I can't look away." Orson leaned into Jacob.

"Dude. Look. Away," Jacob begged.

"You're moving away, Ellie! In a week. In a fucking week! Holy fuck. Do you love me?!" I didn't answer. Rory fell back into his seat and dropped his head between his legs. "I think I'm gonna throw up."

"This is horrifying." I turned to Blair and Cameron. "Probably none of this is what I thought it was, or pretended it was. You've probably thought I was just this bitch screwing around with your brother's feelings this whole time."

Because I had been . . . Because I was.

I started shaking with the realization that I was the bad guy. I had a boyfriend, and I was in love with someone else. They'd all probably thought for years that I was a stupid, silly little girl.

Because I had been . . . Because I was.

None of it was real.

"Meanwhile . . . Fine." I was already going to hell. I turned to Rory. "I have loved you since we were twelve years old. I love you, Rory. I'm *in love* with you. Present-fucking-tense. And I've never known what to do about it."

Rory looked back at me from his chair, shell-shocked.

"Rory, say something," Orson quietly pleaded to his friend.

"Say it right now, Rore," Cameron implored, but Rory said nothing. He just stared at me.

"Okay. I can't— Yeah, I can't do this anymore." An uncontrollable cry escaped through my lips.

"Ellie, don't!" Hannah stood.

"You both need to go outside." Blair grabbed Rory's wrist and pulled him to his feet, attempting to snap his brother out of his trance. "Go talk to her."

But it was too late. I was up and out. "No, thanks. I'm good." I pushed myself through the swinging door.

"Oh shit!" Hannah exclaimed, and everyone was out of their seats and following me into the warm summer air. It hit me like I was under a blow-dryer, but I charged ahead to an empty taxi waiting at the corner.

"Rory, get in the car!" I heard Cameron call from behind.

"Nope! Not necessary!" I shouted as I grabbed the handle.

"Then jump in-fucking-front of it, Rore! Don't let her go!" Cameron bellowed.

"Shut up, Cameron!" I snapped, then ripped the door open.

That's when I finally heard Rory scream, "ELLIE!"

I slammed the door shut, and the cab took off. My phone was ringing off the hook. It was Rory. It was Hannah. It was Blair. It was Cameron. It was Rory. It was Rory. It was Rory. I ignored every call, dialed Matt, broke up with him, then turned off my phone.

Chapter 15

NEW YORK
21 years old

BEN WAS UP EARLY ON MY BIRTHDAY, MAKING BREAKFAST. I HAD been watching him try hard to be quiet at the foot of the pushed-together beds for about ten minutes before he realized I was awake. He was creeping around the one-room apartment, grilling breakfast sandwiches, when he saw me smile. Hannah and Kara were still sleeping.

Ben mouthed, *Did you sleep?*

My eyes grew wide, and I slowly shook my head. *No.*

He swallowed a small laugh.

Did you? I asked with a finger point.

He shook his head just as slowly. *Nooooo.* He smiled sweetly, then mouthed, *Can I kiss you?*

Now? I pointed downward.

He shook his head while flipping the spatula back and forth, then whipped it in a circle. *In general.*

Ohhh . . . I looked at my sister and friend, neither of whom had any idea what was going on. I turned back to Ben and mouthed, *Would that be weird for them?*

"Would it? They cheered for us after you sang me a love song," Ben said with a confused expression.

I threw my finger up to my lips to shush him, then looked over to the two sleeping beauties. Kara turned over.

Do you want to? I mouthed.

Yes. Ben's nod was exaggerated. His scruff had grown in the night, his dark-blond hair was moving in all sorts of directions, and he was holding a birthday breakfast sandwich made just for me. Oh man, I was in trouble.

Really? I mouthed. My sister stirred beside me.

Yes, Ellie. I like you. A lot. Like . . . I really like you. He pointed at me with the spatula. Though he was saying he liked me, the look on his face was calling me an idiot.

I like you *a lot!* I mouthed back, angrily, mirroring his face.

He smiled. *Well, let me fuckin' kiss you!*

I choked down a laugh. *Gimme a fuckin' minute!*

"Are you two talking?" Kara sat up in bed, causing Hannah to roll over and rub her eyes.

"Uhhhhhhhhhh." I had nothing else. I looked at Ben blankly.

Kara eyed us both suspiciously and then blurted out, "Did you two have sex last night?"

My jaw dropped, and Ben folded over with a laugh.

"No, we did not, Kara." I glared at her. "What's wrong with you?!"

"Uh-huh." She grinned, then flipped her finger between us accusingly.

"I've got breakfast in five, ladies. Put your panties on." He pointed at them with a breakfast sandwich in one hand and the spatula in the other. When Hannah and Kara spun themselves around to get out of bed, he looked over at me and mouthed, *Not you.*

As my sister pulled on a sweater and Kara stood with a stretch, Ben grabbed his phone and pressed a couple of buttons. From our apartment speakers, out blasted the Cranberries' "When You're Gone." He winked at me, sending me a silent message, before turning to the small portable grill and throwing down a couple of extra strips of bacon.

The plan had been for me, Hannah, and Kara to spend the day at the spa before the three of us went out for dinner. We would meet Ben, Lucas, and

Zoë at Key One Lounge later in the night for birthday celebrations. Ben and I had been texting throughout the day, and when I told the girls, "Surprise, surprise, I touched Ben's dick," they jumped up and down excitedly.

Hannah and Kara weren't bothered by my distraction. I could see how happy they were for me every time I got an unprompted hug or squeeze. That, and my sister got Lucas's number the night before, and Kara and Cameron had been texting nonstop. They, too, were distracted.

"Where are we going again?" Kara asked for the fifth time while we were in the cab heading downtown. My lottery commercial popped up on the screen of the cab's divider.

Hannah gasped and pointed. "Holy crap! That's you!"

"Key One Lounge," I answered Kara, ignoring my sister.

"Okay." She buried her face in her phone, typing.

"What's going on?" I asked while reapplying my lipstick.

"I don't know. Cameron's being cagey. He keeps asking."

"Well, tell him to leave you alone. You're on vacation," Hannah said.

By the time the three of us got to Key One Lounge, Ben, Lucas, and Zoë were already inside. We walked up to their table, and they rose from their seats to greet us. Zoë ran to Hannah and Kara to hug them even before introductions were made.

Seeing Ben hit me differently. I had to let my eyes catch up with my heart. His eyes fell straight to my mouth, but he caught himself and lifted them back up. I hadn't yet given him the official "Go." As far as the Bronwyn crew knew, we were just buddies who had had an epic make-out session in a bar the night before.

"Hi." His voice was deep.

"Hi." I smiled.

"Hi." The third voice was familiar. Very familiar. Too familiar. It was Cameron. "Happy birthday, Cainey."

"Oh . . . my god." My sister grabbed my hand and held on for dear life.

I turned around. Standing beside Cameron was Jacob. Directly behind them was Blair. And standing behind Blair . . . was Rory.

Chapter 16

VANCOUVER
20 years old

"ELLIE, I CAN'T BELIEVE I DID THAT."

Kara sat on the edge of my bed. I had finally started packing my two suitcases to take with me to New York, and a whole shitload of baggage. But even though she had thrown our status quo into disarray, part of me was relieved to have the weight finally released from my chest.

Kara pressed her hands against the sides of her head, overwrought with guilt. "I'm so sorry. Cameron was so mad at me." She nervously twirled her short hair around her finger until it was knotted. "He was going on about the time you and Rory stopped being friends when you were sixteen and how it ruined everything. He said it destroyed Rory. And everything changed because Hannah and I disappeared, too. I guess he's afraid of that happening again."

"It's okay, Kara. I'm not going to pile on. Everyone already knew how I felt, anyway. It's not like it wasn't obvious."

"Have you spoken with Rory?" She pulled on my comforter.

"No. And I don't want to. I said I loved him, *again*, multiple times, point-blank, in front of everyone, and he just looked at me. Granted, we were in the middle of a fight, and I had a boyfriend . . . what the fuck is wrong with me?" My arms fell to my sides, and I took a deep breath. I was clearly in the midst of a fight-or-flight response, and I had chosen to flee. "I was such an asshole to Matt . . . and Rory. I ruined everything. What a way to go," I sighed.

"Has he called or texted?"

"Yeah. I'm not answering. He's tried the house, too, but Hannah's on guard. I can't deal with it. What's he going to say? 'I don't love you'? 'It's too late'? 'You're moving to another country'? Like, I know! I need to get some space between us."

Kara hesitated before she spoke. "You're going to have another country and a whole continent between you. Are you sure it's a good idea to ignore him now?"

"Nope. I'm not sure of anything." My chest heaved. "I'm leaving, Kara. I just need to go. I need to be excited, and I need to go."

My sister lightly knocked on my bedroom door, interrupting Kara and me. She let herself in. "He called again," Hannah said, peeking through the open door.

I stopped in my tracks, closed my eyes, and took in another deep breath.

"Why does it feel like you're running away?" Kara asked, as Hannah sat cross-legged on the carpet next to the bed.

"Bronwyn's orientation is Saturday night. I literally have to go," I grumbled.

"We know that, but you're also running away. You're doing both." Hannah backed Kara up.

"I have felt so small here for so long. I mean, someone drew a caricature of me on my locker in the eighth grade. Kids threw crap at me when I was onstage for *A Midsummer Night's Dream* in the tenth grade. I once had to fake an orgasm on camera when I was fifteen. So that exists somewhere. That's really fun to think about." I slammed my clothes into my luggage. "The only place where I liked myself was Juniper. I used to love my life, and now I don't know how to feel. Other than sad, and stupid, and small. I think, in New York, I could become the person I've always pretended to be." I took a deep, shuddering breath. "I'm doing something I've wanted to do since I was a kid. I'm actually doing it! And I can't do that halfway. Maybe I'm running away, but I'm also trying to run toward something. I have to try."

Hannah and Kara looked at each other, then my sister stood and placed her hand on my chest. "We love you, Ellie. We love Vancouver you, and we'll love New York you. Then we'll love whoever you turn into next."

My parents threw me a party at our house the night before I was set to leave for New York. At the end of the night, Rory showed up in his hand-me-down, black Jeep Cherokee. It was midnight, and I had an early flight, so we had to kick everyone out, but that didn't stop Rory from making a scene. Instead of coming into the house, he blared the Jeep's horn for a minute straight as people, including Cameron and Orson, filed out of the house.

I stared Rory down from the door, and when I turned to go back inside, he blasted the horn again. The party was over, everyone had left, and Hannah gave me a meek smile and a gentle push. Then she closed the door and locked me out.

"Open the door, Hannah!" I banged on the door. Hannah refused to answer, so I turned to face Rory again. From behind his windshield, I could see a smug smile etched across his face. "UGH!" I stormed over to Rory and opened the passenger door. "What?"

"Get in."

"No."

"You're leaving tomorrow." His voice softened. "Please get in."

"No," I said again.

His eyes darkened. "Ellie. Get in the car."

I took a deep breath and stepped into the Jeep, closing the door behind me. "What do you want, Rory?"

"You! I want *you*!"

"It's too late!" I wasn't even listening to the words I had been waiting my whole life for.

"I know that!" He matched my volume, but then steadied himself. He gripped the steering wheel and closed his eyes.

"So what am I supposed to do with that information?" My skin was already growing a thick protective layer.

"There are billions of people in the world—"

"Here we go." I cut Rory off with a dismissive snort and slammed my head against the headrest.

"Just let me finish!" Rory shook the steering wheel angrily. He stopped himself and took a deep breath. "There are billions of people in the world, but I think you only get three big loves. The first love, the one that got away, and the true love. Ellie, you're all three." Rory cleared his throat. When my quiet gasp revealed that I was crying beside him, Rory finally looked at me. "I applied for transfers to all those schools because I couldn't live in the same place as you anymore. It was killing me. But then I worried that you would go to LA, so I lined up USC because I couldn't live without you, either. I never even considered New York." His head fell back to the headrest, but he kept his eyes on mine. "I love you, Ellie. And like you, I've never known what to do about it." He sounded defeated. I brushed my tears from my face. "Now you're leaving. It's a day I've been dreading since we were fourteen. I knew it was coming. You were always going to fly away eventually."

"For you, Rory, I would have been an ostrich," I said, remembering our longstanding joke about being the worst kind of bird—one that couldn't fly. "I thought we'd get married one day. *Ellie Campbell* is written all over my diaries. I have a crawl space in my bedroom, and your name is on the walls in there. If you were murdered, I'd be the first suspect."

He breathed a sad laugh through his nose, then turned his head away from me. His eyes flickered in the streetlight.

It dawned on me that we were saying goodbye, but it wasn't like when we were younger and went our separate ways at the end of summer. The next time Rory and I saw each other, we'd have already started growing apart. We'd have less in common. And we'd know each other a little bit less well than we did right then.

"I can't move to New York but leave my heart here, no matter how much I might want to. And that's not to say I want to fall in love with someone else, but if I don't take my heart with me, I can't love New York. I can't love new friends. I can't fall in love with who I could become. I don't know who she is yet, but what if I like her? You have my heart, Rory, but I need it back now." I couldn't prevent my tears from slipping down my cheeks and off my chin. I tried to wipe them away with the heel of my palms, but I couldn't keep up.

"I don't want to give it back," Rory whispered, turning back toward me. "It's mine." He dropped his forehead heavily on my shoulder, a familiar move. I wasn't expecting him to kiss my collarbone, however. My body hardened. He slowly lowered his lips once again, but this time into the base of my neck. He nudged my chin with the top of his head and kissed beneath my jaw. His soft tongue lined my jaw in a string of kisses until he reached my ear, where he whispered, "Don't go."

"Rory, I—"

I couldn't finish the sentence. Rory kissed me like his life depended on it. His tongue fought against mine, and we were instantly moaning into each other's mouths, frantically gripping each other's faces, pulling on each other's bodies. He climbed on top of me, pressing his weight into me, and dropped down the reclining passenger seat. His fingers dug into my hair as he tasted me, devoured me, before he bit into me. I lifted my hands up his sides, feeling every contour, and pulled his shirt off. I pressed my hands down his toned chest and abs, and was shocked at the body I found. He kept his mouth on me until he pulled off my shirt. Rory slipped my bra straps down and was kissing my neck, my shoulder, my chest, until my bra was off entirely. He lifted one of my hands next to my head, our fingers locked in place, crushing each other. His other hand squeezed my rib cage, and suddenly, my breast was in his mouth, and he sucked on me, hard.

"Oh god," I gasped.

Holy shit. What the fuck. Holy shit. What the fuck. This can't be happening. Is this really happening? What is happening?

My brain somehow both went into overdrive and completely bottomed out. Rory lifted his head to look back up at me. He let go of me and placed his palms over his eyes for a brief moment, appearing to be in as much disbelief as I was.

"Fuck. I can't think." He was out of breath, and his eyes branded me. "Take your pants off." Instead of waiting for me to do it, he pulled them down himself. He placed his hand over my lacy white underwear and gently grazed his fingers between my legs, then tugged off my underwear in one quick movement, practically ripping them off me.

Rory parted my legs with his body, looking down at me. "You're so beautiful." He hovered over me before he let his mouth roam, sliding down my body. I squirmed up the passenger seat so my head fell over the headrest toward the back seat. His strong hands grabbed onto my hips, and he pulled me back down again, bringing his mouth between my legs.

"Rory . . ." I tried to control my heavy exhales, but I was becoming erratic. Feeling and hearing Rory Campbell take what he wanted from me made me borderline feral. I was going to come. I was going to fucking come. *With. Rory.*

He pressed his fingers into me and pulled me from the inside out with his mouth still on me. I lurched forward involuntarily, but he pushed me back and held me down. I could feel myself start to tense, then shake, and every part of me drew into the center of my chest.

"Oh my god, Rory. I'm . . . Rory . . ." I was gasping.

"Do it, Ellie. Come for me," he demanded, with his mouth and hands forever ruining me.

It was like a bomb detonated inside my body at his command. No one had ever talked to me like that before. No one had ever wanted me so desperately before. And. It. Was. *Rory!*

I let go. Everything inside me released in rolling, shuddering waves, and my guttural moans only left him hungrier. Once I finally stopped trembling, I lifted Rory's head to bring his face back up to mine, and he kissed me. Our tongues demolished each other through groans and sighs, and our bodies pushed into one another to the point where I couldn't tell us apart.

"Holy shit. This is chaos. I want everything. I want all of you. I want fucking *all of you*."

"Rory, stop talking and take your pants off," I said, as if I were having a fever dream.

"Is this real? Are we really having sex?" he asked, somehow still shocked that I was peeling his pants and underwear off.

"Yes, we are absolutely having sex," I answered without thinking. When I finally took him all in, I had to steady myself. Rory Campbell had always been gorgeous, but I wasn't prepared. His kissing and sucking became more frenzied once I finally had him in my hands.

I could feel his teeth against me, biting me. I knew he was marking me up and staking claim like we were a couple of wild teenagers, and I didn't care. I wanted the whole world to know that I was his.

"I want you in my mouth."

"Jesus," he breathed. "I won't last."

"Let's try. Climb up me."

"I mean it, Ellie. It will take five fucking seconds, and then we'll have to stop."

"Rory . . ." I bit his bottom lip, still stroking him. "Right now."

His hooded eyes glazed over. "Jesus fuck. Okay. Yes." He crawled his naked body up mine as I scooted down the reclining seat. He grabbed hold of the roof with one hand and gripped the top of the back seat with the other, pinning me beneath him. I had never in my life felt so wild and reckless and carnal. It was either me losing all sense of myself when I was with Rory or becoming exactly who I was always meant to be.

"Oh my god." He grunted every time his body twitched or his hips thrust forward. I couldn't believe what was happening, who I was holding in my hands, in my mouth, who was hovering over me. I was somehow in the moment and out of it at the exact same time. I gripped him harder and let him take my mouth in a way I had never done before. "Fuck . . . Ellie. I've got to stop. We need to stop." Rory was shaking as he fell back down my body. "I need to be inside you. I want to come inside you."

My raging heart expanded, pressing into my lungs until I was short of breath. "Do you have any condoms?"

He turned and opened his glove compartment, emptying it, and furiously searched through his belongings. "No, like a goddamn idiot I do not." Finally, we slowed, and our mania stilled.

Rory turned back to me, and we wrapped our bodies around each other. Our kissing turned tender, passionate, and all-encompassing. He traced my jawline with his finger as his tongue rolled over mine. I took gentle fistfuls of his hair. Eventually we looked into each other's eyes, and I quietly said, "I'm on birth control . . ."

His eyes went black. "I've never had sex without a condom."

"Neither have I," I admitted. Our hearts were thrashing against each other, but our stillness remained as we silently decided to be with one another. "Only you."

Rory clutched my face with both hands. "Always you." He kissed me deeply, holding me as if letting go would never be an option. Then he slowly pushed himself inside me. I stopped breathing, and my mouth opened in a moment of pain, but he met the moment with his mouth on mine.

"Are you okay?" he whispered against my lips.

"I love you, Rory."

"I love you so fucking much, Ellie." Rory kissed me as his hands found my legs. He gripped me under my thighs and wrapped my legs around his body. He pushed himself all the way in, filling me, over and over again, deeper, and harder, his lips never straying from mine, floating over me, brushing against me. I felt dizzy when my contractions started again, squeezing him rhythmically inside of me. My throbbing surged from between my legs, through my stomach, up my back, and into my heart.

"Rory . . ."

He tangled his hands in my hair and pulled my head back to look into my eyes. He pressed our foreheads together, and our mouths reached for each other. I was still coming when he came too. We held tightly to each other, breathing heavily, and he collapsed on top of me, giving me all his weight. Rory trailed his bottom lip gently along my collarbone and then kissed it softly before digging his face into my neck.

"You can't leave me," he mumbled. He twisted his head to put it on my shoulder once more, where it all began. "Don't leave me. What am I going to do? What the fuck am I going to do . . . ?" The first time he said it to me. The second time, he said it to himself. After a moment, I could hear his breathing go ragged, almost like he had forgotten how. And then he said something I never expected. "Ellie, what the fuck did we do?"

Chapter 17

NEW YORK
21 years old

I WAS HUGGING BLAIR, BUT I COULDN'T BELIEVE I WAS LOOKING at Rory. It had been six months since I left. Six months since he finally told me that he loved me. Six months since he shattered me in the very next breath. And six months of me rebuilding my life.

Rory had his hands deep in his pockets. He was wearing a thin black sweater that hugged his lean, toned frame, and dark-gray slacks. His shaggy, curly brown hair was pushed back as best as it could be, framing his lightly freckled face. His jaw was tense; his lips were tight and slightly downturned.

"When did you get so pretty?" Blair pushed my long, wavy hair over my shoulder.

"Timed it perfectly with moving away, I guess," I said.

Blair grinned, then reached over me to pull Hannah toward him and away from Lucas for a hug.

I looked at Rory and forced out a small smile. He did the same. His dimple twitched, and it caused him to look away, but only for a moment.

"I hope it's okay we're here, Ellie-Bee." Jacob threw his arm around Kara.

"Of course, of course. I'm so happy to see you."

No, it's not okay! It is absolutely not even a little bit okay!

Cameron smiled at me sweetly, then pushed Jacob aside to kiss Kara.

I turned to Ben, who was stiff and confused. He, Zoë, and Lucas stood uncomfortably inside the loud, dark blues bar. I felt guilty. I felt awful and guilty, and I didn't know who those feelings were directed toward, Ben or Rory or both.

The band took the stage, and everything felt louder and brighter. My breath felt shallow; my vision went fuzzy. I looked at Rory and saw his look of recognition morph into worry as he watched my eyes start to go vacant. His back straightened, his eyes focused, and he stepped forward, but Ben beat him to it.

"Breathe, buddy," Ben whispered so low that only I could hear him. He carefully leaned into me, and a rush of calm washed through me.

"Okay," I started. "So, introductions. This is Jacob, Kara's brother." I turned my body away, unable to look at any of them. "And, ummm, this is Blair, Cameron, and Rory." I said their names as quickly as possible. Apparently, it wasn't fast enough, as Lucas and Zoë froze.

Ben stepped forward first. He was tense. It was clear he was upset, and I *knew* he was jealous, but he didn't dare admit it. He extended his hand. "Hi, I'm Ben. I'm . . ." He hesitated.

"The roommate?" Cameron finished his sentence with a speculative tone.

"Yup. That is something that I am," Ben said awkwardly, sounding staccato. His eyes flicked over to me.

Jacob stepped up to meet Ben and took his hand. "I've heard so much about you, Ben. It's nice to meet you."

I exhaled a sigh of relief and noticed Ben do the same. "I've heard a lot about you, too, Jacob. You, Ellie, Hannah, and Kara go back to the diaper years, right?"

"Basically, yeah. Ellie is like a little sister to me." Jacob nodded, and though no one else could hear Jacob's subtle warning to Ben, *I* could.

Blair joined in. "It's your birthday, also, right? How old are you?"

"Twenty-four, as of a couple of days ago."

"Oh, you're our age." Blair tossed his thumb back and forth between him and Jacob. I glanced over to Rory as he leaned against a chair. Rory had turned twenty-one in February. I hadn't wished him a happy birthday.

"So, this is Lucas," I pointed to Lucas. He had moved next to Hannah again when Blair stepped away and draped his arm over her shoulder. Blair's eyes narrowed, silently screaming, *Back up, Frenchie.*

"Zoë is that one."

Zoë brushed her thick curtain bangs to the side and tilted her head. I could see Jacob start to sweat as his eyes roamed her face and body. I watched Zoë look Rory up and down, skeptically, then scrunch her nose and squint her eyes, not wanting to approve, but clearly doing so. Zoë moved her attention back to me, and I shot daggers at her through my eyes and silently shouted, *Stop it!*

She looked at me through her bangs with a casual shrug, and I knew what she was saying: *Okay, I get it now. He's sexy.* Hannah and Kara both snickered.

"And as you know, this one is Ben, the roommate." I grabbed Ben's bicep. "We'll be back." I smiled, then pulled him away from the group. I got Ben alone and let go of his arm. "I didn't know they were coming," I insisted.

"I know. It's okay," he said, avoiding the truth. "Do you want me to figure out a way to get more tables?"

"Okay." I nodded, looking around.

"Ellie, relax." Ben pulled a chair out for me at the small round table they had already reserved.

"Okay," I said again, not listening at all.

"Hey." Ben subtly hooked his finger through a belt loop on my jeans. I saw Rory and Cameron both clock the touch. Cameron looked over his shoulder to see if his brother was watching, but Rory didn't flinch. He kept his hands in his pockets and his dark eyes on me.

"Yeah?" I was entirely unfocused.

"Hey." Ben gently tugged me toward him with his finger. He lightly pressed his hand on my stomach, and his thumb slipped under my shirt to graze my skin. Rory shifted his weight uncomfortably.

"Ellie," Ben whispered. My eyes finally met his. "If you want, we can get out of here. Or you, Hannah, Kara, and Zoë can do a girls' night, and the guys will leave. It's whatever you want." Ben's earthy green eyes were bouncing back and forth between mine.

"I think I need to talk to Rory." My words ran into each other. I saw a momentary flash of hurt behind Ben's expression.

"Like I said, whatever you want." He let out a quick, strained breath.

I shook my head, feeling my brain swell with panic. "Ben, I . . . I don't—"

"It's okay. You don't have to say anything." He released his fingers from my stomach.

I grabbed Ben's hand and held it to my chest. His eyes darted back to mine. "Whatever's happening between us, I want it," I said, repeating Ben's words from the middle of the night back to him. We shared a private smile, and I released his hand before saying, "I'll be back."

I walked through my group of friends, quickly clutched Hannah's hand for a confidence boost, locked eyes with Kara, and then with Zoë, and then moved past Rory and out the door. I may as well have had eyes in the back of my head. Rory stood from the chair he was leaning against. He looked at Ben. Ben looked at him. Then Rory turned and followed me out without having uttered a word.

I had my arms crossed and kept my eyes trained on my black boots. Rory was leaning against a parked car next to a streetlight, appearing more natural on the streets of New York than I had felt in the last six months.

"Why are you here?" I looked up at Rory, and he answered me with his sad smile. His eyes fell to my wrist, and his mouth pinched together. I was wearing the rose gold bracelet he'd given me at his prom. "Whose idea was it to come?" My words were clipped as I brought my hands behind my back.

"Mine," he said. I popped my eyebrows, not believing him. "It was my idea," he assured me, unflinching.

"Yeah, well . . ." I looked at a flashing tattoo parlor sign a few doors over.

After a long moment, Rory adjusted his lean. "So, your roommate—"

"Ben," I said, laser-focused.

Rory closed his eyes and tilted his head back. His loose dark curls were perfectly styled to gleam under the streetlight like a model's. It was *deeply* inconvenient. "Ben. Are you together?" He kept his eyes shut, waiting for my answer.

"Why do you care?"

"Because I care." He was unprepared for me to be so closed off. It wasn't natural for either of us. We didn't know how to navigate the obstacles we put in each other's way.

"No, you don't. You don't choose this, and you don't choose me. That's what you said. You also said you loved me, but then you took it back." Fire rose up my belly and barreled through my throat to the top of my head. "So how am I supposed to believe you when you say you care now?"

Rory contorted his mouth. I could tell he was trying to control his emotions. He unexpectedly moved toward me, surprising me, and his hand raced down my arm. He quickly thumbed my bracelet, then grabbed my hand, threading our fingers together. He was sweaty, and his pulse pumped rapidly against my wrist. He took my hand as if it were his.

"That night was the best night and the worst night of my life. What I did . . . the things I said . . ." He shook his head with his eyes closed. "Ellie, I can't believe the things I said."

I couldn't believe the things he said, either.

"I don't want to do this." I strained for breath, and my stomach dropped. I let go of his hand.

His eyes fell to my hand pulling away from his. His jaw clenched. "I was devastated that you were leaving. Everything was just . . ." He brought his hand up to cover his eyes and pinched his face like he wanted to crush his skull. "To finally have you while knowing that I was also losing you was an absolute mind fuck." He looked at me. "You are and have always been *everything* to me."

"Please stop. You said it was a mistake, and clearly you were right." I couldn't breathe.

He squeezed his eyes shut, pained by the memory of the last time we saw each other. He put his hands on his hips and hung his head. "Ellie . . ." He looked back at me and pressed his fingers into his forehead. "Please hear me out before you break up with me—"

"We were never together," I said firmly.

"Yes, we were." Though he matched my obstinate tone, his eyes started watering. "We've been together the whole time. We've just never said it out loud."

Tears finally fell to my cheeks. "Whatever you're doing right now, please don't," I pleaded.

"But if I don't—"

I cut him off. "Rory."

"Don't do this." Tears escaped him, and he quickly wiped them away. "Ellie, please. You know I didn't mean it." He sucked in an unexpected gasp. I couldn't look, so I closed my eyes. "Please don't do this. You know, Ellie. You *know* I didn't mean it. It's me." I shook my head. "Ellie, look at me." I shook my head again. "Please. Look at me." The desperation in his tone opened my eyes. His face was now streaked with tears, and every muscle in his body was tense. "It's me."

"Rory, you are the only person in the world who has the ability to destroy me. I would put my life in ruins for you. I would throw it all away. Please don't ask me to. I don't want to. I'm happy. I'm right about myself here, and I need to be right about myself. I need this." I stepped forward and wrapped my arms around Rory, hugging him, not realizing what I was doing until I had already done it. His forehead fell onto my shoulder, and his face buried into my neck. He folded his arms around my waist.

"I don't want to lose you." I felt his wet face against the skin of my neck.

"It shouldn't have happened. You were right." I wondered if he knew how difficult that was for me to say, or if he knew I didn't believe it myself. My falling tears betrayed my words. I pushed them away, just like the rest of my feelings.

"I'm so sorry." He struggled to catch his breath. "Please don't go."

I gently ran my fingers along the nape of Rory's neck as we held each other. I dipped my fingertips into his hair. I was totally present and fully aware that I'd likely never touch him like this again. My heartbeat battered against my chest until it slowly transformed into a gentle knocking. "I'm already gone."

Rory finally let out a quiet, shuddering sob into my shoulder.

"I think it's good that you came. It helps us move past it." I moved out of his hold. He looked out into the distance, his gaze unfocused and vacant. "I feel different here. I feel like a different person, and I think I like this me. Actually, I *know* I do." I wiped away the last of my tears. Rory exhaled deeply, trying to compose himself. "Before anything else, we were friends," I said quietly. It was the same thing I had said to him on the night of his prom.

It took Rory some time to collect himself before he was finally able to choke out, "I miss you." He blew out his breath, then brought his eyes back to mine and whispered, "Your turn."

I bit my lip when I realized it was quivering, then forced myself to smile. "I'll see you in there, okay?" I turned around and grabbed the railing to help steady me as I walked back up the stairs and into Key One Lounge.

Chapter 18

NEW YORK

21 years old

I WAS SITTING WITH THE GIRLS AT OUR TABLE NEXT TO THE BAR. Zoë won Hannah and Kara over within minutes. She had them bewildered when she told them about how her grandparents switched spouses when she was ten. She had them crying, talking about her brother and how he died in a plane crash. And she had them in hysterics when she told them she was in a handstand position the last time she had sex. Every time Hannah or Kara shared one of their stories, Zoë's emerald eyes were locked on them, listening intently and asking a thousand questions. They all exchanged phone numbers, and I knew that our foursome was locked in.

Ben had gone for a walk around the block with Lucas. Blair, Cameron, and Jacob were huddled together at the bar, having shots. When Rory stepped through the front door, twenty minutes after me, he made his way to the guys, then leaned forward to get into the bartender's line of sight.

Cameron whistled for Kara's attention. He signaled to her quickly, asking if she wanted another drink. She nodded, then rose from our table to join the guys at the bar.

I overheard Blair ask, "How'd it go?" He passed Rory a beer that had already been ordered on his behalf.

Rory took a sip and turned his body, not answering the question. He leaned on his elbows, with his back to the bar.

"Is she with the roommate?" Cameron handed Kara a shot.

I kept my eyes shifting between the sticky circular table I was sitting at and the bar, trying not to get caught listening to their conversation.

"I think so." Rory picked at his beer's label.

Kara's shoulders slumped sympathetically. "I hate to say it, but Ben's great. I think you'd like him. I know you don't want to hear that, but they're good together."

"What are you doing, Kare?" Cameron's face pulled, then he turned back to his brother. "Don't listen to her. I'm not counting you out yet, Rore."

"Me, either. Put it all on the line. Do what you came here for." Blair backed Cameron up and put his hand on Rory's shoulder, squeezing it.

Rory kept his head down. He had peeled off most of the sticker with one clean rip. He balled it up and tossed it on the ground.

Ben came back into the bar with Lucas, and his face lit up to see me back at the table. Out of the corner of my eye, I could see Rory stretch his neck around to watch Ben silently communicating with me from afar. Ben pointed at me, then gave me a subtle thumbs-up in one swift movement. *You okay?* Rory's head twisted to see my response, which was a slight nod.

Everyone sat around two round tables pushed together. Hannah and Zoë flanked me on either side, and Ben and Rory both sat across from me, but next to each other. As the night went on, the music, the talking, the laughing, the noise . . . when it got loud enough that conversations were overlapping, Rory decided to break the ice.

He leaned toward Ben. "Hey. I'm sorry we crashed your party."

Ben's eyes flipped over to me quickly, checking my reaction. "All good. Happy to have you. You came a long way."

I lowered my eyes, hoping they didn't notice I was trying to listen. Did they notice *everyone* was pretending not to listen?

"So, what's your place like?" Rory asked while taking a swig of his drink, trying to take the high road.

"It's small and every cliché in the book. Within two weeks, we were both slapping cockroaches with our bare hands."

"Ellie can be pretty tough when she needs to be," Rory said.

"You have no idea." Ben locked eyes with me. I could see Rory recoil at the thought that he had "no idea" about something to do with me. "In our Stage Combat class, she got a hard piece of lead paint wedged just under her fingernail. Our teacher tried to take it out with a needle. She almost passed out. I almost passed out. But it was stuck. We ended up going back to our apartment, where she filed off her entire nail from the top down to get it out."

Rory's eyes shot over to me. He was trying to temper his reaction, but I could tell the story jarred him, especially Ben's use of the phrase *our apartment*.

"Anyway, that's all to say . . . yeah, New York is incredible. It's also tough. But like you said, she's tough, too." Ben leaned forward and rested his elbows on the table, creating a little more privacy. "Obviously, I know about you, Rory, and I know you know nothing about me." I lifted my head. Rory's stare secured onto mine as Ben continued. "I'm sure you're probably worried about her, but she's okay." Ben cleared his throat. "I also know that she's been yours for a long time, and I'm not here to take all that time away from you."

Rory's jaw set, and his eyes hardened. He was unnerved by Ben's confidence.

"Do you love her?" Rory asked, matching Ben's boldness.

I saw Blair's and Cameron's eyes widen, even though they were supposed to be talking to Lucas. Kara and Hannah zeroed in on me, even though they were supposed to be talking to each other. And I heard Zoë accidentally say, "Oh shit," when she was supposed to be talking to Jacob.

Ben looked over at me calmly. He knew I was listening.

"Yeah, I do. I love her." Ben's lips curved into the smallest of smiles, knowing I could hear him. "I don't know if she loves me, though."

I felt myself expand from my bones to my blood to my skin. My eyes turned from Ben to Rory, and I emptied into a vacuum of longing and regret. I regretted being with Rory, and being without him. And I longed for a life with Ben, and a life without him. I was perfectly split in two.

Rory's gaze lifted to the ceiling as he swallowed, calming himself down. After an extended period, Rory lifted his beer bottle and tipped it toward Ben. Ben met his gesture and gave Rory's bottle a tap. "I'm glad to meet you, too, Ben," Rory finally said.

"Do you guys come here a lot?" Blair asked the table as loudly as possible, likely changing the conversation on purpose to steer it away from the two loves of my life.

"We travel around, but this bar is in the rotation. It's not far from where I live." Lucas tapped the tabletop and pushed his drink over to Hannah so she could give it a taste.

Blair pinched his mouth together with annoyance. Hannah looked back at Blair from over the drink with a flirty smile, leaving me wondering what the hell that look was about.

Lucas continued, oblivious to Hannah and Blair's silent exchange. "Usually, we go to where Ben works."

"That's where we were last night." Kara threw back her drink as if she were determined to win a competition. "It was the best. Ellie sang."

"Sang? Cainey, I didn't know you sing!" Blair gave a clipped laugh.

Rory's eyes whipped over to me. He was disturbed. Apparently, he, too, didn't know I sang.

"You guys have never heard her sing?" Jacob asked.

Blair and Cameron shook their heads.

"Haven't you seen any of her plays?"

They shook their heads again.

"Seriously?"

Cameron decided to stop Jacob's line of questioning. "No. She never invited us." Cameron put his arm behind Rory's chair protectively.

"You think she sent out handwritten invitations or something?" Jacob laughed, then finished off the rest of his whiskey.

Kara and Jacob had been seeing me in plays since I was a kid, and Hannah ran lines with me regularly. Lucas, Zoë, and especially Ben were profoundly familiar with the performer in me. The Campbells were the odd men out. I had been intimate with Rory. But as I noticed his eyes glued to the table, I wondered if I could say that he knew me the most intimately when he didn't know this side of me.

Rory had come with me to a couple of auditions over the years, but he never saw beyond the curtain. He was never in the room. He never saw what happened when I lost myself inside a character or a song. It was a piece of my insides exposed to the outside, and though it was never "real," it was always real to me. Onstage, I turned into a version of myself that only I knew. I became every diary entry I ever wrote. I drowned in every feeling I ever felt. The idea of the Campbells ever seeing me like that was unbearable; I would never survive it.

"All I'm saying is, you could have just gone." Jacob twisted the knife.

Rory remained still, despondent. I could see Ben notice Rory's unraveling.

"We've never seen her golf." It was Ben's turn to show grace. A small smile tugged on my lips in appreciation of the gesture.

"Don't be too upset about that," Blair piped up. "Hannah's always been better. Cainey can hit the shit out of it, but she's inconsistent, and her short game is garbage," he teased me with a smile.

I laughed loudly. "Don't ruin the illusion!"

"Rory's the real golfer in the group. He'll go pro," Cameron jumped in proudly, pumping up his brother.

"Remember your black hat, Rory?" Kara slurred, and I felt a pinch of concern.

"How much have you had to drink, Kare?"

Hannah giggled. "Oh! Rory! I remember you always used to flip that hat around and wear it backward. The way your curly hair popped out . . . so super cute."

Rory's shy smile finally made an appearance. "Still have the hat, still wear it backward."

"Still super cute," Ben quipped.

It surprised Rory, and he let out a small laugh. For a flash, it looked like Rory could like Ben, then melancholy washed over him as that realization took hold.

"Didn't you write a poem about that hat once, Ellie?" Kara tossed me a wink.

Cameron, Blair, Jacob, and Hannah all quietly chuckled as blood surged to my cheeks. Rory's small smile dipped, and I hid my face in my drink.

"Jesus Christ." I laughed uneasily. I looked over at Lucas, whose eyes were wide. I pointed at him. "Don't you dare."

All eyes shot to Lucas, and he covered his mouth giddily. He was bursting at the seams.

"Lucas, don't!" Zoë squealed, but it was too late; she was already laughing, fully aware of what was about to happen.

"I have to," he whispered excitedly. I started sliding down in my chair, trying to get myself under the table as fast as possible. "Ellie read that insane poem in our scene study class once as preparation for a scene."

I went all the way under the table, humiliated, as everyone laughed, including Rory and Ben. Hannah grabbed my arm and pulled me back up.

"You weren't there that day, Ben. It was wild. I've never laughed so hard in my life." Lucas's cocky grin was aimed in my direction.

"No, I know. I've read it, though. It's in her diary." Ben smiled at me from across the table.

"You've read Ellie's diaries?!" Hannah roared.

The table got quiet again. Heat rose up the back of my neck. Rory closed his eyes, pained. It was evident that in just six short months, Ben and I had already experienced a lot together. I wasn't sure Rory was expecting that. From Hannah's stunned expression, I wasn't sure *anyone* was expecting that.

"Ummm . . ." Ben smiled apprehensively. "Yes? But I wasn't an asshole about it. She was there. She let me read them. She gave them to me."

Hannah slowly turned her head to me, appearing shocked. "Wow . . ."

"So you know *all* about Rory, then," Kara slurred, unable to stop herself.

"Kara," Jacob warned his sister.

Rory's demeanor changed instantaneously. He stiffened and stopped breathing.

"No, not everything. He hasn't read everything." I stepped in before Ben could answer. "There's stuff that's private." I was surprised that I was able to respond, considering how difficult it was to find my voice.

She directed her drunken glare at Ben. "I'm warning you, Ben. Don't you hurt her, too. Don't fuck her then fuck her over at the exact same time."

"Kara!" Cameron growled. He was more than upset. He was enraged.

Cameron leapt to his feet, hauled her up out of her seat, and took her away from us.

All the oxygen in the bar was sucked into oblivion. My soul emptied out entirely. I looked at Rory, and he looked back at me, expressionless. He appeared as hollowed out as I was.

Hannah dropped her face into her hands. Zoë's mouth hung open in a silent gasp. Lucas's eyes looked anywhere but at me. Blair's hand went protectively to Rory's shoulder. And Ben didn't waste a second before standing up from the table.

"Want to get out of here?" Ben asked me directly.

"Yeah." I stood, then walked out of the bar and didn't look back.

Chapter 19

NEW YORK
21 years old

BEN AND I WERE SITTING ON THE SNOWY CURB OUTSIDE OF KEY One Lounge. He released an uneasy breath before saying, "Well, tonight didn't go as planned."

I shook my head. "I don't want to talk about it."

"I do." He played restlessly with his lip, pinching it between his thumb and his index finger. He lowered his hand from his face and leaned forward, resting his arms on his legs. "I love you. I wasn't planning on saying that tonight, even though I've felt it for a while, and I didn't think the first time I'd say it would be to your ex." Ben shook his head, looking discouraged. "I didn't want any of this." I placed my hand on Ben's leg. He sighed, then pulled my hand into his chest and laced our fingers together. "I don't want to be compared to Rory. I'm not him, and this Ellie is not his Ellie. This Ellie is mine." Ben kissed my hand softly.

I nodded slowly, then asked quietly, "When did you first feel it?"

"I don't know. Slowly over time. When I realized it was you and me." Ben looked out at the softly falling snow. "When did *you* first feel it?"

I laughed faintly through my nose. "You told Rory you didn't know if I loved you."

"I lied." He lifted his finger to beneath my chin, forcing me to look at him. "I know you do."

I smiled and took my time to answer, setting my past aside and Rory with it. This, New York, Ben . . . It was another life. Another me. "It happened slowly . . . over time, when I realized it's you and me."

I looked at Ben, and he was already bending toward me. He moved his hand to hold my neck, and our lips found each other. His tongue pressed down on mine, and blood surged through my veins, bringing me back to life. When we pulled apart, I softly touched his lips with my thumb.

"I spent my life dreaming of one day moving to Los Angeles, but I moved to New York instead. I think there's a reason for that. I think I was meant to come here because I was meant to meet you."

Ben pulled me toward him again, and our mouths opened and closed, connecting and dancing with one another. And as we slowed, taking in the moment, we kept our eyes shut. He kissed my nose ever so slightly, then my cheeks, then my eyelids, then my lips once more. And that's when I heard Rory clear his throat. Ben kept his hands on me, like he always did.

"I'm sorry to interrupt." Rory didn't break eye contact.

"No worries," Ben responded.

"Ellie, I wanted to say goodbye. Can I talk to you for a minute?" Rory's voice sounded pained.

Ben looked to me for my response. I nodded, and he gave my hand a small squeeze before gathering himself. He nodded toward Rory, then left us alone.

Chapter 20

NEW YORK

21 years old

I STAYED WHERE I WAS, AND RORY TOOK BEN'S PLACE BESIDE ME on the curb. I knew this moment like it had happened before.

"Are you okay?" Rory asked. I didn't respond. He cleared his throat and kept his eyes on the ground. "I think Blair and Jacob are still staying until Wednesday. But I'm going to go. Cameron, too." Rory's breath was shaky. "The thing is, Kara told Cameron about Ben at Christmas. So I came to New York to get you back before it was too late. Not back to Vancouver. Just back to me. I wanted to tell you that I choose you and you choose me. And I wanted to be the one kissing you tonight . . ."

Rory closed his eyes and tilted his head back.

"I wanted to tell you that he could never know you like I do, or laugh with you like I do, or love you like I do. I wanted to say a lot of things." Rory drew in a massive inhale, as if he were breathing directly into his soul, where our past haunted our present. "But then I got here." He kept his eyes closed and shook his head. "We had a life together . . . Now it's clear that what you need isn't our life, it's this one. I'm too late." He opened his eyes and finally looked at me. Tears spilled down his cheeks. "I'm in the way."

My heart fell. It tripped and stumbled in the moment, just like I had through life. Just like I had with Rory. I had to put the past behind me. He was saying goodbye. I had to, too.

"Do you remember that time on the golf course when we got caught in a storm?" I asked.

"Yeah . . ."

"Remember how we took off our shoes because we thought the metal spikes would attract the lightning? And we ran?"

Rory nodded.

"One in a million. That's the odds of getting hit." My voice trembled. "You and me . . . We didn't get hit by lightning, but we sure got close."

Rory and I looked at each other, painfully aware of how close we really had been to belonging to one another.

"I'm sorry I ran. I don't know what I was so scared of . . . Next time I'll keep my shoes on," I whispered, tears streaming down my face.

Rory let out another slow, shaky breath before saying, "Me too." He palmed his face, brushing away his tears, and nodded. "It's time for me to go."

Rory stood and walked toward the door to get his things. He gripped the doorframe and hesitated. I wondered if he was going to turn back around, or change his mind, or say goodbye, or give me one last kiss. And I knew, in that moment, he was wondering what I was going to do. For so many years we hadn't known what to do, so for all those years we had done nothing. And that's what we did now. Nothing.

Part 11

Everything After

Chapter 21

LAS VEGAS
29 years old

IT WAS ZOË'S THIRTIETH BIRTHDAY. ME, ZOË, KARA, HANNAH, and Maddy, the newest addition to our group and Zoë's best friend from Boston College, were at a bar called Manor House in downtown Las Vegas. It was a fancy two-story cocktail bar with a rooftop dance floor. I genuinely had no idea how we'd ended up there, other than Zoë had made it happen. Zoë could make anything happen. She had become a concert producer in Los Angeles, and her job often brought her to Vegas. She knew and impressed a lot of people, and a lot of people wanted to know and impress her.

I started drinking in our penthouse suite on check-in. When the welcome channel on our TV flashed highlights from the Celebrity Pro-Am Golf Tournament taking place in Vegas that same weekend, I had hightailed it for the nearest bottle of alcohol.

I saw Maddy, who was having her first weekend away since becoming a new mom, notice me go dead behind the eyes the moment Rory Campbell popped up on screen, fixing his glove while fist-bumping Steph Curry. I hadn't seen Rory in person in years, and seeing him playing golf on TV always made me feel a little bit sick to my stomach.

At twenty-nine, Rory had only gotten sexier. His lean but muscular body was evident from the way his polo hugged his shoulders, and his ass was shockingly sculpted beneath his tighter-than-necessary pants. His unruly brown hair remained flawlessly unruly beneath a black Titleist hat, newly upgraded. His eyes were hidden beneath those goddamn Ray-Bans, now one of his many sponsors. His dimple had shape-shifted into a perfect crease against his scruffy almost-beard when he smiled. It was devastating to look at. Especially for a woman wearing a ratty, ten-year-old, homemade tank top that read "Canadian Women's Drinking Team."

Maddy drooled, saying, "I'm sorry . . . who is that?" while looking at Rory on the TV, and Hannah had to remove me from the room. The bottle of champagne was still shoved down my throat, and already half consumed.

I was miraculously able to forget that Rory was also in Vegas when we hit the Daylight Beach Club at Mandalay Bay. He didn't come up once during our incredibly expensive sushi dinner. And even Kara didn't bring him up when his face appeared on one of the many outdoor digital billboards put up by MGM, which was sponsoring the tournament.

While being bullied by too many club promoters, we tried three different bars before Zoë brought us to Manor House.

"To Zoë!" Kara exclaimed as she raised her Manhattan. "A wild woman who came into our lives like a beast and regales us with tales of sexuality that none of us can compete with—"

"Pro tip." Maddy leaned toward me. She spoke out of the side of her mouth. "When Zoë says 'this one guy,' and I'm anywhere in the vicinity, she's talking about my brother and doesn't want to say his name." Maddy side-eyed me clandestinely.

Turned out Maddy fit in perfectly with our girl group that had originally gotten together on my infamous twenty-first birthday. The foursome of Hannah, Kara, Zoë, and me crystalized when we went to the Finger Lakes in Upstate New York for what turned into a debaucherous spa weekend later that same year. We had needed it. Well, I had needed it. My friendship with Kara had struggled for the first time. The only other time in our relationship when things had been dicey was when I stole her marbles when we were eight, lied to her and told her it wasn't me, then gave them back to her, like an absolute asshole, on her sixteenth birthday.

At the Finger Lakes, Kara and I talked about Rory, Cameron, and us late at night around a pitiful crackling fire that took us three hours to make. Cameron had broken up with her. He couldn't forgive her for how she unintentionally destroyed the Campbell boys' longstanding friendship with the McCain girls. I forgave her because it was never Kara's fault. It was mine and Rory's.

"Zoë, when we met, I thought you were Ellie's freaky New York, flash-in-the-pan friend who would come and go once Bronwyn was over. I had no idea how important you would become to us Canadians." Kara pushed her drink forward as we toasted our cheese-hating American best friend. "We love you!"

"You just like living vicariously through my roommate's sex stories." I stared accusingly at Hannah.

Zoë and I had moved to Los Angeles four years ago. We first lived in Marina del Rey, then moved to Beachwood Canyon, and now we were in a cute, tiny house in Highland Park. She had become my lifeline and security blanket, and was just as significant to me as Hannah and Kara.

"She never lets us down." Hannah giggled while lifting her drink to her lips. Her engagement ring sparkled beneath the twinkling string lights that lit the dance floor. I frowned when looking at her ring. Hannah was engaged to someone back in Vancouver whom she had been dating for a few years. She had met him online, and he was . . . what's the word? Unmotivated? Basic? Boring?

"I'm not gonna lie; my stories are fabulous." Zoë turned to Kara. "Did I ever tell you about the time this one guy ate me out on a table at a dinner party as an appetizer?"

"Yes, Zoë," Kara said flatly. "And that's not a dinner party, that's an orgy."

Maddy's eyes went wide when Zoë said "this one guy." She turned to me stiffly, and I bent over with laughter, believing wholeheartedly that Zoë probably *was* talking about Maddy's brother.

"To Zoë!" I laughed as we lifted our glasses once again.

Zoë took a sip of her Negroni, dropped her drink onto the table we were standing around, and started dancing when Whitney Houston's "I Wanna Dance with Somebody (Who Loves Me)" blasted throughout the bar. She shimmied as if she had no control over her body.

"Oh shit!" she cried out. "I don't know what's happening." She dipped herself, bending her body back so her head almost hit the floor.

"You're so flexible!" Hannah shrieked, deeply impressed.

"It's the music. Something's happening to me!" Zoë started spinning in circles. If anyone was going to get the party started, it was Zoë. Her energy had always been intoxicating. Kara and Maddy joined in.

My phone vibrated. I lifted it out as stealthily as possible to check if it was work. Since moving to Los Angeles, I had worked my way up behind the scenes and become the director of development at Marie Street Productions. My hours were intense, and the job was incredibly demanding, but my boss, Ken Caplin, had given me a first in my career: He treated me like a person. I still didn't have the job title I wanted, but before Marie Street . . . well, it took a lot to get to Marie Street Productions.

I had heard rumors about the sixty-year-old director and producer Ken Caplin for years. He was not just one of the most influential tastemakers in the television industry, but also had a reputation for being a true champion for his team. I had run across many of his former assistants, executives, or producers over the years, and they were always my favorite people.

The downside to my job? I was living off no sleep and on the brink of stress-induced ulcers twenty-four hours a day, seven days a week. Also, Craig Sinicki. Craig was ten years my senior and the creator and showrunner of Marie Street's long-running, critically acclaimed post-apocalyptic drama.

Unsurprisingly, the text came from Craig.

CRAIG SINICKI: What happens in Vegas . . . happens in LA, too?

I rolled my eyes and pushed my phone back into my pocket. I turned to Hannah, handing her my drink.

She stared me down. "Put your work away," she demanded.

"I am! I will! I have to pee. I'll be back."

The moment I sat on the toilet, my phone blew up. I had placed it on the toilet paper holder, and it started vibrating so violently that it almost fell onto the piss-stained tile.

KARA: Ellie!

KARA: Sound the motherfucking alarm!

KARA: He's here!

HANNAH: E, stay in the bathroom. I'm coming.

ZOË: I don't see him!

HANNAH: Look for the only person wearing a black hat.

KARA: Oh my god.

I picked up my phone and started reading the texts, which were flying at me so fast, I almost got whiplash. I was very aware that I was sitting in a dank and dark bathroom. I was on the toilet, with my panties around my ankles, wild-eyed and frozen in place. A random EDM remix of "Shallow" by Lady Gaga and Bradley Cooper was thumping through the speakers and burning into my frazzled brain.

KARA: He saw me.

KARA: He. Saw. Me!

Maddy has been added to the Group Chat

MADDY: We all know that we're standing next to each other, right?

The bathroom walls were closing in on me. My breath left my lungs and pushed through the top of my head. I was "off the deep end," as the truly relevant song would say. My friends hadn't said it outright, but I knew they were talking about Rory.

I had seen him only once since my twenty-first birthday. However, I had been following his career, watching him dominate the world's biggest golf tournaments and championships. He had won the PGA Championship, the US Open, and the Masters. From a distance, I watched Rory become the person I'd always known he would be. I stumbled through the years toward a life I had decided upon as a kid without a fully developed frontal cortex.

I ran, and by the time I realized I didn't like what I was running toward, I had already run away from anything and everyone I ever loved. I ran away from Rory. I ran away from Ben. And when reality washed over me, turning back around wasn't an option. I had already passed the point of no return. Whereas Rory had achieved everything he had dreamed of, everything he had dedicated his life to, over the last four years of my life in Los Angeles, I had come to very successfully hate myself.

"Ellie?" My sister called out my name in the busy bathroom.

"Here." I kicked my foot against the back of my stall door.

"Are you coming out?"

"Nope."

"Ellie, you need to deal with this."

"That would be ideal, but I actually can't move right now . . . so that's a thing." My laughter started to bubble up from within. I worried it would come out sounding exactly how I felt, which was unhinged.

"Ugh." I heard my sister grunt, then slap against the floor. Her hands landed in front of my stall. Her ring was blinding. I saw her head and face twist between the bottom of my stall door and the dirty floor. She was directly in line with my dangling, slightly ripped underwear. "Get up."

"Um, that's disgusting," a random girl called out.

"Mind your business, Lindsay!" Hannah snapped her head back at the faceless voice.

"Lindsay?"

Hannah shrugged. "I took a guess. It felt right."

"I can't see Rory, Hannah." I shook my head, feeling my stomach hollow out.

"Yes. You can. Put it all behind you and talk to him." She pulled herself into my stall and crouched down, using her therapist voice. I was in a very strange position as a twenty-nine-year-old woman sitting on a public toilet and holding hands with my sister, but it wasn't our strangest position as sisters.

KNOCK. KNOCK. KNOCK.

"Get a room!" another faceless voice called out in the crowded bathroom.

"Go away, Lindsay!" Hannah screamed back.

Whoever it was banged on the stall door again. This time, it surprised both of us. Hannah crashed forward. To steady herself, she gripped the rim of the toilet between my legs. We both started gagging, then shouted at each other to stop because we were going to make each other sick.

Hannah and I left the stall but stayed huddled in the bathroom as she furiously texted. I wasn't getting any notifications, so it wasn't with our Lover Ladies group chat.

"What are you doing?" I asked.

She held up her finger, silencing me, continued texting, then cleared her throat. Finally, a notification came through on our group chat.

HANNAH: Ellie and I are coming out of the bathroom. Anyone want to see if they can get Rory's attention and distract him?

I looked at Hannah, and her eyes flipped over to me quickly, then back to her phone. She was acting cagey.

"What are you doing?"

"Nothing!" she snapped, then continued typing.

HANNAH: Anyone? Come on, ladies.

ZOË: He doesn't know who Maddy is. She can show off her boobs! They're out of control. When was the last time you pumped, M?

MADDY: 7 hours ago . . .

KARA: Your tits are MAGNIFICENT.

ZOË: He'll never notice you sneaking out the back.

KARA: You won't upstage Maddy's boobs, Ellie. This is a guarantee.

MADDY: Wait, I don't know how I feel about this.

HANNAH: Okay, this plan sounds legit! We're walking out in 30 seconds. You have 30 seconds! 30 SECONDS!

KARA: LET'S DO THIS!

ZOË: AHHHHHH!!!

MADDY: CAPS LOCK!!!!!

I closed my eyes, practiced some deep breathing, and counted to thirty. I looked up at my sister just as her phone dinged with another text message. Hannah looked down at her phone, then her eyes shot back up to me, wild as ever.

Hannah shouted, "OKAY, GO! NOW! NOW!"

I pushed through the door and walked straight into my first love. Rory blinked at me, stunned. I had smacked Manor House's bathroom door directly into his rock-hard body.

"Hannah, you set me up," I said through a tight jaw as my sister slinked out of the bathroom beside me.

"Byeeeeeeee," Hannah said as she hurried over to Kara, Zoë, and Maddy, who were bumping into each other and scattering behind Rory like cockroaches exposed to daylight.

Useless.

My eyes dragged over Rory; it was as if I had been stupefied. He was gorgeous. He looked strong. He looked like a man. It was hard for me to process. I had admired Rory's life and accomplishments from afar, but other than one brief encounter when we were twenty-five, he lived inside my memory. Rory was frozen in my past, and I wanted him to stay there. In my memory, we still mattered to each other. Seeing him again catapulted me into the present.

Eight years. It had been eight years since my twenty-first birthday, and I had discovered that I still couldn't let Rory go. I didn't know how.

"Ellie?" Rory's voice was low, steady.

"Hi," I said breathily.

Rory's eyes moved slowly up my body, taking me in. I was thankful I looked cute, in a tight black, long-sleeved, scooped-neck minidress. My wavy hair was cut halfway down my chest and lighter now, blonder, which he had never seen before. I had on minimal eye makeup, but I'd gone bold with my lipstick, as I often do. If there was ever a time for me to wear this outfit, it was tonight.

I saw Rory's Adam's apple bob as he swallowed, then parted his lips ever so slightly. Rory was wearing fitted gray pants, a black T-shirt, and a black bomber jacket to go with that black bloody hat. It was turned to the front, his curls flipping out to the sides. His eyebrows were pulling together into a thought pattern that I couldn't quite pinpoint. His dark-brown eyes were familiar and warm. His jaw was strong beneath his short beard.

"It's good to see you." Rory let out a small smile, creasing his dimple, and I wanted to die.

"Yeah, definitely." I jumped over his words.

"Are you still in LA?" he asked as a leggy brunette pushed me out of the bathroom doorway and stopped mid-stride to salivate.

"Yeah. Where are you these days?" I willed my legs to work and sidestepped along the crowded hallway to stand with my back against the wall.

"I'm in Vancouver."

"Oh." I bobbed my head around and noticed him shift his weight, also likely uncomfortable. I lifted my foot to step away from the wall, and Rory lightly placed the tips of his fingers onto my stomach to keep me in place. It felt like I had just been stabbed.

"What are you doing in Vegas?" Rory cocked his head.

"My friend's birthday. I should get back to them." I slipped out from beneath his fingers, but Rory moved his hand to my arm.

"Wait. Where are you going?" he asked.

I looked down at his hand gently gripping my forearm, unintentionally claiming me for that brief moment. "Um, not sure yet." I laughed softly.

I looked out to the bar, not too far from where I was standing. I could see Hannah staring back at me. Kara, however, was looking up at the ceiling, pretending to be interested in the building's architecture. Zoë gave me a wave, then pulled Maddy's top down for a better look at her cleavage. Her boobs were about to explode. Maddy shook her head solemnly and called out in distress, "I don't know what you want from me!"

Fucking. Useless.

"Well, how long are you here?" Rory let go of my arm, which was so hot from his touch that I was certain it had been left branded.

"Just the weekend."

"I'm here for the weekend, too."

"Yes, I know. Your face is sort of everywhere." I nodded, finally making proper eye contact.

"Ahh . . ." Rory's beautiful, softly freckled face flushed. He scratched his scruff.

I lifted my hand and gave him a limp wrist-wagging. "Get off my TV, will ya? It's super inconvenient to just . . . always see your fuckin' face." I started laughing uncomfortably, but Rory didn't laugh along with me.

"Yeah. Speaking of, I saw that Ben's in a new movie with Ryan Gosling. He's getting really big. Can't get rid of that guy." Rory held my stare.

"Yup. Gotta love it when your exes are so publicly successful." I attempted to control my sarcasm.

"Are you two not together anymore?" His chest had risen, and I saw it stay in place. He was holding his breath.

"No," I answered quietly, hoping he'd read the room and see that I didn't want to go into any details. My eyes flipped over to my friends again, and they had all clandestinely shifted ten steps closer to Rory and me.

"I'm sorry." Rory's eyes dropped. He bit his bottom lip, thinking. "I didn't know that."

"Well, I really am gonna go now. I'm here with Hannah and Kara. I don't know if you remember my friend from New York, Zoë?"

"Of course I remember her." He kept his eyes on the ground.

"Anyway, it's her birthday. So, here I go." I turned to leave.

"Wait, just wait." Rory grabbed my arm again. It was my bicep this time. I slowly looked down at Rory's hand. Surely my skin should be melting off, no? He noticed where my attention lay and removed his hand. He took off his hat to rake his fingers through his hair and readjust. With a deep breath, he asked, "What are you doing tomorrow?"

"I'm— I'm in Vegas with my friends, so—"

Hannah cut me off, shouting from even closer now, "SHE'S DOING NOTHING, RORY! SHE'S SINGLE AND DOING NOTHING!"

Rory gave Hannah a closed-mouth smile and dropped his hands into his pants pockets. "Hi, Hannah," he called out, with a nod.

"Hi, Rory," she called back, with an enormous self-satisfied grin. Hannah apparently still had a penchant for dramatically inserting herself into our . . . whatever this was.

He turned back to me. "It would be nice to catch up. Can I take you out?" Grown-up Rory's confidence was disarming. He had never been so forward with me before.

"Um, I don't . . ." I wanted to turn to the birthday girl to see her reaction to Rory's offer, but I couldn't because her chin landed squarely on my shoulder. Zoë had snuck up behind me.

"Yes, I think that would be a lovely idea, Rory. How nice to see you again." Zoë's voice was a deep whisper. They were all eavesdropping.

"Jesus Christ," I sighed, then shook my head, silently apologizing for my friends.

Rory responded with a sly smile that creased his dimple. Zoë slowly backed away from us and straight into Kara. She stepped on Kara's foot.

"Motherfff— OWW!" Kara screeched. Her knees gave out, and she tumbled over, elbowing Maddy directly in her engorged boob, which had borderline mastitis.

"Holy shit!" Maddy called out, grabbing her tit and bending over.

"Same number?" Rory asked, ignoring the chaos behind me.

"I'm not sure. Did you ever get my New York number?"

Rory just barely shook his head. He went into his pocket and handed me his phone. I grabbed it from him and sent myself a text message that simply said "Ellie." I cleared my throat, hoping to clear away the awkwardness between us. "Haven't switched my number over to LA. Can't seem to let go of that nine-one-seven area code." Rory kept quiet until I gave him back his phone. "Alright, well, I guess . . . text me?" I laughed warily and lifted my eyes to his.

"I'll see you, Cainey." Rory relaxed as he called me by my forgotten name. It was a name I had lost a long time ago, back when I lost myself as well.

Chapter 22

NEW YORK
21 years old

AFTER MY BIRTHDAY, BEN TOSSED OUT OUR TWO TWIN BEDS AND bought us a queen. We tried to keep our relationship under wraps at school, but would find dark corners to sneak away to. Zoë and Lucas knew the truth, but we didn't want our personal lives to become fodder for everyone else.

At school, the only time we weren't together was during dance classes, but we would pass each other in the halls before and afterward. One day, we were sitting next to each other on one of the long benches in the lobby. "Try a Little Tenderness" by Otis Redding was blasting from the dance studio, where class was starting. Ben was drinking water on his way out, and I was lacing up my jazz shoes on the way in. He pressed his hands into his thighs, ready to leave, but before he did, he leaned over, dripping with sweat, and gave me a kiss on the lips.

"Alright, see you later, buddy."

My eyes went wide, and I snorted. He squeezed his eyes tight, realizing what he had just done. He opened one eye to see five other classmates watching us, slack-jawed.

"Well, I guess that's that." He laughed, then bent down for another kiss. We'd lasted a month before everyone knew that Ben and I were "Ben and Ellie."

My parents came to visit, and we took them to all our favorite spots. They watched him reach for my hand every time we walked. He took my dad to his first baseball game. They also went golfing, and Ben didn't say a word when my dad tried to give him tips and correct his swing the entire time. Ben was just so instantly my live-in boyfriend that my life in New York started to feel permanent.

We kept our Central Park tradition alive, lying out in the sun on the Great Lawn, walking the snowy paths, and picnicking in the rain under the Glen Span Arch. I was slowly shedding my past life with every passing season, every passing day.

When school was out for the summer, I decided not to go back to Vancouver, much to my parents' dismay. Ben and I would bring a thin floral sheet and spend entire days in the park. We would lie flat, fall asleep, eat, blast music, play games, and watch people set themselves up in encampments for the day and break them down in the late afternoon. We would lie out there at night, too, and count how many people made us nervous, then make up silly stories about each person to suppress our fear of them.

One morning, I looked over at Ben, baking in the summer sun, shirtless, shorts on, sunglasses on, and I reached for his hand, assuming he was asleep. He wasn't. His parents were flying in from Seattle and had splurged by getting two rooms at the Plaza Hotel, one for them and one for us.

"My mom and stepdad will get into the city around six tonight, and our check-in is at three. So we'll have three hours to kill." He moved his other arm around the back of his head, making himself more comfortable.

"That's fun. What do you want to do when we get there?" I lifted my hand to block the sun.

"A whole lot of sex would be nice." Ben smiled mischievously.

A teenage girl lying out on a blanket not too far from us pulled a face as she overheard our conversation.

"Also, my mom was hoping to get in a girls' day with you while they're here. Would that be okay?" Ben flipped over onto his stomach and placed the side of his head on his hands so he was facing me. I did the same.

"I can take the heat. Tomorrow we've got the commercial shoot, but the next day?" I shifted my body so I could press my lips into his arm.

"Yeah, I'll let her know." Ben pulled himself toward me for a quick kiss.

I had been working under the table at a casting agency as a background talent wrangler ever since my internship with Justin Bordin ended. My boss, Sal, was nice enough, but I couldn't help but notice that every time he made an inappropriate comment about one of the actors on set, he would dismiss it by saying, "It's okay, Ellie's here." I never quite knew how to feel about him using me as his protective shield.

Sal would slip me in front of the camera whenever an opportunity popped up for a featured extra. It wasn't glamorous, but it was a start. I was excited when he decided to throw me a bone and give me a tiny part, with one line, in a commercial for a European gin company. Ben asked to come along for the ride and be one of the extras so he could cheer me on.

"Do you even know yet what we're doing tomorrow?" he asked.

"No, Sal said it would all be on the fly."

"Feels a little amateur hour that we're going in knowing nothing." Ben picked some grass off my arm.

"Oh, there is nothing about this that screams legitimate," I agreed. "But whatever, it's an experience."

We checked in at the Plaza, and the first thing we did was locate the massive soaker bathtub. Ben ran the bath and stripped off his clothes.

"Get in! This is so big. We can actually take a bath together. Bathtub Ethan can suck it!"

In the bath, we watched a movie, ate pizza, engaged in some naughtiness, tested each other on how long we could hold our breath, and drank way too much wine. It was our first time in water together; Ben didn't like company in the shower, and I couldn't persuade him no matter how hard I tried. "There's always a weird moment when both of us are bending over at different times, and not in a sexy way" was one of his reliable excuses.

We were acting like we were in a luxury hot tub at an all-inclusive resort. We kept topping up the bathtub with hot water. We knew full well we could have gone to a real hot tub, but then Ben wouldn't have been able to start referring to himself as Bathtub Ben.

His phone rang as we started our second bathtub movie, *The Sandlot*. We still had an hour before his parents arrived, and we intended to use every minute of it.

"Shh!" He brought his finger to his mouth. "It's my mom."

I pulled a stink face. "Don't answer it! She'll know we're in the bath." I pinched his nipple.

"Ow!" He swatted my hand away as he answered his phone.

"Hi, Mom. What's up?" Ben's eyes widened when he heard his echo in the bathroom.

I mouthed, *What are you doing?*

"No, no . . . I'm just . . ." Ben's smile shifted into discomfort as he pressed his mouth into the phone. "Taking a shit?"

I accidentally snorted, revealing my whereabouts.

"Yeah, she's here." Ben's eyes went wide again. "I mean, no, she's not literally with me. The door is closed. Mom, I'm a grown man. Let me . . . shit in peace." Ben closed his eyes and sighed. "Yes, Mom, she still likes me."

I sank beneath the water to stop myself from laughing. When I came up for air again, I could see that Ben's face had turned red, and his mouth was in a tight line. He was trying not to laugh.

"Okay, I'm glad it was a good flight. Text me when you're in the lobby, and we'll come down. Yes, she's excited, too. Love you." Ben put the phone down, then turned to me. "That wasn't great." He laughed.

"That whole conversation was alarming. I feel like I need to reconsider some stuff." I lifted my hand out of the soapy water, and Ben lifted his to meet mine, intertwining our fingers.

He pulled me toward him. "Too bad. You're locked in." He flipped me around so I was sitting between his legs, with my back pressed into his chest. "My parents are going to love you."

"Yeah?" I lifted my toes above the water.

"Yeah. Please don't get freaked out if they start saying some crazy things." He kissed the side of my head, then leaned back against the tub.

"What do you mean?"

"They just know how I feel about you, and they've asked how serious this is. So they might get a little weird." Ben turned up the movie's volume.

I turned it back down, causing him to chuckle. "And just how serious is this?" I teased.

"It's pretty serious, McCain." I could hear him smile from behind me.

It was my turn for my phone to ring. It was Kara.

My anxiety started to spike. It hadn't been smooth sailing for me and Kara since my birthday.

"Can I put it on speaker?" he asked.

"Yeah, but don't say anything."

Ben tapped my phone, answering it for me.

"Hey, Kara. What's up?" I asked.

"Hey, Ellie-Bee. I just needed to talk to you." She sucked in a shaky breath, and I bolted upright in the bath, concerned to hear her so upset right out of the gate.

I picked up my phone but kept it on speaker. "Where are you?"

"I'm at Juniper."

The air emptied from my lungs as she spoke. "You're going to Juniper again? When did that start?"

"It didn't. Jacob asked me to drop something off, but I just saw Cameron. I haven't seen him since we broke up. It did not go well."

I slumped. "I'm sorry."

"No, it's . . . my fault." Kara let out a deep, loud sigh. I could tell she was trying not to cry.

"I promise, there will come a time when this is all in the past." I hoped to believe that myself one day. Ben gently trailed his fingers along my back.

"Umm, yeah. Hold on." She was distracted.

A muffling sound clouded the mic, but then I could hear him. His voice was in the background, but it was clear as day. Rory was there with Kara.

"Hey, Kare. You okay?" His voice was quiet, but it was Rory.

"Yeah, I'm fine," she answered hurriedly.

"I caught the tail end of what happened in there and wanted to check on you." Rory's voice was growing louder. He must have been walking up to her. I wondered where they were. Was she leaning against the bag stand by the drop-off? Were they at her car in the parking lot? Were they anywhere near the putting green where Albert Davis had rammed his sweatband up my arm and sunk his fingernails deep into my wrist, hoping to hit bone?

"I'm just talking to Ellie. Can you give me a few minutes? I'd really like to talk to you, too."

I stopped breathing. I didn't hear Rory respond. There were only a few seconds of silence before Kara said, "Hey. I'm back." I wondered what Rory was thinking, knowing that I was on the phone, assuming that I could hear them. A heaviness grew inside my chest, like I was being compressed from all directions.

"Hey," I whispered.

"I'm sorry." She sniffled. "Rory's here. I'm sorry." I could visualize her pressing her hand into her forehead.

"It's okay, Kara." I sounded stronger this time. "I'm with Ben right now. So I should go. Go talk to Rory. I'm sure he's got some insight, and I know he'll make you feel better. Just remember that whatever Cameron said, or says in the future, I love you. Cameron needs to move on. Rory has. I have. Okay?" I envisioned her nodding, and Ben kissed my shoulder blade. He rested his cheek against my back, still listening. "I love you, Kare," I said again, for good measure.

"I love you, too," she choked out. "Bye."

After I hung up, Ben pressed another kiss into my shoulder before saying, "That was sad. She doesn't sound like she's doing well."

"No, she doesn't," I agreed, then sank back into Ben's arms. My thoughts swirled between Kara and Rory. What were they doing? What were they saying? What was he thinking? Was Kara okay?

"You should invite her to come visit this summer. It sounds like she needs a break." Ben moved my wet hair to the side and off his chest. "Or you two could go someplace together? That might be nice for you both. Maybe upstate?"

"That sounds like a really good idea, actually. What if I organized a trip with all the girls? Kara, Hannah, and Zoë? I feel like they could be good friends if I gave them a little push. What do you think?"

"Go for it, buddy. Just let me know when, so I can plan something with Lucas."

I flipped my body around, with a little splash, so my head was on Ben's chest. "We should get out now. Your parents will be here soon. And I don't want to be any crinklier and wrinklier for tomorrow's shoot."

"I'm still convinced tomorrow is gonna be a shitshow."

"I have a feeling you might be right."

I smiled as Ben lifted my face for a soft kiss before we finally pulled ourselves out of the bath.

The next day, everything went as expected until it didn't. Ben and I showed up at 6 a.m., and we were excited and surprised to learn the commercial was Marie Antoinette–themed. All the extras' costumes were jaw-droppingly gorgeous.

Unfortunately, the woman in charge of wardrobe tried to fit me into seven different pastel-toned rococo-style dresses. They were all too big, too small, or too similar to someone else's. It got to the point where every time she looked at me, she groaned—until she made a fateful decision. "Okay, we'll put you in the back somewhere, so no one can see you, and you can be a butler. At least that way it's not a wasted day for you. Sound good, honey?" She then shoved a tuxedo into my hand and pushed me through to hair and makeup, where I was fitted perfectly with a Hungarian mustache and a powdered white wig.

I came out of the trailer and looked at Ben just as he was taking a sip from his water bottle.

I was dressed exactly like him.

"Ellie!" Ben laughed, doing a full-on spit take.

I tried to contain my smile and not reveal my amusement at the insanity of the moment. I lifted both arms, pointed my middle fingers to the sky, and did a full circle with my arms while Ben bent over in hysterics.

"Wait. I need a picture." He scrambled to get his phone out of his pocket. "I need to remember this for the rest of my life."

I playfully thumped his shoulder with my fist. "Get me out of this hellhole, Ben. When are we moving to LA?"

Chapter 23

LAS VEGAS

29 years old

IT WAS THE EARLY AFTERNOON, AND I HAD DONE EVERYTHING IN my power to avoid any mention of the Las Vegas Celebrity Pro-Am where Rory was playing. Instead, we somehow managed to get into a cab that had a poster of Ben's movie advertised on its digital rooftop banner.

Hannah shoved me into the back when she saw Ben's face scroll across the top of the cab, simultaneously saying, "Oh, for Christ's sake. We should have taken an Uber."

After grabbing lunch at Shake Shack, Hannah, Kara, Zoë, Maddy, and I found ourselves at a lively piano bar, singing along and dancing to every song that people randomly threw out to the singer-slash-pianist-slash-jukebox.

We were listening to our pianist absolutely crush "Brown Eyed Girl" when Kara asked, "When are you expecting Rory to reach out?"

"I have no idea. I think he's done golfing for the day, but who knows what kind of commitments he has for these sorts of things with sponsors or advertisers, or the tournament itself. I really have no clue what his life is like. I'm just waiting for my phone to ring at any time." At that exact moment, my phone vibrated. All our eyes shot up and connected.

"I need a drink." My voice was lower than normal.

I put my phone on the table and unlocked the screen. Everyone gathered around to get a good look.

CRAIG SINICKI: I'm imagining you at a pool right now. I want to see your bathing suit.

My stomach knee-jerked into my throat. I quickly grabbed and hid my phone as another text popped up.

CRAIG SINICKI: I'll show you mine . . . ?

"Um, who's Craig Sinicki?" Maddy asked curiously.

I saw Hannah and Zoë exchange strained looks.

"Just someone I work with." I put my phone back in my pocket and felt myself flush.

"Do you have a dirty little work relationship you're not telling anyone about?" Kara continued Maddy's line of questioning.

"No. I do not." I leveled my eyes at Kara.

"Think of the role-play. Hot, Ellie. Hot," Maddy purred. "Do you have elevators at your work? Because I always imagine shit happening in elevators. Or a roof? My god. Please tell me you have a roof. Does he call you a good girl when you balance a budget?" We all turned to Maddy, and her face turned stoic. "I haven't had sex in a really long time, and I've been listening to a lot of audiobooks, okay?"

"Why haven't you been having sex? Georgie is one." Zoë licked the salt off her rim.

"Because my vagina was torn all the way to my asshole, Zoë. And when my period came back, it turned into a tsunami. And I have clots the size of fists falling out of me for days at a time. Shall I go on?"

All of us leaned in and said, "Yes."

"You've got to get your iron checked," Hannah said, unperturbed, while sipping her drink.

Kara turned back to me and placed both elbows on the table. She put her chin in her hands. "Who is he? What does he do? What does he look like?"

I stumbled through my thoughts on how to accurately describe Craig's and my dysfunctional work relationship, if that's what one would call it.

"His name is Craig Sinicki. He's the showrunner for *Black Cross*, which means he's the head writer and basically the creative force behind the show. The writers' room is down the hall from Marie Street. So he comes into the office a lot. He's fine."

Kara ran a quick Google search on her phone, then pulled her lips into an O and sucked in a breath. "He's pretty handsome." Her eyes widened, and she popped them back up to me.

I looked over at what Kara had pulled up. It was a photo from Craig's IMDb profile of him and his girlfriend on the red carpet for the season six premiere of *Black Cross*. His blond hair was swept back, and his piercing blue eyes stared into the camera lens. Somehow, even through a photo, his sleepy bedroom eyes still managed to look like they were undressing me. I looked away.

"Maybe we should just drop this, guys." Zoë tried to come to my rescue.

"Yeah, clearly Ellie doesn't want to get into it." Hannah backed her up.

"It's okay." I closed my eyes. "He's someone I have to work with. That's it. He sends me emails and texts, and I don't love them. I don't like him, and nothing has ever happened between us, nor will it. I don't fuck around with people I work with. Let's leave it at that," I pleaded, then changed the subject. "Where's that drink we talked about?"

"Did we talk about a drink, or was that just you?" Zoë asked me with a sly smile. With absolute precision timing, a shot girl showed up at our table, and I threw back a shot of tequila.

"I need to have some fun!" I declared. "I want to have some fun right now. I feel like I need to . . ." I waved my arms in circles, trying to pump myself up. "I don't know, do something."

"Speaking of fun, you'll never guess who I heard from last night after we saw Rory." Kara put her margarita to her lips and didn't give us time to respond. "Cameron."

"What?" Hannah gasped. "Are you serious?"

"Who's Cameron again?" Maddy asked excitedly.

"Cameron is Rory's brother. Kara and Cameron used to touch each other. Hannah and his other brother, Blair, also used to touch each other," Zoë stated matter-of-factly.

"Blair and I did not used to touch each other!" Hannah said defiantly, though none of us believed her.

"What did Cameron say?" I grabbed Kara's arm, bringing her back to her revelation.

"Just that he heard Rory saw us, and he asked how I was doing. I haven't responded."

"Why not?!" I demanded.

"Because I haven't decided how I feel about it." Kara took a sip of her drink, but I could see her also swallow whatever lump she had in her throat. Cameron had ripped Kara's heart into shreds and then stomped on it like he was a rhino. I wasn't shocked that she didn't know how she felt about him reaching out, but I would be shocked if she didn't eventually reciprocate.

"Did you love Cameron as a little kid, like Ellie loved Rory?" Maddy asked Kara.

"Oh, I *loved* Cameron. But not when we were kids. He wasn't my sexual awakening or anything." Kara grinned at me.

"Rory wasn't my sexual awakening! How dare you!" I scoffed.

"Oh, that's a fun question! Who was it?" Maddy probed. "Wait! I'll go first. I really liked Max from *A Goofy Movie*. Like, I *really* liked Max. Oh! And Chip from *Chip 'n Dale*. I don't know. He was so bossy." She grinned.

"Those are both cartoons!" Hannah laughed.

"Mine was Elijah Wood." Kara chuckled. "But only because Ellie shoved him down my throat and forced me to watch every one of his movies a hundred times each. Eventually, I buckled. But I don't regret it. He's a beautiful owl. I still love him."

I feigned tipping my hat to Kara and gave a haughty "You're welcome."

"That's insanity, because he's not even Ellie's." Hannah jumped in. "It was Devon Sawa, in the final scene of *Casper*. I saw you pretend to be Christina Ricci, with your face all squished against the TV and a pillow between your legs."

"Hannah!" I shrieked, with a horrified laugh. "I was *eight*! Shut. Up!"

Zoë's phone dinged with a message, killing the conversation. "Okay, everyone. I've got confirmation for tonight." She read her text. "We're going to Planet Hollywood. Dress to dance your faces off."

"Are you joking?" I threw myself back into my chair, needing another shot.

"What?" Zoë asked, smiling mischievously.

"You're going to see Gwen Stefani, aren't you?" I already knew the answer.

"I don't know what you're talking about." Zoë pressed her hand into her heart, faux-bashfully.

"What?! Seriously!" Maddy shrieked. "I'm never returning to my family, am I? Have I run away from them? Do I live here now?"

"Ooooh, that's going to be fun." Hannah turned to me with a shit-eating grin. "I'm so sorry you're missing it, sister."

"Whatever. I'm done with this." I left the girls and chased down the shot girl at another table. I did a shot with that table, then came back to our table and said, "I'm not missing out tonight."

"You're not bailing on Rory, Ellie-Bee." Hannah narrowed her eyes at me. "This is like . . . the night we've all been waiting for. You haven't seen him in four years. It's been eight years since you broke each other's hearts. And you've been in love with him—he's been hidden away in the back of your heart—every day of your life for *seventeen years!*"

"Don't say that! That's not true!" I threw my head down on the table with a slam, knowing it was completely true.

"You just need to let out some stress. Maybe you should masturbate." Zoë calmly rubbed my back.

I scoffed at her, which turned into a cough, and she grinned back at me playfully.

"No, what I need is to have a little fun, and I need some Gwen." I stood up from my seat and walked over to the pianist, making a request.

"Aaaaaand she's back, baby!" Zoë laughed.

"Uh-oh." Kara's eyes were wide. "Here we go, folks!"

"What is she doing?" Maddy watched me with eagle eyes.

"Maddy, we'd like to introduce you to New York Ellie." Zoë laughed.

The pianist began playing No Doubt's "Just a Girl." I lifted the microphone to my mouth and started singing with 100 percent commitment. I let it rip like a raging lunatic, and in a matter of seconds, I had everyone in the whole dinky bar on their feet.

Chapter 24

NEW YORK
22 years old

BEN AND I WERE SHARING AN UMBRELLA THAT WE'D HAD TO PICK up from Duane Reade after an unexpected downpour pummeled us during our walk home from school. Hannah was in town. The arrangement of her and me sleeping on the bed and Ben sleeping on the floor had worked out for the first two days, but when she suggested things might be a little less cramped if she stayed with Lucas, I kept my mouth shut and my smile smug.

Along with Zoë, we were all heading back to Grayrock, dodging enormous piles of garbage that lined the street, when Ben spotted a glowing orange sign in a window that read "PSYCHIC."

"Let's do it." Ben tugged on my arm.

"Oh! Fun!" Hannah did an excited little jump. She and Lucas were sharing an umbrella as well, and Lucas didn't appreciate the jostling, which caused the rain to slide off the umbrella and onto his shoulder.

"Hey! Settle down, Canada!" Lucas yanked the umbrella away from Hannah entirely. She shrieked and grabbed his arm, cuddling for cover.

"No. Ben, no." I leaned back, away from the psychic, trying to keep him on track. We were going to the movies, and I still wanted to change out of my tights from our last class of the day.

"I'm with Ellie. I don't like psychics," Zoë said, walking behind all of us with her head tilted back, letting the rain fall on her face. "Now, find me a witch, and we can have a real conversation."

"Watch this." Hannah switched one of her rings around, putting it on her left ring finger. "Lucas, you keep your hands in your pockets, and I'll bet you all thirty dollars that the psychic thinks we're married."

"Yes. I'm in." Lucas jumped under the eave of the psychic's door and closed their umbrella.

Ben gave my arm another small pull. "You don't have to do it, but you're gonna watch, because now I want that money."

The door chimed as we opened it, and we stepped into what looked like the waiting room of a doctor's office. We all sat stiffly on a long white couch in front of a coffee table. Ben and I exchanged a glance as a woman appeared from behind a closed door. She pulled up a seat and sat in front of us. I looked around the empty, musty room with dying plants and said, "Oh, are we doing this here?"

The psychic's attention dropped down, sweeping across our bodies. Hannah noticed the psychic note her "wedding ring." She and I made eye contact, and I could see her attempt to restrain her bubbling excitement.

The psychic turned to Zoë first. "At times, you find yourself doubting decisions you've made, which have led you to where you are today. Try not to look back on those crossroads in your life. If you are constantly looking back, you'll never see where you are."

Zoë nodded kindly. The psychic moved her attention away, and Zoë looked at me, rolled her eyes, and mouthed, *Where's the witch?*

The psychic adjusted herself in her seat, gently touched her temple, and closed her eyes. "I sense there is some type of marriage in this room."

Hannah's mouth tightened as she eagerly anticipated the psychic's next comment. Ben pressed his elbow into the coffee table and covered his mouth with his hand. I could tell he was trying to mask his excitement as well.

"This love will last a lifetime, but with it comes hardships."

Ben snorted at the most generic and basic piece of wisdom any of us had ever heard.

Zoë tapped into her acting, and tears welled in her eyes. She looked over at Lucas, then at Hannah, and back again. She breathed dramatically. "I knew you'd break her heart eventually, you bastard."

Ben chuckled again, causing the psychic's focus to shift to him. She grabbed his hand and closed both of hers over it. His eyes went wide. I could see him trying to hold in his smile.

"This is a recent development." She nodded back and forth between me and Ben.

"We're well over the year mark, so . . ." His eyes flipped over to me. I had to look away to stop myself from breaking into a smile and accidentally offending anyone.

"He's been hittin' that for a long time." Zoë gave an affirming nod.

"Zoë . . ." I said under my breath, as everyone else choked back their laughter.

"There's something significant bound to happen between the two of you." The psychic kept her eyes closed. "I see sun and palm trees." She patted Ben on the hand. "You'll be happy."

I gave Ben a little nod and a smirk. Los Angeles had been a topic of conversation between us lately, so I was pleased that the psychic was on my side. It wasn't that Ben was opposed to moving once we graduated. It was something he was interested in, but he wavered. He just wasn't sure anymore. But I couldn't shake the image of LA I had cemented inside my heart and head. Since I was a kid, I had been wanting to know who I could be there.

"We would need a solid reason to go," Ben had said one Friday night while mixing drinks.

I was sitting at Lifers bar, waiting for his shift to end. We were nearing graduation, and I had been suggesting that we sublet our apartment and try LA for a couple of months. At first, he was all in, but then he started auditioning in New York, and casting directors kept calling him back. He was booking jobs, surprisingly big jobs. He had already been cast in his first off-Broadway show and was a recurring character in a TV teen drama. His momentum was building, and I knew he was afraid to kill it. The worst part was that I understood where he was coming from. He had a point that was hard for me to argue with.

"I need that thing that knocks it over the line. Like a job, something like that," Ben said while pulling up a bill and handing it to the person sitting next to me.

"There will be more opportunities in film and TV there. Everything gets developed in LA, so if you want to find your way into the right rooms and meet the right people, that's where you need to be. Random auditioning isn't going to do it." I maintained my argument.

"I don't know. I think I'm doing okay." He shrugged, dismissing me. "We're trying to climb a mountain. We've made connections here, and I don't want to go back down again. You gotta go up."

"There are more ways than one to get up a mountain," I debated. I was certain I was right, but had no idea how to correlate the mountain metaphor to our choice of career with any discernible path.

"I don't know why you're so dead set on it."

"It's hard to explain, and I've tried before. I think it's that I've always been restless. It's just a feeling in my gut, and it's never gone away, you know?"

"Again, a feeling in your gut is not a solid reason for us to go." Ben side-eyed me while reaching for a bottle of gin. "You're not going to get magically cast in movies just because you're in LA. It's not like the city is going to know you're there and be like, 'Oh! Ellie McCain? We've been waiting for you!' It's going to take the same hard work that it takes here. If you're not willing to put in the work, it doesn't matter where you are." Ben shook his head.

"Ben, I put in the work." My head flew backward. I was offended.

"No, I know. That's not what I mean."

"I'm writing almost every day." My back stiffened.

"So let's take one of your scripts and make something. Let's do it here, because we know people here and we can get it done here. Who do we know in LA?"

Ben and I never fought. Ever. We battled playfully and debated each other all the time, but we never fought. I felt myself shrink. "I don't know, Ben . . . But I feel like we're living a lot of *your* life right now, and not a lot of mine."

"We're living *our* life, Ellie. New York is working. You might need to be a little more realistic."

I sat back in my seat, at a loss for words, overcome with a feeling I had tried to run from before.

Now I looked over at Ben inside the psychic's blindingly white foyer-turned-office. Hannah's energy changed beside me as we all waited to hear Ben's reaction to the psychic's reading. The rain was battering the windows, and Ben's smile twisted.

"Sun and palm trees, huh?" Ben said to the psychic. "I think you're holding the wrong hand for that one." He tilted his head toward me. "That's this pretty girl over here."

The psychic opened her eyes and stared right through me into the back of my head. "No. It's not her. She doesn't belong in the sun."

I nodded, widening my eyes even more, feeling unnerved. "Cool. Good to know. Thank you. Should we get going?" I stood and straightened my pants.

Hannah looked at me, concerned. "Sure. But you don't want to—"

"Nope," I said curtly.

Ben paid the psychic, and we all walked out. I regretted making things uncomfortable, and my friends could sense the tension. Lucas, Hannah, and Zoë walked ahead of Ben and me, all huddled under one umbrella.

"So . . . New York it is, since you don't belong in the sun?" Ben fastened his lips together, holding back his teasing smile. I shoved him playfully, but he grabbed my waist and dropped the umbrella, soaking us. "Look at how beautiful you are in the rain."

I smiled as he bent down to kiss me in the storm.

Later that night, I woke up at one in the morning to Ben, wearing pajama pants, digging through our fridge. He was dimly lit by the Grayrock sign through our terrible curtains. He pulled out corn on the cob leftovers and bit into the cob one-handed, like it was an apple.

"Seriously?" I mumbled from my side of the bed. "Cold corn on the cob? That's your decision?"

Ben turned his head to me, with a cheeky smile. "Have you ever *had* cold corn on the cob? Delicious." He took another bite. "Why are you awake right now?"

"I don't know. Maybe the movie. Maybe the psychic. Maybe the corn. You pick." I sat up and rested against the headboard.

"What are you thinking? What's freaking you out?" Ben brought his corn with him to sit at the edge of our bed and hold the tops of my feet.

"I don't know." I adjusted my pillow.

"You don't know what you're thinking, or you don't know what's freaking you out?" Ben took another crunch.

I lifted one knee, hugging it to my body, then rested the side of my face on my knee. I looked at the vertical Grayrock sign through the crack between our curtains. "I don't know . . ."

Ben stopped eating, stretched his body so he could reach the non-kitchen area, and put the corn down. He scooted up the bed and positioned himself in the exact way I was positioned, with his face on his knee, only he was looking at me. "It's you and me, Ellie."

"Yeah." I matched the softness in his voice. My eyes lifted over his head to focus on Grayrock's glowing red *R*.

"I'll go," he said quietly.

"What?" My eyes fell back down to Ben. He was looking at me intently, searching for something, but I wasn't sure what.

"To LA. Once school is done. We'll go." Ben lifted his head, and I did the same, mirroring him, perfectly in sync with each other as we always had been.

"Ben, it's okay." I lifted my hand and gently stroked his cheek with my thumb. "You don't have to say that. You've got a lot going on right now. If it didn't work for you there, you'd always blame me, and you'd always wonder, *What if?*"

Ben pulled me toward him, and we fell into each other like converging streams into a waterfall. He lifted my arms, and I left them in the air as he took off my tank top, never taking his eyes off mine. My hair cascaded back down over my body, and he kissed my collarbone, prickling my skin with goose bumps. I closed my eyes and felt every touch, every kiss, every movement as if I needed to remember it.

Once Ben had fallen asleep, I brought my computer onto my lap and googled flights to Los Angeles, wondering, *What if?*

Chapter 25

LAS VEGAS

29 years old

HANNAH AND I WERE LYING UNDER THE COVERS IN BED TOgether, watching the day's golf highlights. The rest of the girls were hitting up a couple of blackjack tables before they came back to the room to get ready for the concert. Rory's face flashed across the screen. He was hitting a shot out from a bunker, and sand sprayed before him. His smile was wide. Steph Curry appeared to be making a joke at Rory's expense. Rory looked lighter. Happier than he had been on the clips from the day before.

"Why can't I let him go, Han? It's been so long . . . Why can't I let him go?" I asked as I watched Rory cross his lean but muscular arms, pushing his strong chest together. He had flipped his hat on backward and looked like he should have been posing for a picture rather than watching his teammate hit his ball. "I can't let things go, and it's ruined my life so many times."

My sister turned to me. "What do you mean?"

"Think about my move to LA. I decided who I was, where I would live, and what my life would look like when I was fourteen, and I couldn't let it go . . ." I bit my lip and closed my eyes. "I'm chasing the dragon."

I remembered what my parents used to say to me, how they used to worry about my never-ending quest for fulfillment. My dad was ambitious, but he became a doctor. There was an end to his goals, and a moment when he could say, "I did it." I didn't know where my end was.

"Well, sister. I don't know about dragons, but I know about Rory and why you can't let him go." Hannah kept her eyes trained on the TV. "You're a pancake."

I snorted out a surprised laugh.

"It's true. Rory's your maple syrup, and you can't scrape him off. You taste like him. You smell like him. He's in you. And I don't think you moving to LA is necessarily the reason why you and Ben didn't work out."

"Don't say that. That's not true, and you know it." It wasn't the first time my sister had implied that my lingering love for Rory was somehow indirectly responsible for my breakup with Ben.

"Maybe not, but it's certainly why you haven't found anyone else you want to be with."

"You've got to give me a break here, sissy. I haven't been a nun. I've dated, just not the right people."

"Because you compare everyone to your two great loves."

I sighed. "Listen, the moment I'm laughing to placate rather than actually laughing, I'm out. Or if we don't move through life the same way, I'm out. That's not me comparing anyone. That's just something I haven't found in LA. I know so many people who have married their partners simply because they were already together. They reached a certain age and said, 'I guess this is the person.' I don't want to get stuck in a trap where being without someone is scarier than finding the right someone." I fluffed the massive white down comforter up and tucked myself in tighter.

"The problem is, you've found two 'right someones.' Therefore, you believe that kind of connection is something natural that just happens. It doesn't. It's rare. Sometimes, you have to decide to be happy," Hannah said firmly. "Maybe you decide to be with someone because they're a good person and you can try to make yourselves right together."

"I mean, I'm not going to lie, Han, I think that sounds incredibly healthy. Is that what you feel with Brandon? Are you making yourselves right together?" I tilted my head toward my sister, and she snapped her mouth shut. I knew she wasn't entirely happy or in love with her fiancé, and wondered if she'd ever say it.

Hannah shook her head, not biting my bait. "You can't let Rory go because you know what it's like to be in love with your soulmate. You know what it's like to be with him, and you know what it's like to be without him. Not everybody knows what that feels like."

"I don't believe in soulmates."

"Says the only person I've ever known to have two." Hannah casually flipped the channels and stopped on *The Devil Wears Prada*. "I'm telling you, Ellie, you're a pancake. Ben's the whipped cream, and Rory's the syrup. You're soaked all the way through. Everyone else is just a sprinkle to you, and it's your own fault that you've decided sprinkles aren't delicious."

"You've taken the metaphor too far, Han." I chuckled.

Hannah cleared her throat to ask her next question, which she knew would be a hard one. "So, this Craig guy from work—"

"I don't want to get into it." My voice changed. I didn't want to discuss what I should and shouldn't put up with at work. I constantly had to explain myself to anyone who wasn't in the entertainment industry. I even had to give my therapist an education on basic company culture, and I was tired of making excuses for everyone's behavior to justify my own. Even Hannah and Kara didn't understand my life and choices, and I could feel the space between us grow thicker with every story I told.

"Okay, we don't have to talk about it."

"I've made my career in the entertainment industry, and I grew up on a golf course. Trust me, I can handle it," I quipped, and my sister laughed.

"Remember the time Dad said that knowing how to golf would help our careers because we wouldn't get left behind, and we could impress the men we worked with if ever a time came when they wanted to go golfing?" Hannah tucked in closer to me in the bed.

"Yes. Imagine someone saying to a ten-year-old boy that he should take up ballet in case he worked with women one day," I said, and Hannah's face pinched with her smile. "Real talk, and don't tell Dad I said this, but knowing how to golf has definitely come in handy at some super-unexpected times," I admitted through a grimace.

"Oh my god. I know. Me, too. How depressing is that?!" Hannah laughed.

We lay there for a couple of minutes, letting our giggles settle, before I decided to change the subject.

"A million years ago, Rory said he believed that there are three great loves in your life: the first love, the one that got away, and the true love. Who do you think those people are for you?" I turned to my sister, already assuming she wouldn't answer the question.

"It doesn't matter. You and I are very different, sister. Your life can be messy, and that's okay. You're allowed to be a bit of a mess. You're creative, and it keeps you interesting. But I keep my life tight," Hannah said, still watching the television. She wasn't wrong. "The biggest difference between us is that I look forward, never back."

The Devil Wears Prada flipped over to a commercial, and it just so happened to be a trailer for Ben's movie. I sighed and pointed at the TV. "It's impossible not to look back when your exes are in every direction."

"If there's the first love, the one that got away, and the true love," Hannah said, nodding toward Ben on the TV, "which one is he?"

I looked at Ben on the small screen and knew I had no idea who he was to me now, or who he would be to me in the future. I only knew who we had once been to each other. Then I thought about Rory. Then I realized I was a pancake.

Chapter 26

VANCOUVER

24 years old

BEN AND I HAD GONE BACK TO VANCOUVER TO CELEBRATE OUR birthdays. Hannah, Kara, and Jacob wanted to take us out to dinner, and Jacob suggested the Hideaway. He didn't realize I had no idea that the Hideaway was the restaurant Blair and Cameron had opened that year. We walked into the dark brewhouse and barbecue joint, which sat along False Creek in downtown Vancouver, and I tripped over my own feet, shocked to see the eldest Campbell boy greeting us with open arms.

"Blair?" I hugged him and looked at Hannah. Her eyes hit the floor so fast she could have won a world record.

"Hey, Cainey. Jacob told me you were coming to town. I got you a good table."

Jacob and Blair still lived together, and even though I saw Jacob every time I came back to Vancouver, I hadn't seen any of the Campbells in three years, since my twenty-first birthday.

Blair stretched out his hand to shake Ben's. "Hey, good to see you again, man. Although I feel like I see you every time I turn on the TV now."

Ben was starting to get real work in New York. He no longer needed a side job. He was a working actor and was even recognized on the street now and then. It was expected, but also bizarre.

"Yeah, good to see you, too. It's been a minute." Ben smiled warmly as he took off his coat.

Blair walked us to our waterfront table.

"This is *your* restaurant? It's amazing." I was flabbergasted. I had never thought about Blair as a fully functioning adult, and here he was, running his own restaurant. It was beautiful, and cool, and packed to the rafters.

"Cameron's and mine."

"Oh." My eyes flicked over to Kara. "Is Cameron here?"

"No, not tonight," Blair answered quietly. "Although word spread that you were all coming in, so . . ." Blair nodded to the bar, where Juniper's own Orson Whitlock was having a beer.

"Holy shit. I haven't seen Orson since my going-away party. This is weird."

"Good weird?" Blair asked.

"Yeah. Yes. Of course." I looked down at the large table, and there were too many seats. I knew what was happening next.

"Okay, good. Orson and I were hoping to eat with you tonight. It's just us. No other surprises." Blair crinkled his forehead, and I knew what he was implying: Rory wasn't coming. "That okay?"

"Yeah. That's awesome." I nodded, though I wasn't sure if anyone believed me.

Our table was packed with deliciousness. We had smoked rib tips with andouille sausage, pork belly burnt ends, smoked brisket, baked beans, cornbread salad, creamed corn—you name it, we had it—and after we ordered our third bottle of wine for the table, the questions started coming.

"So, how long have you two been together?" Orson asked Ben, sipping his freshly poured glass of wine.

"Three years now," Ben said confidently.

Orson nodded, then turned to me. "Think you'll ever come back?"

"To Vancouver? Um, honestly? No?" My eyes jumped from person to person around the table. "Not if I can help it."

"You could always do a green card marriage, if it comes down to it," Jacob suggested casually, as he dipped the last of the burnt ends into barbecue sauce and shoved them into his mouth. I saw Orson's eyes flick to Blair to assess his reaction, which was muted.

"Are you thinking about that? About getting married?" Orson probed.

"The thought has crossed my mind." Ben laughed softly.

"So, you live together, and you want to get married."

I wasn't sure Orson knew he was speaking his thoughts.

"Orson," Blair warned with a steady voice. He subtly shook his head, silently communicating to Orson.

Ben laughed again, this time uncomfortably. He was reading the room correctly and recognized that we were being scrutinized.

"Guys, I see what you're doing." I stepped in on Ben's behalf. "Don't grill us."

"Cains, I promise, that's not what I'm doing," Blair said genuinely, and I believed him.

"Fine, that's not what you're doing. But what are *you* doing, Orson?" I demanded. A blush crept up Orson's neck to his cheeks.

"I'm sorry to interrupt . . ." A soft, chirping voice came from behind me. We all turned to see two teenage girls with heart eyes looking at Ben. "Are you Ben Winters?"

"Um, yeah. Hi." Ben's face reddened.

"Can we get a picture with you?" The girl giggled sweetly.

Ben looked at me. I rarely saw him embarrassed, but in this moment, I could tell he was dying. Our entire table was silent as we watched Ben stand in between these two sweet young girls and have his picture taken by their mother.

"Alright, nice to meet you." Ben let out a long exhale as he sat back down, and didn't lift his head to see everyone's prying eyes.

Kara was the first person to speak. "That . . . was wild."

We all started laughing quietly.

"Does that happen a lot?" Blair asked, confounded.

"No," Ben answered quickly.

"No, but it's starting to happen every once in a while. So it's not totally unusual. It's strange, though." I laughed.

"Damn, Ben." Jacob shook his head, in awe of Ben's trajectory. "You guys moving to LA soon?"

"Um, not sure. I'm on hold for this thing, and I'll need to stick around New York if I get it." Ben pressed his hand into my thigh.

"Isn't LA your dream, though?" Orson directed his question straight at me.

Ben's face fell.

Hannah saw the ticking time bomb and stepped into the conversation, defending him. "Ben's on hold for a show with Julia Louis-Dreyfus," she bragged on his behalf.

Ben gently caressed my leg with his thumb. I smiled back, but knew it didn't extend across my face.

"Rory had his first celebrity encounter type of thing the other day, too. Did you know he's gone pro?" Orson continued the conversation.

"Yeah, I heard. Of course I heard." I nodded. It was my dad who'd told me about Rory's success, and when I first saw him flash through a random highlight reel online, my heart stopped.

"Some kid asked him to sign one of his balls. It was really cool," Orson said.

"What about you, Ellie? Any auditions lately?" Hannah flipped the conversation over to me, and I wanted to kill her.

"Oh, you didn't hear the news? I'm a regular on one of those courtroom dramas." I feigned excitement. Kara laughed. She knew where I was going with my joke. "It's called *Court of the People*. Ever heard of it? I sit in the audience." Since graduating, my acting could be summed up with four words: *Background. Talent. Featured. Extra.*

"You're too hard on yourself, Hollywood." Orson shook his head, and I saw Ben smile at Orson's old nickname for me—a nickname he recognized from reading my diaries.

"Funny, I was just gonna say the same thing," Ben agreed. "Did you hear that Ellie's an official casting associate now? She's doing film and TV and everything. They're sponsoring her visa, too, so no green card marriage just yet." Ben lifted his glass to Jacob.

"Yes, it's true." I nodded agreeably. "I'm officially aiding and abetting other people's dreams coming true, instead of my own."

Based on all the awkward glances, it appeared I was exceptionally effective at making everyone uncomfortable.

Ben covered my hand with his own, protectively. He whispered, "Don't do that. You've worked your ass off, and I'm really proud of you."

I did work my ass off, and I was working my way up, slowly but surely. But I wasn't proud. Every time Sal brought me into a casting session, he would comment on the actor's looks in some snide way. He needed to be the funniest person in the room, and that was the only way he knew how to get everyone laughing. One of the most surreal moments of my life was when I was sitting behind a table at a commercial audition, watching a young woman dance, and then had to listen to everyone talk about her body after she left.

On long, hard days, we reviewed actors' taped auditions alphabetically. If your last name was at the start of the alphabet, you had a much better chance of getting the part. Sal would scroll down the list, click on a few other names and tapes, and add them to the short list we would send to producers. But it was random. "It's fine. If they weren't good, they wouldn't have made it far enough to get their tapes in front of me," he would assure me. "There are only so many ways someone can say two lines in a throwaway scene," he promised. Sal also set timers for his emails to be sent to executives, giving the illusion that he was working all hours of the night, when I knew he wasn't, because I was. The "dream" was slowly dismantling, and I could feel New York me flaking into the air and slowly disappearing right along with it.

Ben squeezed my hand under the table.

"I know you're proud of me." I shook my head, disappointed with myself. "I'm sorry."

Blair and Orson looked at each other. They were having a separate telepathic conversation.

"Sorry if I brought the mood down, everyone," I said shyly.

"All good, sissy," Hannah insisted. She turned to address the table. "Ellie's also been writing. She's got a play that's being produced and everything," she boasted.

"No, I don't," I corrected my well-meaning sister. "I have a play that's going to have a staged reading with actors, Ben being one of them, but it's not being turned into anything."

"I didn't know you wrote plays," Blair mused.

"It's a showcase with a small audience. It's nothing." I downplayed my writing, as always.

"Doesn't sound like nothing." Jacob smiled.

"Because it's not nothing," Ben defended me against myself.

Blair's phone, which was face up on the table, lit with a notification. It was a text from Rory, but I couldn't read what it said. He lifted his phone and typed back. Orson leaned over to read the conversation, then nodded before returning to his seat.

"Sounds cool, Cains. Very New York." Blair smiled as he put his phone back on the table, face down. "I can see why you don't want to give it up." He nodded to Ben, unintentionally picking at our scab.

"What are you guys up to for the rest of your trip?" Kara asked.

"Not much. Just hanging out. Walks. Dinners. That sort of thing," I said, looking at Ben.

"You going to Juniper at any point?" Orson asked.

"No." I shook my head.

"You should come back, Hollywood. It would be fun to see you up there again." He smiled softly.

"Sometimes you can't go back. It'll never be what it was. And experiencing that with the same people, but without the magic . . . it would break my heart."

"Well, you're missed up there," Blair said quietly, and I had a sneaking suspicion he was saying one thing but talking about something else entirely.

I nodded, then turned to Ben. "Shall we?"

Ben brought my face toward his and kissed me. He softly slipped his tongue against mine. I knew what he was doing. He wanted everyone to see him kiss me. He wanted to subtly and gracefully acknowledge the underlying conversation that had gone unsaid all evening. I knew it. Ben knew it. Hannah, Kara, and Jacob knew it. They had all seen Ben and me love each other deeply for three years. But Ben kissed me right there at the table because he wanted to leave a lasting impression. He wanted Blair and Orson to understand that I'd chosen him. Not Rory.

Hannah, Kara, Jacob, Blair, and Orson got up from the table, leaving Ben and me alone. He opened his eyes and stared into mine. "Let's do it. Let's go to LA."

"Really?" I whispered, hopeful, pushing away reality. "Are you sure?"

Ben nodded. "I want to. I do. I really want to."

He kissed me again, and that's when I felt it. For one brief second, for just a flash, for one skipped beat of his heart, something happened for the very first time. Maybe it was only to himself, but Ben was lying.

Chapter 27

NEW YORK

25 years old

I WAS TRYING NOT TO WATCH RORY ON THE SMALL TV BEHIND Ben's head, but it's hard to turn away when you're watching the dreams of someone you used to know coming true. Ben and I were at Lifers, drinking wine and having appetizers. Ben was flipping through a script, memorizing lines for an audition the next day, and Rory was playing at Pebble Beach. Rory was in California.

The camera kept coming back to him. He adjusted his black Titleist hat as he stood next to his caddie and laughed. He was waiting for the other guy he was playing with to tee off, and I couldn't take my eyes off him. The feeling that had overcome me was almost indescribable. I was so happy for him. I was so proud of him. And at the same time, I was utterly and totally gutted that I was missing it. I wasn't there. For a large part of my life, I had known every thought that crossed Rory's mind. And I didn't know him anymore. A wave of grief rolled through me as I watched him laugh. I didn't know what made him laugh anymore. It used to be me.

I looked around Lifers, a bar I loved, sitting next to the person I loved, and even though neither my bar nor my person had changed in the four years I had been living in New York, there was something about it all that felt very different. It all felt bigger. Or I felt smaller. I wasn't sure which. And as I looked up at the TV, watching Rory golf, living out his dreams, I knew I didn't fit inside New York anymore. I didn't fit inside my body anymore. I didn't fit inside my life anymore.

The smell of bacon stung my nostrils the next morning. The weekend breakfast sandwich was a gesture that Ben followed through with religiously. I had loved that smell. That morning, I hated it. I looked in the mirror, and I could have sworn I saw my soul pushing out of my body. I looked out the window, and an echo of myself in the windows of the building across the street floated away from the city that I loved toward a city I had only ever dreamed of.

To me, Los Angeles was a city where black sheep found their herd, where outcasts found their place. It was a city where chasing dragons wasn't silly; it was celebrated. It was a mix of cultures and realities, a collision of people coming together, with many of them sharing the same purpose. It was a blue-collar city with big dreams and a grounding heartbeat that only Los Angelenos could understand, and I wanted to understand it, too. It was a city that didn't just call to me. It screamed.

"I'm going to LA, Ben." I couldn't even hear myself speak. I was in a daze.

"What?" Ben put his spatula down. "What are you talking about?" He turned off the small electric element and turned to face me.

"If I don't do it right now, I never will." I sat at the edge of the bed. My arms were stiff, and my hands were against my knees. My soul had already left. I saw it out the window.

Ben pressed his fingers against the side of his head, confused. "Wait. What's happening right now?" He joined me on the bed and grabbed my hand. "This isn't the plan."

"What *is* the plan?" Tears sprang from my eyes. "We said we'd go; we haven't gone. What's the plan? What am I doing? I don't know what I'm doing." I shook my head, and Ben wiped my tears.

"Whoa, whoa, whoa. Hold up. You were just in a play—"

"It was a part that my old teacher handed to me. I'm not an actor, Ben. It didn't work out for me. And that's okay. I'm okay with that." I was not okay with that.

"Yes, you are. I was there every night. You were amazing—"

"Please don't. You were there every night because you love me, not because I'm winning any awards or making any money in the shitass fifty-seat black box theater. I need to pivot, and I need to do it now." I grabbed Ben's hand from my face and brought it down to my lap. "I don't get anything out of acting when I go on auditions anymore, and that's all I do. I don't get the parts. I have seen behind the curtain. I work in casting. I know how this works. I get more out of writing than I ever did out of acting."

"So pivot. I support that. But you can write from anywhere." Ben shook his head, determined to fight me on it, but I wasn't going to listen. "What about your job? Sal's asked you to partner with him. You went from under-the-table wrangler to associate to full-blown casting director. There's huge growth there. And he's sponsoring your visa. How are you going to work in LA?"

I looked at Ben and bit my lip.

He closed his eyes and tilted his head back, answering his own question. "Have you already talked to him about moving to the LA office?"

"No, I wouldn't do that without talking to you first," I answered honestly. "But it is something he mentioned a while ago, so it's always been in the back of my head."

"I'm on hold for HBO. And we're starting to film the Amazon show next month. The timing . . ." Ben ran his fingers through his hair. "Are you breaking up with me?" He pushed his face into his hands.

I shook my head. "Of course not." Another tear slipped down my cheek.

"I literally can't leave for you right now." I could hear a sob escape through Ben's words.

"And I can't stay for you anymore. Between my writing and my job . . . Maybe I can turn it all into something. I could shift into development. There are more companies out there. There's more opportunity out there. For you, too, you know. More than half of your auditions are taped and sent to LA. This would work," I insisted.

Ben's energy dropped, and he slumped. "I'm not ready."

"I need to try, Ben. I have to. And if I'm really going to try to become a writer or a producer or . . . I don't know . . . I need to get in the room, and the best shot I can give myself is in LA."

A voice appeared in my mind and rocked through my heart. It was saying something I hadn't thought about in years. Something that finally made total and complete sense to me.

"I'm a bird," I said, choking back tears. "I feel like I'm spending my life watching everyone else fly, and I can't get off the ground. I need to try."

Ben gasped, struggling for air. "Fuck." He wiped at his face, flicking away his falling tears. "You're breaking up with me, Ellie."

"I'm not. No, I'm not," I insisted. "I love you."

"You have a life here. You have friends here. You have me."

"I know. But I don't think I have *me* here anymore." I pressed my hands over my eyes and could feel my weeping start to bubble. "I've come this far, and I owe it to myself. I'm so proud of you, Ben. You deserve it all. You deserve the world. Now I want to see who I can be, too. I've stayed here for you for so long. It's your turn, Ben. Come with me, please." I cried, knowing he wouldn't.

"I can't. Stay with me. Please . . ." Ben whispered, knowing I wouldn't.

There was something untamed howling inside of me, screaming that I wasn't finished; I wasn't there yet. If it wasn't Vancouver, and it wasn't New York, then it had to be LA. I had believed it to be true when I was a kid. It had to be true. It *had* to be.

"I can't . . ."

Ben and I spent the next two weeks loving each other, crying together, making false promises, and breaking each other's hearts. We said we would make it work long distance until we could be together again. And at the airport, we both knew deep down that it wasn't true.

Zoë came with me, and just as I had with New York, I packed my whole life into two suitcases.

As the plane lifted off from JFK, heading toward LAX, I felt a thunderous clap of fear, grief, and an overwhelming amount of intense regret. A small voice poked through the noise that muddied my mind. I wasn't sure what prompted the voice to rise from my memory, but there it was, as clear as day: *She doesn't belong in the sun.*

Chapter 28

LOS ANGELES
25 years old

ZOË AND I BEGAN OUR LIVES IN LOS ANGELES ON HER AUNT'S hardwood floor. She lived in a 500-square-foot one-bedroom apartment in Marina del Rey, and for two months, while we set ourselves up, our bodies lay in the living room while our heads slept in the kitchen.

The LA office of the casting company I worked for was vastly different from its counterpart in New York. I no longer worked in an office building, but in a small house in North Hollywood. My boss was funny and smart and took every single person she talked to as seriously as they took their craft. However, the number of times I said, "I'm not sure if we have the bandwidth to take on this project; let me circle back," was disturbing. After only a couple of months, I overheard one random manager say to an actor, "Did you not want to look skinny today?" and then follow it up with "You're a prop, sweetheart, try to make it look good," and I decided it was time to move out of casting.

If I were going to have any creative say in storytelling, I needed to work directly with producers and in development. I had a few ideas, but I wasn't going to assume anyone would listen until I proved I could make other people's ideas a reality. That meant I needed someone to take a chance on me and sponsor my visa; otherwise, I would be shipped back to Canada.

I got a job with an older independent film producer named Dan Burke, who had jet-black hair and a salt-and-pepper beard that fell halfway down his neck. His shark eyes were as alarming as his hair dye. I thought it was strange when one of his questions during my interview was "When did you realize you were pretty?" but I shrugged it off as a question from an older man of a different generation. His company had produced two award-winning films that I loved, and he was going to sponsor me. My discomfort grew when Dan opened his jacket by casually propping his hands on his hips, revealing a handgun holstered to his side during meetings. It seemed strange to me how it always magically happened when the conversation wasn't going his way, but again . . . a different generation? I didn't know what to tell myself.

Ben grew increasingly wary after I told him that Dan was encouraging his team to take yoga together at lunch.

"Is it just the women he's asking, or the men in the office, too?" Ben asked through the phone as Zoë and I were unpacking our new Beachwood Canyon two-bedroom apartment.

"I don't know. There are barely any men on our floor. It's this strange gray area where I don't know what's happening. I think he's just weird."

"Are you going to do it?" Ben asked.

"I don't know. If everyone in the office is doing it, and I'm all uptight, what does *that* look like? I don't know what to do. I don't *want* to. I don't want to get sweaty at work."

Ben groaned loudly. "I don't like this."

"Do you think *I* like it?"

"No, obviously not."

I heard a light knocking on Ben's trailer door. He was filming on location. His pilot had just gotten picked up for a full season order, and his hours were just as ludicrous as mine.

"Hold on," Ben said to me.

I heard him open the door, and a cheerful voice bouncing in the background. "I'm here to take you to set."

"Okay." Ben pressed his mouth back to his phone. "I gotta go. I'm sorry. I'll call you later on tonight, though, okay? I love you."

"Okay. I love you, too." My shoulders slumped.

Zoë pushed herself through my bedroom door and hung her body half off the frame. She held out my lucky golf ball. Her thick, dark bangs hung over her eyes, and she forced them back by blowing through her lips. "Where do you want this?" she asked.

It was the golf ball from the Women's Long Drive competition when I was a kid. It had traveled with me from Vancouver to New York to LA. It was always with me, and I had no excuse for keeping it all these years, other than that I couldn't let it go.

"Oh, um . . ." I looked around. "Maybe the car? Let's put it in the cup holder or something for the traffic gods."

"Yes. Love it." Zoë noticed that my phone was on the bed. "Where's Ben?"

"He got called to set."

"Oh, shitty." She pinched her mouth together. "Are you okay?"

I sat on my bed and threw my clothes on the floor. "Yeah. It's just . . . we haven't talked much lately, and when we do, we're in this weird dynamic. Like, I think both of our hearts are broken, but we can't say that out loud, so we say 'I love you' instead."

Zoë sat on my bed and pressed her hand into my leg.

I continued, "I just feel a bit empty right now. Sometimes it's easier to miss him than to talk to him and walk away feeling even more empty." I shook my head and closed my eyes. "I made a mistake. I shouldn't have left. I shouldn't have left him. I shouldn't have left New York. I just . . . I miss him, and I made a mistake."

"You didn't make a mistake. You love Ben, but you stopped growing in New York. Listen, Dan Burke is a dirty dick, but right now you're working on a movie that the entire world will see one day."

"I'm just an assistant, Zo." I sulked.

"You didn't break through in New York. I'm sorry, but it's the truth. You didn't make it. And you didn't in Vancouver, either. And right now, in LA, you're getting the chance. And I know it's hard. And I know people suck. And I know you're just an assistant. But you've made it into the room, Ellie. Sure, you're standing at the back, but you're in the room. This wasn't a mistake. Every choice you make is preparing you for when opportunity hits. You're smart, you're scrappy, you're good at the politics, and you have no idea where this job is going to take you. You don't know who you're going to meet along the way. You don't know who is going to read your scripts. You. Don't. Know." Zoë slapped my leg and stood up. "As for Ben, have phone sex. Get on FaceTime and shove your vagina right against that screen."

I laughed and covered my eyes with my arm, still lying on the bed.

The next time Ben and I talked, we were on the phone for only three minutes. The time after that was five minutes. The time after that, three again. We had only been apart for a handful of months, and I could feel him fading into a past version of my life, a version I was saying goodbye to and was slowly losing touch with.

I found myself cycling through a memory of a conversation I had on my twenty-fourth birthday: *Sometimes you can't go back. It'll never be what it was. And experiencing that with the same people, but without the magic . . . it would break my heart.*

Every time I spoke with Ben, the magic slipped and fell between us. It was stuck somewhere between New York and Los Angeles. I could feel myself breaking.

"What are we doing, Ellie?"

I could hear Ben crying softly through the phone. I had driven up to Mulholland Drive to look out at the cityscape below me. It was a city I had dreamed about. It was a city I had had nightmares about. I clutched my lucky golf ball in my hand and held back my tears.

"I just think we need to live the lives we've chosen," I sobbed.

By the time I was in Los Angeles for six months, the magic was gone . . . and so was Ben.

Chapter 29

LAS VEGAS
29 years old

"OH SHIT! RORY'S TEXTING!" KARA WAS HOLDING HER TOWEL against her freshly showered body when my phone lit up on the bedside table in the suite's primary bedroom.

From the bedroom's ensuite, I could hear Maddy run to her side. They were picking out their outfits for the evening while Hannah, Zoë, and I were in the bathroom, putting on our makeup.

Kara snatched the phone first and called out "What's your code?" so she could unlock the screen and read the text.

"Nine-one-seven-eight," I bellowed back. Hannah, Zoë, and I had all brought our hands down from our faces, and our eyes shifted back and forth between one another, waiting for Kara's report.

"It says, 'Hey, Ellie. It's Rory. Thoughts on Topgolf? We can grab food there, too.' "

Maddy was the first to break the prolonged silence that followed, shouting out, "Dude's probably a millionaire, and he wants to take you to Topgolf for dinner? Red flags, Ellie. Come to Gwen instead!"

Hannah snorted and brought her mascara brush back up to her eyelashes.

"Topgolf?" Zoë asked, confused. Hannah and I were sharing the mirror, and Zoë shifted over to the toilet, where she sat to apply her eye shadow. "That feels random. Like, we get it, Rory, you're a golfer."

Hannah released her laughter this time.

I shook my head, dismissing their initial reaction. "I think he's trying to be nice and thoughtful, and maybe nostalgic. I'm not surprised by Topgolf."

"Where were you the last time you saw Rory?" Zoë asked while combing and perfecting her eyelashes. Hannah kept quiet, but her eyes met mine through the mirror.

"At his dad's funeral." I plugged in my curling iron to enhance the waves in my hair, but then remembered I was going golfing and threw on my blue Dodgers hat instead.

"Oh, that's right," Zoë mumbled to herself.

"That was a rough couple of days." I dug into my sister's makeup bag to find her lipstick.

"Couple of days?" Zoë dropped her eye shadow kit down to her knees. "Why am I not remembering that? His dad's funeral lasted a couple of days?"

Hannah let out a heavy exhale, anticipating my next comment.

"The day after the funeral was the last time I talked to Ben." My body panged with the back-to-back memories, and I realized I wasn't breathing.

"Oh, shit . . ." Zoë dropped her voice. "Yeah, rough couple of days," she said quietly, remembering the series of events.

Hannah, Zoë, and I stayed quiet until Maddy hollered out excitedly, "Another text!"

My palms started to sweat. It wasn't that I was worried about what my friends thought of Rory. It was that, after all these years, I still thought about him too much.

"He said, 'Unless you have something else in mind,' with a question mark!" Kara bellowed. "He's freaking out right now that you haven't responded. I bet he's just sitting there, looking at his texts, waiting for your thought bubble."

I could hear Maddy laugh, then quietly say, "Let's write something back."

I dropped my makeup and sprinted out of the bathroom. I snapped my phone out of Kara's hands and quickly typed.

ELLIE: Topgolf @ 8. See you there.

I brought my phone back into the bathroom, leaving my meddling friends in the living room to finish getting changed so they could see Gwen Stefani in concert. My big Las Vegas night out was going to be remarkably different from theirs.

Chapter 30

VANCOUVER

26 years old

I HAD BEEN IN LOS ANGELES FOR A YEAR WHEN HANNAH TOLD ME that Rory's dad had passed away from pancreatic cancer, and the wake was going to be held at Juniper Golf Club. I felt sick. It had been five years since my twenty-first birthday. More than that, it had been ten years since I had been to Juniper. But there was no way I was going to miss being there for the Campbell brothers.

Hannah and I drove to the funeral together, our parents separately. We hid at the back of the church during the service. Mrs. Campbell, Blair, Cameron, and Rory sat in the front row. I could see Cameron continually wiping his eyes throughout the service, and Blair rubbing his brother's back. Rory was wearing a black suit, and his wild hair looked tamed. He still had loose curls, but they were controlled. He sat stoically next to his mom as she crumbled in his arms. Kara and Jacob were also at the back of the church. I knew Kara was nervous about seeing Cameron, but like me, she was going anyway.

Blair stepped up to give his eulogy, and Cameron and Rory stood by his side. They kept their eyes down as Blair spoke beautifully of his father, telling his life story within the space of five minutes.

Five minutes. You just get five minutes.

If someone were telling my life story and they only had five minutes, what would I want them to say? I knew it would never be what I actually *wanted* them to say; it would be how that sole person saw me. It would be one person, and how they felt about me, speaking for me for the last time. I dropped my eyes and could feel the walls closing in. Who in the world *really* saw me for who I was, well enough to make those five minutes count?

As Blair was finishing, Rory looked up and spotted me at the back of the crowd. I saw his dark-brown eyes soften. He took in a long, deep breath through his nose. I fastened my lips together into a small, downturned smile and tilted my head to the side. I subtly lifted my chin to silently tell him everything I could say in that moment: *Hi. I'm sorry. I'm here.*

Rory nodded ever so slightly, receiving my unspoken message. His chest lifted after another big, deep breath, and he sat back down with his mom when Blair's five minutes were over.

We pulled up Juniper's driveway and drove past the bag stand where I used to wait to get picked up. I could see the putting green off in the distance. I could see the boys having their putting competition, and Albert Davis sitting in his golf cart, looking at me. I could see Rory and me running toward the clubhouse in the pouring rain, our socks sloshing, and hear both of our dads shouting at us. I could see us in the back of the pickup truck, legs pressed against each other, sunset seeping into our pores. My entire childhood lay before me in vignettes. Everything I'd loved first. Everything I'd never have again. I let out a shaky breath.

I can do this.

Hannah and I walked into Juniper's ballroom in silence. Everything was exactly as it had been. The cherrywood floors, the cathedral ceiling, the twinkly white lights strung around the windows. A slideshow was playing on the same old projector, showing photos of Mr. Campbell throughout the years with friends and family.

Orson Whitlock was the first to notice us. He walked over, handsome as ever and dressed in a dark-gray suit. He opened his arms for a double hug. "The McCain girls have entered the building." He turned to me. "How's New York?"

"I'm not there anymore. I'm in LA now."

"No shit? Hollywood really did it." He smiled.

"Yup." I looked down and winced at Orson's old nickname for me. "I really did it."

"Yeah, you know what? Now that you say it, I think I already knew that." Orson pointed his finger, trying to remember. "I think Jacob told us you made your way out there. How long has it been? You're a movie producer now, right?"

"One year. I'm an assistant."

"Very cool. Where's Ben?"

I shouldn't have been surprised that Orson asked about Ben. The last time he'd seen me was at Blair and Cameron's restaurant for our joint birthday dinner.

My phone vibrated. Instead of answering Orson, I said, "Just one second," and popped my phone out of my pocket to see if it was anything urgent from my boss.

DAN BURKE: Where are you? I heard you're not coming in today. You're aware that we sponsor your visa.

My throat calcified before I texted back.

ELLIE: Hi Dan. I'm at a funeral. We talked about this yesterday, and you approved it. I'm on a 6 am flight tomorrow and will be back in the office by no later than 10:30.

Hannah looked over my shoulder. "Everything okay?"

"Yup, all good," I replied curtly, locking my phone and putting it back into my pocket.

"Where are you these days, Hannah?" Orson turned to my sister.

"I'm in Kits." Hannah was in an apartment close to the beach, and she had vowed never to move again.

"Me, too!" Orson's face brightened.

"We should get together." Hannah smiled.

"I'd love that." As Orson poured himself a glass of water from one of the buffet tables, Blair approached us and warmly put his arm around Orson for a side hug.

"Blair." Hannah's eyes started watering.

Hannah and Blair's history was kept very private, but I knew enough to know that there was a lot of love between them.

Blair opened his arms for a hug, and Hannah fell into them. "I'm sorry," she said as he smoothed her hair and kissed the side of her head.

"Thanks for coming," he said quietly. He then looked at me while still sealed in his hug with Hannah. "Good to see you, Cains."

"I'm sorry, Blair."

Orson and I decided to give my sister and Blair some privacy.

"Do you know if anyone else is coming?" I didn't want to ask Orson outright if Caleb Davis or his dad planned on coming, but I hoped he could somehow read my mind.

"I don't know," he answered, then immediately changed the subject back to his favorite topic. "So, I see that Ben is sort of famous now. How's that going? How are you doing?"

When will it end?

My phone dinged again.

"Excuse me." I pulled out my phone.

"Ellie!" Kara called out and waved me over to her and Jacob. They were in the corner, next to the wall of windows, with our parents and a few other club members that I hardly recognized.

"Just a sec," I called back, unlocking my phone.

DAN BURKE: We're in the middle of cutbacks. You know this. I'd like to have a meeting with you tomorrow to discuss your future at this company.

I closed my eyes and let out a deep breath. I opened them again, and standing in front of me was Rory. I gasped, and stumbled to the point where he had to reach for my arm to steady me.

"Hi," he said quietly.

Instead of saying it back, I hugged him. I wrapped my arms around his head to try to hold him harder, to try to somehow melt into him. He brought his hands up my back, and his thumb trailed down my shoulder blade.

"I'm sorry," I whispered.

Rory hadn't cried in the church, but he was crying now. He placed his forehead on my shoulder and let out a sob. I closed my eyes, breathing him in, and held him tighter. I brought my hands around his neck, and my fingers stroked his hair. His wet face buried into my neck.

"Rory, I'm so sorry." I cried, too. There were many reasons why I was sorry.

I knew at least a handful of people were watching us—Hannah, Kara, Jacob, Orson, Blair, and Cameron—but I refused to let their stares hold me back. I felt Rory's lips gently press into the bottom of my neck, against my collarbone, for a soft kiss. Then, as if suddenly realizing what he had just done, he pulled his face away and pressed his fingers into my neck where he had just kissed me, wiping it away.

He whispered, "Sorry."

"Rory . . ." My eyes scanned his face. I was desperate for him to look at me like he used to.

Orson stepped toward us, breaking us apart, and patted Rory's back.

"Just give us a second," Rory said, and Orson moved away, toward Cameron.

Rory tenderly stroked my arm. I heard him catch his breath when his fingers found the rose gold bracelet wrapped around my wrist. I always wore it. I didn't even think about not wearing it. Perhaps I should have. His index finger slipped beneath the bracelet, and he gave it a small tug.

"I'm surprised to see you," he said, still staring at the bracelet, but not saying anything about it.

"I . . . I wanted to be here for you. I'm sorry if I shouldn't have come."

"I'm glad you're here. I just wasn't expecting it. It's good to see you. You look so beautiful," Rory said casually, knocking me off balance, as he pushed away the last of his tears.

"I'm so sorry, Rory . . ." I quickly flicked my tears away.

He nodded, eyes on the ground. "I know . . . How's LA?"

"Um, it's . . . You know. It's good," I lied.

"Good." He nodded.

"I've been watching . . . I've—" I stumbled through my thoughts. "Everything you've done with your career, and golf, and all of it. I'm so happy for you, Rory. I've . . . I've . . ." My lips trembled, and my voice grew weak. I bit my lip to stop myself, but I couldn't be stopped. "I've missed you," I whispered so quietly that I didn't even hear it myself.

Rory raised his tear-stained face, and his eyes finally lifted to meet mine.

"Rory?" Cameron called from the back of the room.

Rory kept his eyes on me.

"Rore!" Cameron called again, causing Rory to finally pull his gaze away. Cameron beckoned for Rory to join him and Orson.

"I should probably go." Rory's words came out with difficulty. "I'll say goodbye now, just in case I'm not able to get back to you. There's just a lot going on right now, you know?"

"Okay. Yeah, of course."

"Tell Ben I say hi." He dropped his attention to the ground again.

"Rory, I'm n—" I started shaking my head. I was about to tell him that I wasn't with Ben anymore. I hadn't been with him for six months. I didn't know where my sentence would go from there, but I knew that's where it would start.

But I couldn't start. We were interrupted when a beautiful woman with long, bone-straight black hair, wearing a knee-length, cap-sleeved black dress, stepped up to Rory. She looked familiar, but I couldn't place her. Her hand fell to Rory's.

"Your mom is looking for you," she said in the smoothest, silkiest voice I had ever heard.

Rory nodded, then looked at me, still holding her hand. His stare pierced through me, causing me to become short of breath. He didn't introduce us, and I don't think I was the only one to notice. "When are you heading back?" he asked.

"Tomorrow," I choked out.

"Well, thank you for coming. I know you're busy."

I felt sick. I felt so fucking sick I almost passed out on the spot. Did Rory think that I could ever possibly be too busy for him? In that moment, I had no idea what came over me, but I grabbed his free hand and lifted it to my face, then closed my eyes and pressed a kiss inside his palm. As I lowered his hand, his brow crinkled, and his eyes flicked back and forth between mine.

"Okay, bye." I let him go, then turned to leave Rory and his girlfriend.

Across the ballroom, Hannah was looking back at me with a sad smile. She mouthed, *Let's go*. And I nodded, struggling to keep more tears from falling.

Chapter 31

LOS ANGELES
26 years old

I PARKED ALONG MULHOLLAND DRIVE AND STOOD IN FRONT OF my car, looking out at the smoggy night scene laid out before me. The lights of downtown Los Angeles, the winding curve of Highway 101, the blur of speeding cars, and the scattered homes of the Hollywood Hills were below me. Beverly Hills and Century City were to my right.

I'd left Rory and Juniper Golf Club feeling exactly the same as I had when I left them at sixteen. Empty.

When I'd gotten to work that morning, after waking up at 3 a.m. to make a 6 a.m. flight, my boss, Dan Burke, had asked me to lunch. Instead of giving me a formal performance review, as he called it, he sat me down and, over salads, asked me only one question: "Do you spit or swallow?"

My focus blurred, and the restaurant's walls and ceiling pressed against my body. My blinking was heavy and strained, as if blinking wasn't ever meant to be a reflex.

I didn't tell him to fuck off. I didn't scream or slap him. I didn't storm off or go to HR, because there was no HR at the company, or any production company I worked for. I thanked my boss for his generosity. I thanked him for sponsoring my visa and for the opportunity he had afforded me to build my résumé and learn from him. I asked him to be a reference. And then I quit my job.

I closed my eyes. I didn't know my next step. With the job went my visa, and the life I had built and fought for. I needed to immediately find a new job that would sponsor me, or I would be sent back to Canada, proving that everything I had said about myself was wrong. That nothing I believed about myself was true. None of it was real. Everything I gave up . . . everything I left behind . . . none of it was worth it.

As I stepped back into my car, my phone rang.

It was Ben.

"Hello?" My nerves darted up my spine. Ben and I hadn't talked much since we'd broken up six months earlier. It was too difficult. The distance and the air between us felt tangible, like we were separated by quicksand, and when we finally stopped struggling to grab hold of one another, we could actually breathe again.

"Hey," Ben said quietly.

"What are you doing? It's . . ." I looked at my phone to see the time. "It's two in the morning for you."

"I wanted to talk to you."

"Are you okay?" I didn't know where to look, so I fixed my stare through the windshield on the stream of red and orange rear car lights streaking the freeway beneath Mulholland's overhang.

"I'm okay . . . I got a movie. Kind of a big one."

My pulse picked up. "What? Really?"

"Yeah. It hasn't been announced, and I had to sign an NDA, but I'm going to Atlanta for four months," he said as if he didn't know how to feel about it.

"Wow, Ben. Wow."

"Yeah," he whispered with uncertainty. "There was no one else I wanted to tell."

The silence between us had substance. I could taste it.

"How's LA?" he eventually asked.

"Not great." I couldn't be honest with Rory, but I could be with Ben. Ben already knew the answer.

"No? What's going on?"

"Just a bad day at work." I felt myself splinter.

"Dan?"

"Yeah." I knew it would take only one more knock against my broken glass for me to shatter completely, but I somehow managed to keep myself together. I pulled the phone away from my face for a brief moment and covered the microphone, trying not to get caught catching my breath. He caught me anyway.

"Don't let them break you, Ellie. That's not who you are."

I nodded and tugged on my lips, trying to stop them from trembling. "Show 'em I'm not someone they can fuck with, right?" I looked up at my stained car ceiling, trying to keep my tears in place.

"That's right. You're Ellie Fucking McCain. You took ninety-fourth place in the Women's Long Drive when you were fourteen, goddamn it."

I wanted to laugh, remembering the first time Ben tried to pump me up, back when we were just friends. A sob slipped out instead.

"Why didn't we get married? Why didn't we do that?" He let his words linger, then softly said, "I wanted to marry you, Ellie."

I pressed my hand over my mouth and nose. I couldn't breathe. My focus blurred through my tears. I looked out at the Los Angeles skyline, and I saw my life split in two. I saw everything I was running toward, and everything I'd left behind. I saw everything I wanted, and everything I hated. I saw all my dreams, and everyone I'd sacrificed for them.

I closed my eyes, dropped my hand, and whispered, "I wanted that, too."

His inhale was jagged. "Come back . . ."

"I want to." Silent tears poured down my face. "Come to me."

I knew he wouldn't leave New York, and he knew I wouldn't go back. I didn't know what in my life or my career I was still fighting for in Los Angeles, but I knew I wasn't done fighting. Zoë had been right. Within a year, I had found more opportunities and built a more extensive network in LA than I could ever have imagined in New York. And Ben's career was thriving there. He'd been right, and he was turning into exactly who I'd always known he would be. He couldn't chance messing that up. His life was too big. He was too close. The only thing I had in New York was him. And the only thing he had in LA was me.

"I want to." His voice was quiet.

My heart cracked open. Ben knew me better than anybody. He was a dreamer, like me. He still knew what made me tick, because it made him tick, too. We were the same. I couldn't go back to New York, and Ben couldn't come to LA, because we couldn't let our dreams break us. That's not who we were. It's what we loved about each other. It was also the reason we couldn't be together.

When I opened my eyes again, they landed on my golf ball sitting in the cup holder. I didn't want to admit that I thought about Rory, but I did.

I always did.

Chapter 32

LAS VEGAS

29 years old

I SHOWED UP AT VEGAS'S TOPGOLF WEARING CUTOFF JEAN SHORTS and a black T-shirt. I wondered if I'd match Rory, considering that his day-to-day uniform, including the night before at Manor House, was always some sort of black shirt and a black hat. I was wearing minimal makeup again, with a pop of lip color, and my hair was down underneath my blue LA Dodgers baseball cap.

I'd tried to beat Rory to the entertainment-venue-meets-restaurant-meets-sports-bar-meets-driving-range by showing up ten minutes early, but he was already waiting for me when I arrived. He was sitting on a small couch inside our private bay, leaning back and typing into his phone. No hat. Perfect, messy, curly brownish hair that was magically pushed away from his face. My guess is he had spent some time watching YouTube tutorials on how to tame his wild hair. He looked like he belonged on the cover of a magazine, which seemed fitting considering he *had been*, including *Men's Health*. I lost my appetite for three days when I stumbled across that issue at my local Ralphs grocery store.

Rory saw me walking up to him and placed his phone down on the coffee table, flipping it over so I couldn't see the screen. He stood, saying, "Hey." He smiled sweetly and moved around the crowded furniture.

I opened my arms, assuming we should hug. I saw him hesitate as he stepped toward me, and I regretted my life choices. He hugged me regardless. I felt every sharp point on his body poking uncomfortably into mine. I took in a deep breath, and after a moment, he did the same. His arms dropped from holding me across my back like the Tin Man and wrapped around my waist, sinking into the hug. After our bodies relaxed, I could have drowned in that hug.

I cleared my throat and pulled away after I realized too much time had passed with us in this position to be considered acceptable.

"This feels familiar." I gestured to the bay and the clubs laid out for us. "Haven't had enough golf for the day?" I knew he had already played eighteen holes for the Celebrity Pro-Am.

"Oh." He frowned. "I thought you would like this. We can do something else if you want. Do you want to go to dinner somewhere? Or we could see a show?"

I smiled. "No, no. It's just . . . all a bit surreal. You must be a big deal at a place like this, huh?" I shifted toward two Titleist bags that were set up for us. They were decked out with top-of-the-line clubs, one left-handed and one right-handed. I lifted my eyes to see Rory watching me move my hand carefully over the clubs. His eyes followed my hand, moved along my arm up to my shoulder, neck, and mouth, then flicked up to my eyes.

"No one cares that I'm here." Rory shook his head but didn't shift his stare.

"They care." I lifted my hand and pointed to the group of twenty-something guys in one of the bays beside us, all pretending not to sneak photos. "Rory Campbell!" I called out to them while popping out my thumb toward Rory. "You boys better be good, or it's gonna be hella embarrassing."

Rory swiftly moved to block my view of the guys. He clasped his hand over my pointed finger and pressed my arm down. "Well, you're still you. That's good to know." His smile dipped. "Also, 'hella'? You've been in LA way too long."

"I don't think an Angeleno has said that word in the last twenty years. It just came out of me, from some untapped darkness. I think I was possessed."

"Your voice did change into something demonic with that word only, so . . ."

"Checks out. I forgot about that time I sold my soul at Duke's in Malibu."

Our smiles lingered, and we held our stare just as the music ringing throughout the sports bar shifted to "Sweet Child O' Mine."

"Whoooooooaaa!" My eyes went wide, and my voice dropped. "Guns N' Roses? Did you do this?!"

"I did not." Rory laughed. "I guess the Devil works hard."

"Not as hard as you," I teased.

His laugh grew, and his dimple intensified beneath his scruff. "I didn't do this. If I had, I would have made them play our song, but the acoustic version to try to be subliminal about it."

"*Our* song? We had a song? Which one was that?"

He grinned. "I'm not falling for it, Cainey."

It was shocking to me how quickly we settled back into ourselves, as if no time had passed, as if our history hadn't been complicated, as if we hadn't absolutely shattered each other's hearts multiple times, as if he wasn't dating a model that he'd met on a photo shoot whom I inadvertently met at his father's funeral.

Suddenly, we were sixteen again.

"You did, though, right?" I asked. "You made them play this?" I poked my finger into his chest and was reminded by his pecs that, nope, Rory wasn't sixteen anymore.

"Give me a little more credit than that." Rory lifted out a driver from one of the bags and tipped the club head toward the other bag. "That one's yours. I took a chance that you still play with men's clubs."

"I haven't played in a long time. No joke, this is gonna be awful, but luckily, you've seen me play at my worst, so I've decided not to care." I grabbed the other driver. "Ooof. These rentals are faaancy!"

"Not rentals. I got them for you."

"What?" I spun my head around, my face flattened with surprise.

"They were free. Try not to be weird about it."

"I don't know, that's really hard for me." I smiled.

"I'm aware." He returned my smile.

Rory dropped his ball on the mat and prepared to swing. He was in his element. I could picture him as a kid, standing the same way, in the place where I fell in love with him. My throat closed. The two groups of rowdy adults that flanked us on either side were watching with their phones out. I smiled awkwardly at one of the girls next to us. When she waved, I waved robotically back, not sure how else to handle the situation. Rory hit the ball, and we heard a chorus of whistles and whoops. He then stepped away from the mat, making space for me to take his place.

Oh no. This is . . . intimidating. It's the Long Drive all over again.

I lined myself up with the ball.

Okay, calm down, Ellie. Calm down. It's just Rory. It's just a shit ton of strangers with their phones out. Calm. Down. Ellie, for the love of God, calm—

I was distracted by Rory quietly laughing to himself. He was holding his club against his chest. His smile warmed the night with nostalgia. My back straightened, and a slow smile crept across my face.

"What?"

"Nothing." He laughed again, pulling on his jaw with his hand, trying to stop himself. "Just go."

"Rory?" My voice lowered, and my eyes narrowed.

"I just . . ." He squeezed his eyes shut and let out a shaky exhale. His shoulders were shaking.

"Tell me." I shifted my stance so I was leaning against the club with one hand, and the other hand landed on my hip.

"I just . . . I know what's gonna happen." Rory's hand went to cover his eyes, exposing his perfect smile. He could no longer control his laughter.

I started laughing, too. "And what do you think is gonna happen?" I asked accusingly.

His eyes were lit up, and we shared a smile, knowing we were both thinking the same thing.

"Promise me, if you shank it, to hit the divider and not any of my twenty fans. I need that round number for my ego."

I scoffed. "Okay, Instagram-verified-three-million-followers Rory Bloody Campbell, I'll try my best not to maim or injure one of your twenty fans."

"Just don't kill anyone."

"Ha!" I squared myself to the ball, and as I swung back, I shouted, "No promises!"

THWACK!

Rory was smiling hard as he watched my ball crack down the center of the range. I got a few whoops and whistles myself. I even heard one of the guys off to the side say "sexy" to his friend.

"Alright, back off. She's with me." Rory turned to the guys, who were all laughing. He shooed them away, then shifted back to face me, and our eyes connected. My stomach dropped, and his mouth tightened. He put his hands on his hips again and shrugged, clearly not as self-conscious as I was. "Old habits."

I moved away from the mat so Rory could take his next turn. "We were never together, you know."

As I walked by, he whipped off my Dodgers hat and popped it on his head, flipping it around backward. "Yes, we were." A smile spread across his face, then he stepped onto the mat and hit his next ball.

"You can't just take my hat, Campbell," I protested playfully. I could see his body react to my calling him by his last name, something I had never done before.

"I just did, *McCain*."

"I have hat head. Our first proper hangout in eight years, and you really wanna do me dirty like that?" I plopped myself down on the couch, crossed my legs, and picked up one of the menus that were sitting on the coffee table. "Mini cheesecake balls? Jesus Christ, yes."

Rory walked to his bag and unzipped the side while simultaneously flagging our server.

A beautiful young woman dressed in a polo and a white skirt ran over to us excitedly. She pressed her short black hair behind her ear and gave us an award-winning smile. "What can I get you?"

Rory pulled out his black Titleist hat from the side of his bag. He then walked over to me and placed it on my head, pulling the rim down so it fit me perfectly.

"Apparently, cheesecake balls," he said, not acknowledging that he'd just given me his hat. He sat down on the couch opposite me. "Anything else?" He leaned back, waiting for my order, and picked up a menu himself.

"Um." I had stopped thinking. I was wearing Rory's black hat. Not only was it a hat I had paid attention to throughout my teenage years and early adulthood, but it was a hat that now had its own fan-run social media accounts. A hat I once wrote an embarrassingly atrocious poem about where I rhymed "black hat" with "flat on my back." The tight fabric wrapped around my head. It was the only thing I could feel. "Um, what?"

"Do you want the cheesecake balls?" the server asked, unaware that my brain had left my body.

Rory's brown eyes were on me, studying me over the menu.

"Oh, yes, please. And can I get . . . I don't know, a Stella or something?"

"You got it." She turned to Rory. "Mr. Campbell?"

"Please, I'm Rory. This is Ellie. What's your name?"

"I'm Tessa." Her voice trilled like a nightingale.

"Nice to meet you, Tessa. Thanks for helping us out." Rory turned back to me. "You want some buffalo chicken dip to go with those balls?"

I laughed. "A perfect pairing."

He handed the menus to Tessa. "We'll go with that, please, and I'll take an old-fashioned. And if you golf at all, you should come back and hit a couple balls after your shift, if you want."

Tessa was so flustered by Rory's offer that I was secondhand embarrassed for her. Once she was gone, my eyes shot to Rory, and my mouth hit the table.

"What?" He smiled.

"Excellent moves, my friend. I just watched her fall in love with you."

"Those weren't moves. The goal is to get us some free drinks." He laughed.

"Oh man, you're lethal!" I pointed out the women who surrounded us. "I just watched about thirty pairs of legs part for you like the Red Sea," I said.

Rory's surprised laugh had him tipping forward.

My face flushed. "Sorry. I just remembered that you don't know me anymore, and I don't know you. And we don't say things like that to each other, nor have we ever. So, I guess I can still embarrass myself in front of you after all these years. That's fun," I said sarcastically. "Thought I'd grow out of it eventually."

"You know, I wouldn't be mad if we said things like that to each other." Our smiles held before he leaned forward and threw his thumb back to Tessa, who was punching in our order. "By the way, that's gonna be delicious, but it's also gonna be a gut bomb. If I have to go to the bathroom every thirty minutes tomorrow on national television, I'm blaming you."

"You?" I scoffed. "I'm going to the pool in the morning! I had this cute one-piece lined up, but that's now impossible. Running to the bathroom every thirty minutes while peeling in and out of a wet one-piece would be a nightmare."

Rory leaned back with a sigh. "What pool?"

"Cosmopolitan. It's where we're staying. Zoë has all these hookups. We're spending the day there. I don't think it's going to be crazy busy, but it'll still be fun. What time do you tee off?"

"Eight o'clock. Although now I kinda wish I was going to the pool to watch you fight with your bathing suit."

"Listen, if you and any of your celebrity sports friends want to pop on by, I'm pretty sure I can get you in." I winked. "I mean, I'll be hiding under a towel in a cabana and terrified to make eye contact the whole time, but I'll still get you in."

Rory rolled his eyes. "Says the beauty who was dating Ben Winters. Who, by the way, has his face on a building wrap at Sunset and Vine right now!"

"Says the professional athlete who's dating a swimsuit model! Who, by the way, is a LITERAL SWIMSUIT MODEL!" I cried out teasingly. I started vigorously shaking my head. "Nope. Never mind. You're not invited. No pool party for you."

Our eyes sparkled at each other across the table. My heart thrashed in my chest.

"*Was* dating, by the way," Rory said carefully as Tessa arrived with our drinks. "I'm not seeing anyone right now." He turned to Tessa with a nod. "Thanks."

"Oh," I said quietly. "Except for Tessa," I whispered after she left, unable to concentrate knowing that Rory had gone out of his way to tell me he was single.

"Well, obviously," he whispered back with a playful grin.

I took a deep breath before asking, "Have you been broken up for a while?"

"Yeah." He tilted his head to the side, grabbed his drink, and took a sip. "I guess when your dad dies, you start to think about how you want to live your life, and who you want to live it with."

For a long moment, we just looked at each other.

"So, how do you know what's on the corner of Sunset and Vine? Do you go to LA often?" I asked.

"Every now and then." His chest rose slowly and fell heavily.

"You never wanted to call me?" The question fell from my lips faster than I expected.

"I *wanted* to call you." He kept his eyes locked on mine.

"Well . . ." I willed myself to just say the thing I wanted to say. "I wish you would have." I grabbed my drink and took a sip.

Rory's smile washed away, and the light that surrounded him

dimmed for a moment. He let out a weighted sigh. He closed his eyes and scrunched his nose, pinching his face together. I watched him shuffle through a thousand emotions within only a couple of seconds. It was as if the music had turned off and everyone around us had muted. All I could hear was Rory's deep breathing. He opened his eyes again, and they landed on mine, then moved around my face. He dipped his gaze to my mouth and then dragged it up to my hat. His hat.

He nodded at it. "That looks good on you."

I nodded back to mine. "That looks good on *you*."

Rory put his drink down, then took off my blue Dodgers hat. He thumbed it carefully, looking at it. "I remember this, you know. When we were kids, you said you'd get one. I know UCLA didn't happen, but LA did." He smiled to himself. "I don't mean this to sound condescending, so please don't take it that way, but when I heard that you actually went, I was so proud of you."

"Well," I said, my voice thick with regret, "LA hasn't exactly turned out like I hoped it would."

"Still . . . You said you would, and you did." Rory was playing with the hat, adjusting the back so it would fit his head more comfortably.

"I said and did a lot of stupid things." My chest hollowed out.

Don't cry. Don't cry. Do not cry.

"So did I." Rory's eyes pushed back up to mine. He cleared his throat, sniffed quietly, then looked back down at my hat in his hand. "You ever get that yellow Jeep?"

I took in a quick breath and shook my head. "You remember that?"

"I remember everything." He put my hat back on his head, facing forward. "I'm keeping this."

My stomach dropped. "Well, I'm keeping this." I touched the brim of his black hat and tipped it slightly downward.

"I hoped you would." His sad smile dipped.

Rory finally tore his eyes away from me and looked out at the field littered with golf balls and flags. He pressed his hands into his pants and stood up, then pulled one of the clubs from the bag he had just gifted me and said, "You're up."

Rory and I closed the place down. It was 2 a.m. We had moved to the same couch in our private bay. The entire venue was empty except for the cleaning crew and a couple of other employees and managers, who told us not to worry or rush. They promised they would kick us out when they themselves were ready to go.

Throughout the many hours that we'd been there, we'd played friendly competitions with Tessa, a few other employees, and the two parties in the bays next to us. Closest to the flag, long drive, games like that. They all loved it, and I could tell Rory was having fun, too. You would never have known he was a sports celebrity. They were strangers, but he was their pal, buying drinks, sharing food, telling inside jokes that developed over the course of the night. It reminded me of how popular Rory was at his prom. Everyone loved him. He was kind, funny, thoughtful, fun, and easy to love.

Rory had his arm draped over the back of the couch. It wasn't around me, per se, but it was certainly behind me. I had my legs curled into my stomach and was turned toward him, with my head in my hand. My elbow was dangerously close to touching his outstretched arm.

"Do you think you'll stay at your job?"

"Ugh." I hung my head. "I really don't know. My boss, Ken Caplin, is an icon, and he's kind and respects me. He's like a mentor, which I never thought I'd have. And the kind of shows he's making are exactly the kind of shows *I* want to make." I sighed. "But I take all the meetings, manage budgets, help with contracts, coordinate logistics with production managers, work closely with editors, writers, and the studio, and put out all the fires. Truly, the list goes on and on. I can't turn my phone off, ever, because I'm always on call. I'm essentially a producer, but I don't have the title or make the money. So I think part of me is biding time until I meet someone who'll recognize what I do and poach me. Or I'm waiting for Ken to give me a promotion, which I don't think is coming. He's happy with how things are. It's hard, because Ken is . . . different from a lot of other people I've worked for." I swallowed, not wanting to dig any further into that powder keg. "But I feel like I don't quite know how to crack him. I don't know if he's testing me or what."

Rory put his feet on the coffee table, which was still littered with empty glasses and plates of half-eaten food. "How quickly did you stop acting after moving to LA?"

"I figured out before I moved that I wanted to go into development. I was writing a lot. I guess that's the truth of it," I admitted. "I want to write. I want to be a writer. Everything else is just happening along the way."

Rory's eyes softened as he took in my words. "Yeah, Blair told me you wrote a play when you were still in New York. Have you been writing this whole time?"

"Yeah, I guess. It's always been there. I don't think you know this—I don't think anyone knows this—but my mom tried to get something of mine published when I was around twelve. But that was just unrealistic-overly-enthusiastic-mom behavior. The diaries have always been a thing, and I've twisted and fictionalized them, turning them into stories and scripts. I would miss auditions because I didn't want to stop writing." I smirked. "I guess I like the feeling of being somewhere else."

Rory let a small smile slip through his lips.

"What?" I asked.

"Nothing. Déjà vu." He pressed his finger into my knee. "So, you've written stuff based on your diaries?"

I laughed. "I mean, it's not literal, it's not *based on*, but it's inspired by, I guess. Oh god . . ." I closed my eyes with anticipation. "I know what's coming next."

Rory chuckled, keeping his finger poking into my knee. "What am I going to ask?"

I narrowed my eyes at him. "Are you in anything I've written."

His smile grew. "Am I?"

I looked to the ceiling, took a moment to consider my options, then decided to be honest. "You're in everything I write," I admitted. Rory looked at me and blinked. I could tell he was stunned. "Everyone I've ever loved is. You, Ben, Hannah, Kara, Zoë, Lucas, Blair, everyone. It's a nugget of a real thing that happened, or a real feeling I had. All the people and feelings get mixed together, so it's never inspired by just one thing or just one person, but you're all in there somewhere . . . everywhere. You're everywhere, Rory. So, yeah, it's kind of real, but also not at all. Kind of like me." I smiled meekly, but I could feel my voice shaking as I finished my thought.

Rory looked at me. He removed his hand from my leg. "Ellie, when I said that you weren't real, and that we weren't real, the night before you moved away . . ." He let out a deep breath. I waited, letting Rory say what he needed to, even though I didn't need to hear it anymore. He closed his eyes and put his palms together, twisting them in two different directions. "That night and everything that followed . . . it completely altered the course of my life. I can trace everything back to that moment." Rory opened his eyes again and pressed his mouth together. "I'm sorry."

"I forgave you a long time ago." I placed my hand gently on Rory's leg. "Though I've had a harder time forgiving myself. I'm not sure if I ever said I'm sorry for everything I did, too, and all the hurt I caused, but I am. I'm very sorry, Rory. I have a lot of regrets. I made a lot of mistakes." I pushed out a quick breath, trying to release the tension. I lifted my hand. "The good news is, if you can trace everything back to that night, then maybe our disaster is the reason you have the spectacular life you have today. You're welcome." I smiled.

"It hasn't been that easy for me," he said quietly, then straightened his body and cleared his throat. "We can get into that another time. But right now, it's late, and I'm so absolutely screwed for tomorrow. I should really get going."

"Okay. Yes, totally." I stood, adjusting my jean shorts and my new black Titleist hat. I looked at my phone for the first time all night. I had forty-seven unread text messages from my Lover Ladies text thread.

"Wait, your tee time is eight o'clock? Rory, it's two thirty! How did that happen? Did you know that happened?"

"Yes, I knew that happened." Rory stood beside me, and somehow managed to sling both golf bags over his shoulders. "If I'd wanted to leave, I would have." I reached for my bag, but he twisted his body and pulled out his phone to order me an Uber.

"Let me carry my bag," I argued, knowing he would fight me on it.

"No." He took a step away from me and walked toward the exit. "Are you leaving tomorrow?"

"No, we're off on Monday. One more night celebrating Zoë. You?"

"Well, I was supposed to take off after I play in the morning, but . . ."

"But?" My heart leapt into my throat.

Rory grinned but kept his attention forward as we stepped into the Vegas late-night heatwave. "But do you think I could tag along tomorrow? Would the birthday girl mind?"

"I think she would be okay with it."

Rory led the way to the rideshare line and flagged down the black Tesla that he called for me. After storing my golf bag in the car's trunk, he opened the door and leaned in to talk to the driver. "I'm Rory. You're going to the Cosmopolitan, right?" Rory confirmed with the driver then opened his body to me, giving me space to get into the car. "Can you please text me when you get into your room? Just so I know you're safe?" he asked me.

"Okay." My voice was thicker than usual as I stepped toward the open door. Rory nodded. He kept one hand on the door and placed the other on the roof, trapping me in the small space between the Uber and his arms. We weren't touching, but I could still feel him, and I wondered if he could feel me.

If this were a date, this would be where he kissed me good night. Or pressed his hand into my stomach, pushing us both into the car, and came back to my hotel room. But this wasn't a date. I saw his eyes flick down to my mouth, and I couldn't help but bite my bottom lip. He smiled. We were both thinking the same thing.

"Good night, Ellie." He let out a slow breath when his eyes lifted back to mine. His hands gripped the car door tightly before he released his hold and stepped back, giving us distance.

"Good night, Rory." I smirked, and he let out a silent, awkward yet self-aware laugh.

"I'll see ya." Rory stepped back onto the curb.

I gave him a small wave and ducked into the Uber. Once I closed the door, I finally let myself breathe again.

When I got back to the room, Hannah, Kara, Zoë, and Maddy were all up, waiting to hear every salacious detail of my night. I entered the suite carrying my new golf bag with my new high-end clubs, and wearing Rory's black hat, and the silence was palpable.

"Nothing happened."

"Bull. Shit," Maddy stated emphatically.

After that, no one believed me, and everyone lost their minds.

The next morning, as we were getting ready for the pool party, I flipped the television to the sports channel. My heart expanded so violently I could feel it in my neck when I saw Rory teeing off on the ninth hole. He was wearing my bright-blue Dodgers hat.

Chapter 33

LAS VEGAS
29 years old

THE POOL PARTY AT THE COSMOPOLITAN WAS SO LOUD AND SO surprisingly crowded, it was a miracle we were all able to sit together. Well, not a miracle, since we paid out our asses to make sure it happened, and Zoë had to pull some strings. We opted out of hanging out in a cabana or sectioned-off booths. We wanted to be *in* the party, not watching it from the sidelines.

It was scorching hot, and we each had a drink in our hands. Zoë and Kara were dancing in the middle of the pool, while Maddy, Hannah, and I were lying out in lounge chairs that had us half in and half out of the pool.

The text from Rory came around three in the afternoon.

RORY: Hey, are you here?

I squinted at my phone, confused. *Huh?* My eyes lifted, and I did a quick, stealthy scan of the pool.

"What's up?" Maddy asked.

"It's Rory. He's asking if I'm here."

"If you're where?" Maddy shouted over the music. She leaned toward me from her chair, looking over at my phone.

Hannah raised her sunglasses to her forehead and turned her head to see what was going on.

ELLIE: Hey. You must be tired. We're still at the pool.

RORY: Cosmopolitan? Where are you?

I bolted upright and felt immediately nauseous. "He's here."

Maddy and I both removed our sunglasses and twisted around, looking for Rory.

"Don't freak out, sissy. He might be looking at you right now." Hannah didn't move a muscle.

"She's right. Bring it down," Maddy agreed. She and I both slowly returned to our "super-casual" lounging positions.

ELLIE: I'm on one of the loungers in the shallow end. Look for me or Hannah. Kara's in the pool.

I held my breath when I saw the three dots pop up in our open text conversation.

RORY: I see you. Making my way over. Heads up, I'm with Orson Whitlock.

"He sees us. And he's with Orson Whitlock." I practiced some deep breathing.

Hannah straightened in her lounge chair and leaned over my phone. "Really? Orson? Oh man, Kara's going to freak out. I think he's still super close with Cameron." Hannah giggled. "I hung out with him a couple of times back home after Mr. Campbell's funeral."

"Hannah, did you sleep with him?!" I tried not to scream.

"No!" she snapped.

"Okay! Don't get so defensive! Hello, *Lucas*!" I reminded my sister of her on-and-off fling with one of my best friends in New York, whom she not-so-secretly hooked up with every time she came to visit. "Hello, *Blair*!"

"Blair and I were never a thing!" Hannah burned brightly.

"I don't believe you for a second. You two—"

"Ellie. Shut it," Hannah snapped, practically biting my head off.

I took the cue and backed down. I thought about Orson and Rory's longstanding friendship. Orson had asked about my relationship with Ben when we were in Vancouver. He'd been unusually curious at Mr. Campbell's funeral, too. Orson had been keeping tabs on me.

I placed my phone down on a small, elevated table where our drinks were and smoothed out the bottom of my bathing suit. I had switched up my suits that morning and was wearing an athletic-style black bikini set. I went to tuck my hair behind my ears and felt the hat on my head.

"Oh no. I'm wearing his hat. I look—" I was about to say pathetic, but Hannah interrupted.

"Sexy," she said sternly.

I looked over to Maddy, and she nodded in agreement. The ultimate hype women.

Somehow, miraculously, I heard Zoë shout from the middle of the pool, over the screaming crowd and the venue's thumping bass. "ELLIE! RORY'S HERE!"

I slumped down when Zoë pointed over to Rory and Orson making their way through the crowd. Rory was holding a towel and wearing navy-blue swim trunks, Ray-Bans . . . and that was it. I felt like I was going to faint. He looked like he was made of marble, wild curls flopping on top of his head. He was broad-shouldered, defined, and absolutely gorgeous. Suddenly, I remembered exactly how it felt to have him crawling up my body inside an old, cramped Jeep Cherokee and pinning me to my seat.

A couple of guys patted Rory on the back or shook his hand as he walked toward us, but for the most part, he was getting noticed more for his looks than his sports status.

Orson sent a chill through my bones as well. His hair was buzzed to about half an inch in length. He was wearing red trunks, a loose white tank top, and sunglasses. He looked like a sexy lifeguard, and I saw Zoë tracking him from the pool like a hungry bear.

I stayed seated when the boys finally made it all the way to us. I looked up at Rory through my sunglasses, and he squatted down to meet me at my level.

Jesus . . .

He looked like a volleyball player. A soccer player? A hockey player? I didn't even know. He didn't look like what you would imagine a typical golfer to look like. It was no wonder he made so much money through endorsements.

I couldn't see his eyes behind his dark sunglasses, but his mouth curled at the edges. He reached out and gently tapped the brim of my new black hat, his old black hat, with his index finger.

"Hi," he said quietly.

I matched his smile, but it was Maddy who spoke first.

"Hi, Rory. I'm Maddy. Take my seat." Maddy slipped off her lounge chair next to me and plopped herself down on Hannah's, so they were cuddled together.

"Hi, Maddy. I'm not taking your seat," Rory protested.

"Well, I'm not sitting there anymore, and I'm very stubborn. I'm also a mom. So, this is my mom voice." She turned to Orson. "Orson, is it? Feel free to take this wide-open seat that no one is using," Maddy said very loudly.

Orson looked at Rory, unsure what his next move should be, but he didn't have time to think because a guy standing behind us overheard Maddy and placed his hand on the back of the chair. The stranger shifted into position to slip his body into the seat, then looked over at me and smiled. "Hello."

"Nope. Get outta here." Rory threw himself into the seat, splashing in the water.

We all laughed as Zoë and Kara made their way over to join our own little private pool party. Kara and Hannah were excited to talk with Rory and Orson. The next couple of hours were so unnaturally natural that I found myself quieter than usual. Hannah and Rory ended up sharing a chair for a long while so they could catch up properly. Orson sat on the edge of Kara's lounger, comfortably, as though no time had passed between them. Zoë and Orson were also hitting it off, and were buying each other shots as if they were in their early twenties.

"Maddy's bachelorette was out of control." Zoë had everyone's attention as she lay on her stomach in the water, the top of her body resting on Kara and Orson's lounger. We were all sipping margaritas.

"No. *You* were out of control," Maddy corrected Zoë. "That was the night I first met Ellie."

"Oh yeah?" Rory asked.

I still couldn't tell if he was looking at me from behind his sunglasses, and I feared that my sunglasses were revealing how much I was looking at him.

"Maddy and her friends came to LA for the bachelorette, and they stayed with me and Zoë in Highland Park," I confirmed. "Zoë was the maid of honor."

"Okay, I feel like this is where it's going to get good." Orson licked the salt from the rim of his glass.

"You want to take this one?" Maddy turned to Zoë with a cocky smirk.

"Nope." Zoë laughed, then dunked her head into the water, hiding from everyone.

"Cains?" Rory asked me with a grin.

"Oof. This is . . . girl code." My head moved back and forth between all my friends. "Do I tell the story or do I not?"

"You do not." Zoë reappeared from the water. She pushed her wet curtain of dark-brown bangs back in a panic.

"Oooooo-ooo! But it's so good." I laughed.

"I'm doing it. It was my bachelorette!" Maddy stepped up to the plate, and we all cheered.

"Wait!" Zoë bellowed. "Let me preface this by saying this was two years ago. I am *not* the same person."

"Oh no." Rory started laughing before we could even get to the story. "I think you're about to take us on a ride, Maddy. Let's do this."

"Zoë had decided that since it was a bachelorette party, someone needed to have their face smacked with a flaccid dick," Maddy said matter-of-factly.

"Aghhhhhhhh!" Zoë went back under the water.

Hannah choked on her drink, while Rory clutched his chest, his stomach crunching together as he bent forward. Good lord, he was beautiful.

Look away, Ellie! He can see you!

"Since I wasn't a willing participant, nor was anyone else, surprise, surprise, Zoë offered herself up. Aaaaaanyway . . ." Maddy let out a massive sigh. "She got me an exotic dancer, which I didn't want, who showed up at two in the afternoon. We all still had our Sephora hydrating face masks on while he was dancing up on us."

"Oh my god." Orson squeezed his eyes shut, in hysterics at the visual that Maddy was painting.

"After he humped my ear, she bullied Ellie—"

"NO! DON'T BRING ME INTO THIS!" I cried.

"Too late. You're in." Kara laughed.

I looked over at Rory again and could tell he was watching me by his warm, sloping smile.

"Zoë bullied Ellie and me into asking the dancer if he could give her a little *thwap-thwap* in the face."

"Oh my god! A *thwap-thwap*?!" Hannah howled. Tears were streaming down her cheeks.

"It's the most accurate description," Maddy stated calmly. "He was . . . not pleased with us, obviously. So, the rest of the night, Zoë was chasing that D, and she ended up calling her neighbor."

"Martin is the best," I insisted. "Like, otherworldly, and in Zo's defense, he was honored to be called upon."

"After that, Martin took us to the Abbey, where he was dating one of the go-go dancers at the time, and we ended up having the best night." Maddy smiled, pleased with herself.

"More shots, anyone?" Zoë's voice had risen four octaves. I noticed she was looking everywhere but in Orson's direction. She was blushing, and Zoë never blushed.

Hannah grabbed Zoë's arm. "Let me save you, my baby. Take me to the VIP section so we can feel special." Hannah pointed toward a private, roped-off bar area on the other side of the pool. "Who's coming?"

"Me!" Kara said, as she and Orson jumped off their shared lounger.

"Me, too." Maddy raised her hand for Orson to help her stand, then turned to me. "Are you coming?"

"Nah, I'm good here," I answered.

"Rore?" Orson tipped his head back to Rory.

Rory shook his head with a soft smile. He shifted himself into the center of the lounger next to me. "I'm gonna stay."

My heart thumped in my throat, matching the bass in the music as we watched our friends leave us. My hand dangled in the water beside me. Rory was waving his hands, skimming the surface of the water, and when he reached my forearm, he gently moved his fingers down my skin. He found my hand and delicately hooked his fingers around mine. I looked over at him, still unable to see his eyes. He was looking forward, and I was unsure if he could see me until I saw the edges of his lips lift.

"So, how did it go today?" I asked, pretending my mind wasn't trapped in an eternal loop, thinking about how Rory and I were kind of holding hands.

"I'm so tired." He chuckled to himself. "I got two hours of sleep."

"Oh no! I definitely slept in." I laughed guiltily. "You want to have a quick nap? I can tell the DJ to keep it down."

"We Found Love" by Rihanna and Calvin Harris was pounding throughout the venue. People in the pool were jumping to the beat and making the water splash over the edges.

"Yeah, would you? That'd be great." He adjusted his fingers to latch onto mine a little more securely, and my heart seized. "Your friends are fun. Hannah and Kare are a given, but Zoë and Maddy . . . I really like them. Thank you for letting me and Orson hang out."

"Are you kidding? I'm so happy you're here." I allowed myself to give in to the moment. "I thought . . ."

Nope. Stop, Ellie. Too much.

"What?" Rory tugged on my fingers.

"Nothing."

"Say it."

"No, it's nothing." I shook my head.

"Too late. Say it." Rory gripped my hand like he was holding a life preserver.

I looked down at our hands. We had never casually held hands before. I shook my head, befuddled. Sure, our fingers danced around each other when we were younger. We touched and tested each other, but how had we never properly held hands before? How was that possible?

"Ellie . . ." Rory's voice softened. My eyes darted up to see a smile spread across his face, and I wondered if he was thinking the same thing. He tilted his head to the side, looking at me through his sunglasses. "Say it."

I took a deep breath. "I thought this part of my life was over. You've haunted me. You've been like a shadow for years. You were always with me, but I could never get to you."

"I know what you mean."

"I'm almost uncomfortable with how comfortable I feel. It's weird, don't you think? How normal this is?"

"It feels pretty normal," Rory said, squeezing my hand.

"It's been years, and so much has happened, and I don't know you at all anymore, but it still feels like I know you."

"You've said that twice now." Rory shook his head. "Ellie, you know me. We could go a lifetime without seeing each other, and you'd still know me. We were figuring each other out at the same time as we were figuring ourselves out. Because of that alone, you know me in a way that nobody else does or ever will."

I looked at Rory and could feel every point of contact my body was experiencing. I could feel his eyes on me. I could feel his hand wrapped around mine, and his thumb stroking my skin. I could feel the water lapping over us, and the tension in my legs as my feet pressed into the lounger. I could feel the tightness of his hat wrapping around my head and across my forehead. I could feel my wet hair sticking to my shoulders and the sweat forming in the back of my neck. It wasn't the blazing sun burning me up; I was ignited from the inside.

My phone dinged from the small table next to us that was holding our drinks. I tore myself away from staring at Rory and leaned over to find my screen lit up with a text.

> CRAIG SINICKI: How's Vegas? You at a pool right now? Cuz I'm over here thinking about how wet you are.

A sharp, stabbing pain ripped across my muscles. I dropped Rory's hand and clicked off my phone screen as fast as I could.

"All good over there?" Rory shifted his sunglasses to the sky.

"Sorry . . . Work stuff," I said, attempting to slow down my heart rate.

"Everything okay?"

"Yeah, just . . . Um—yeah. I've got some weird . . . No, I mean, it's fine." I pressed my lips together.

"You're really convincing me over here," he said sarcastically. "Do you need to go do something?"

"No. All good." I knew he didn't believe me, so I decided to change the subject. "So, are you thinking about coming out tonight, or was joining us here your plan since you didn't get any sleep?"

"I'm coming tonight. Orson, too. Is that still okay?" Rory reached over to his drink and took a sip.

I put my hands back into the water, hoping Rory would slide his fingers through mine again. I looked over at Zoë dancing in the VIP area. Her back was against Orson, and she was pushing her ass into his crotch.

"I don't think Zoë will be bothered." I laughed. "Did Orson come to Vegas to piggyback off you for a free trip, like a sneaky little devil?"

"He's my caddie. We travel a lot together."

"He is? That's amazing!" I shook my head. "I'm surprised I didn't realize that. I've been following you over the years, and I can't believe I didn't notice Orson there, too."

"Following me?" Rory smiled, and his head cocked to the side.

"You know what I mean. I've seen you on TV and online and all that. Plus, you're my dad's favorite topic. I didn't bury my head in the sand after we stopped talking." Avoidance was my usual go-to when anything in my life went awry, but I just couldn't do it with Rory. Not after Juniper and Albert Davis. Not again.

"Oh, I definitely did," Rory admitted with a laugh.

"Really?" My heart lurched.

"You were with Ben Winters. Every time I saw his face on TV, I wanted to stab myself in the eye. I saw him on one of the late-night shows. It was awful."

"Says you, my friend," I said, remembering how quietly jealous Ben would get over Rory. He never vocalized it, but he would always touch his face and start sighing when Rory came up in conversation or popped up on our TV.

Rory looked back over at me. "So, what happened there?"

"With Ben? Long distance. Things change. Life moves on. He's still a great guy, obviously. But yeah, kind of a lot happened there . . ."

"When did you break up?"

"After I moved to LA."

"Wait." Rory took off his sunglasses and put them in his lap. "Were you broken up when you came to the funeral?"

"Yeah. I'd been in LA for a year at that point, so we'd been broken up for about six months."

Rory pressed his fingers into his eyes. "Seriously?" He pushed his hand up his forehead and through his hair with a tired laugh. His head fell back into the lounger. "I . . . I can't even think about that. Why didn't you tell me?"

"Um, it was your dad's funeral? We hadn't talked in years? Cameron, Orson, and your hot girlfriend kept cockblocking us? I mean, pick your poison."

Rory's laugh died out and transformed into a sigh. "Wow . . . Well, I'm sorry about Ben, even though it was a while ago. I know you really loved him."

"I did, yeah . . . I gave Ben something inside me that I didn't know existed until I met him. He has a piece of me, and he always will, and I don't regret giving it to him."

"Do you still love him?" Rory bit into his cheek uncomfortably.

"Yeah," I answered honestly. "Unfortunately for me, it appears as though once I love, it sticks. It changes with time and all that, but it stays with me . . ."

"Did I stay with you?" Rory's question came at me quietly, but still struck me directly in the center of my chest.

Here we go.

I smiled nervously and then took a deep breath.

Four. Three.

"So, my grandma is ninety-three. She spent her life unhappily married and separated from my grandpa for fifty years. He never gave her a divorce. Now she's in a nursing home, and it's the end of her life, and she turned to my mom, out of nowhere, and told her this story about someone she used to love when she was twenty years old. She asked my mom to find him. My mom was floored. She had never even heard of this guy before. So my mom tracked him down. He's dead. And that's that. My grandma has been thinking about this person, quietly loving him, for seventy-three years."

Rory kept silent, kept watching me.

Two. One.

"I was afraid that was going to be me. I could be surrounded by a field of people . . . by everyone I've ever known, and everyone else in the world, too, and I'd still find you. I'd still only see you, Rory." I let out a soft sigh.

Rory's lips twitched into a downturned smile. "Ellie, look at me," he said softly, using the words we used to say to each other.

"No, I can't!" I cried, and he released his pent-up energy through a laugh. I threw my hands up in the air, then slammed them back down in the water. "And you were holding my hand. You've never really done that before, not like that. Now I wish you hadn't, because I'm afraid I'm going to feel your hand in mine for the rest of my life, whether it's there or not." I laughed, and Rory grabbed my hand again. He knotted our fingers together. I was feeling lightheaded. "I don't know what I'm doing right now. I don't even know how you would feel if—"

"You know how I feel," he said unwaveringly.

My eyes lifted to meet his. The warmth of his stare settled my nerves, and we both took a deep, connected breath as the music flipped over to ABBA's "Dancing Queen." The entire crowd started singing along.

I tried to keep my smile in check. "We have a lot of history and loaded emotions, and I live in LA, and you live in Vancouver, but there's always been a voice inside my head that's said maybe not tomorrow, but the next tomorrow our timing will finally work out. You have my heart, Rory. It's yours. I've let you keep it all this time, waiting for that next tomorrow." I released a massive exhale and popped out my cheeks. "So, there it is. I finally told you how I really feel. It only took me seventeen years."

Peace seemed to wash over him as he slowly shook his head, and his grin grew, tugging the edges of his lips. "I can't believe we're actually having this conversation. The music is so loud."

"I know. But at least it's 'Dancing Queen' and not 'Drop It Like It's Hot' obliterating the vibe."

Rory threw his head back with a loud laugh, clearly remembering his prom, then sighed. "I was going to propose." My heart stopped. "I mean, if we're saying the thing, then I'm going to say *the thing*."

"What do you mean, you were going to propose?" I blinked. "When?"

"When I came to New York. I had a ring in my pocket. I spent those first six months you were gone trying to figure out a way to get transferred to Columbia. I had a lot of plans. But when I saw the way you were with Ben, and the way he was with you . . . You were happy. It was a nightmare." Rory laughed at himself half-heartedly. "You had a whole life that I wasn't part of. And I knew that no matter what I did or where I was, I could never be part of it. It was . . . rough." It was Rory's turn to let out a deep exhale. "So, as I'm sure you can imagine, Blair and Cameron are *very* worried about me right now, knowing that we're talking and I'm seeing you. Cameron has tasked Orson with making sure we don't hook up."

My head was thumping from the blood rushing through my veins, along with the blaring music pumping throughout the pool. My senses were overloaded. I knew Rory was trying to make light of things, but I couldn't think. "Rory . . . You had a ring? I . . . I don't know what to say."

"There's nothing to say. I do want to acknowledge that it's nuts that we're talking about this with hundreds of people singing very loudly around us in all directions."

I let out a much-needed release of laughter, then slipped off my lounge chair and moved onto Rory's. He wrapped his arms around me, and I curled into him. "I'm sorry . . ."

"It's okay. I'm okay." He pressed his cheek into the top of my head. "I didn't tell you to make you sad or make you feel bad. I just wouldn't be okay if our whole lives passed us by and you never knew what happened." Rory took off my hat and placed it on the table beside us so he could run his fingers through my hair. He leaned his head back against the lounger. I was snug between his arm and his body. We were cuddling, and we had never cuddled before. My heart was racing, and I instinctively placed my hand over his heart to feel it thumping against his chest. I looked up and saw Hannah watching us anxiously from the VIP area across the pool.

"I meant it back then . . . I would have thrown it all away for you."

"You also meant it when you said you didn't want to," Rory gently reminded me. "I would never have forgiven myself, you would never have forgiven yourself, and you would never have forgiven me. I wanted you to build this great big crazy life with lots of love and a great career." Rory lifted his hand and rested it on top of mine. "Like you've always wanted."

I controlled my impulse to break down into tears. "It's been hard . . ."

Rory brushed the tips of his fingers along the back of my hand. "Do you want to talk about that?"

I shook my head. "No . . ." I cleared my throat and concentrated on hearing Rory's steady heartbeat through his chest. "How were you going to propose?" Maybe I shouldn't have asked, but I couldn't have stopped myself if I tried.

A sharp breath blew out of Rory's nose. "I had no plan in New York. We were twenty-one. I was going in blind and terrified. But I used to think about it a lot in Vancouver when we were younger. I liked the idea of me saying, 'Do you wanna watch a movie?' We would argue about which one, like we used to. I would give in and say, 'Well, if we can't decide, why don't we just get married instead?' I'd go from the couch to my knee." Rory gently stroked my arm with his free hand. "It's pretty juvenile and dumb, but I couldn't get it out of my head. I don't know." He laughed and pinched the bridge of his nose, squeezing his eyes shut with mild embarrassment. "I couldn't picture you liking this sweeping, grand, romantic proposal, so . . . yeah, that was it. I liked it. It felt like us. Inevitable." I had stopped moving, and Rory stilled alongside me. "What? I said too much, or you would have hated it?"

"No, that's . . . I would have liked that." I struggled to speak. I would have really liked that, and I wondered what would have happened if he had done that all those years ago.

Rory resumed lightly stroking my arm. I wanted to smile, but I tried not to cry instead.

Chapter 34

LAS VEGAS

29 years old

AFTER ZOË'S OFFICIAL GIRLS-ONLY BIRTHDAY DINNER, RORY AND Orson met up with us to go dancing. Between Zoë and Rory, we were well connected, skipped the line, and felt like kings and queens with complimentary bottle service.

"I can't believe you two went to prom together! That's so cute!" Maddy squealed. It was the most she'd had to drink since before getting pregnant, and she was determined to celebrate.

Rory's smile slipped, and before he could say anything, Zoë slapped Orson's chest and said, "Aren't Maddy's tits incredible?"

I blinked rapidly and could see Rory's face shift into a confused expression as well.

"I don't know how to answer that question. Is that a question? Are you asking me that question?" Orson shook his head and stuffed his face into his cocktail.

"Don't do it. Don't fall into the trap," Kara warned, poking her finger into Orson's side. "You'll never hear the end of it." Her voice changed into an impersonation of Zoë. "Remember when you said Maddy's tits were incredible? She had a baby and was married, you goddamn deviant. I want a divorce, Orson. You don't deserve my tits anymore!" Kara widened her eyes and looked at Orson again, sending him another warning, and we all broke into laughter, including Zoë.

"Kara, you need to let your nursing career go. You should have been the actor," I declared.

Maddy turned to Kara. "Didn't you date Rory's brother?"

"Whoa! Left field! Abort!" Kara shouted louder than necessary.

Rory shook his head while popping a bottle of champagne at the table. "Let's not go there."

Maddy then turned to Hannah, like she was taking each of us down one by one with a rapid-fire assault. "Hannah, didn't you date the other brother?"

"What's happening right now? I'm engaged, my friends." Hannah fanned herself with her hand, blinding us all with her ring.

"Are you happy about that, though?" Maddy squinted at Hannah accusingly.

"Oh my god, Maddy. Try to control yourself, or you'll be the new Kara, saying shit you shouldn't be saying," Hannah exclaimed, then tipped her chin to Rory for backup. "Right, Rore?"

"Oookay, Han, let's not go there, either." Rory poured the champagne and tried not to show anyone else the "yikes" expression he was giving me.

I chuckled softly, and Kara hip-checked me.

"Alright, I want to hear about the craziest thing that's happened since Zoë and Hollywood left New York," Orson declared, holding his drink out for Rory's pour.

"I genuinely don't even know where to start." Zoë looked over to me.

"Wait! Pause. Happy birthday, Zoë. You're an absolute knockout, smart, and funny, and I'm so happy to be getting to know you," Rory cooed with a devastating smile, knocking us all down at the knees.

Where the hell did this guy come from?!

The Rory of my childhood would never have said something so effusive and suave. He was so comfortable in his skin that I thought back to Tessa at Topgolf and all those open legs, ready and willing.

"Happy birthday, Zoë!" We clinked our glasses.

Rory winked at me before taking a sip.

"Okay, continue." Orson smiled.

"Oh, right. Well, Ellie and I were accidentally in a porn movie," Zoë stated bluntly.

"ZOË!" I scream-laughed, and buried my hands in my face, horrified.

"What?!" Rory yelled. His jaw practically hit the table.

Hannah and Kara doubled over with laughter. They loved this story and were clearly excited that Rory was about to hear it.

"Okay, fine. We don't *know* it's porn, but I'm at least eighty percent positive."

"I need more information than that." Rory laughed.

"We were booked by an extras casting agency. The only information we were given was the time and location. It was a pool hall. Anyway, these two actors . . . Wow." Zoë shook her head, dumbfounded. "There's no explanation other than they must have been porn stars. Plus, the dialogue, the scene, the lighting. It was too much. So, when the director called action, instead of quietly mumbling 'watermelon, watermelon, banana, banana,' there were twenty-five background actors all looking around suspiciously at each other and whispering, 'Are we all in a porno right now?' "

"Ha!" Maddy dabbed a tear from her eye. "I don't know this story."

"Did you leave?" Orson asked.

"No. We wanted to see how it ended." I laughed.

"Did you see them having sex?!" Rory's eyes were fiery; he was loving every minute of our ridiculousness.

"No." Zoë pulled a sad face. "Which is why I'm not one hundred percent."

"Ellie won a car on *The Price Is Right*!" Hannah jumped in.

Rory excitedly snapped his head around to me.

"Oh, and we once danced with George Clooney," Zoë added on.

"What the fuck?" Orson's eyebrows flew up his forehead.

"Yeah, but that was by accident." I tried to temper the story, which made me instantly self-conscious. I was always worried that my sometimes-seemingly glamorous LA life came across as self-aggrandizing when, in reality, nothing ever is as it seems.

"Have you ever been to the Hollywood Bowl?" Zoë then asked.

Rory and Orson both shook their heads.

"Next time you come to LA, we'll take you."

My heart leapt into my throat at the idea of a next time.

"Alright, let me think," Zoë continued. "Ellie, you want to get into any of your work stories?"

My eyes plummeted to my drink, and I felt heat rise up my neck.

"You have to tell them about the time with the construction workers," Zoë said, turning to Rory and Orson. "Ellie once had a boss who invited her into a meeting with a director, then complained about the construction noise out on the street in front of their office. He said that if she couldn't get the construction workers to stop for the duration of the meeting, she would never be a successful producer. He kicked her out in front of everyone, just for a power trip, locked her out, and would only let her back in if she got the workers to stop doing their job."

"That's so messed up." Orson's face morphed with disgust.

I couldn't look at Rory. I didn't want to even imagine what he was thinking.

"Did you get them to stop?" Orson asked.

"Um, yeah. I did." I laughed weakly.

"How the hell did you do that?" Maddy asked, baffled.

"Oh, I don't know. I got pretty good at talking myself into and out of bizarre work situations. I've had worse," I said, minimizing the story. "And my boss now isn't like that. Ken's great."

"Yeah, but don't you have to work with that Craig guy a lot?" Maddy kindly reminded me.

I gave her a poisonous glare. "Craig's fine." My voice was clipped. When I finally flipped my attention to Rory, I could see that his jaw was tense. He kept his dark eyes on me. "Alright, let's be done with this. No one wants to talk about work. We're in Vegas! Let's dance!" I took Kara's hand and led the ladies to the dance floor.

The dance floor was packed. People were pressed into each other. Drinks were sloshing about and making the hardwood floors ever stickier. All the girls were dancing together, and when Rory and Orson joined us, Rory spun me around, away from the girls and toward him.

"Hey," he said. "Is everything okay at your work?"

"All good." I shook my head and continued dancing.

"I don't know if I believe you." Rory lifted his hand to brush my hair away from my face.

"I'm okay. It's in the past. It's not that bad anymore." I took his hand into both of mine and pulled it to my lips to kiss the inside of his palm. I held my lips on him and opened my eyes, looking directly into his. I could see that my kiss surprised him. I had done this with him before, at his dad's funeral, and it surprised him then, too. My stomach collapsed, and I wondered if his had, too. "I promise you, I'm good. Now, for the love of God, Rory, dance with me."

Rory and I danced all night. We may as well have been at the club by ourselves. I would usually have been concerned about how my friends felt about me abandoning them, but every time I looked over at any of my girls, they gave me an enthusiastic look. Kara even went so far as to give me a thumbs-up. Hannah looked nervous, but I could see the light in her eyes and knew she was excited, too.

We were sweaty, and our heartbeats pumped along with the music. Our foreheads collided, and we could feel our hot, alcohol-tinged breath on each other's faces. Our hands tangled with each other as we swayed. Rory found my stomach and pushed my shirt aside in search of my bare skin. I draped my arms over his shoulders. His body pressed into mine, his chest, his hips. His hands roamed me openly and fearlessly. The music raged, and we felt every beat thrumming through us.

Rory tugged me all the way in to him and placed his forehead on my shoulder. Still bouncing to the music, I became a time traveler. I had felt him in this exact position so many times in the past. I could see us as teenagers on a couch, I could see us at prom, in his car, in New York, at his father's funeral. Back in the club, I could feel him breathing on my bare shoulder. Then I could feel him pressing his lips into my shoulder. He gently lifted my arm as the music carried us away. He moved his mouth down my arm and kissed my bicep, the inner crook of my arm, down the soft inside of my forearm, my rose gold bracelet against my wrist, all the way to my palm, as I had done with him.

"Rory." I was breathing heavily. He lifted his dark eyes to mine and bit the top of my thumb. "What are you doing?"

I might have said it out loud, but it also might have been in my head, because before I could think straight, or think at all, Rory brought his other hand to the back of my head and dug his fingers into my hair. His mouth landed on mine.

My heartbeat thumped against his chest, pounded in my neck, pumped through my lips. I pushed one of my hands through his curly hair and belted my other arm around his body until there was no space between us. It was exactly like how we were in the Jeep all those years ago. It was the same overwhelming, intense desire for each other. As we kissed, we clung to one another as if my arms were his and his arms were mine. Our hold wasn't close enough; it wasn't tight enough. We needed to breathe each other in more than we needed air.

His tongue plunged into my mouth, and we ruined each other once again, right there on the dance floor. I couldn't hear our soft groans against the music, but I felt them against our sweaty skin.

We both stopped to take a breath and held each other's hungry, desperate stare. Rory was a drug to me. I craved him. He was my center of gravity, and my life had been pulling toward him since before I even knew him. It was just like the first time I ever saw Rory Campbell. A steady knock had been rattling inside me, waiting for something to be let in, and when Rory and I finally connected, the quiet knocking stopped.

I brought our lips together again, and he pressed his hands into my ass, lifting me like he owned me, like I was his to grab, like I was his to take. My legs wrapped around him, binding to his waist. He spun me around, moving us away from the dance floor, until my back landed against a wall.

His hands dragged up my rib cage, pulling on my sticky skin, pushing up my shirt. My back pressed into the wall as his one arm moved around my waist. He held me tightly while his other hand slipped beneath my bra. Our kissing was feverish.

His thumb grazed over my nipple, and he squeezed, pulling out from me an unexpected moan that reverberated against his mouth. He groaned back, still squeezing my breast, and started sucking roughly on my neck.

"Wait, Rory." My heartbeat was thumping louder than the music, throbbing against the top of my head.

He pulled back, immediately stopping. "What? What's wrong?"

"People can see us." I couldn't control my shock as I sat perched on his hips.

"I don't care. Ellie, I don't fucking care." He put his mouth back on me. His tongue pressed into my salty skin as he kissed me hard along the underside of my jaw. He bit into my neck, marking me up just as he had once before. His hand moved from my breast, down my side, and back to my ass, where he held me against the wall. He brought me down his body, then thrust against me, hitting me perfectly between my legs.

"Oh my god," I gasped. Thank the good Lord I was wearing pants, because had I been wearing a skirt or a dress, things could have gotten out of control. Although let's face it, they already had.

Rory kissed me again, holding my face with one hand, only this time I could feel him tear through my reality. My body started to contract. My skin buzzed and burned, and our electricity pulsed through me as he pushed himself hard against me once more.

"Holy shit . . ." I started shaking, feeling every sensation pull toward my center. "Wait, baby. Wait." Rory stilled, and my heart jolted up into my throat. "I can't— I can't just come in the back of a club. I . . . I . . ." My mind was spinning. "We can't do this here."

I must have been having a stroke. I had never done anything like this in my life, and there was simply no other excuse for my delirium. Other than the fact that only Rory could eviscerate my self-control. Only Rory could unravel me. Only Rory could both bring me back to life and then dismantle it entirely.

Rory's forehead fell to my shoulder again. His curls stuck to the side of my face. "Okay. Christ. Okay. You're right. I'm sorry." He was out of breath. "I need a minute."

I gathered all my willpower and untangled my legs, then slid them down his body until I was standing again. I felt Rory's labored breathing against my collarbone, his head still locked in place on my shoulder. I closed my eyes and burrowed my face into his neck, then started quietly laughing. "I'm so afraid to look at everyone. Do you think they saw us?"

Rory's solid body started to shake, matching my muffled laughter. "I hope not. I think I started humping you."

I let out a loud laugh. He might have pulled out my boob as well, but I didn't need to bring that to his attention. We kept our faces hidden in each other's bodies as we continued to laugh and catch our breath.

"Okay, let's look over at them at the same time," Rory offered, and I nodded against his neck.

"Yeah. Let's do it."

"Ready? Go." Rory lifted and turned his head, never taking his hands off my waist. He looked back at the dance floor we had moved away from.

I tilted my head to the side to look over his shoulder and opened my eyes. All five of our friends were staring at us, motionless, mouths gaping. Rory snorted, puffed his cheeks out, and dropped his head back down to hide.

I threw my hand over my eyes, unintentionally slapping my own face. "Don't make me look at them again!" I cried out with laughter.

Rory lifted his head. His eyes softened, and he peeled my hand from my face as he laced our fingers together. After a moment of just looking at each other, he said, "Do you realize you called me baby?"

I pressed my lips together, feeling my entire body heat and flush. "I . . . It just slipped out," I said quietly.

A warm smile spread across his face. "No, it didn't. We do that now."

Somehow, I knew he was thinking the exact same thing as me, at the exact same time. *We're doing this now*.

"Come on," he said softly, tipping his head over to our friends. "We've got to face them."

"Zoë's gonna say something outrageous. I know it."

"I can't wait to hear it." He laughed.

I dropped my head, then said under my breath, "Fuck me."

"I'm going to." Rory smiled as he walked backward, tugging me back to the dance floor, toward our friends.

My head shot up as my thumping heart dropped. "Rory!" I pulled on his hand, stopping him dead on the dance floor. It felt like I was malfunctioning. He wrapped his free hand around me, slipping his fingers beneath my waistband with a dangerous smile. "Is this crazy? Are we being crazy?"

"What do you mean?" He lifted my hand and kissed my palm.

"What is this?"

Rory looked peaceful, like his entire being had quieted. He slowly shook his head. "I'm not falling for it, Cains. You know what this is." He kissed my palm again, with his eyes locked on mine.

I could feel my brain start to fog, so I decided to stick to the immediate future. "Okay, but right now, in this exact moment, are we going to go dance with everyone and try not to be perverts?"

"No promises." Rory smiled devilishly, repeating my words from the night before at Topgolf.

I slammed my hand into my forehead, and Rory just laughed as he brought me over to our friends.

When we got to everyone, Zoë looked at us, wide-eyed. "I'll be masturbating to what you two just did for the rest of my life."

"Zoë!" I threw my hand up to cover my eyes again, truly mortified.

Rory moved behind me and wrapped his arms around my waist, pulling me in so my back was pressed against him. It was the first time he'd ever held me this way, but it was like we had been comfortably living in each other's personal space for years.

"And your tits? Perfection. You're giving Maddy a run for her money." Zoë dipped her cocktail napkin into her drink and dabbed her chest.

"Oh . . . my god." Rory's head fell to my shoulder, this time with a shuddering laugh. "I'm sorry."

"All good," I said, trying not to laugh with him. "I think that was happening at the same time as the humping." Rory pressed his face into my neck to try to stifle his laughter, but I could feel him shaking behind me.

"Cameron dry-humped me against a wall once." Kara jumped into the fold like a real contender. "In your house. Your games room." Kara knocked her elbow against Hannah. "Those Campbell boys, am I right?"

"I literally don't know what to say right now," Hannah said.

I crossed my arms around my stomach and folded my fingers into Rory's. He kissed my shoulder softly, reminding me that we were in this together. With his lips, I felt our lightning bolt pierce through me from my shoulder to my feet, rooting me to the ground. My back fused into his chest, and we breathed together. I wondered if we had always been in it together. Did we still have moments, even while apart, when we thought the same thing at the same time? Was the reason I could never let him go, no matter how hard I tried, because he was always "in it" with me?

"Cameron's going to be so mad at me." Orson laughed, covering his face with his hand, then scraping it over the top of his head.

"Cameron knew this was going to happen. He can deal with it." Rory stepped out from behind me, holding my hand. "Well, this has been very fun, guys, but we're gonna go."

"What?" I spun around to face him. "What happened to let's dance and try not to grope each other?"

"Baby, we're not doing that." Rory smiled, amused with himself for saying "baby" in front of everyone. He held my surprised stare.

I glanced over at my friends, and they all awkwardly looked down at their drinks, attempting to avoid eye contact. I looked back at Rory.

"They know we're leaving together," he said. "We know we're leaving together. It's time we finally leave together, Ellie."

Maddy looked up at me. "Oh wow. I'm so excited for you right now."

I couldn't blush any harder.

Rory began giving out goodbye hugs. "Happy birthday, Zoë."

I dragged my hand down my face and mouth, trying to stop myself from smiling. Or crying, maybe? I actually had no idea what emotion was about to pop out of me. I was feeling too many.

"Well, it certainly went better for you this time around, didn't it, Rory?" Zoë teased.

Rory chuckled, accepting the light ribbing.

"Wait, are we seeing you before we fly out tomorrow?" Hannah asked as she and Rory hugged.

"I'll bring Ellie back to you ladies in the morning. And I changed our itinerary when you were all at dinner, so Orson and I are on the same flight as you now."

"You guys are in first class, aren't you?" Kara sulked.

Rory lifted his shoulders, his response a mix of "oopsies" and "oh well." He captured my hand again and squeezed. "Let me go settle everything up."

"No, absolutely not. You're not paying!" I interjected. This night was for Zoë's birthday, and Rory had only met her twice.

"No, Rory, don't . . ." Kara faux-whined as she mimed pulling out an invisible wallet from her purse, making Hannah and Maddy laugh.

"No way," Zoë argued alongside me. "These are my contacts; you need to let me show face here."

"Zoë, forgive me and forget it, because this isn't a negotiation. You're the birthday girl. I'll be right back." Rory gave my hand a quick kiss before jogging to the bar to try to flag down our table's host.

My heart was expanding and pressing into every other organ in my body.

Once Rory was gone, Hannah looked at me, wearing her big sister hat. I could tell she was balancing a few precarious emotions. Elation, fear, worry—I could see them all behind her gray-blue eyes. "Be careful, Ellie." She tapped my chest, right above my heart. "I'm worried about this little ticker of yours."

"Hannah, it's Rory." I still wasn't fully processing the weekend.

"Exactly."

"I'm okay, sissy." I hugged my sister, then turned to Orson. "It was so good to see you, Orson." I hugged him, but could feel his trepidation.

"Wait. Hannah, I know you're worried about your sister's heart. I get that. But I'm worried about Rory's, and Cameron and Blair will kill me if I don't at least say something." Orson turned to me. "Ellie, I know he's hurt you, but you've hurt him, too. Rory's been in love with you since you were kids, and even after everything that's happened between you two, he still is. It took him a long time to find himself after you moved away. Don't hurt him again."

Everyone was quiet.

"I won't."

Rory jogged back up to the group, oblivious as to why everyone was staring at him. "Okay, we're good to go."

Everything came into focus. My sun. My gravity. His force, pulling me toward him. My eyes inspected Rory's beautiful face. I ran my fingers across the side of his cheek, and my thumb stroked his scruff. I brought his head down to me and gently held his jaw to kiss him. He smiled against my mouth, and I pulled away to look into his dark-brown eyes.

"You're the love of my life. Only you." I said it right there, in front of everyone, as clearly as I felt it. I needed to say it, so I did.

Once the words passed my lips, they hung heavily in the air, but I didn't care. Let them hang. I had made too many mistakes. There had been too many missed connections. Too many almosts. Too many regrets. Too many times that I didn't grab the moment when my heart screamed for it, and my heart screamed for Rory.

My love for him had never gone away. It had never diminished. It had dissolved into my body. Everywhere I went, Rory was always with me, holding my heart. It felt like he was never close enough, because our bodies were always in the way. But our past, our future, our love lived inside me.

Rory looked back at me. I heard him suck in a breath and let out a short exhale. He searched my eyes and pressed his thumb into my bottom lip. "You're the love of mine. Always you." Rory's smile tugged his lips downward. He tilted his head. "Let's go."

He put his arm around my shoulder and walked us out of the club, leaving behind our friends, who were once again staring at us, gobsmacked.

Chapter 35

LAS VEGAS

29 years old

RORY AND I KISSED IN THE CAB. WE KISSED IN THE HOTEL LOBBY. We kissed in the elevator. His hands were on my face, and he leaned me against the hallway wall with his hips. He spun me against his door as he dug through his wallet to get his key card. It was as if I were having an out-of-body experience.

This was happening.

This was all really happening. Again! With Rory.

With my Rory.

I was having a difficult time believing it, even as it was literally and physically happening.

Rory pushed the door open and backed me up into the room with one hand lightly pressing against my stomach. His tongue explored mine as if he hadn't been kissing me nonstop for the last hour, as if he hadn't kissed me when we were teenagers. Even so, it felt like we had done this all before, from beginning to end, an infinite number of times, in an infinite number of ways, in an infinite number of lifetimes.

We crossed the room until the back of my legs pressed against his bed. I leaned back fluidly, and he slid on top of me just as seamlessly. He wrapped his arm beneath my body and lifted me up the bed so my head fell into his pillows.

"I'm in your bed, Rory."

Rory's mouth drifted from my lips to my neck as he mumbled, "I know. Never leave it, okay?"

"Okay . . ."

His lips fell into mine, and his hands found the bottom of my shirt. He slowly dragged his fingers up my sides, lifting my shirt over my head. My hair fell over my shoulders, and he brushed it away. He kissed my collarbone as he slipped off my bra straps, unhooked my bra, and dropped it to the floor. He sat up, and I sat with him. I watched his gaze roam my body, truly looking at me for the first time. His eyes sparkled, and his dimple creased from his small smile as I pulled his shirt over his head.

We both rose to our knees and pulled each other into a full embrace. Our bare chests and stomachs collided, mirroring our first kiss on the couch when we were only sixteen. His hands dragged along my shoulder blades, and he delicately kissed my neck. My hands slipped beneath his waistband and trailed to the front, where I unbuttoned his pants.

"I have thought about this a thousand times," he said quietly while pulling off the rest of my clothes, as well as his own.

"Me, too. In Vancouver, New York, LA . . . It doesn't matter where I've been . . ." I smiled. "I was always going to love you."

Rory leaned back and tangled his fingers in my hair. His eyes searched mine. I had never felt so willing to hand my body and life over to someone. He pressed his face into my neck and moved his arms around my body to hug me. His warm breath coated my skin. "I was always going to love you," he muttered. He lifted his head, looked into my eyes, then leaned me back on the bed. He pressed his lips into my navel and traveled down my body, landing between my legs.

"I can't believe we're doing this again," I said, breathless. "I think about that night all the time," I admitted.

"Tell me what you think about," he demanded softly.

"All of it." I sighed. "Your weight on top of me. How you felt inside me. Your mouth on me. My mouth on you . . ."

Rory once again discovered my every moan, gasp, and twitch, and a surge of tension moved through me. Our fervor and obsession with each other only heightened every time I called his name, or raked my fingers through his hair, or he held me down. I felt heavy, and my release was ruled entirely by his mouth and fingers. He smiled against my skin once I started trembling, and I lifted his face to mine.

"I want you to feel me."

Rory climbed on top of me, and our lips found each other as I guided him inside me. My body adjusted to him, stretched for him. It was as though it remembered every which way he had already been let in. As Rory filled me, he stole all the space inside me—the air in my lungs, the thoughts in my head—and the only thing I needed was more.

He pushed himself all the way in as I pulsed and contracted around him. A surge of heat overwhelmed me as Rory watched and felt me come for him. He was enraptured, smiling his quiet, soft smile, his warm eyes bouncing all over my face. He appeared in awe of how I moved, how I looked, how I sounded, how I felt.

Once my shivering subsided, he released his breath, exhaling softly. "Always you, Ellie." He brushed his lips gently over mine.

I pressed my hands into my eyes. "You can't say that."

He leaned on one arm and moved my hands from my face, still deep inside me. "Why not?"

"Because you're going to make me cry. I can't be the person who cries within seconds of having sex with you for the first time in almost a decade. That person is not awesome."

A couple of uncontrollable tears spilled down my face. Rory brushed them from my cheeks with his thumbs, and we laughed softly together until our laughter faded and we were left gazing into each other's eyes.

"I love you," he whispered.

"I love you." I kissed Rory, knowing I would never again kiss anyone else.

We started moving again as one, our bodies never leaving each other. When we eventually both started coming, he wrapped his arms around me so tightly that I didn't know where I ended and he began.

Rory and I spent the whole night together, lost in his sheets. The second time we made love was more urgent, more desperate, more everything. It was like we both needed to satiate our addiction to one another.

"My god," I huffed, as Rory pulled me in to his chest. His breath steamed the back of my neck with his steady panting.

"I feel like we should high-five after that." Rory breathed out a laugh.

I laughed as well, then lifted my hand over my head, and he happily slapped it.

Rory moved my hair away from my sweaty neck and gently turned my face toward his so he could kiss me. I twisted and shifted into the crook of his armpit and pressed my hand into his chest so I could feel his thumping heartbeat on my palm.

It was the small moments that I told myself to memorize. The sunrise glowing against his closed eyes and downturned smile. *Remember that, Ellie.* Him sitting in bed, his legs hidden in the white sheets, his chest bare, carefully picking finely diced green onions off his eggs. *Remember that, Ellie.* How he closed his eyes and tilted his head back in the shower. How the water fell from the tips of his hair and defined his curls. *Remember that, Ellie.* How he pressed my back into the cold wall, with his hand on my neck, while kissing me under the falling water. *Remember that, Ellie.* How his face transformed into sadness when I said it was time to go. *Remember that, Ellie.*

"Do you want me to throw the rest of your stuff into your suitcase?" I put on one of Rory's T-shirts. I still wasn't wearing pants, but my underwear (well, a clean pair of his underwear) was finally on, so that was a step in the right direction.

"Yeah, please." Rory was already dressed in gray sweatpants that looked like they were made for him, a white T-shirt that hugged and hung off his body, and my blue Dodgers hat. He gave me a quick kiss on the nose before going into the bathroom.

I collected every stray item in the hotel room, assuming it belonged to Rory. Rory stepped out of the bathroom, leaned against the doorframe, brushed his teeth, and watched me sit on the suitcase, trying to close it.

"You good, Cainey?" he asked with his mouth full of toothpaste.

"Yup," I grunted while wrestling with the zipper.

Leaving the toothbrush in his mouth, he came over, lifted me from the suitcase with both hands on my hips, and popped me onto the bed. He then knelt on the suitcase and zipped it closed.

"Thanks." I smiled from the bed, then put on my pants from the night before.

He tossed me a wink and went back into the bathroom to spit. When he came out again, he sat next to me. He pressed his hand into my thigh and fell backward onto the bed with a sigh.

After putting my shoes on, I fell back with him. "What are you thinking?" I asked quietly.

He turned his head so he was facing me. "Well, I'm feeling pretty bummed that I'm about to get on a plane, but I think I'm doing a good job pretending I'm okay."

I lifted my hands behind my head. "You're not regretting anything, are you?" I bit my lip and looked up at the ceiling. "Because this all feels a little spooky . . . and familiar, with last night happening and then us leaving each other this morning."

Rory sat up, his face showing immediate concern. "Regretting anything? No. Everything feels different. Everything *is* different. Why would you say that? Are you regretting anything?"

I sat up, too. "No, of course not. But we still live in different countries, and we can't pretend we don't."

He shook his head. "What are you doing right now?" I could see his eyes start to go vacant. "Ellie, you can't do this. What are you doing?"

I held Rory's face, forcing him to look at me. "I'm not doing anything. I'm scared about what you're thinking."

"Why would you be scared about what I'm thinking? What are *you* thinking?" Rory pulled my hands down from his face and interlocked our fingers.

"I think this is it for me, Rory."

"But?" Rory held his breath, concern straining his expression.

I swallowed hard. "But . . . I've tried long distance before, and it didn't work. It was awful, and heartbreaking, and if that happened with you, I wouldn't recover."

"What *we* have tried before is not being together, and *that* wasn't working. For me, *that* was awful and heartbreaking." Rory lifted my hand and kissed my palm. "I'll come to LA, you'll come to Vancouver, and I don't know when, but eventually . . . maybe not tomorrow, but the next tomorrow . . ." He smiled, recalling my words. "We'll be in the same place at the same time for the rest of our lives. So we're not *trying* anything. We're doing it. You just have to love me every day in between."

"I already do. I already have. Even when I wasn't supposed to." I shrugged. "Whoops."

Rory kissed my hand again. "Look at me, Ellie."

I let my eyes fall over Rory's face as he sat beside me, holding my hands. His brown hair curled out at the sides of my blue Dodgers hat; the honey mixed inside his dark-brown eyes flickered against the light; his subtle scruff defined his already chiseled jawline; and his freckles were scattered across his nose and the top of his cheeks. My eyes lifted to connect with his again, and my heartbeat slowed. I knew his face better than my own.

"It's me," he said. "Are you *really* worried about us not being able to make this work?"

"No."

Rory smiled, carving out his creased dimple. "Okay. Good." He stretched over me to grab his black Titleist hat from the bedside table. He placed it on my head with a loving tug, grounding me against his gentle calm. "Because this is it for me, too, you know." Rory leaned in and kissed me just beneath my ear, then stood. "Time to go, Cains." He stretched his hands to help me up, but instead of bringing me to my feet, he grabbed my waist and threw me over his shoulder.

"You can't carry me like this and drag your suitcase around the hotel lobby," I squealed.

"That's what bellhops are for." Rory left me hanging over his shoulder, picked up the phone, and called the front desk. "Hi, I'm ready to check out. Rory Campbell. Could you please send someone to grab my suitcase? I picked up a girl last night and now my hands are full of trouble."

I howled with laughter. He hung up and shifted my weight on his shoulder to pull out his wallet and toss two hundred dollars onto the nightstand.

"You're an idiot." I bit his back.

"Ow!" he cried out, before smoothing his hand over my ass, then spanking it hard with a stinging slap.

"Oh yes! A little more of that next time. What do you think? Do we have ten minutes so you can spank the shit out of me?" I teased playfully.

Rory tossed his head with a loud laugh and threw me back on the bed. He ran to deadbolt the door, tore off his hat and shirt, then jumped on top of me before I could move a muscle.

Zoë, Maddy, and I followed Rory, Orson, Hannah, and Kara's Uber to the airport. I was still wearing Rory's underwear, shirt, and black hat. The girls pressed their feet into the curb and leaned against the door of my tiny silver Toyota Yaris while I sat cross-legged on the hood. Rory, Orson, Hannah, and Kara pulled their luggage from the black SUV.

I slid down the hood as Hannah walked up first and gave us each a massive hug, telling us how much she loved us.

Kara was next. She pointed at Zoë. "I'm coming to LA soon, so we should plan something. I want to go to Palm Springs."

Zoë nodded. "Ooooh, definitely!"

Orson was next. He planted a kiss on all our cheeks, then pinched my face and gave it a light tap. "See you later, Hollywood." He grinned.

Rory gave Zoë and Maddy hugs, and when he finally made his way to me, he stepped between my legs, tugged on my hips, and pulled me into him, shooting a flare up my spine and through every nerve ending. He quietly muttered, "This is terrible."

"Yeah," I sighed, and he leaned down to kiss me.

"I don't want to go," he whispered so no one else could hear him. The busy drum of the airport dulled around us.

"Always you, Rory."

He pulled his face away and tapped the brim of my hat, then brought me in for a hug.

"So, I was thinking," I mumbled into his neck. "I did a little research this morning, and you said you've never been to the Hollywood Bowl."

"Yeah?"

"And as luck would have it, Guns N' Roses—"

He didn't let me finish. "Yes."

"Are playing there—"

"Yes," he interrupted again.

"In a couple months."

"Yes." He brought his mouth down to mine one last time.

"Okay." My heart fluttered.

"Okay," he murmured, opening his eyes and smiling against my mouth.

"Let's go, first class." Kara pulled on the back of Rory's white T-shirt, tightening it around his body and taking him away from my arms.

He walked backward, smiling, not taking his eyes off me. He adjusted his Dodgers hat, but his auburn-tinged hair still flipped out from the sides. I looked at him, and my throat closed. *Remember this, Ellie.*

Drive safe, he mouthed.

I nodded and moved to the driver's side of the car. Before I ducked into my car, I called out, "Text me when you land."

He nodded and brought his hand next to his hip, where he bent his middle finger and his ring finger into his palm, subtly telling me in sign language that he loved me. My arms were still on the roof of my car, so I flipped my wrist up, doing the same. He smiled and then disappeared into the airport.

Chapter 36

LOS ANGELES

29 years old

I WENT TO GREENSBORO, NORTH CAROLINA, TO WATCH RORY PLAY in a tournament. I brought Zoë with me so I wouldn't be sitting in the stands or walking the course alone. Orson was there as Rory's caddie, and Zoë was more than thrilled to spend some more time with him.

"Nothing's happened between you two?" I whispered to Zoë as we watched Rory make his way to the tenth tee. We were surrounded by full trees, lush greenery, and a crowd of spectators.

"Literally nothing. He slept with me in my bed last night, and I felt . . . things in the morning." Zoë's eyes went wide. "Very exciting things. At one point, I woke up in the night and he was cuddling me, but that's it." Zoë sulked as we watched Rory drive the ball. We clapped along with everyone else, then she leaned in again. "I don't think he likes me like that."

"He's looking at you right now," I noted, but Zoë still wasn't so sure. When they made eye contact, Orson turned away, putting his attention back on Rory.

"See? What was that?" Zoë asked.

"I don't know." I frowned at Orson's reaction, wishing I hadn't said anything. "He's working, though. Don't worry about it."

"Do you remember him being shy when you were young? Because he wasn't shy in Vegas. I'm getting some crazy mixed signals here."

"Yeah . . . Maybe. I really don't know, Zoë. Rory's told me that he's into you," I admitted.

"Well, can someone tell Orson that?" Zoë joked.

It was a thrill to see Rory in his element. Fans, employees, commentators, even his competitors were fawning over him. I tried to keep my distance, so as not to crowd or distract him, but every time he saw me standing at the back of the crowd, he would shoot daggers at me with his eyes, then crank his head for me to come closer.

At night, the four of us would go to dinner, and Rory would parade me around as if the night were mine, introducing me to everyone. When Rory threw out "Ellie golfs, too" to a journalist he was making small talk with, I choked on my drink, bringing up some backwashed wine into my glass.

"No, I don't." I shook my head, full blush. "I used to when I was a kid."

"She's really good." Rory winked at the journalist. "She's also a writer."

"Rory! Stop." My body curled in on itself as the journalist smiled at me. "No, I'm not."

"Yes, she is. On the record. Ellie McCain. Los Angeles. Writer."

The journalist nodded at me politely, then clapped Rory's back before wishing him luck on the tournament.

"You're crazy." I laughed, and Rory pulled me onto a nonexistent dance floor in the middle of the restaurant, where no one else was dancing and everyone was watching. A pianist was playing softly in the corner. Rory brought my hand up to hold against his chest and wrapped his other arm around my waist. "What are you doing?" I whispered as we began to sway.

"I want to dance with you," he muttered into the side of my head.

"But everyone is looking at us."

"Yeah, well . . . fuck 'em." He kissed my temple.

I looked over to Zoë and Orson, who were sitting at our table, and saw Zoë's wide smile as she watched us. I pulled back to look at Rory, and he leaned down to kiss my nose.

"What do Cameron and Blair think about all of this?" I asked, just as I noticed the journalist that Rory had been talking to snap a picture of us on her phone.

"About all of what?"

"Us."

"They're happy for me, but they're also nervous. They're worried about the distance, but I'm not, and you're not, and that's all I care about."

A few other diners joined us on the makeshift dance floor. I smiled at them before turning back to Rory. "They're just being protective. Hannah's the same way."

"Did I tell you that Jacob talked to me?" Rory laughed.

"Are you serious?"

"Yeah, he gave me a big brother, if-you-hurt-her-I'll-kill-you talk, and I had to remind him that you weren't his sister and it's not 1995. I told him you were a big girl."

"I'm sorry, did you say I was a 'big girl' or a 'bad girl'?" I joked.

Rory chuckled. "You dummy," he said lovingly, then breathed me in.

"I feel so lucky, Rory. I don't think everybody feels this way. I hear people talk about their partners, and . . . I just don't think everyone gets this. Lightning struck twice."

He was staring back at me calmly, carefully, scanning my face. "Thank you for not taking your shoes off this time . . ." he murmured.

"Back atcha." I smiled. Rory looked into my eyes, lost in his thoughts. "What?"

Rory shook his head and whispered, "Nothing."

"Well, you're looking at me right now like you want to ask me to go watch a movie with you." I narrowed my eyes at Rory, teasing him about the way he once envisioned proposing when we were young in Vancouver.

Rory squeezed his eyes shut, looking embarrassed. "I'm better than that. It will be better than that," he declared.

I put my head back on his chest, tucking our hands under my chin as we finished the song in silence.

Before Rory could lead me back to the table, he cleared his throat. "I'm going out with Orson in the morning, if that's okay. I'll slip out before you're up."

"What are you going to do?" I pressed my face into his neck.

"Just grabbing breakfast and meeting up with some of my team. But I didn't want you wondering where I was when you woke up." He tucked his chin and lightly kissed the top of my shoulder.

"Okay. But I get you for the rest of the night, right?" I released myself from my hiding spot and looked up at Rory.

"Ellie, Cainey, baby, my love . . . you are getting fucking destroyed tonight." Rory smiled wickedly. He captured my jaw, tilting my head so he could kiss me deeply, public forum be damned. Our lips slowly fell away from each other, and with his eyes still closed, he mumbled, "How'd I get so lucky?"

"Hey!" I smiled. "That's my line."

Rory kissed me softly once more. We returned to our table to find Zoë and Orson holding hands.

After Greensboro, Rory started coming out to Los Angeles almost every weekend, staying with me and Zoë in Highland Park. I showed him all my favorite places and taco trucks. We did the Hollywood sign hike. I took him to see an outdoor screening of *The Lost Boys* at Hollywood Forever Cemetery. My neighbor Martin brought him along as a substitute player for his West Hollywood dodgeball team, Fleetwood Smack, where Rory was so popular, he may as well have been King of WeHo. Martin had never been so proud to show off a beautiful new friend. Rory moved seamlessly into my American life as if he'd always been there, and I anchored into his. If he wasn't in LA, I went to Vancouver or off to wherever his golf took him.

When the Hollywood Bowl concert finally came around, we packed a picnic, wine, and blankets, and Rory finally understood what all the fuss was about. The sunset had lit the sky lavender, and the Hollywood sign sat in the hills just beyond the iconic bowl. We arrived early to sit on the bleachers and enjoy our picnic while watching the crowd filter into the world-famous outdoor amphitheater.

"This is incredible." Rory opened our bottle of wine.

"The coolest thing I've seen here was a screening of *The Nightmare Before Christmas*, and the cast sang with a live orchestra to the movie. Oh! Wait, maybe not." I scanned my memory. "Maybe it was seeing Steve Martin play the banjo here."

"No wonder you don't want to come back to Vancouver."

My heart sank. I tilted my head at Rory. "When did I say that?"

Rory shook his head, clearly upset with himself. He kissed my shoulder delicately. "You haven't. Not to me. I'm sorry. I shouldn't have said that."

"Ellie?" The voice came from behind me, and my body tightened. I turned slowly to see Craig Sinicki looking at me, bemused. He was with a friend, and they were taking their seats six bleachers below us. I let out a slow, deep breath, and could tell from Rory's shift in position, moving closer to me, that he could feel my energy change.

"Hi, Craig." I forced out a smile.

"Guns N' Roses? I never would have pegged you." He let out a smarmy smile as he ran his fingers through his blond hair. "Who's this?"

"Craig, this is my boyfriend, Rory. Rory, this is Craig. We work together."

"Well, she works for me." Craig reached his hand out to shake.

Rory looked down at the hand, not wanting to accept the pleasantry but doing so anyway.

"I don't work for you," I said flatly, then turned to Rory. "Craig is the showrunner for one of the shows Marie Street produces. The writers' room is in the same building as us. So our paths are always crossing." I nodded. Hopefully, that was the end of the conversation, and we could all go on our merry way.

"Well, apparently, we have a complicated relationship that we're still trying to figure out. Ellie, you can set me straight later." Craig laughed with his friend.

Goddamn it.

"Excuse me?" Rory said, his jaw hardening. His hand stopped gently skimming my back, and he pressed his palm into the side of my hip, scooting me closer to his body.

"I'm just messing around. Ellie's one of the good ones."

I stiffened and pressed my lips together tightly.

"We have a lot of fun together, right, El?" Craig winked and then sat down with his friend, turning away from us to face the stage.

Rory moved his hand from my hip to around my shoulder. "What was that?" he whispered into my ear.

I barely shook my head, silently communicating with him to please drop it.

"Do you want to go?" He lightly brushed his lips against my temple.

I turned toward Rory. "No, I absolutely do not want to go. I— I . . ." I stumbled.

"I don't like the way he was talking to you, Ellie."

"I know." I closed my eyes and nodded. "I didn't like it, either . . . Okay, give me a second. I need to collect my thoughts." Rory waited, watching me. I could see the concern growing behind his eyes. "I know that in Vegas, when Zoë brought up my work, there were some alarm bells for you." I shook my head, changing my mind. "I don't think I want to get into this right now."

Find your words, Ellie.

"It's been a long, hard road, Rory."

"I know that." Rory knew that my job demanded my time, and that my work-life balance was essentially nonexistent, with often sixteen-hour days and being on call for my boss twenty-four hours a day, seven days a week. But he didn't know the whole story.

"It's complicated, but I like the company I work for, which is a first.

Ken is amazing, even though I'm not technically a producer yet. But that's okay." It wasn't okay.

"You are a producer. Maybe you don't have the title, but that's what you are. And you're a writer. You think I'm not with you when you wake up in the night because you need to write or you won't be able to sleep? I'm with you, Cains. I know you've been through a lot to get to where you are—"

"No, you don't, Rore. You don't know." I started to tear up.

Keep it together. Why am I about to cry?

"But I'm okay, okay? I am. Craig Sinicki and his stupid games are nothing. I've had worse."

Rory chewed on his lip, thinking. He slowly put his hand in my lap, holding mine. "Ellie, you saying that you've had worse is like a nightmare for me because I don't know the bar that's been set . . . You've said that before, and I don't know what it means." His face was washed with worry. "I want to know everything, including the long, hard road. You could describe what your shit looks like at this point. I'm not going anywhere."

I laughed softly as a tear slipped down my face, surprising me. I palmed it away. "Okay, well, I won't do that." Rory gave me a soft kiss. My chest heaved as I breathed in as much air as humanly possible. "I've got this. I've got really thick skin—like, I'm basically all rock. I've had to learn how to be pretty tough. I can handle it." I nodded confidently.

"I know you can. But I'm gonna be here for you anyway." He brushed his thumb along my cheek. "You don't feel like a rock."

"Well," I said, smiling softly, "that's because with you, I'm an ostrich."

"No, you're not. California condor, all the way. Mate for life, baby." Rory smiled, then gave me another kiss.

"Hold up." Craig spun around in his seat, and a wave of recognition fell across his face. "Are you Rory Campbell?"

Rory's smile subsided and was replaced with a sigh. "Yeah, I am."

"That's awesome, dude!" Craig slapped his knee.

"Oh shit. The golfer?" Craig's friend perked up.

Craig stood and turned to the two people who were sitting next to Rory and me. "Do you mind switching with us so we can come up and sit with our friends? Better seats?"

My mind went blank. My breath shortened, my skin tingled, and I was chilled even though I had started sweating. "Oh . . . umm." I was about to stammer through a response, but Rory beat me to it.

"No, let's leave it as is. It's just us tonight. I'm sure you get it." Rory placed his hand firmly on my outer thigh so his arm draped over the front of my body like a seat belt protecting me. He was subtly putting himself between me and Craig.

"Oh, yeah. For sure. Maybe we could grab a drink after?" Craig sat back down.

"Not tonight. Enjoy the show." Rory gave them his million-dollar dimpled smile, not moving a muscle.

"Alright. El, you coming in on Monday?" Craig asked his last question.

"Yup." My voice was clipped.

Rory held the side of my thigh tighter, securing me in place and reminding me he was there.

"I'll see you then." Craig turned back around and bent down to finally settle in and start pouring their drinks.

Rory and I sat in silence for a moment before I kissed his shoulder, which was still in front of me. Rory didn't let me go for the entire concert, whether we were sitting, standing, or dancing.

Later that night, when Rory and I were in bed, I draped my leg over his and cuddled into him. I kissed his chest and pressed my hand over his heart to feel it pumping. It was my favorite thing to do while he was sleeping, but tonight he wasn't. He hummed peacefully with his eyes closed. I took a deep breath.

"I once had a boss . . ."

Okay. Here we go.

Four. Three. Two . . .

". . . make me watch porn with him."

Rory stilled and opened his eyes. His heart began hammering under my hand. "What?" he asked quietly.

"It was his birthday, and he called me into his office. He looked at his assistant and jokingly said, 'She's come in here of her own free will, right?' The assistant laughed, because what else was he supposed to do without getting fired? My boss closed the door and played a video of a naked woman with an enormous candle stuck in her asshole. The guy in the video blew it out, and my boss then asked if I would do the same." I remained calm.

I could tell that Rory had stopped breathing.

"Being Canadian, I need companies to sponsor my visa to stay in the country. So, when something like that happens, I don't do it, but I also don't feel like I can ever really do anything about it without the threat of losing my job. If I lose my job, I lose my sponsorship and my visa. Everything comes tumbling down after that. I would get deported, lose my home, country, network, career, friends. My whole life."

"Ellie . . ." Rory's voice was strangled.

"It's scary for me, because sometimes it feels like, to survive it, I need to be 'one of the good ones.' " I used air quotes, echoing Craig's line from the concert. "So I stood there, laughed, and did nothing except hate myself."

Rory clearly didn't know what to say, so he said nothing.

"Same guy," I continued, letting out a shaky breath this time. My eyes locked onto the spinning ceiling fan. "He threatened cutbacks, which, to me, meant I needed to fight for my job and everything that came with it. He called it a performance review, and for that review, the only question he asked was how I liked to give head."

Rory shot up into a seated position like a rocket. I sat up with him, holding the sheets under my armpits to cover my body.

"I quit. I was about to be kicked out of the country, but miraculously got another job, another sponsorship, with a demotion and a sixty percent pay cut, where I was bullied and publicly humiliated by a supervisor for over a year." I inhaled sharply. "It's not always like that. I've met and worked with some incredible people, but now and then someone comes along . . . There are a lot of stories, Rory."

"I don't . . . Ellie . . ." Rory was at a loss for words.

"At my job now, we used to have these development meetings, with ten or so people, sometimes more, all trying to build a show together." My heart pumped in my throat. Rory gripped my hand, anticipating what would come next. "Craig, who you met tonight, used to sit across from me at our conference table during these meetings. And he would send me emails about the very graphic, very explicit things he wanted to do to me on that table. He would sit there, hear my computer ding when I received his emails, and get off on watching me read them, silently . . . in front of everyone."

"Ellie." Rory's voice was thick.

I looked at him for the first time, and his eyes were black as night.

"So it's not that I don't want to come back to Vancouver. When I came to LA, I was running away from everyone I've ever loved. I ran, and I ran, and I ran. By the time I finally realized that no one was running with me, and that I didn't like where I was going, I was already lost."

Rory put his hand on top of mine.

Tears dropped to my cheeks. "When I first got into the water, I was just a kid going on auditions, doing what I was told in a room full of adults. I twisted myself in knots, doing whatever I could for my dreams to come true, hoping they would pick me. The water wasn't boiling then. I don't know when that happened." I moved my unfocused stare to the end of my bed, to the dresser that held my TV. Sitting on the dresser was my lucky golf ball.

"Every day, I think, 'Was it worth it?' I'm good at my job. People at home think what I do is cool. My parents are proud. But was it worth it? I lost you to New York. I lost Ben to LA. I ran away from my family and friends. Now I feel like I don't have anything if I don't have this career that I've sacrificed everything for, including myself."

Rory placed one hand over his mouth. We sat in silence. I knew his brain was turning, trying to find the right words. The whir of the ceiling fan seemed to be getting louder.

"I waited my whole life to see who I could become in Los Angeles . . . I never thought this was who I would be." I shook my head, defeated, then broke through the silence again. "They say LA will chew you up and spit you out. I feel pretty chewed, but now I just want them to fucking choke on me. I've worked too hard and I've put up with too much to let them spit me out." I closed my eyes. "That's why I'm still here. I need to prove to myself that everything was worth it."

"How are you going to do that? What do you need to feel that way?" Rory choked over his words.

"I don't know . . . My parents used to say I was chasing dragons. But I think I'm the dragon. I'm pursuing some version of myself that I've only ever caught small glimpses of and that won't ever exist. I'm the dragon, and I'm chasing my own tail."

Rory's rasp cut through the dark and quiet. He slipped his fingers under my bracelet, tying us together. "I know you might not feel this way, but when I look at you, Ellie, time stands still. I see you as you were, and as you are, and I love every version of you. If you run, I'm running with you."

I let out one more sigh, then said, "Thank you . . ." I smiled meekly, needing to stop myself from crying. "I can take a picture of my shit now, if you want." I laughed softly, but Rory wasn't laughing with me.

"I'm going to kill Craig on Monday. You know that, right?"

"Nothing has happened in over a year except for some random texts and tonight's weirdness. I need you to believe me. Most of this stuff is long in the past. I just wanted you to know about it. About me."

Rory was nodding, but I could see his brain working a mile a minute.

I twisted my fingers into his and kissed his hands. "Rory, listen to what I'm saying. I'm okay."

"Okay." Rory nodded solemnly, blinking again. Life was making its way back into his distressed expression. “Do you promise you’ll tell me if something else happens?”

“Of course I will.”

“Good, because I have a guy.”

I chuckled. “Is it Orson?”

“It is.” He matched my laughter, but his tears fell, revealing how he was really feeling.

“I can’t hide a body. I don’t have the muscles.”

“I do.” Rory’s voice lifted. He sounded more sincere than he should have.

I gently laid Rory back down onto the pillows, having forgotten that we were naked. He pulled my entire body tightly in to him, protecting me from whatever boogeyman was haunting his mind. I moved his loose curls away from his forehead and held on to the back of his head as he kissed me. I moved my legs around Rory to straddle him, but he pulled me down and wrapped his strong arms around my back, stopping me, steadying me, holding me.

“Are you okay?” I asked quietly.

He shook his head against me. I pulled away, and he looked back with wetness in his eyes.

“Just . . .” Rory wiped his face with his open hand. “Hard conversation.” He shifted me off his body, so I cuddled into him.

“I know.” I nodded. “I’m sorry.”

“I would move here for you. For us. Tomorrow. I would move tomorrow.” He left his lips pressed into my forehead.

“I know,” I whispered.

“Would you want that?” he asked carefully.

“I would.” Everything inside me hurt. I was bruised and fogged and confused. “But, Rory, I know you don’t want to be here.”

“Ellie, I would—”

“Rory, I know you don’t. And the truth is . . .” Along with my deep, shaky breath came a quiet cry that I wasn’t ready to release. “I don’t know if *I* want to be here anymore, either. I'm waiting on that next tomorrow. I just don't know when or where that is yet."

I didn't sleep all night, and I could tell he didn't, either.

Rory didn't tell me until after my workday was over that he had spent all of Monday sitting in his car on the street in front of my office, on his phone or reading a book. He promised he wouldn't do that again on Tuesday, but he did. On Wednesday, I forced him to go golfing and said I would call if anything happened. Thursday and Friday were spent entirely in bed, ordering food, watching movies, having sex, talking, laughing, falling deeper and deeper in love. When he left on Saturday to meet up with his brothers for the weekend, I cried. I cried all of Sunday, too.

Chapter 37

VANCOUVER

29 years old

WHEN I WENT BACK TO VANCOUVER FOR CHRISTMAS, I DECIDED to stay with Rory instead of my parents or sister. He had a two-story penthouse in Yaletown with floor-to-ceiling windows that overlooked the water. Flickering lights surrounding Science World's enormous globe and BC Place lit up his modern apartment. A two-story solarium sat in the corner of the main space, and his balcony had a tree that towered through the clouds. The bottom floor of the solarium was his breakfast nook, and the top floor had a small TV surrounded by pillows and an old-school DVD player. That area, where we watched movies, listened to the rain patter against the windows, and made love surrounded by the city's twinkling lights, became my favorite place in all of Vancouver. Rory told me it had taken him two years to find the perfect apartment, but he would sell it in an instant to move into my 800-square-foot, moldy Highland Park rental, with Zoë as our roommate, if I only asked.

"When does she land again?" Rory wondered.

I was in a matching pajama set, and Rory was wearing gray sweatpants and a thin white T-shirt. He was leaning against the window of the solarium, and I sat between his legs on the pillows. We had hooked up a Nintendo Switch to the TV and were battling each other on a perfect rainy morning.

It was New Year's Eve, and we had a full day of nothing planned before we went to Blair's for his annual Jingle & Mingle New Year's Eve Party. It was my first time attending, and I would have been lying if I said I wasn't nervous.

Rory had his arms around me, clutching the controller in front of my stomach, lightly jostling me with every flick of the button.

"This isn't fair, you know. I've got no movement."

"I need an edge. Just be happy I'm not bouncing up and down on your lap, distracting you that way." I smirked.

"I accept your challenge," Rory said, still focused, still playing.

I looked out the streaked window and pressed my fingers against the falling raindrops. "Zoë's getting in around seven, so I think the plan will be for me to pick her up, and we'll go straight to the party."

"Orson's not doing it?" Rory lunged forward, jostling both of us, to make some sort of move that was supposed to be impressive.

"They're not together. She's sworn up and down that he doesn't like her."

"Yes, he does! What an idiot." Rory shook his head, befuddled.

"He's super confusing. And listen, maybe I shouldn't say anything, but—"

Rory dropped his controller dramatically, lifted me by my waist, and twisted me around to face him. The look of youthful glee on his face was nothing short of beautiful and hilarious, and was exactly why I loved him. "Do you have . . . juice?" Rory dragged out his question.

I laughed and waved my hands back and forth. "Never mind. I'm not saying. I've changed my mind."

His eyes were sparkling. "Do you have any . . ." Rory tapped his forearm with three fingers, as if he needed a hit of heroin. "Hot goss?"

I fell forward, giggling into his chest. Rory's broad smile was beyond contagious. "No!" I shouted playfully. "I always give you such good gossip, and you're always shit at giving it in return. You're being punished."

"No! Don't say that!" He laughed. "I'm just bad at remembering the details."

"Rory!" My smile was a mile wide. "You didn't tell me that the reason Blair had gotten divorced was because his wife cheated on him for *months into our relationship*! That is *not* a small detail. That is the *pinnacle* of hot goss."

He laughed even louder. "I thought you knew!"

"You're terrible."

"Come on, baby. Don't do this to me. Love me for who I am." He grinned, already knowing he was going to win the battle.

I sighed, caving in, but only partially. "I'm not giving you any hot gossip about what Zoë said this trip means for her and Orson." I nodded my head toward Rory to silently communicate that her making the effort to spend the holidays in Vancouver was make or break for them.

"I see . . . I see. I see," Rory said happily. "I need to tell him to pick her up at the airport, don't I?"

"No." I nodded *yes*.

"Should I tell him to take her back to his place, so she stays with him instead of us?"

"I'm not saying anything." With my eyes wide, I nodded again. *Yes!*

"Oh, this is gonna be fun!" Rory's eyes were wild with excitement. "I'm just going to put this out there: I'm not going to be able to take my hands off you. Like, I want it. I need it." Rory squeezed my waist. "But I am going to be ignoring you the entire trip and watching them instead. You get that, right?" Rory said teasingly.

"Oh yeah. I definitely get that."

Rory met my smile and pinched my chin for a delicate kiss. "I'm so happy we're not there anymore."

I pressed my thumb against his lips. "Do you think being nothing to each other for all those years was worse than the maybe years?"

"No, I don't think so," Rory answered. "I think we became who we were always meant to be *because* we were apart. And the people we eventually turned into . . . turns out *they* were always meant to be together." Rory studied my face.

We looked at each other for an achingly long time, listening to the rain fall all around us from the solarium. Tension grew, and I wondered if Rory was about to ask me to "watch a movie with him."

He moved his hand to the back of my head, and his lips melted into mine. I shifted my body so I was sitting on top of him, and felt him smile against my mouth. He let out a soft laugh through his nose.

"What?" I asked.

"I mean . . ." His lips pulled down with a cheeky grin. "You *are* on my lap. And I *did* accept your challenge." His eyes flicked up to *Super Mario Bros.*, and I cackled, tossing my head back. I crawled backward, away from Rory, and he chased after me.

When Rory and I got to Blair's house in East Vancouver, the party was already in full swing, the place filled to the brim with people I didn't know and lit with multicolored Christmas lights. The dress code was holiday formal, and Rory was looking mouthwateringly good. He'd gone all out with a tailored tuxedo, and had slicked his hair back in a way I had never seen before. His curls were still intact, but contained. I was wearing a full-length, long-sleeved black dress that fell to my lower back. Rory had been right; he couldn't keep his hands off me.

Blair's front door opened, and his three-year-old daughter, Grace, ran to greet us. Rory dropped to his knees to hug his niece.

"Uncle Rory!" she squeaked happily. Grace was wearing a onesie, had toothpaste crusted around the edges of her mouth, and had tangled, unkempt hair, probably from trying to tie it into a ponytail herself.

"Hi, honeybee. Say hi to Ellie."

Grace turned to me and clammed up.

"Hi, Grace." I laughed. "It's okay. You don't have to say hi back."

Grace ran back into the house, and Rory let out a sigh. "I mean, come on. Is it so hard to say hi?"

"Sometimes." I shrugged as we stepped inside.

I placed our bottle of wine on the entrance table, and Rory helped me out of my jacket as Blair made his way through the crowd to greet us.

"Come in, guys," Blair called out. "Gracie! I don't want to start counting. Get up there!" Blair tossed his thumb up the stairs, then turned back to us. "It's like two hours past her bedtime. I'm gonna kill someone."

Blair had only grown more handsome, with his sleepy brown eyes and dark, wavy hair. I had no doubt that he had made a dent in Vancouver's population of straight women over the years, though Cameron had taken over that mantle once Blair finally settled down with the wrong person.

"Who's putting her to bed?" Rory shook his arms out of his coat and brought both of our coats to the hallway closet.

"She wanted Cameron."

"Well, there's your first problem." I pulled my best "yikes" face. "He's probably up there scrolling on his phone. Do you want me to help?"

"No. She doesn't like you yet," Blair said, defeated.

I slumped. "I know . . ."

Blair laughed, then pulled me in for a hug. Blair had been divorced for a year, and being a single father suited him. He dedicated his life to Grace, and his relationship with his ex was remarkably strong, despite her having cheated on him. I had always been curious about what would happen if Blair and Hannah ever spent any significant time together. My sister had called off her engagement after Vegas. She said that once she saw Rory and me together, she realized she was missing something in her life, and I always wondered if that something was Blair.

Cameron, on the other hand, was still a wild child. He hadn't had a committed relationship since Kara, nor did he want one. Cameron spent all his time at their restaurant, working and picking up women who were far too young for him.

"Alright, well, come in. You both look great. Grab some food. Jacob and Kara are here somewhere. Also, Orson brought Zoë, and apparently she didn't know she was supposed to dress up?" Blair narrowed his eyes at me.

Rory pumped his fists back and forth, excited for the drama.

"Oh shit. My bad." My heart sank for Zoë.

Blair's house was beautiful, warm, and homey. A massive, crackling stone fireplace sat at its very center, and all the rooms wrapped around it. Instead of background Christmas music, a live band was playing in the corner of the living room, and everyone at the party was taking turns as lead singer. Being a legitimate first-rate open-mic night was the Jingle & Mingle's tradition.

Kara looked stunning. She had gone back to the brown bob of her younger years, only now it looked sleek and was slicked behind her ears. Her chestnut-brown eyes popped through her mascara and bright-red spaghetti-strap dress.

Zoë, on the other hand, was wearing jeans and a tight green turtleneck. Her long dark hair was pulled into a clip, and her bangs were moving in all directions. When she saw me walking up to them, she shook her head and said, "You asshole." She sighed, then laughed softly.

I gave her a hug. "I didn't realize I didn't tell you to dress up."

"Whatever. Also, when Orson picked me up, he hugged me, but somehow his dick was still seven feet away." Zoë rolled her eyes. I tried to restrain my reaction, but I was looking forward to giving Rory that juice later. "He said he wanted me to stay with him, but I can't stomach the mixed signals. It's officially over and done with Orson. I'm not doing it anymore. I want to have fun with my girls."

"No problem. Let's go back to the original plan. You'll stay with us," I said with a quick nod.

"Ew." Kara stuck her tongue out in disgust. "Rory barely has walls. Zoë, you're staying with me."

"Yes. Okay. I like that better." Zoë pointed at Kara, accepting the offer.

All three of our phones vibrated simultaneously, and we knew it was from our Lover Ladies group chat. I grabbed my phone so we could read the text together.

MADDY: Happy New Year from the East Coast! Zoë, have you touched Orson's privates yet?

Zoë narrowed her eyes at me.

HANNAH: Happy New Year, friends. I wasn't invited to the big party and am home watching When Harry Met Sally, but thanks for the reminder, MADDY!

I had my sneaking suspicions that Hannah wasn't invited because Blair's ex-wife was. Zoë grabbed my phone, and her fingers flew.

ELLIE: Crash the party. Blair is looking foxy. Dress in something your boobs can accidentally fall out of.

I pulled my phone back from Zoë's tight grip and typed.

ELLIE: That was Zoë. Don't come. Carrie's here. Might ruin Blair's night.

Rory slinked behind me, moving his hands inside the fabric of my backless dress and inching his fingers across my bare stomach.

"What's going on over here?" He pressed a kiss into my shoulder. His thumb trailed over my belly button and down to the top of my pubic bone.

I turned my head, shooting him an accusatory look, and he grinned back at me, acknowledging our secret touching.

"Just texting the girls."

My phone dinged, and without looking at it, I showed the screen to Rory. His fingers, which had moved dangerously close to being between my legs, stilled. He pushed his mouth into my shoulder again, but he didn't kiss me this time. The muscles in his jaw rippled with tension.

"That's not the girls." His voice was low, raspy, and . . . angry?

I flipped my phone back around so I could see what Rory was looking at.

CRAIG SINICKI: Happy New Year, Ellie.

Before I could say anything, Rory growled, "I'm going to hit him."

"What's going on?" Kara leaned forward to look at my phone, confused about what made Rory so instantly furious.

"Excuse us." I moved my body free from Rory's grip and grabbed his arm, pulling him away from Zoë and Kara and toward the hearth to sit. Rory was seething and crackling as much as the fire behind us.

"It's nothing, Rory. Totally innocent," I said, trying to soothe his rage.

"It's not nothing. It's purposeful, and it's inappropriate." Rory's face was turning as red as Kara's dress.

"He's just wishing me a Happy New Year. What am I supposed to do? Call him out for being nice?"

Rory ran his fingers through his hair, frustrated. "He's not being nice, Ellie. It's him subtly reminding you that he's still around. It's manipulative, and I'm going to fucking hit him."

I touched Rory's chest as it rapidly rose and fell with his strained breaths. I locked eyes with him. My blue against his brown. My coldness against his warmth. Balancing each other out.

Just as Rory began to calm down, two women sat next to us on the hearth. "Can you settle a debate for us? Ryan Gosling or Ben Winters?"

My eyes shot to Rory, and I couldn't help but snort with laughter.

Rory looked back at me, then lifted his eyes to the women and deadpanned, "Ben Winters." He lightly shook his head, but a faint smile revealed itself against his tightened mouth.

"Ellie-Bee!" Jacob called from the other side of the room. He jogged over to sit next to Rory at the fireplace. "I haven't seen you in ages. When are you moving back?"

The question came at me hard, like I had just been punched.

When am I moving back? As if everything I've done up to this point was just a phase?

My eyes flipped over to Rory, who was leaning his elbows against his knees and loosely holding his hands together. He was looking between his legs.

"Uh . . . Yeah, I don't— I don't know."

"I might be going down there. We're still undecided." Rory leaned back and crossed his arms, saving me.

Just then, Blair's little girl popped her head around the fireplace, surprising us. Cameron sat down on Rory's other side, having given up on bedtime.

"Uncle Rory, can you put me to bed?" Grace asked.

Rory grabbed Grace's little hand and stood. "I would love to." He gave me a small smile, then took her up the stairs.

I took Rory's seat on the hearth, between Jacob and Cameron, as Orson, Kara, Blair, and Zoë made their way over to us.

"How's work?" Jacob asked.

"Work is, you know, work."

Cameron jumped in. "Rory told us you're writing a lot. Is that why you're still there?"

"Wow. Okay," I mumbled to myself. "Not really. I'm a development executive at a production company. I work with writers and other creatives, and producers, but yeah . . . Anyway, it's a whole lot of everything and a whole lot of nothing at the same time." I swallowed, reverting to the same insecurities I had always felt about acting or being creative in any way. I didn't want to admit what I really wanted, to save the embarrassment of the inevitable follow-up questions: "How much money do you make?" "What have you been in?" "What have you written?" "Would I know anything you've done?" Nothing. Leave me alone.

Blair was next to speak. "Rory says you're a producer. And he talks a lot about your writing. He thinks it's great."

"Well, Rory's very supportive, and as my boyfriend, I'm sure he feels like he has to say all that."

"That's not true," Cameron asserted, his face twisted. He was looking at me like I was a moron.

"Do you like writing more than producing?" Orson jumped in.

"Uh . . ." My eyes shot over to the stairs, in hope that Rory had magically put Grace to bed in seconds and was already on his way back. "Yeah, but I need to make a living, and my day job sponsors my visa and keeps me in the country." My back tightened.

"Why'd you stop acting?" Blair followed up.

I pushed my face into my hands. "What's happening right now? Why am I being interrogated?"

"Because Rory's our brother, and we want to know what's up," Cameron answered confidently.

"You know you ambushed her the second Rory walked away, right?" Kara snapped at Cameron, defending me.

Things between Kara and Cameron had remained strained since they broke up almost a decade earlier, but at least they were talking again and had learned how to be in the same room.

"Are you coming to Vancouver, or is he going to LA?" Cameron continued, ignoring Kara.

I blinked, and my thoughts crystallized. "I've been gone for almost ten years, Cameron. I've made choice after choice that's led me to where I am. And beyond that, I've had tunnel vision about my life for twenty years. Reconciling with the idea that perhaps I've been wrong for all that time is a hard thing to do." I turned to Orson. "Do I miss acting and performing? A little. Do I love writing? Yes. When I'm writing, I can live inside my big, annoying feelings without fear, and I can turn my life into whatever I want." I took a deep breath and closed my eyes, very aware that everyone was looking at me. "But I'm not a writer. I produce and I develop, and that career wouldn't exist for me here in the same way as it does there. I miss Rory every second of every day. And even though I haven't loved my life in LA, I don't know who I would be without it. So I don't know what to do." I opened my eyes and tilted my head toward Cameron.

"Just know that your choices affect Rory, too." Cameron wasn't giving an inch.

"Let's back off." Jacob placed his hand protectively on my leg.

I remembered what Rory had said that morning and felt a calmness wash over me.

I think we became who we were always meant to be because *we were apart. And the people we eventually turned into . . . turns out* they *were always meant to be together.*

My eyes flipped between Blair and Cameron. Blair was now thirty-two. He had softened over time and was a divorced single father. Cameron was thirty and had hardened after Kara. The brothers continued to be fiercely loyal and protective of one another, and though they were concerned about Rory, I knew they felt the same loyalty and protectiveness toward me, too.

"Blair, Cameron, I love your brother. I always have. We haven't figured out the future yet, but we're figuring it out together, because it will always be Rory."

Cameron nodded, and Blair bit his cheek, trying not to smile. I shifted my eyes to Zoë and Kara, who were smiling at me. Jacob gave my leg a loving squeeze. I turned back around to the stairs.

Where the hell is Rory?

"So, have these guys heard you sing yet?" Zoë nodded toward Cameron and Blair.

"No." I sighed.

"Well, tonight's the night." Blair pressed his back against the fireplace. "We already heard Zoë rock out to Alanis Morissette before you got here. And Jacob sounded like shit. I don't even know what he was singing.

"Post Malone. I was incredible." Jacob took a sip of his drink.

"Not so sure about that," Zoë teased Jacob from across the group.

"I don't think I'll be getting up there tonight, guys." I shook my head.

"It's tradition, and this is your inaugural Jingle & Mingle. You're doing it," Jacob determined.

"I'm not even that good." I was digging my heels in.

"That's a lie," Kara and Zoë said in unison.

"Cains, you shattered our brother's heart and then dated a famous person," Blair stated bluntly.

Zoë spat her drink into her glass, surprised by his comment.

Blair pointed at Jacob. "Do you remember the time Rory was at our apartment and Ben was on *The Tonight Show*?"

Jacob leaned forward, hiding his face in his drink, trying to cover his laughter. "Yes."

Blair continued, "Jacob and I were sitting there, pretending we didn't like the guy, even though we secretly wanted to be his friend. So he's on TV and telling this hilarious story about the time he walked in on a girl he liked while she was on a date with a magician in a bathtub—"

I puffed out my cheeks, trying not to laugh. I could hear Zoë and Kara start snorting.

"We all eventually realized that THE STORY WAS ABOUT YOU, CAINEY!" Blair shouted. "Worst. Case. Scenario." Everyone was laughing. "So I'm sorry, but you singing tonight is the only way I will ever be able to forgive you for that moment from hell you put us through," Blair challenged me with a grin.

"Blair! That's evil."

"You should have seen Rory's face, Ellie. I wish I had taken a picture." Jacob laughed.

"Alright, it's happening." Cameron slapped his legs and stood. He made his way over to the band, talked to them briefly, then turned back and called to me from across the room. "Radiohead. 'Fake Plastic Trees.' You know it?"

Blair could tell from the way my chest was hollowing out that, yes, I knew the song. He dragged me over to the band, and Cameron placed the microphone in my hand.

The music started playing, and Blair and Cameron made their way back to their spots on the hearth. I kept my eyes on the ground, took a deep breath, and told myself not to think. Not about the small room. Not about what others were thinking. Not about the fact that I was about to show Blair and Cameron a different version of myself while singing a song about desperately needing to be something you're not. A song about striving for a life that could never be real, and just how exhausting and emptying it is to pretend. The lyrics hit me in the marrow of my bones. Everyone sees the shine, but no one knows about the toxins it takes to make it all look so pretty. My fake plastic life.

Don't think about that, Ellie.

I started singing, eyes stuck on the ground in front of me. Being vulnerable in front of people didn't used to scare me. But now? Now it did. I could be goofy and sing in front of strangers, but singing sincerely in front of people I cared about felt paralyzing. I used to be good at this. I used to be a lot of things.

Breathe. Calm down. Don't look.

As the song built, my self-preservation mode clicked on and took me somewhere else. I wasn't in the room anymore. I went to the place I used to go in my darkest moments, driving around the streets of LA, pretending I wasn't alone. I went to where I used to go onstage. I went to where I go when I write. I began belting. I closed my eyes, protecting myself from judgment, trapping myself safely inside my head, where I liked myself better. Where I was real and somehow not real at the same time.

By the time it was over, you could hear a pin drop. People had been watching me from every direction in the house. Blair and Cameron whistled first, and the loud applause followed. But when I lifted my eyes to the room, I didn't see any of them. I saw Rory. He was sitting by himself on the stairs, watching me become someone else. He had leaned against the railing, with his elbow pressed into his knee. He was holding his mouth and jaw in his hand and had tears in his eyes. We made eye contact, and his eyebrows ticked, and I saw his lips tug into a soft smile between his fingers. It took him a moment to move his hand away from his mouth and slowly join in the applause.

Rory eventually stood up from the staircase, but instead of joining us at the fireplace, he pressed his fingers into my stomach. "Let's talk, Cainey," he murmured as he moved me backward and away from our friends and family, out the back door to Blair's covered patio. "How have I not seen you do that before? How is that the first time I've seen you perform in any way? There's a whole part of you that I don't even know, Ellie. I keep missing out, and I'm not doing it anymore." His eyes roamed my face. "I'm moving to LA, even if we don't know if that's where we'll end up, even if we move somewhere else the next day. I'm moving," he said definitively.

"You don't want to live in LA, Rory. Your family is here. Your friends are here. You love Vancouver." I was certain my lip was trembling, because my words were shaking.

"I love you more." Rory's hand wrapped gently around my waist to find the exposed skin on my back. "I've already been talking to my lawyers. It'll take a minute, but I can get there. It's New Year's Eve, Ellie. This time next year, everything is going to be different."

My heart leapt into my throat. "Okay," I whispered.

"Okay." He smiled, then carefully tucked my hair behind my ear with his fingers. "You're gonna marry me, you know."

I softly pressed my lips into his as he wrapped his arms around me. "I know."

Chapter 38

LOS ANGELES

30 years old

SPRING AND SUMMER CAME AND WENT, AND RORY WAS STILL TRYing to sort out his US status by the time fall rolled around. Just like when I was a teenager, I found myself looking for him everywhere I went, even though I knew he was somewhere else. My eyes never landed anymore, unless they were landing on him. Until one day, when they landed on Ben.

It was a scorching-hot November, and Ken had thrown me into the fire. I was working closely with him on a brand-new prestige, hour-long drama that had already been picked up for series. There was something about how Ken was working with me that felt different. He would sit at the edge of my desk and shoot the shit. He would eat lunch with me and review the casting packages from various agencies. He took my script notes seriously, and he had hired a new assistant named Cheyenne and was inviting her into meetings to take notes instead of me. I was now seated at the table instead of standing in the back. He said nothing about it, but Ken was starting to feel more like a mentor than a boss.

We had been searching for our leading man, holding general meetings with actors for months, when an agent named Rhonda Milk gave us her agency's pitch package. Ken tossed it on my desk, saying, "I'm meeting with one of the actors from Driven in five minutes, Ellie. I'd like to know your thoughts. Cheyenne's going to read with him."

I followed Ken into his office, and when Ben walked in, I almost fell over. We smiled at each other, my eyes bugging out of my head, shocked to see him, but we kept things professional.

"Ben Winters. Thanks for coming in." Ken stretched out his hand to shake Ben's.

I watched Ben work in awe, and when his audition finished, he asked me to walk him out.

"Holy crap," I whispered as we moved through the echoey hallways. "I can't believe I'm looking at you."

"I know. You look good. Are you good?" Ben was still so devastatingly handsome, towering over my coworkers in the office. His eyes seemed even greener and darker, his hair was longer, waving along the top and sides of his head, and his beard was thicker.

I smiled. "I am. Are you?"

"I am." His eyes darted back and forth between mine.

"It's been a long time." My attention fell to my feet.

"Yeah." Ben held his lips together tightly and looked at his feet, too.

"How long are you in LA?" I opened Marie Street Productions' heavy black front door to the building's long hallway, where we passed multiple production offices, editing bays, *Black Cross*'s writers' room, a kitchen, accounting, and legal, and guided Ben out the emergency exit to the private staircase that was used only by employees and celebrities.

"I don't know, am I getting the job?" He smiled as we descended the outdoor metal stairway to the ground level and designated private parking.

"No-brainer, in my opinion, but sadly it's not my call."

"Maybe you can put in a good word."

"I think I can probably swing that."

"So, what's been going on? How's life?" Ben flicked my hand with his own, trying to gauge our comfort level. Even before Ben and I were together, when we were just friends, our touch was how we showed each other how we felt. With only half a second of contact, even after years apart, it all felt so familiar.

I flicked him back. "I'm still living with Zoë. We're in Highland Park now, on the east side. And Rory and I are together." I held my breath, waiting for Ben's reaction.

"You are?" Ben said, sounding surprised. He exhaled through his nose as he crossed his arms. "He's doing well for himself. It seems like I can't watch any sports without seeing his face in some commercial. I mean, Rory Campbell." Ben chuckled. "Get that guy off my TV."

"Funny, he says the same thing about you." I leveled my gaze at him.

"But you live with Zoë?"

"Yeah. He's still in Vancouver. For now."

"Got it."

Long distance had been a path Ben and I tried and failed. I couldn't survive LA while still clinging to New York. But with Rory, I had chosen the path I didn't ultimately choose for Ben, and he didn't ultimately choose for me.

"Well, from everything I remember, Rory's a good guy. I'm happy for you."

"Thank you, Ben. What about you?"

"Ah, I'm with someone pretty great. Her name is Emma." Ben pulled out his phone to show me his lock screen. He had his arm around a woman who was drop-dead gorgeous. They were both wearing bathing suits on vacation and making playful faces for the camera.

"Well, it's too bad she looks like that, but I'm assuming her personality shines," I said sarcastically, and Ben laughed.

"Ellie!" A voice boomed from the other side of the parking lot, next to the building's main visitor's entrance. It was Craig Sinicki. "Hold up. I'll come to you."

"Give me a minute, Craig," I called back, but he kept walking toward us. I rolled my eyes.

"Big fan?" Ben asked through a smartass smile.

"I can't stand this guy," I whispered.

"Who is he?" Ben whispered, mirroring me as he always had.

"He's the showrunner for *Black Cross*. He created it."

Ben nodded and looked at Craig as he made his way across the parking lot. "I stopped watching that stupid show after season one. Don't tell Craig how dumb and stilted I think his dialogue is."

I laughed, and Ben looked back at me, his face softening.

"I should go." He brushed my hair behind my ear, still quietly caring.

"I hope this isn't inappropriate, but I've talked to Rory about it, so he knows, and I feel like I can say it to you because it's you." I took a moment to compose myself. "One day we're all going to be gone, and none of it will have mattered. But I want you to know that I am who I am, because you were who you are. And I loved you."

I watched tears build in Ben's forest-green eyes,

Deep breath, Ellie.

"You're the one that got away. And I don't mean that romantically because my love for you went beyond that. I mean our friendship. When someone settles in your bones, they never leave you. And every time my bones creak and ache, I wonder if it's because you're not in my life anymore. You were my best friend, Ben. And you and New York . . . I'll miss it for the rest of my life." A few stray tears fell to my cheeks. I bit my lip, worried I had gone too far with my honesty.

Ben let out a sigh and wrapped his arms around me for a hug. He kissed the top of my head. "I miss you, too, Ellie."

I smiled and pressed my face into Ben's chest, a place I had lived and loved in a past life. "Was that weird?" I asked nervously.

"Yup." Ben let out a small laugh. "But I wouldn't have expected anything less."

"Okay." I felt lighter. I hadn't realized that Ben's absence from my life carried so much weight.

When I stepped out of his hug, I noticed that Craig had slowed his pace and was looking at us like he was trying to put together a puzzle.

"I should see what this idiot wants now," I whispered, barely audibly, as Craig closed the distance between us.

Ben chuckled softly. "I travel to LA a lot these days. Next time Rory's in town, see where I'm at. We should all grab a drink or something."

"I'd love that."

"Okay. I should go." Ben reached into his pockets, searching for something. "Actually, I think I left my sunglasses inside. It's good to see you, Ellie." Ben gave me one last smile before he jogged up the private staircase and ducked back into the building.

I turned to Craig. "What's up?"

"Where's your boyfriend?"

"Right now? New York." I smirked to myself at the irony of Rory in New York and Ben in Los Angeles. "Why?"

"So, what was that with Ben Winters?" Craig walked around me in a way that forced me to move behind the stairs.

"He's an old friend."

"Seemed like more to me. You fucking around on Rory Campbell? That's pretty hot."

"What?" I sneered. "No. I've got to go. I need to run to a meeting," I lied.

I tried to walk out from behind the stairs, but Craig leaned forward and kissed me. I was stunned—frozen solid for a full two seconds as his mouth moved over mine. When I lifted my arms between us to push him away, he took my hand and pushed it down his pants, then closed his hand over mine, over his dick, locking me in place. He quickly unsnapped his top button with his other hand to free himself, then groaned. "You like that? Fuck . . ."

Everything went blurry, then got prickly. It all happened so fast that I looked down and had no idea how my hand had gotten down his pants. It felt as if my head were crashing on top of my body like a boulder crushing a paper bag. I was caving in on myself. I lost my voice. I lost my words. I lost my thoughts. I lost everything.

And then everything inside me went black and rigid. I gripped Craig's dick, beneath his hand, and throttled the shit out of it. He let go of my hand and started yelling at me, I think—I couldn't be sure—but I screamed, too, right in his fucking face. I dropped his dick, and he darted up the private staircase, through the emergency exit door, and into the building. Again, so fast.

I don't know how I got upstairs, but I did. It felt like I was floating. I walked down the long hallway, past legal, accounting, a kitchen, *Black Cross*'s writers' room, editing bays, and multiple production offices, then pushed myself through Marie Street's heavy black front door.

"What the hell is going on out here?" Ken emerged from his office, confused. "Did I hear screaming?"

I didn't fight. There was no flight. I didn't even freeze. I didn't fall to the ground, but my body still played dead, like a possum in front of a predator. I'd had panic attacks before, but I didn't know what this was. This wasn't anything. I'd turned into nothing.

"Ellie?" I think it was Ben talking. I wasn't looking at him. I was looking through him. "What happened?"

"Ellie McCain's a liability to your company and your reputation, Ken. You need to fire her."

"What the fuck did you do?" Ben snapped his head toward Craig.

"Me? Nothing!" Craig looked like he was actually surprised and confused by Ben's questioning. "She's been acting fucking cra—"

Ben ripped his arm back and punched Craig, connecting with the side of his face and knocking him straight to the ground.

"BEN!" Ken screamed.

"I quit," I said. I was breathless, like I had been punched in the gut.

"What is happening?!" Ken asked, but I didn't answer.

I don't know if I ran, but somehow, I was gone, already through the emergency exit, and Ben was with me. As I made my way down the stairs, Ben grabbed my waist and picked me up like a feather. It felt like I was flying. When we got to his rental car, he opened the door and set me inside, then got into the driver's seat and peeled out of the private parking lot before either of us could buckle up.

"Ellie, what happened?" Ben implored, driving quickly through Beverly Hills down Wilshire Boulevard. I couldn't speak. "Jesus Christ! Ellie, give me your phone!"

I was clutching my phone, unable to open my hand. It was as if I were experiencing rigor mortis. Ben pulled it from my grip and punched in my four-digit code. 9178. He remembered. He went to my call history and pressed the screen when he saw Rory's name. Ben put the phone on speaker and set it on the dashboard as Rory's phone rang on the other end.

"What's up, babe? Are you late to work?" Rory answered, without saying hello.

"Rory. It's Ben. I'm with Ellie." Ben's voice was clipped.

"Uh, hi . . . ? Is everything okay?"

I could imagine Rory sitting straighter, the hairs on the back of his neck prickling. Ben calling him from my phone and saying we were together would have been, to say the least, surprising.

"No, dude. Everything is not okay," Ben answered. His eyes jumped between the road and me in the passenger seat.

"Give Ellie the phone," Rory ordered.

"I can't. She's not talking."

There was a beat. I could almost hear Rory shaking. "What the fuck is going on?"

"Something happened at her office."

"Okay . . ."

"I came in to meet Ken Caplin. She and I were catching up on my way out, then she got called away by someone. Something happened between them. Now she's having a panic attack."

Rory was silent. His brain was likely firing in a thousand different directions.

Ben gave him a couple of seconds to catch up before asking, "You still there?"

"Take her home. Get her head under cold water. Give me your number, and I'll text you the address." Rory's voice was cutting.

Ben gave Rory his phone number. There was an immediate ding from Ben's back pocket. He pulled out his phone and tapped in his passcode. 9178. His eyes flicked over to me for the briefest of seconds. I blinked, then was flooded with a lost memory of us making our passcodes the same, back when we were together and living at Grayrock. Neither of us had changed it since. I wasn't sure either of us even remembered we had done that until this very moment, when Ben's muscle memory kicked in.

Ben mapped out the directions to my address, then placed his phone on the center console.

"Who was she with?" Rory demanded.

"Someone named Craig."

The silence on Rory's end of the phone was so thick the car became suffocating.

Ben continued, "Then he said some shit about her to Ken. It wasn't pretty."

"Can you put me on speaker?" Rory asked.

"You are. You've been on speaker the whole time."

"Ellie, you've got to talk. Tell me what happened," Rory said.

We pulled up to a red light, and Ben turned to look at me, waiting for a response. "Come on, buddy."

I wanted to talk, but I had forgotten how to find my thoughts. They were there, but I couldn't catch them. Rory and Ben had both seen me suffer through panic attacks. It wasn't a common occurrence, but they knew when it did happen, I would find my voice eventually. But I knew they needed to hear it right away. I put my elbows on my knees. The fact that I was moving at all was a good sign. I pressed my eyes into my palms and kept them there as I strained to grab my words.

"He . . ." I started. I kept my face in my hands. "Kissed me." I pushed out the rest of my sentence through sheer force. "Shoved my hand down his pants."

There was nothing but silence on the other end of the phone. The light had turned green, but Ben wasn't driving. We were being honked at, so Ben pulled off to the side of the road and turned on the car's hazards. Rory and Ben were both quiet, waiting for me.

I finally lifted my head and met Ben's eyes. If looks could kill. "I don't know how it happened."

"Okay. Ellie, can I hold your hand?" he whispered, but loud enough so Rory could hear.

I nodded through my fog, barely noticeable. Ben picked up my phone from the dashboard, composed. He held it to his mouth, though it was still on speaker. His other hand took mine. "Rory?"

The sound on the other end of the phone changed from deafening silence to the drum of city life when Rory finally barked, "Yeah." His angry voice sounded strained. He must have put himself on mute. I could imagine him holding his phone with two hands, bent over and screaming *"FUCK!"* as loudly as he could while standing on the sidewalk of a busy New York street. "I'm on my way to the airport. I'll probably get in late. Ellie, baby, when you wake up in the morning, I'm going to be there."

I nodded.

"She's nodding," Ben said, taking over for me. "Hey, Rory, I think you should know that I punched him."

"You did?" Rory sounded surprised.

"Yeah. I hit him pretty hard."

Rory cleared his throat. "I'm glad you're there, Ben."

"I'll take her home, but I'm going to stay until you get here. Is that okay?" Ben was asking Rory but looking at me.

"Whatever she wants. Whatever she needs."

I nodded.

"Okay, she's nodding," Ben confirmed to Rory.

"I love you, Ellie." Rory's voice was heavy.

I nodded again.

"She loves you, too. See you when you get here."

Ben clicked the phone off, and we drove the rest of the way to Highland Park in silence, with him clutching my hand.

Chapter 39

LOS ANGELES

30 years old

RORY ARRIVED AS BEN AND ZOË WERE EATING LATE-NIGHT VIETnamese food at our kitchen table. I was pretending to sleep but was really watching them through my open bedroom door.

"Where is she?" Rory asked before I could even hear the front door close.

Zoë answered. "She's sleeping. If you wake her, I'll kill you."

Rory nodded and then wiped his hand down his face before hugging Ben as if they were old friends. "Jesus, Ben, are you gonna get arrested for assault?"

"I don't care, but also probably not. He assaulted her first." Ben sat back in the chair, already comfortable in my house.

"Is she okay? I know that's a stupid question, but I'm asking it." Rory placed his hands on his hips.

"She's upset, obviously, but she'll be okay," Zoë said. "By the end of the night, she seemed like herself, but she was still quiet, and a little distant. I think it's the weight of everything that goes along with quitting her job, and not just Craig."

"She's quitting her job?" Rory asked, surprised by this new piece of information.

"She said so on her way out, and again to us tonight," Ben confirmed. "What do you think she's going to do?"

"I don't know. Ken and Marie Street sponsor her visa, but she's been in this position before. So she's either gonna have to get scrappy, which we all know she's good at, or . . . I don't know." Rory rubbed his chin. "It's not like she wouldn't get another job. She's had two production companies approach her in the last couple of months."

"Maybe this is the moment for her to go back to Vancouver," Zoë said, more to herself than to anyone else.

"I don't want that, though." Rory pressed his fingers into his eyes, frustrated.

"That's bullshit, Rory," Zoë huffed. "I know you want to be in Vancouver, and you want her to be there with you."

"Not like this." Rory gripped his hair.

Ben instinctively jumped in on my behalf. "Why not?"

"I don't want that choice forced on her. She'll never have closure if it is. If she ever wants Vancouver again, she needs to come to that decision herself."

"Then why aren't you here yet?!" Zoë was unable to control her anger, and directed it at the wrong person.

"I'm working on it, Zoë! I was ready to move here straight from Vegas last year. When we were twenty, I got in to USC for her. I went to New York on her twenty-first birthday to propose!" Rory threw his arm out to Ben without looking at him and shook his head. "I'm sorry, I don't mean to make this uncomfortable for you."

Ben bit his bottom lip. He nodded, letting whatever discomfort he had slide.

"Where she lives and what she does is wrapped up in her identity. I don't want what the rest of our life looks like to be decided for her. You can't tell Ellie what to do. She has to find it. And I wouldn't want to, anyway. I love that she's a wild fucking bird! It's always been the scariest thing about her, and it's always been my favorite thing about her. She doesn't know where she's landing yet, but when she does, wherever she does, I'm gonna fucking be there!"

Rory tipped his head back, then brushed his hands forward through his hair, landing them on the back of an empty kitchen chair. He nodded at the Vietnamese food. "Can I have some of that?"

Ben pulled out the chair next to him so Rory could sit. "Go nuts."

Rory didn't look at Ben as he sat down, but he tilted his head slightly. "I'm glad that Ellie can still count on you." He closed his eyes and took in a deep breath before continuing. "I hate that I wasn't here. It kills me."

"Don't do that to yourself," Zoë said quietly.

Rory sighed heavily and kept his attention on Ben. "But I'm glad it was you with her, because I don't think anyone else would have punched his face in. So thank you."

Ben leaned forward to take a moment. He placed his elbows on the table and lifted his fist for a bump, which Rory reciprocated before diving into the leftovers.

I woke up the next morning with Rory's hard, warm body pressed against mine. He was shirtless and wearing only his boxer briefs, his hand limp on my stomach. I turned toward him and pushed my face into his neck, kissing him. He stirred. I moved my mouth to just below his jaw and kissed him again. Instead of opening his eyes, he tilted his head down to meet my lips and kissed me back.

"I quit my job," I whispered.

"I heard." He kept his eyes closed.

"I squeezed his dick so hard, I think I broke it."

Rory's eyes flicked open, and the tiniest smile reached the edge of his lips. "That's my girl."

"What a nightmare." I burrowed my face into his chest.

"Do you want to press charges?"

I didn't want to admit that I feared an earthquake would tear my life apart if I did anything. I recalled an old boss, sitting at the head of a conference table, laughing with other executives over lunch that it wouldn't be difficult to ruin one's life. All it would take was six phone calls, and they'd never work again. What if that was the end of my career? Every sacrifice I'd made, every person I'd loved and lost . . . would it have been worth it? What would "one of the good ones" do? What would a precocious little girl nicknamed "Hollywood" do? What would the girl on the plane do, leaving her love and life behind, determined to figure out what she was made of? What would fourteen-year-old Ellie do, driving through the Airport Tunnel, dreaming of her future?

"I just need to think," I answered, not moving.

"I'm so sorry I wasn't here." Rory sat up and pressed his back into the headboard.

"Don't be sorry. I just don't know what I'm going to do." I traced my fingers along the indentations of his abs.

"It's whatever you decide. You want to rebuild, I'll get the bricks. You want to burn it all down, I'll bring the lighter. You want to run, I'll lace up our shoes." Rory pulled me onto his lap.

I adjusted myself to straddle his body and wrapped my arms around his neck. "Only you, Rory. I love you. I'm sorry I didn't get to say it yesterday. I forgot how to talk." I kissed him, and our tongues folded together.

Rory's hands moved up my sides beneath my shirt. His mouth trailed along my neck and jawline with a series of kisses until he pulled me into him for a tight, warm hug.

"Yesterday was pretty shitty . . ." I murmured.

Rory pressed his face into my neck and inhaled deeply. "Yeah . . . Have you thought about talking to Ken?"

"I don't know. You should have seen it. I think Ben knocked Craig out. Then we were out of there like we were Bonnie and Clyde."

"Remind me to buy Ben all the alcohol that's left in the world," Rory said. I laughed softly as Rory placed his head against the headboard. "Hearing you go through that over the phone and not being able to do anything about it . . . was difficult." Rory squeezed his eyes shut. I pressed my fingers into his twisted brow, smoothing it as best as

I could. He let out a deep breath and opened his eyes, then pulled my hand down and kissed my palm. "It took me ten hours to get to you. That was the longest ten hours of my life."

"You're here now." I leaned forward and kissed his forehead.

"Yeah . . ." He swallowed, and his face crunched together again.

"What?"

"Blair and Cameron both reached out separately to ask for help while I was on the plane. My mom put the house up for sale without telling anyone. I don't think she's doing well right now. They plan to talk to her tomorrow, and I need to be there for that." Rory rubbed his palm into his eye, clearly frustrated.

"Oh no. I hope she's okay. So are you leaving today?"

"Yeah, but I'm coming right back after we see her. I didn't tell my brothers what happened, but I said I needed to be here to sort through some things. They didn't ask questions, so I'm assuming they realized shit was hitting the fan. I saw Zoë texting Cameron last night. I think he's worried about you."

"You should stay in Vancouver. I don't want you to not be there for your mom or your brothers."

"Ellie, I'm showing my face and will be there for them, but I'm coming back tomorrow night. You are my priority." Rory brought his hands to the outside of my thighs and gently rubbed my legs. He let out a giant sigh before continuing. "You should know that Ben's still here. He slept on the couch, and he's making breakfast this morning."

The surrealness of having Ben in my kitchen and Rory in my bed was overwhelming. "Did you guys stay up late?"

"Yeah. After Zoë went to bed, we talked and had some drinks. It was good." Rory stretched his body beneath mine. "I like him. I liked him when we met in New York, too, but it was impossible for me to say back then."

"Is it weird for you that he's in the other room right now?" I hadn't decided if it was weird for me yet.

"No. You and me are getting married soon, so I'm pretty sure I've got nothing to worry about." Rory smirked impishly. His brown eyes bounced between mine.

"Have you already proposed, and I didn't know it?" I let my tired smile reach my eyes. I could feel myself coming back together again, piece by piece.

"When I do, you'll know it's happening."

I became grounded again in Rory's presence, with his love surrounding me and centering me.

He brought his hands to my cheeks and pulled me in for a soft kiss before saying, "Come on, baby. Let's go eat."

Chapter 40

LOS ANGELES

30 years old

AS RORY BIT INTO HIS BREAKFAST SANDWICH, HE FLIPPED HIS chin up at Ben. "What are you up to today?"

"Just going to the gym. That's my only plan," Ben answered, biting into his sandwich, then flicking away the crumbs from the black T-shirt of Rory's that he was now wearing. Bizarrely, it fit him perfectly.

"What about you, Cainey? What are you thinking?" Rory switched over to my childhood nickname with ease.

Zoë grabbed an apple from the fridge and sat across from me at our round glass kitchen table.

"I'm going back and forth about whether I should go talk to Ken."

Rory's face softened. I could tell he liked that answer.

"What's stopping you?" Zoë perked up and crunched loudly.

"Ummm . . . well . . ." My eyes lifted to Ben, then moved over to Zoë.

Rory reached for my hand on top of the table. He stroked his thumb against my skin, quietly comforting me.

"I'm embarrassed," I admitted.

"Why would you be embarrassed?" Zoë lowered the apple from her mouth.

Ben tracked my sighs and twitches, clocking my nerves.

"There's been so many times like this that I've accepted, laughed over, joked about, even thanked people for. The only time I've ever done anything about it was when I was a kid at Juniper. I told a bunch of people what happened between me and this older man, and I was dismissed. I felt so much shame that I stopped going. My entire childhood was consumed by that golf club, and then it was gone." Rory squeezed my hand, and I continued. "I learned how to adapt in these types of situations so I wouldn't lose it all again."

Zoë put her apple on the table. "You're not going to lose anything, Ellie."

"I could lose everything, Zo. If I lose my job, I lose my sponsorship, visa, and status, which means I lose the country I live in, which means I lose my home and community, which means I lose the network, career, and life I've built for myself and sacrificed everything for. I can say something and maybe lose my reputation, too. Or I can say nothing, find another job, and lose my integrity and self-respect instead."

Ben stretched his arm over the back of my chair. I knew he wanted to comfort me, but he wasn't going to overstep.

"It's all a game, and I don't know how to win it." I let out a shaky breath. "And I'm part of the problem because I've never said anything. Even with Craig—"

Zoë put her hand on top of Rory's and mine. "Whatever you're going to say right now, this is not your fault."

I buried my face in my hands. "But it feels like—"

"It's not." Zoë cut me off again. "You are not responsible for Craig's actions. And as for other people you've worked with who have pulled this kind of shit with you, or bullied you, or made you feel small, they had power and control over your job, and therefore your visa, which has acted as the linchpin of your life thus far, Ellie, and they abused it." Zoë's words ran into each other. She was filled with adrenaline.

"Zoë—" I shook my head, but she wasn't having it.

She waved her hand, silencing me. "You can do this. Are you someone who dies in the night while climbing up the mountain, or are you someone who gets to the top? You've trained for this. I know your fingers are tired. I know your rope has been cut. But you've worked hard for your career, so get to the top."

I pushed a burst of air out through my tight lips, then looked at Ben and shook my head. "Don't."

"Don't what?" he asked smugly.

"I know what you're going to say. Don't do it."

Ben shrugged his shoulders casually. "I'm not going to say anything about you being Ellie Fucking McCain—"

"Ben—" I closed my eyes.

"I don't need to remind you that you took two-hundredth place in the Women's Long Drive when you were fourteen. Goddamn it."

I opened my eyes, and Ben was smiling. I looked over to Rory. The warmth in his gentle stare settled in my belly.

"Where's the ball?" Ben asked. "I know you have it. Where is it?"

Rory stood, went into the bedroom, and came back with my lucky golf ball. He tossed it to Ben, who looked at it with a smile, then placed it on the table. Rory sat back down and took my hand once again.

"Anyway," Ben continued, "I don't need to tell you about that." He nodded toward the ball, then leaned forward. "I would like to tell you, though, about a girl I know. She once got a chip of paint jammed under her fingernail. It was as thick as a wood chip. And when she was told that there was nothing she could do about it, she said fuck that and sawed off her whole hand."

I laughed, feeling a small cry escape at the same time. "These stories have gotten bigger over the years."

"You know, I know a girl who accidentally threw her golf club into the middle of a driving range." Rory's eyes dropped to our hands. "She must have been so embarrassed when everyone had to stop and watch her walk out into the rain to get her club, all by herself. But when I saw her come back to try again, soaking wet, determined, and mad as hell . . . I fell in love with her." Rory flicked his eyes up to mine.

I turned my focus to my lucky golf ball. I had been holding on to it since I was fourteen. I had been holding on to it for the same length of time that I had been holding on to my dreams of living in Los Angeles. I had saved the ball specifically to remind myself that I was "a piece of shit." I let out a small laugh, thinking about how ridiculous that was. Over sixteen years, that ball had transformed into something else entirely. Now, when I looked at my lucky golf ball with the Juniper logo on it, I saw Rory, I saw Ben, I saw Zoë, Hannah, Kara . . . everyone who'd traveled through life with me. And I saw the fearless little kid I used to be.

"I knew that girl. She was okay, I guess," I said quietly. "She'd probably go back to the office, because she actually really liked her job, loved her boss, and would want him to know that Craig tried to break her, huh?"

Rory nodded softly. "I think she probably would."

I thought of what I had overheard Rory say to Ben and Zoë the night before. *You can't tell Ellie what to do. She has to find it.* Rory had always let me find my way. He wanted me to be exactly who I was, and he loved me through every transition, through every version. I tilted my head upward in an attempt to prevent any tears from falling. My love for Rory had been a thread throughout my entire life. We'd been tangled in it. We'd tripped over it. But it had pulled us together over and over again. It had always been there, connecting us.

I had lived so much of my life in the shadow of my regrets. How much more was I willing to sacrifice? I could drown in my past, wondering, "Was it worth it?" Or I could live for tomorrow, knowing it would be. I felt my chest expand as I looked at Rory and realized I had finally made it to my next tomorrow. I breathed in an old memory: *There's before this moment, and everything after. For the rest of your life, you're living in the after.*

"Can I go with you to talk to Ken?" Rory asked, unaware that I was on the precipice of a breakthrough.

"No. I need to do this myself."

"She said, surprising no one," Ben added with a wry smile.

"Okay." Rory lifted his arm to pull me from my chair and onto his lap, then wrapped his arms around me. "I'll probably be on the plane by the time you get back."

"Okay." There was something twisting and pulling inside me that knew this was going to be the last time Rory would leave me. It was certainly the last time I would leave him.

"What are you gonna do before you head to the airport?" Ben asked Rory, finally taking another bite of his sandwich, resuming breakfast.

Rory reached across my lap to pick up his sandwich and shoved the last little bit into his mouth. "Want to go play some golf?"

"Yeah, dude. That sounds awesome," Ben said, with his mouth full of food.

"Ben Winters and Rory Campbell, hanging out together? You guys are gonna cause a scene." Zoë took a bite of her apple.

"Oh shit," Ben said. "I don't have anything to wear golfing."

"Here." Rory lifted me from his lap and stood up. "Come into the bedroom. I've got more clothes that'll fit you."

Ben followed Rory into my bedroom without a second thought.

My eyes went wide, and Zoë came over to give me a quick kiss on the cheek. "Is this full *Twilight Zone* for you?"

I listened to Rory and Ben chatting inside the bedroom, and that's when I realized what was happening. They were becoming friends.

"Yup. Full *Twilight Zone*."

Chapter 41

LOS ANGELES

30 years old

I PULLED MY CAR UP AROUND THE BACK OF MARIE STREET'S building, into the private parking lot, and looked at the metal staircase that led to the building's emergency exit. I knew what was happening in that building without having to set foot inside. Interns were binding scripts. Assistants were rolling calls at their temperamental boss's whim. Production assistants were already preparing lunch orders for each department. Lawyers were reviewing contracts. Creative executives were setting up general meetings with people they likely never intended to see again, or follow up with, for the sake of a busy schedule and optics. Ken was avoiding emails and calls from line producers who needed to talk about how everything was over budget.

I'd had a lot of "last times" in my life. But as I looked at the staircase and along the wall, I saw the flashing red light of a small surveillance camera hidden in the corner, and I thought maybe this "last time" could be different.

I held my breath as I walked through the office's heavy black front door, fully aware that everyone was looking at me, and knocked on Ken's closed office door.

"Come in," Ken called out from behind his desk.

The office was filled with memorabilia of Ken's career, but that wasn't what struck me. He was the only boss I'd had who displayed pictures of his family. He had birth announcements of his kids framed on the wall, but photos of him with multiple presidents loosely scattered on the bookshelf that framed his desk.

I looked out his enormous window and could see the Hollywood Hills. I knew that lost inside those mountains was Mulholland Drive, where I used to park and look down at where I was standing now. It was there that I would think about every mistake I had ever made.

The sky was blue, as always. Houses were scattered along the rolling hills. The view seared into my soul and pushed through who I was now all the way to who I had been when I was fourteen. I had memorized it. Every hill. Every house. Every side street. Every freeway. Every palm tree. None of it lived outside anymore. It all lived inside me. And I knew I was saying goodbye. Not just to Los Angeles. To my life. To this version of myself. To the dreams that made me who I was. But life evolves, and dreams change, and it was time for me to be okay with that. It was time for me to finally learn how to let go.

I shifted my gaze back to Ken. "Craig Sinicki assaulted me." It felt impossible to say, mainly because a part of me was still trying to justify what had happened. I still had a hard time believing myself. I tempered every impulse to tell myself that maybe I had led him on. I took a deep breath and forced myself to keep going. "I've known Ben Winters for years. He was trying to protect me. Please check the camera by the stairwell, under the emergency exit."

Ken stood up from his desk. "Ellie, are you okay?" I nodded, and Ken grabbed his office phone to call his assistant. "Cheyenne, can you get the tapes from our security cameras. I want to see yesterday's footage." He hung up, and I could hear Cheyenne start walking down the hall. "Craig's been fired."

"He has?" I gasped. *But that's not possible* was my immediate thought.

"I was very confused by what happened, so I did some investigating. I called Mary in our IT department. About four hours later, I got a call about some emails that he had written to you, and some recent ones to Cheyenne."

I closed my eyes, and tears streamed down my face. Intensely confusing feelings of relief mixed with guilt swept through my body like a raging river.

"Ken, I don't want to quit. That's not who I am. I love working for this company, but more than that, I love working for you and learning from you." I pushed my tears away from my face with my palms and composed myself. "But I also don't want to be in Los Angeles anymore." I couldn't believe I was saying that sentence out loud.

"Ellie, after I got the phone call, I went into your computer, too. I hope that's okay." Ken opened the top drawer of his desk and pulled out three scripts that I had written. "I did some reading last night."

I looked down at my scripts, shell-shocked. He'd had them printed and bound, and they were already marked up with notes in red ink.

"This is who you are." He pressed down on the scripts. "I think you should keep writing because I think you could be good at it, and I want you to keep producing because I *know* you're good at it. So I'd like to talk to you about what that might entail if you choose to stay at Marie Street."

I looked back out to the Hollywood Hills and repeated something someone once said to me a long time ago. "I don't belong in the sun."

"Nobody likes this kind of sun in November. You don't want to quit, so I'm willing to make this work. If you don't want to be in LA anymore, work remotely and come down for essentials only." Ken nodded. "I don't want you to quit, either."

"Thank you, Ken." I wiped the tears from my face, then hugged him.

By the time I got back home after an entire day sitting on boulders at the side of the Pacific Coast Highway and looking out at the ocean, Rory had already left. I'd called him while he was playing golf with Ben to tell him about my conversation with Ken, how Craig got fired, and that I was keeping my job. He wanted so much to be there for me when I got home, but our timing wasn't going to work. When did it ever? I didn't tell him, however, that I had decided to leave LA and was about to give him the life that he wanted . . . that both of us wanted.

Ben was at the house in Highland Park, waiting for me when I got back, warming my heart with the same ease he had ten years earlier when we got pizza that first night in New York. I looked at Ben and told him it was time for me to go home.

"I know." Ben folded his arms around me. "You're a bird."

The next morning, Zoë drove me to the airport. We went under the Airport Tunnel on Sepulveda Boulevard. I watched the yellow lights blur around the car. And as I felt them burn into my soul, I closed my eyes, cried, and said goodbye.

Chapter 42

VANCOUVER

30 years old

I WAS STANDING IN FRONT OF RORY'S PENTHOUSE DOOR IN YALE-town with my two suitcases by my side. It was pouring outside, and I could hear him moving around in his home, entirely unaware that I was at his door. I grabbed my phone from my pocket and called him.

"Hey, baby," Rory answered. "No FaceTime?"

"Not right now," I whispered as I pressed my hand into the wooden door.

"You're so quiet." Rory matched my whisper, and I could hear the smile in his voice.

"What are you doing?" I asked.

"Just making some tacos before I head out. I'm meeting Cameron and Blair at my mom's in about an hour. What does your day look like?" I could hear Rory rattling away with pots and pans.

"Um, I don't know yet." I tapped the door gently with my finger. "Ken gave me a couple of days off."

"Oh, that's good. When I get back, let's just do absolutely nothing. Oh! And is there any chance you can pick up The Sandwich from Roma for me today? I get in after nine tonight and have been craving it for like two weeks."

"Maybe . . ." I put my forehead on the door.

"You okay, Cains? You sound a little off."

"Yeah. Ken told me last night that we're offering Ben the part."

"Holy shit. Damn. That was quick. Does he know yet?" Rory seemed genuinely happy for Ben, and I closed my eyes with a smile.

"No, not yet. He'll have to figure some stuff out. He's been in New York for a long time. It's crazy how things work out sometimes." I flipped my eyes up to the ceiling, waiting for Rory's reaction.

"Totally." I could hear him grab a plate from his cabinet.

"He's finally going to LA, and I'm not gonna be there anymore . . . It's just weird, don't you think?" I opened my eyes and could feel my stomach flutter.

"What do you mean?"

"Remember how we talked about the next tomorrow? Before last year, I was so afraid it would never exist. Like, a time and place we could never get to."

"Yeah . . . ?"

"Are we there yet?" I asked.

"What's going on?" I heard Rory stop moving.

"I'm asking if we're there yet." I smiled and wished I could see his face as he worked through what was happening and what I was saying. I waited for Rory's next thought to form.

"You tell me . . ."

"I think I just did," I whispered.

"Ellie, where are you?" I could hear that he was short of breath and imagined his heart thumping through his chest. I wished I could place my hand over it and feel it beating rapidly.

"Where do you think I am?"

"I don't know . . ."

"Yes, you do." I moved my forehead away from the door and took one step back.

After a moment, the door flew open. Rory was still holding his phone and stood in the doorway wearing a black long-sleeved shirt, sweatpants, and my Dodgers hat on backward. His hair flipped out, exactly how I loved it. He looked down at my two suitcases, my whole life.

"Ellie, what are you doing here?" Rory's expression was pure shock.

I thought about what to say next, then decided to just answer the question.

"I live here."

I watched Rory's chest rise and fall with his staggered breathing. I watched his dark-brown eyes dance between mine. I watched his dimple appear then disappear with his changing emotions. I watched him take a step back to steady himself. He released his hold on the door, and the hand that held his phone dropped to his hip. His other hand gently rubbed his mouth. He closed his eyes.

"Ellie?" Rory's voice was low, trembling. When he opened his eyes again, his face transformed to match my teary-eyed smile.

"Yeah?"

Rory's tears fell with mine as he asked, "Do you wanna watch a movie?"

I held my lips tightly together to refrain from letting any sobs escape, remembering how Rory had once said he wanted to propose when we were younger. He was right. When it happened, I would know. I took a sharp breath and smiled through my tears.

"Yes, Rory. I really do," I whispered.

Remember this, Ellie.

Rory grabbed me by the front of my jacket, pulling me toward him, and kissed me. It was right there, back in Vancouver, back in the November rain, where we began . . .

Again.

Epilogue

LAS VEGAS
30 years old

IT WAS THE NIGHT BEFORE MY THIRTY-FIRST BIRTHDAY, AND BEN had just turned thirty-four. We were celebrating together in Las Vegas with his girlfriend, Emma, Rory, Blair, Cameron, Orson, Jacob, Hannah, Kara, Zoë, Maddy, and Maddy's husband, Reid. Even Lucas had made the trip from New York. We were all in a roped-off area at a club in the MGM Grand. Rory, Jacob, and Lucas had popped some champagne at our tables and were serving everyone drinks. We all lifted our flutes, and Ben winked at me when we finally clinked our glasses together.

Happy birthday, buddy, Ben mouthed.

Happy birthday, I mouthed back, smiling.

I'd moved into Rory's apartment the day I landed in Vancouver, and we'd turned the breakfast nook in the solarium into my office. I only had to go to LA for work once a month, for a couple of days. Because of my job, Los Angeles was still very much a part of our lives. When I was in LA on my own, I stayed with Zoë. When Rory came with me, we got an Airbnb.

Ben and Emma moved to Los Angeles together for our show. They didn't know many people there, but they knew us. After Craig Sinicki, a dam had been broken, and Rory welcomed them into our lives in a way that was unexpected. Ben and Rory hung out whenever Rory was in town. They even sent each other pictures of their drinks when they were having a noteworthy cocktail. It was strange to see Ben become "Ben Winters." You could see people in his orbit who didn't care about him but only about being seen with him. Rory had some similar experiences, but it wasn't nearly the same. Even so, Ben and Rory had something between them that only they could understand. Ben was even planning on going to Augusta with Blair, Cameron, Hannah, Kara, Jacob, and me to watch Rory play.

It was our first time back in Vegas since Zoë's thirtieth birthday, and we intended to make it just as memorable. Lucas had started putting the moves on Hannah within five minutes of landing, and though Blair kept his mouth shut, it was clear by his shifting eyes that their flirting bothered him. Maddy and Reid were experiencing their first trip away from their kid. Kara and Cameron had somehow gotten more contentious, and when a random guy approached Kara as we first entered the nightclub, Cameron pulled her away without exchanging a word.

"Stop it, Cameron!" Kara snapped. "You don't own me. You're not with me. And you're barely nice to me. I'm going to meet someone tonight, or tomorrow night, or the night after that, or every night, and every morning when you show up at breakfast, you're going to wonder if I was just having sex." She flipped her brown bob and walked away, leaving everyone speechless, especially Cameron.

Ben leaned in to Cameron. "You're telling me all about whatever just happened within the next ten minutes, or we'll never be friends."

Rory was the next to lean in. "Can I be a part of that conversation? Because if I find out in Augusta that I'm missing out on some juicy gossip, I won't be able to concentrate."

"I got you, dude. We'll come up with some hand signals." Ben lifted his fist to Rory for a bump, which Rory gladly tapped back.

"Rory, I swear to god." I started laughing. "If you 'forget' any details of that conversation with Cameron, you're sleeping somewhere else tonight."

Rory threw his arm around my shoulders with a loud laugh and kissed the side of my head.

Meanwhile, Zoë had given up on Orson and started sleeping with Jacob. When Orson pressed himself against Zoë at the pool party earlier that day, it was clear he wasn't aware of her new sleeping arrangement with his longtime friend. Rory and I both froze, margaritas in hand, when we saw Orson finally make his move. We were the only ones who knew Jacob and Zoë's dirty little secret. Even Jacob and Zoë didn't know we knew. But we *definitely* knew.

Overall, our second big trip to Vegas had been a success so far. Zoë, Orson, Jacob, Maddy, and Reid were now gossiping around one of the tables in our sectioned-off area. Orson had put his arm around Zoë on the couch, and Jacob was playing it off coolly, giving a master class in confidence.

Hannah, Lucas, and Kara hit the dance floor, and I watched Blair sneaking glances at Hannah, eyeing her proximity to Lucas, every other minute. I also noticed that, though Lucas was laying it on thick, clearly wanting to restart what they'd had long ago, Hannah wasn't letting him get too close.

Rory, Blair, Cameron, Ben, and Emma were at another table, doing shots. When Rory saw me looking at him, he cranked his neck, calling me over. Cameron was filling Ben and Emma in on his complicated history with Kara and everything that had happened after my twenty-first birthday debacle.

Rory pulled me down onto his lap. His hands roamed my thighs, and he ended up inadvertently pulling up my short white lace dress so his fingers could graze my skin. "Sorry," he said quietly into my ear when he realized he was accidentally exposing me. He pulled down my dress and switched sides so he could keep his hand in place, gently trailing his fingers along my leg beneath my dress, sending chills up and down my spine. Blair turned his back to us, unintentionally cutting Rory and me out of the conversation, but we weren't fussed.

"Do you like my dress?" I asked Rory quietly, so no one else could hear.

"You know I do." He turned his head and nibbled on my ear. "I almost cried when you came out of the bathroom in that dress."

"It's white."

"I noticed." He smiled, then pressed his forehead against mine, keeping our conversation for only each other. "Did you notice that Hannah's also wearing white?" Rory's eyes flicked over to the dance floor.

"Yes, I did. That bitch," I joked, and Rory tipped his head back with a silent laugh. "Good thing it was just an accident, and she doesn't know, or I would have had to kill her."

"You don't have the muscles," Rory teased.

"It's okay. You know a guy."

"Do you like my suit?"

Rory was looking exceptionally dapper. He was dressed in my favorite dark-gray fitted suit, with a white shirt and no tie. His top three buttons were undone, and his hair was perfectly unruly, as always.

"You know I do," I whispered. "We shouldn't stand next to each other, or we're gonna give it away."

"I don't care if we give it away. I'm standing next to you. I'm kissing you. You're literally on my lap right now. They're all dumb if they haven't figured it out. We're in Vegas, and we look pretty obvious," Rory said, and we both started laughing.

Rory played with the antique citrine engagement ring he'd given me the day I moved back to Vancouver. Citrine for the month we met and, entirely coincidentally, the month we got engaged. He told me he'd gotten it the first time I saw him play golf in Greensboro. He decided to propose while we were dancing at the restaurant, and I called him out on it. He went with Orson the next morning and bought the ring. It was on my finger before we even brought my luggage in from the hallway.

"Are you nervous?" I asked.

"No." Rory shook his head. He closed his eyes and took a deep breath. "Are you?"

"Are you kidding? They're going to be so pissed when they realize we went and got married, and they weren't invited."

"They're going to be even more mad when we tell them we've been planning this since November. Think about how much fun tomorrow's gonna be once they all find out. I can't wait."

"Me, too." I threaded our fingers together.

"Let's go now," Rory said against my lips.

"But I still want to dance."

"We can go dancing after. Just us. And then we'll all celebrate tomorrow. We can dance at the pool. We can go to a dive bar. We can slow dance in the hotel lobby or by the slot machines. The long-ass bridge walkways out on the street. Elevator music." Rory was laughing now. "Literally anywhere. But right now, Ellie, baby, my love, my Cainey . . . Marry me." Rory's dark eyes were filled with excitement and adventure.

"Okay, let's do it."

Rory's smile spread across his face, deepened his dimple, and reached the edges of his eyes. He helped me to my feet, then turned to our friends and said the same thing he had said the last time we were in Vegas. "Well, this has been very fun, guys, but we're gonna go."

Zoë snapped her head toward us from the other table. "Here we go again. You need to keep your hands to yourselves."

"Where are you going?" Blair asked, confused.

"They did this last time," Maddy answered for us. "They're gonna go fondle each other. Watch out for them on the dance floor, it's gonna get naughty."

"See?" Rory turned to me. "They know we're leaving together. We know we're leaving together." His smile dipped down as he kept our secret. "It's time."

Rory lifted my wrist, his fingers slipped beneath my rose gold bracelet, and he kissed my palm. He held on to the moment for longer than usual as he closed his eyes and breathed me in. When he flicked his eyes back up to mine, I saw that they were holding back tears.

I nodded slowly, looking at the love of my life, staring into the eyes that held my past, present, and future. "It's time."

Acknowledgments

Sixteen years ago, after losing my job due to some confusion with my visa, I started writing about a girl named Ellie. I turned to my computer instead of my journals and typed out the first line: "HOW IT WAS, KIND OF WAS, WISH IT WAS, AND WISH IT WASN'T." Over the years, there have been many different iterations of Ellie. She has been written and rewritten into different books, pilots, screenplays, and pitches, but I couldn't quite figure out the way through her story. It took me sixteen years to realize that was because I hadn't figured out the way through my story yet.

To those who have been there since the very beginning: my mom, dad, sister, and Chelsea. To my incredible friends, who have supported me always. To the boy I loved first, all the way to the boy I'll love last. You've all cracked me and filled me with color and life like a stained-glass window that shines light directly into my heart. I am lucky to have loved you, and to have been loved by you.

Alexis McKechnie, Allison Mattison, Sarah Bakker, Chelsea Dunn, Pia Inglis, Sheila Dong, Christina Reichelt, and Adina Beier, thank you for being my readers along the way, for your thoughtful notes, edits, tears, and laughter. You've shaped this book, sharpened its edges, and softened its curves, much like our friendships have shaped me over the years.

Allison, I sent you this book a chapter at a time, and to feel your excitement over text messages was one of the main driving forces that kept me going. Without you, I don't think the book I started sixteen years ago would ever have been finished.

Mia Vitale, Sarah Passick, and Krista Carnegie, on May 6, 2024, I sent you an email that said, "I found myself completely caught up in a flow that I couldn't get away from." I am so grateful that you three fell down that waterfall with me. Calling you a dream team is an understatement, because you've made my dreams come true. Mia, your instincts and intelligence are astounding. You helped structure this book with deadly precision and immense care, and I'm forever indebted to you for guiding this wild journey.

To my powerhouse editor Jennifer Lambert and the extraordinary team at HarperCollins Canada. Though I wrote this book in what felt like a fog, some moments were difficult for me to put into words. Jenn, you seemed to understand that immediately and saw beyond the love triangle. You believed in the story I wanted to tell, and you masterfully led this book toward centering Ellie, not on boys, but on those difficult moments. You not only love Ellie, but you became her as much as I am her, and your partnership has been one of the greatest gifts of my life.

To my phenomenal, deeply thoughtful editor Caroline Weishuhn, it is an honor to work with you and Harper. Because of you, I'll one day be able to pick up this book at a bookstore in the country and cities that forged me. I am thankful for your passion and belief in this book. From the moment we met, I knew Ellie, Rory, and Ben would be safe in your steady hands.

It is not lost on me how many dedicated, talented, and brilliant women have come together to make this all possible. But there are two men in my life without whom none of it would be happening. Bill Mechanic, you gave me my first professional writing assignment, you read my scripts, you noted my pitches, and you believed in me when I was just an assistant. I am eternally grateful for your priceless mentorship, encouragement, and kindness.

And to Mike, my husband, my sword and shield. I now believe that Los Angeles was always calling to me—a gentle knocking on my soul—because you were there. I love you.

Maude and Birdie, my daughters . . . Have big feelings. Make big choices. Chase dragons. I believe in them, and I believe in you.